The Body in the Bracken

Marsali Taylor

Published by Accent Press Ltd 2015

ISBN 9781786150783

Cover photo: Paul Bloomer

DEDICATION

To my sister, Joan, and my brother, Niall, and in memory of our parents, Margaret and Douglas Gordon Baxter, who took us year after year to Gavin's remote loch, to a cottage three miles by boat from the road's end, with neither water nor electricity, and so gave us the most wonderful childhood memories of messing about in boats, checking out Foxy's lair and Otter's slide, watching seals and red deer, finding incredible furry caterpillars, reading by candlelight, and brewing 'fizzy' over a driftwood fire on remote beaches.

The proverbs heading each section come from the wonderful collection *Shetland Proverbs & Sayings*, edited by the late Bertie Deyell. Thank you to Bertie's family for letting me use these.

For those who enjoy finding new words, there is a Shetland glossary at the back of the book.

Monday 23rd - Tuesday 31st December

Monday 23rd December

Low Water Mallaig UT	*03.26, 1.7m*
High Water	*09.05, 4.5m*
Low Water	*15.59, 2.2m*
High Water	*21.31, 4.2m*

Sunrise	*09.07*
Moonset	*11.14*
Sunset	*15.38*
Moonrise	*22.52*

Moon waning gibbous.

If I dunna see dee in Lerook, I'll see dee in Liverpool.
Said by sailors accustomed to travel.

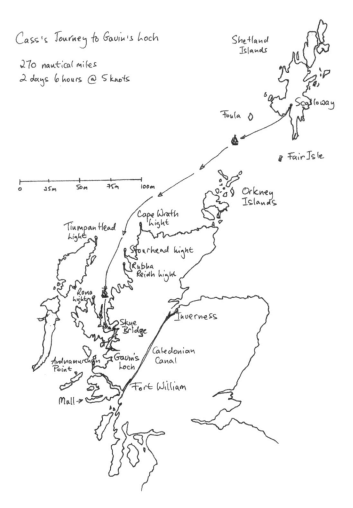

Cass's Journey to Gavin's Loch

270 nautical miles
2 days 6 hours @ 5 knots

Shetland Islands

Scalloway

Foula

Fair Isle

0   25m   50m   75m   100m

Orkney Islands

Cape Wrath Light

Tiumpan Head Light

Stoarhead light

Rubha Reidh light

Rona light

Skye Bridge

Inverness

Ardnamurchan Point

Gavin's Loch

Caledonian Canal

Mull →

Fort William

(For Cass's passage plan, see appendix)

2

Chapter One

It was like sailing into another world. The north-westerly wind that had blown me down from Shetland funnelled behind me as I turned into the outer loch, and *Khalida* flattened as I let the mainsail out and goose-winged the jib. The slap of the waves turned to a gentle rolling. Cat came up from my berth, stretched his white front paws on my varnished cockpit bench, and hunkered down, looking around. The sun picked out the faint white stripes running through his glossy grey fur, and the paler owl tufts behind his ears. I reached for my binoculars to check the position of the rock I wanted to avoid, picked a shore-mark to steer to, then gave an enormous yawn.

I was dog-tired. We'd set off from Scalloway at half past five the day before yesterday, anchored for a sleep yesterday afternoon, then pressed on southwards. Now the hills of one of Scotland's dramatic sea lochs enclosed us; the giant Ladhrbheinn soared up to the right, its ridged summit fissured with snow, its lower slopes rust-red with dried bracken and heather. Ice-hardened brown kelp silvered the sea's edge.

It was a crazy voyage, going down to spend Christmas with the family of a man who was barely even a friend. We'd spent so little time together, DI Gavin Macrae and I. He'd invited me down, and I'd taken a deep breath and decided to risk beginning a relationship I was scared to want. I got cold feet even thinking about it, but I'd said I'd come, and so here I was, threading my way down an unknown loch sprinkled by unmarked rocks and sandbanks, with two extra jumpers keeping out the

December cold, and my only pretty dress hanging in the locker, protected by a plastic cover. I kept an eye on my passage plan and list of compass headings, and my primitive GPS pinged as I neared each of the waypoints I'd typed into it. I was just thinking I should phone and say I was almost there when I heard the steady put-put of an outboard somewhere ahead, and saw a white wash at the head of the loch, two miles away. I reached for the spyglasses again. It was just the sort of boat I'd have expected Gavin to own, an old-fashioned clinker dinghy, varnished the colour of Oxford marmalade, with what sounded like a genuine Seagull outboard on the stern. He was alone.

I turned my own engine on and left the autopilot in charge while I stowed the sails. By the time the boom cover was on, the ties snicked, and my mooring rope ready on the stern, the varnished dinghy was curving round *Khalida*. Gavin raised a hand, and spoke in Gaelic. '*Fàilte!*' Welcome. Then he switched to his soft English, with the consonants precise, the S sounds lingering: 'I thought you might like a pilot through the narrows, with the water low and the tide falling.'

'My very wish,' I agreed. When pride and seamanship clashed, pride went overboard. 'Your chart gives me less than a metre below my keel.'

'About that,' he agreed, and set off before me. One of my *Khalida*'s glories is that she goes as smoothly in reverse as forwards. I turned her and stood facing the stern, looking over her aft locker at the rocks on the bottom of the clear water, with the bladderwrack curving upwards from them, and the darker channel between rippled by the wash from Gavin's dinghy. If we touched, I'd get advance warning, and she'd have her full forward power to push her clear. The shore was only five metres away when he turned in a smooth U-shape towards the north side. *Khalida* moved in his wake. Great squared boulders like a wardrobe and grand piano left on the beach topped the opposite shore. We came within spitting distance of them, then turned at last and came diagonally into the pool at the head of the loch. The mooring buoy was in the middle. I putted up to it, threaded my rope through the ring, and made it fast.

'I won't come aboard,' Gavin said, from the dinghy. His russet hair was covered by one of those fishermen's hats whose brim bristles flies (his ghillie grandfather's, I'd have bet), and his tanned cheeks were reddened by the wind that fluttered the green folds of his kilt and the tabs on his socks. 'Would you like to come up to the house now, and meet everyone over a cup of tea, or do you want to sleep first?'

'Sleep,' I said. 'Give me two hours, and I'll be human again.'

'I'll come back at five.' Without any fuss, he backed the dinghy away and rowed smoothly for the little stone jetty that jutted out from the shore. I hung up my lifejacket, crawled into my berth, and was out cold in five seconds flat.

When I woke, the wind had fallen away. The sun was gone, the moon not yet risen, and only starlight glimmering on the surface of the loch let me see water from shore. I hoisted the anchor light, a white star to beckon to the yellow light that shone from Gavin's farm. I'd just changed my sailing thermals for my best jeans and navy gansey and put Cat into his travelling basket when I heard the creak, dip of oars. Gavin called, 'Ahoy, *Khalida.*'

'My taxi,' I said, and handed down Cat's basket. There was one of those awkward silences as we rowed over, but by the time I'd caught the jetty and helped secure the ropes it was all fine; we fell into step together up the dark road as if we were walking along the seafront in Scalloway. A light on the farm wall flicked on as we passed it, showing a cobbled yard with wide byre doorways and a grange window facing us, and a corner doorway with two steps up to it. It opened as we came to it, and Gavin's mother held out her hand. 'Come in, Cass. You must be cold now, coming all this way by boat.' She waved me past her. Her voice was softer than Gavin's, the lingering Highland S sounds pronounced. 'Come in to the fire.'

I was glad he had warned me. 'My mother had an accident to her face when she was a girl, with a threshing machine. She was lucky not to lose her eye.' Her scar was far worse than mine, even after sixty years, puckering up the whole of one side of her face in a network of white and red. I smiled at her, straight on. I knew how it felt to see others looking at the bullet-scar across my cheeks, then glancing away. She was even smaller than I, barely reaching five feet, with her grey hair coiled in a bun, and a print pinnie covering her dress.

'Thank you for having me.' I gestured at the basket. 'And Cat – I hope there won't be trouble with your cats.'

'Only Solomon comes indoors.' She nodded at Gavin, busy hanging up his oilskins in the passage. 'Has Gavin told you about him? Half-wildcat, and speaks to nobody else. He probably won't come in with a visitor here. This is my older son, Kenny.'

Gavin was only half a head taller than I, and compactly built, so I wasn't prepared for the man-mountain that rose up from the couch. Kenny was well over six foot, broad-shouldered and dark-haired, with a ruddy outdoor complexion and green-hazel eyes that crinkled in laughter. His hand was twice the size of mine. 'Sit ye down, Cass.' He motioned me to the armchair beside the fire. He had a resonant voice, honed with years of directing sheepdogs, a stronger lilt than Gavin's, and a hesitant way of spacing his words, as if he was translating from Gaelic in his head. 'Let me have your jacket.'

I took my slippers from my pocket, hauled off my boots

and jacket, and handed them to Kenny, then unfastened the straps and opened Cat's lid. He put his paws on the basket edge and jumped out, ready to spend the next half hour sniffing round, trying each chair for size and checking out any windowsills. I sat down on the couch and looked round.

It was my sort of room. The walls were lined with varnished pine, darkened with age to honey-gold, the armchairs differed from the couch, and all three were piled with non-matched cushions. On the mantelpiece, a pair of black-and-white china dogs with foolish King Charles faces jostled envelopes, newspaper clippings, and complete sea urchins – scaddy man's heids, we called them in Shetland – and the fire below crackled between a set of brass fire irons and a wicker kishie of sawn driftwood. A tall clock ticked in the corner, and the smell of roasting meat drifted in from the kitchen. I didn't need to surreptitiously dust off the seat of my jeans before sitting down, or worry about the carpet. It was all homely and worn and welcoming. It was going to be all right.

Chapter Two

The days sped by. I helped Gavin's mother with preparations for the Christmas meal, and we all decorated the tree on Christmas Eve, with the men reminiscing and occasionally disputing over who'd made which cardboard snowman or toilet roll angel in primary school, and their mother arbitrating: 'Ach, no, Kenneth, it was you made the blue angel, and Gavin the green one. I remember it well. You boys have no memory at all.' Midnight Mass was in a little chapel an hour's drive away; the men were magnificent in their scarlet dress kilts and black jackets, and we sang the carols with gusto. On Christmas morning, we exchanged presents: I'd found a Shetland cattle book for Kenny, and a lace wool shawl for Mrs Macrae. I gave Gavin a daft present, a Shetland children's picture book called *The Grumpy Old Sailor,* and he responded with equal lightness: a thirties copy of Olivia Fitzroy's *The Hunted Head.* We ate a huge Christmas dinner of one of their own geese, surrounded by home-grown vegetables, and followed by a home-made Christmas pudding, then collapsed in front of the Queen's speech and the TV's film offering, which turned out to be *Casablanca.* Even Solomon had come in to the house then, lured by goose skin scraps. He was just as Gavin's mother had described, a lean, tawny wildcat with tufted ears and eyes green as sea running over sand. He came in warily and leapt to the back of the couch, then settled on Gavin's shoulder. Cat sank into the couch, pressing closer to my leg; Solomon looked, hissed, and ignored him thereafter.

On Boxing Day, I was initiated into the life of the farm.

Mrs Macrae showed me how to coax the sweet-smelling milk from the cow's pink udders, and I carried the warm enamel can proudly to the table. I scrunched short walks with Gavin and Kenny along the shore and helped count the sheep; we carried buckets of feed to the long-horned Highland cattle, and nets of hay to the Lodge's two Highland ponies – garrons, Gavin called them – which were kept for the stalking in the autumn. They were Luchag and Ribe: Luchag was the fawn of dried bracken, Ribe dappled silver. 'Mouse' and 'Cobweb', Gavin translated.

One day, taking the evening haynets, the wind in our faces, Gavin touched my arm and crouched down among the shore boulders. I imitated him and looked. There, two hundred yards away, half a dozen deer were coming down to drink at the river. I'd never seen Scottish deer in the wild; they were bigger than I expected, and so delicately made, with their slender legs that stepped among the shore stones like dancers. The stag had a great sweep of antlers that turned like a fencer's foil as he checked out his kingdom before drinking. We watched them for ten magical minutes before they turned away and dissolved into the dusk.

Evenings were spent with Cat sprawled between Gavin and I on the couch. Gavin tied trout lures, the finished flies nesting in a round tin like dandelion clocks, or made notes in his small, neat script for the history of the loch that he was writing ('Not that it'll ever be finished,' Kenny interposed, from his armchair by the fire, 'for as soon as he thinks he's got everything, then another letter comes in from Canada with a whole new branch of family tree.'). Their mother knitted by the driftwood fire that blazed with blue and green flame and scented the room with woodsmoke. I found their bookshelves and began working my way through Scott's *Waverley*, a leisurely tale of a young Englishman getting caught up in the Jacobite rebellion of 1745, bound in three volumes that you could never take to sea, with gold embossing on velvety red leather. I joined Gavin's mother with her knitting, and completed an all-in-one for an African baby, with a stripe of Fair Isle pattern across the chest. The comfortable, friendly silence was broken every so often by an exchange of news. At last I understood why Gavin thought I'd fit in there, and I relaxed, and felt that this was a winter land-life I could live.

Before I'd come, five days had seemed long enough. Now, with the days slipping by, it felt too short; but there was a low moving across the Atlantic, and I'd need to get home before it.

'You must come for a ride,' Gavin said, on my second-last day. We caught the ponies and bridled them, then Gavin gave me a leg-up on Luchag before swinging himself up on Ribe's bare back in a swirl of pleats, looking instantly as if he was part of the beast. I knew now that Luchag was trustworthy, though I'd have felt safer out at sea in a force 8 than I did perched perilously bareback, with only her mane to hold on to, but by the time we'd scrunched along the shore and wound through the Lodge plantation of rhododendrons and resin-scented pines, the ground felt less far away, and I was starting to feel at home. The hairy hooves squelched through the last marshy piece and began climbing, up to the shoulder of the hill.

'Just keep yourself vertical,' Gavin said. I swayed and jolted until we came out on top of the rise, and the loch was spread before us: the pool at the head, with *Khalida* nosing the orange mooring buoy, the Z-shape of the narrows, then the loch twisting and turning from headland to headland until it reached the Sound of Sleat. The Cuillins reared up like organ-pipes of snow-covered stone. The colours were glorious: the smooth grey of the loch, the striped line of foreshore, the rust of the heather and gold of dried grass below the dazzling white of the snow caps. I drew a long breath and sat back, contented just to look. Luchag dropped her head and began tearing at the olive grass.

'It's strange,' Gavin said, 'how you can't remember the summer colours once the winter comes.'

'Shetland's the same,' I agreed. 'Though the other way – the minute the sun shines, it feels like it's always shone.'

'The mind's protection. Otherwise we'd all go "*Why* do we live in a place with six months of winter?" and move to Benidorm.'

I made a face. 'I've done the Med in winter. Trust me, you don't want to. Besides –' I spread my hands, trying to marshal my thoughts. Luchag lifted her head at the tug on her reins, then pulled them out of my hands. I leant forward to take them back. Ribe remained statue-still. 'You need to have lived through the winter to enjoy the summer. If you went to Benidorm, it would always be warmer there, so you'd just freeze when you came back.'

'I put it down to the Reformation,' Gavin said. 'The belief that you have to suffer six months of cold and wet to have earned the summer.'

'The Scots psyche.' I agreed. 'I wonder how long it took the emigrants to get used to Australian sunshine.'

'They never got used to it.' Gavin was suddenly serious. 'Not the first generation. This loch –' he swept an arm outwards along its length – 'once supported a whole clan. Sixty families, cleared to Canada. My family was only kept because we were the laird's servants, his farmer and his best ghillie.' His grey eyes caressed the loch. 'My great-grandmother's sisters prospered there, but their letters show how they never forgot their own country. Every so often we have a Canadian Macrae who comes home. There was one, a fourth cousin, who was so like me that I could have shaved by him.' His voice lightened, teasing. 'At the entrance to the loch there was one of the best attested kelpie sightings, by several ministers, no less, and one of them a distant cousin.'

'Kelpie?' I thought of the giant silver horses tossing their head near the Falkirk wheel.

'Ach, it's the water horse, a great dark hump in the water. You'll meet it on a dark night, just like an ordinary Highland pony, grazing by the waterside, with its saddle and bridle, all of the best quality, but if you're so daft as to jump on its back then it'll take you down to the depths of the loch.'

'Oh,' I said, recognising the description, 'a njuggle.'

'And what's a *nyeugle*?'

'A Shetland pony, all black, with a silver harness. It lived in burns, and scratched its back on the millwheel, or it would lead you through bogs until you were muddy and exhausted. What about these ministers?'

'It was August, 1872, and they were on the yacht *Leda* when a creature came up beside them, a dark slatey brown, with a long humped body and a fin on the back of its neck. They had a very clear view of it for about an hour, until it was frightened off by a steam launch coming up behind them.' He gathered up his reins up, and Ribe lifted one foot. 'We'd better turn around – downwards is always harder going. Just let Luchag pick along, and shout if you feel insecure.'

We did my passage plan that evening. I spread my pages of downward plan, my charts, tidal atlases, and pilot books out on the floor, then coaxed Cat out from under the chart and persuaded him to go and annoy Kenny's ancient sheepdog, Luath, instead. I just had to reverse all the compass bearings of my route down and re-work my timings to fit tomorrow's tides. It would be an easier journey, with the tricky Kyle Rhea and Kyle of Loch Alsh got through first, then just the long run up the west of Scotland. The second day, when I'd be more tired, was straight across the North Sea to Shetland, with no coasts to worry about, and only oil tankers to dodge (the fishing boats didn't leave till the New Year), so I'd be able to cat-nap all the way. I was just heading my paper 'Back to Shetland' when Kenny looked over the top of his cattle studbook.

'Cass, bairn, you're behind the times. You should just be using Gavin's iPad.' He gave his brother a wicked smile. 'He was watching your voyage down every step of the way.'

Gavin reddened. 'Potential voyage,' he corrected. He brought out his iPad, tapped it a few times, and passed it over. There, on a chart on the screen, was my course here. I looked at the logo.

'Navionics. It's frighteningly easy to use.' I scrolled up 'route' and tapped 'return'. Immediately the waypoints reversed themselves. At the side of the screen was the really useful bit, compass bearing and distance from one waypoint to the next. I passed the iPad back to Gavin. 'Can you check each of my paper bearings as I do it?'

Kenny set his stud book down, and moved to the couch to look over his brother's shoulder. 'It looks very bonny, but would you actually use it to steer your course?'

'People do,' I said. 'Literally – they create the route, like this, then tell the autopilot to steer it. That's why it's frighteningly easy. You could get yourself into such trouble. Look at this – a nice, neat dog-leg through Kyle Rhea and Kyle Akin, with nothing to say how dangerous they are at the wrong state of the tide.'

Gavin looked up, smiling. 'So what would a real sailor do?'

'Distance. 270 nautical miles. Hours of journey at five

knots. Hazards.' I flourished the first page of my passage plan at them. 'Starting with one unmarked and one marked rock in your own loch.'

'Ellice shoal,' Kenny said, and gave a grin at Gavin that said one of them had ended up on it.

'Then helps – lights, towers, anything that'll tell me where I am as I head north. Boltholes, places I can go if the weather turns nasty, and the exact page in the pilot book for each one. When things are going wrong isn't the time to scrabble for information.'

'So what are all these books you're using?'

I flourished each one. 'Imray's *Yachtman's Pilot to the Skye and the North-West of Scotland.* That gives me all the lighthouses and anchorages, and advice about routes and tides. The Admiralty *Tidal Streams Atlas* tells me what the tide is doing every hour, direction and strength.' I opened it to show him the charts with arrows. A faded photocopy fell out. 'This is from a book that's out of print, but it's a clear guide to Kyle Rhea.'

Kenny considered. 'We're at springs now.' He leaned forward to the chart. 'So you want to be at the end of the loch for the first of the west-going tide, five hours after high water.'

'Four and a half hours after,' I said. 'The hour is from the half hours.'

Gavin opened Safari. 'Tides at Kyle of Lochalsh on Sunday. High Water at 03.58 or 16.14.'

'Perfect,' I said. 'So it turns to go in the direction I want around half past eight. Two hours to the end of the loch, so ETD 06.30, and the tide with me.' I wrote it down on my piece of paper. 'Eyeball navigation to there. Okay, Gavin, Kyle Rhea to the Skye Bridge, how far does the machine reckon it is?'

'Waypoints 5 to 9, 11.4 nautical miles.'

I spun my dividers over the chart, and nodded. Kenny grinned. 'You're not trusting the machine at all, are you?'

'Not an inch. Here, you try.' I showed him how to lay the parallel ruler on the line I wanted to sail, then walk it to the compass rose on the chart, while Gavin checked the angle on the iPad, and by bedtime we'd worked out timings, tides and compass bearings for the whole journey, along with when I'd see each lighthouse and what its flashing pattern would be, all written clearly on three sides of A4, and stowed ready for cockpit use in a clear plastic wallet.

'This navigation is easy once you know how,' Kenny said, yawning.

'I've still got to actually sail the course,' I pointed out.

'Ach, there's no fear of you. We'll be expecting that phone call to tell us you've made it home at 15.36 precisely.'

A smoor of rain swept over us as Gavin walked me down to the jetty. 'It'll clear tomorrow, though,' he predicted. 'Are you game for walking up to the Bonnie Prince's cave?'

We'd talked one evening of a walk to the waterfall, then along to Prince Charlie's cave. It was Gavin's grandfather's great-grandfather's great-grandfather that had guided the Bonnie Prince to it, when the head of the loch had been stiff with red-coats camped all around the farm, and he'd been rewarded with one of the buttons from the Prince's coat.

'Our only heirloom,' Gavin had said, when he'd worn it to the Halloween party I'd got volunteered for judging at, 'and my heart's in my mouth every time I wear my black kilt-jacket, for fear I haven't sewn it on firmly enough. Mother would never forgive me if I lost it.'

'A perfect last day walk,' I agreed.

Chapter Three

Saturday 28th December

Gavin knew his own loch. By mid-morning, the wind had fallen; the sun had come out in a glory of rainbows, and was picking up the silver twists of the burns cascading down the rust-red hills. The fretted sea had turned from sullen grey to polished pewter, and there were enough blue chinks in the sky to make a Dutchman's trousers.

We left Cat sleeping by the fire, took a picnic of scones and his mother's freshly made crowdie, like cream-textured, salty cottage cheese, and scrunched off along the pebble shore.

'The tourist side,' Gavin murmured, nodding across at the gravel track running above the opposite shore. 'Our going's a bit harder.' He picked his way up a network of narrow paths to the height of the headland, then down again until we came out at the boulders and were swinging along the shore, walking boots scrunching in time, breath smoking in the crisp air. The grass above the tideline was the yellow-green of newly gathered mermaid hair weed, the shore pebbles coloured like jewels: rose granite, milk quartz, green serpentine, mica-glinting gneiss. The fronds of kelp just breaking the surface at the sea edge of the wide river were crinkled with ice.

We threaded through an oak wood with mossed boulders between the trees. I could hear the waterfall now, like a distant drum roll; then suddenly we came out to a polished basin brimming with black water, and turbulent with zebra ripples of current in the centre. The still edges had comma-shapes of coffee coloured foam swirling around the sanded-smooth rock. The distant drum roll became a throbbing roar.

'The bottom of the falls,' Gavin shouted in my ear, and gestured me upwards. A clamber upwards through heather stems, a twist in the path, and we were half way up the great cascade, falling the height of a tall ship's mast from a twisted spout in the rock above us. The path was slippery with spray, but the rooted heather gave a grip underfoot, and the slender trees made good handholds. Half an hour of breathless climbing brought us to the top, beside the lochan that fed the river, with the cascade below us. We paused to unpack our picnic.

'Though we'd better keep moving,' Gavin said, glancing at the dark shadows on the hills. 'Kenny said he'd pick us up from the Smugglers' Bay half an hour before dusk. We can eat as we go.'

He used the little dagger in his stocking to spread two scones each with crowdie, and we munched companionably as we sidestepped down to mid-hill level. The ice-hardened bracken crunched beneath our feet, and the air was cold and crisp. I was glad of my best sailing socks and gloves. Before us, a mile away on the hill, was the cave we were heading for, a dark mouth half-way up a rock face, with a thin ledge of heather as pathway.

I was nervous about arriving there. Although we'd achieved a comfortable intimacy in these five days, the closest we'd been physically had been touching fingers as we hung up tree ornaments. At some point we were going to have to get closer. Part of me wanted to: I loved the way he moved, the economy of his hand gestures, the neat way his kilt pleats swirled as he turned. His brown hands were square in shape, hands made to work, yet delicate as a spider spinning a web when he was tying one of his tiny flies. At the same time I was terrified. Convention was closing over me like cold deep water. I could do swinging along the hill path like this, but there would be police functions, and he'd want children, and soon my unfettered life with *Khalida*'s sails bent on, ready to take me where the wind blew, would just be a memory. And the Bonnie Prince's cave, with Gavin's kingdom spread below us, would be a romantic place for a first kiss –

We were half way there when Gavin wrinkled his nose. 'A dead deer,' he said. So much for romance. I was getting the faint scent of it too, a sweet decay overlying the sharp frost, when he stopped dead, with a shocked exclamation in Gaelic. His hand came up to hold me back. My feet halted obediently, but I couldn't help looking forward.

I saw the skull first. It was lying in a hollow of dried bracken, below a grey-lichened rock, with the sockets gazing straight at us below a mop of dark hair. The jaw was pushed sideways; the teeth grinned. Something that might have been an ear clung still to the dirty bone. The neat ribs, the spine and breastbone, lay in their pattern, tarnished with vestiges of black flesh. The shoulders were there, but the arms had been pulled away. There were foxes in these hills, and badgers, wildcats, ravens, golden eagles. One leg lay straight; the other kneecap was slightly raised above the dried-fern ground, as if sinews still held it to the thigh. That foot was a jumble of gnawed bones. The smell came from the tangle of dried intestines within the rib cage, like blackened seaweed on a beach.

Bile rose in my throat. I took a couple of steps back, and choked the sickness down.

Gavin retreated with me, and reverted to DI Macrae of the Inverness branch of Police Scotland. 'Scene of Crime are going to be delighted with this.' He took a handkerchief from his pocket and skewered it flat with bracken stems, a square signpost, then turned to give me a wry smile. 'Is it you, or I, or just the combination of the two of us, that attracts murder?'

'Murder?' I managed to keep my voice steady.

19

'A hillwalker who'd died of a heart-attack or exposure would still have his clothes on.'

I looked at the exposed bones. There was no sign of torn cloth; only the dark, matted hair.

'Besides,' Gavin said, 'this isn't the tourist side of the loch. A very few go up the track from the back of the Lodge and along the ridge until they get to Arnisdale. Almost nobody comes rambling here.' He took several photos with his mobile, not stepping any nearer to the body. 'The last person here was the murderer. There may still be clues. It's amazing what the SOCOs can find.'

Sooner them than me. 'Can you tell how long he – she's – been there?'

'After the 21st of July.' Gavin's tanned cheeks reddened. 'I always climb up on the anniversary of the Prince being here. Late August, September, maybe. Forensics will narrow it down. But what was he doing up here?' He shook his head. 'We can't carry on to the cave. It may be that was where he'd been, or was headed.' He sighed. 'Oh, I'm going to be popular. Every uniform in our force will be doing a sweep of this hill for two days, and finding nothing but bracken.'

We fell back into step, heading diagonally downwards towards the bay. Above us, the handkerchief shone white against the auburn foliage. 'Some student going off for a highland ramble, and not being specific about where he was headed?'

'Don't forget the missing clothes. Two or more students, with the others able to cover up the dead man's absence, or tell a convincing story of a tragedy, like a drowning where the body wasn't recovered. I don't remember one of these from this area, and we've certainly not had a missing person reported from here.'

'Why take the clothes? It can't have been easy, undressing him.'

'To speed up decomposition. To make identifying the

body harder.' He grimaced. 'Teeth are only any good if you have a name. We'll see what missing persons comes up with UK wide.'

I thought about what clothes could tell, as we tramped downhill. Gavin's kilt would narrow it down to a Macrae with that waist size and height. My T-shirt had been bought in Bergen, and my thermals, knitted gansey, and Musto jacket would mark me out as a sailor, so you could begin by circulating my description among Norwegian yachting folk: woman, thirty, 5'2", long dark hair in a plait. I reckoned that would get my name within twenty-four hours.

It was three o'clock by the time we reached the bay Gavin had called Smugglers'. The upper half of the clouds blushed in the last of the sun, the colours were filtered through an amber gel, and the varnished dinghy gleamed bright as a marmalade cat as Kenny curved it round towards us, cut the motor, and sculled it to the shore. Gavin broke into rapid, urgent Gaelic. Kenny followed Gavin's hand; he nodded as he pin-pointed the white handkerchief, caught now by the last rays of sun on the mountain's upper slopes, then asked a question, with a gesture of his own towards the cave. Gavin nodded, and added a sweeping movement of his hand and a short phrase which evidently meant 'They'll have to search the whole place' for both brothers grimaced, suddenly looking alike: their private kingdom being trampled by interlopers. I knew how that felt. Gavin had had to search my *Khalida*, the first time we'd met, and I remembered still my stab of outrage as his space-suited minions had stepped over her guard-rails.

The men left me on the boat to do a final rig-check before tomorrow's voyage. By the time I got to the farm, Kenny had explained to their mother, while Gavin went from phone to computer, to download and send his photos, and finally came through to the sitting room, rubbing one hand through his hair. The curls he tried to cut away sprung back. 'Cass, I've told them you must get away tomorrow, so they're sending the local man from Kyle of Lochalsh to take your statement. I can't do it, because we were together.' He grimaced. 'A round trip of a hundred and forty miles for him. Mother, I invited him to dinner.'

When the local man arrived, just after six, he turned out to be from Orkney. 'They try not to put us back to our own place,' he explained in the familiar lilt, like a Welshman speaking Scots. 'I'm trying to learn the Gaelic. A lot of the words are the same; the Western Isles folk are almost as Norse as the Northern Isles.'

'The Minch used to be the Viking Corridor,' I agreed. I'd sailed it in the replica longship *Sea Stallion.* 'I'm sorry to drag you out tonight, but tomorrow and Monday are my weather window to get home.'

'To Shetland, yea, yea. Gavin explained that. I'll get your statement in a peedie minute.'

It was a constrained last meal, with Sergeant Pearson an extra on one side of the table, and the staring eye-sockets of the skull still vivid in my memory. Gavin's mother had intended it as a special goodbye, with a steak pie of golden crispy pastry covering melt-in-your-mouth beef from their own animals, Brussels sprouts and potatoes from the garden, and a lemon meringue pudding which was almost enough to convert me to life ashore. We women cleared away the plates, then left Gavin and Kenny to wash and dry while the sergeant wrote down my statement in his black notebook.

'I had a look on the computer at the station,' he said, 'and you're right enough, Gavin, there's nobody reported missing anywhere round here this summer, on hill or at sea.'

'Aye,' Gavin said. 'But he may have been reported missing from his home area. We'll be able to start looking once forensics give us a sex, height, and age. Will you be okay, Kenny, to lead the Scene of Crime folk up the hill?'

Kenny nodded gloomily. 'Will there be many of them?'

'Two trips, at least, and an extra one back, with the body.'

It was almost nine o'clock by the time Sergeant Pearson left for his long drive home. 'It's a good thing he has nobody waiting up for him,' Gavin's mother commented. 'Cass, see what you would like for your journey. Here are fresh rolls, and ham, and I have portions of stew frozen, you would just need to heat it up and have bread with it.'

She made a picnic of it, everything I'd need at hand for the first day, and wrapped the carton of stew in newspaper, so that it would defrost slowly and be ready for when I needed it. She had made me a whole crowdie too, and wrapped it with bubblewrap inside a cardboard box: 'It will keep for a week, easy. This tub is fish for Cat.'

'Thank you,' I said. I wouldn't be expecting her to get up at six thirty. 'Thank you for everything.' I resorted to my native Shetland. 'It's been a most special Christmas.'

She gave me a steady look from the grey eyes that were so like Gavin's. 'I hope you'll be back, now you've found your way.'

I wasn't sure what to say to that, so I was glad of Gavin coming into the kitchen. 'Are you needing a porter, Cass? Creator Lord, will you have room aboard for all this?'

'I'll make room,' I assured him.

'You're a pleasure to cook for,' his mother said. 'I was afraid you might be one of these girls who's so concerned about her weight that she only eats salad.'

'There's nothing like sailing to keep the pounds off and the appetite up,' I said. 'Thank you.'

It was black dark outside. Once we got into the dinghy, the sea glinted coal black around us, and the anchor light half-way up my mast shed a moon-clear circle around *Khalida*'s white hull. I climbed aboard, and leant over for

Gavin to hand Cat's basket and the provisions up. 'See you at six thirty.'

'Six thirty.' He looked up at me, face whitened in the LED light. 'Don't be having nightmares, now. Sleep well.'

Sunday 29th to Tuesday 31st December

Sunday 29th December,

High Water Kyle of Lochalsh, UT	*03.58, 4.6m*
Low Water	*10.08, 1.8m*
High Water	*16.14, 4.6m*
Expecting to arrive Ruba Reidh light	*16.45*

Sunrise	*09.07*
Moonset	*12.58*
Sunset	*15.42*
Moonrise	*03.49*

Moon waning crescent.

Monday 30th December

High Water Ullapool, UT	*02.06, 3.9m*
Low Water	*07.55, 2.0m*
High Water	*14.27, 4.2m*
Low Water	*20.59, 2.0m*

Sunrise	*09.07*
Moonset	*12.58*
Sunset	*15.42*
Moonrise	*03.49*

Moon waning crescent.

Forecast: westerly force 3-4, Sunday a.m., and backing S to SE during Sunday evening with strong gusts, then SW from midnight.

Mackerel skies and mares' tails
Make tall ships carry small sails.

Chapter Four

It was still black dark when I awoke, but the crescent moon cast her yellow gleam over the loch, so that every headland stood out black against the burnished water. Half past five. I squirmed out of my berth and put the kettle on to boil while I dressed. Cat got his breakfast and litter tray, then I headed up on deck. The wind was exactly as promised, a westerly that would give us a fine beam-reach up to Cape Wrath.

I rolled the cover off the mainsail and freed the tiller. By the time I'd done that the kettle was whistling; I filled my flask and secured it to the table with bungee cords. I put the stew on to heat while I buttered several of Gavin's mother's rolls, added a generous layer of crowdie, and put them in an ice-cream tub. The hot stew went into my wide-necked flask. I wouldn't starve this voyage.

Back up on deck, I saw Gavin's dark figure stepping from the pier into the boat, and heard the oars creak, then the clink and splash of him lowering the engine. A moment, then it put-putted into life. I started my ancient Volvo Penta and hauled my mooring rope from the buoy. The anchor light would double as a steaming light, if there was anyone about to be particular.

'*Halo leat,*' Gavin greeted me. 'All set?'

'*Tha,*' I agreed. 'Lead on.'

Ten minutes, and we were in the loch proper, with the twisting path we'd seen from on high glinting before me. Gavin throttled back and came alongside, holding up a newspaper-wrapped parcel. It was warm as he handed it to me.

'Bacon rolls,' he said. 'They'll keep in a jumper till you're ready for them.'

'Thank you,' I said. I hated those awful railway platform moments. 'It was a lovely Christmas.'

'Thank you for coming.' He held out his hand and I laid mine in it, glove to glove. 'Now you know your way, come back.'

'I'd like to,' I meant it. 'Let me know how you get on with your skeleton.'

'I will. *Beannachd leat.*' Goodbye, a blessing on you.

'*Beannachd leat.*' I leaned forward and kissed him on the cheek. His breath was warm on my lips as I drew back. 'Thank you. *Taing mhor.*' Then, before I could make a fool of myself, I stepped back and put *Khalida* into gear. 'I'll text as I go, if I get a signal.'

He raised his hand as I pulled away from him. 'Safe journey.'

ᚼ

It would be a long day and night. I had a bacon roll just after seven, when the hills began to be outlined in blue, and another at eight. The first creamy light, the colour of a duck's egg, lay in a streak above the eastern hill, though the western sky before me was still dark, with the crescent moon as flat as if it had been painted on, and the stars fading points of light against the violet sky. As *Khalida* putted on, the light behind us strengthened to a line of cream above the cut-out hills, and the old-brass moon bleached to a curved silver line. Daylight replaced the starlight glimmer on the water; now I could see the shore, its colours dulled, and by the time we reached the end of the loch it was fully light, with the early sun turning the western hills to shades of gold: the bleached long grass, the olive heather, the varnished brown of tree branches. We passed the last skerry, then I brought *Khalida* head to wind to raise the mainsail. I sheeted it in, loosed the jib, and she surged forward under her own power. I glanced down into the cabin. 08.35. Yes, I should have the tide with me now – and on the thought we came out into the stream, and I saw the log figures creep up from 4 knots to 5, then to 5.3, 6.2. At this rate, we'd make a swift passage. Cat crept up to sniff the air, then crouched down on the thwart, paws braced. I reached down for his lead and clipped it to the harness I'd trained him to wear at sea.

'Going home, Cat,' I told him.

The sky was clear now, but the water was overshadowed by the mountains, and the low sun magnified every bump and hillock. On my left, the shore was bare; on my right, there was a row of cottages by a pale beach, their lights glimmering in the water. Glenelg, Bernera, the ferry pier and the end of the road. The Kyle Rhea turbines flickered fibreglass-white above the pale blue water. After that the hills were wooded on each side, then the sound opened out into Loch Alsh. The sun dazzled in my eyes from the east, and the wind was in my face. I tightened the sails and pointed close to the wind, and *Khalida* tilted over. Cat slipped back into my berth, where he'd be snug, however much the boat tipped. The log had gone down to 5.6 knots, but we were broadside on to the tide, so we'd be pushed towards the next narrows, at Kyle Akin. On shore, a hunch-shouldered heron flapped into life above the whisky-gold water at the loch edge; behind me, the sun's reflection made an oval too bright to look at. Three ducks crossed my path.

By ten thirty we were bumping under the arches of the Skye Bridge, with *Khalida* rocking to the overfalls of wind against tide. I'd come down under sail, and been rocked closer to the massive piers than I'd liked by a passing fishing boat. This time I set the engine going, rolled the jib away, and headed dead centre of the wide arch. Now the Sound of Sleat lay open before us. I cut the engine, restored full sail, set *Khalida*'s nose for the gap between Longay and Eilan Mor, hooked up the windvane, and settled back to relax.

The views were spectacular. On my left, the Cuillin rose sheer from the sea, Bla Bheinn and Sgurr Alasdair, jagged slabs of rock topped with fissures of snow. On my right, Loch Kishorn and Loch Carron cradled the green oasis of Plockton, where palm trees grew. The sky arched blue above me now, with long cumulus gathering smoke-grey from the west. Behind me, slanting lines of rain fell to the water, blotting out Ardnamurchan. If I'd had longer, I'd have sailed on down and round that headland, and earned my little *Khalida* the right to wear a bunch of heather at her prow. Properly speaking, of course, it was a sign that boats coming up from south had made it round the notoriously tricky point and into the Highlands, but we Shetlanders had to do it in reverse. Another time …

Under sail, with the tide pushing her on, *Khalida* kept up her speed. The Course over Ground on the GPS in the cabin read 8.3 knots. By midday we'd come level with the point of Rona, and the sea horizon had opened out before us. The sun had climbed as far into the sky as it was going to go, and the water deepened to hard, bright winter blue. On my right, the headlands to the north lay one after another like the landscape glimpsed through a window in a medieval painting. I'd done forty miles of the journey in under six hours. I should easily make Rubha Reidh, and maybe even the Stoerhead Light, before the weather closed in.

By 14.00, the sky had darkened. A mirr of rain blew over. I pulled up my hood and fastened it under my chin. A last shaft of sunlight hazed the hills and brightened the colours: scarlet roofs, cornflower-blue tarpaulins over boats and tractor, the glistening orange weed at the water's edge. Then the grey clouds closed over the sun. Rain by 1800, the forecast had said, and the wind backing to the south and rising. I hove-to, took in a single reef, and made sure the ropes ran free to take in the second, then ate a bowl of Gavin's mother's stew sitting at the table in the cabin, added an extra jumper under my oilskins, and wrapped a scarf around my neck. I sent Gavin a text: *Making gd progress how is skeleton?* His reply came just as the kettle boiled: *Organising hill search bad time of year. Everyone busy with N Yr. Safe voyage.* Fed and clad, I took my mug into the cockpit and freed off the sheets again. We sailed on into the dusk.

It was a long, cold passage over the coal-shining water, with the cliffs of Scotland an outline in the distance. The rain came on in the early evening, as forecast, and the wind swung with it. Soon we were running goosewinged under a double-reefed mainsail and half jib, and I didn't dare leave the tiller for more than seconds. I could reach into the cabin for the log-book, or make drinking chocolate from the flask, but that was all. *Khalida* surged forward with each gust, surfing down the long wave-backs. I was glad when midnight came, and it began to back westerly at last. I let the jib slip over to the same side as the mainsail, and unrolled it a little, then I put the chain over the tiller, to hold *Khalida* on course, and made myself comfortable under the cabin awning, standing up every five minutes to look all round for the lights of passing ships hurrying down the Viking corridor to have their New Year at home. I slipped below for a midnight snack, then alternated between sitting up on deck and doing my own New Year clean: polishing the woodwork, washing the dishes, pans, floor and ceiling, and shining the ship's bell, lantern, and fish brass. I wrote up the log at half-hourly intervals, and had a cup of chocolate every three entries. I listened to the Coastguard weather reports. I fished up a bucketful of water and scrubbed as much as I could reach of the decks.

I cleaned the bilges. I re-stowed the sails in the forepeak. I checked off the lighthouses as we passed them: Tiumpan Head, Stoer, Butt of Lewis, and Cape Wrath at last, as the first grey light began to filter through the darkness. Now I could see the water around me, although the cape was only a dark shape on the horizon.

Another day, another night. I cat-napped through it, with my alarm clock set to allow me no more than twenty minutes at a time. Grey water tumbled around me. I caught a glimpse of the peak of Hoy, far on the horizon as the sun set, and saw the lights of Fair Isle as the 30th of December slipped into Old Year's Day. At last the star of Sumburgh Head light flashed from ahead of me. Gradually the sky lightened; the triple peaks of Foula stood grey and distant off my port bow, and the rocky head of Sumburgh, topped by the Stevenson brothers' first Shetland lighthouse, was off to starboard. By breakfast time, the horizon ahead was violet, shading into the blue east, but behind me there were grey cirrus, dabbed with a painter's brush. *Mackerel skies and mares' tails, make tall ships carry small sails.* The sailor's storm warning. *Khalida* was still moving steadily through the long waves, and the tide was bringing our speed up to 6.3 knots. We'd go faster in the next three hours, when the wind picked up, and I'd be sheltered by the cliffs of West Burrafirth once I'd turned the corner around Papa Stour. College didn't start for another week, so I was heading for my home port of Brae, where my parents still lived – at least, Dad still lived in the house I'd grown up in, and Maman seemed to be dividing her time between it and her elegant town flat in Poitiers. I wasn't sure I'd be awake for the New Year bells, but I'd join them for lunch tomorrow.

We just beat the wind. We stormed past the World War I guns on Vementry isle with the water breaking white around us, skooshed around between Papa Little and Muckle Roe, and ran full tilt for the marina, with

Khalida's mast swaying ominously to each gust. I was thankful to drop the mainsail at last and motor in to my berth. I'd just fastened the last mooring rope when the wind rattled the rigging and tilted *Khalida* over as if she was still at sea. I dived below. The rain drummed on the fibreglass roof. I opened the forehatch for Cat to go out if he wanted to, sent a 'made it' text to Gavin and Maman, fell into my berth, and slept.

Wednesday 1st January
New Year's Day

Low Water, Brae UT	*02.42, 0.6m*
High Water	*08.55, 1.8m*
Low Water	*15.11, 0.6m*
High Water	*21.33, 1.8m*

Moonrise,	*08.25*
Sunrise	*09.15*
Sunset	*15.02*
Moonset	*15.59*

New moon

He wis flyin every fit.
He was flying every foot – said of someone in a great hurry.

THE SHETLAND ISLES

Unst

ATLANTIC OCEAN

Yell

Eshaness

St Magnus Bay

Brae

Muckle Roe

Linga Voe

Papa Little Gonfirth

Papa Stour

Aith

Lerwick

Vaila

Scalloway

Foula

NORTH SEA

Sumburgh Head

Chapter Five

The midnight fireworks woke me, and the cheerful noises drifting down from the boating club bar. I opened my eyes and considered my curved fibreglass ceiling. I could turn over and go back to sleep, or I could go and join the party for an hour or so, then go back to sleep. Cass, the party animal ... maybe not. I made myself a new hot water bottle, got undressed properly, and left them to it.

When I woke, the wind had fallen. The sunrise was tinged with rose; to the west, the clouds were blowing like smoke across the pale blue sky. The spring tide had washed up the slipway until it almost reached the flat in front of the boating club. It was strange to see the concrete empty. I'd worked here all last summer, when it was filled with dinghies: Picos, Sport 14s, Mirrors, our new Feva under its pristine cover. Now they slept in the shed, with the rescue boat in the middle, like a mother hen surrounded by its chickens. The slip was a silent gleam of grey water, instead of being filled with flapping neon-pink sails, and scuffling children shrieking at the coldness of the water, or throwing jellyfish at each other.

It was warmer this morning. I tightened the halyards without needing my gloves, then leant against the mast to look around. The marina was cradled in a rock arm at the head of Busta Voe. The town of Brae (population 2,000), half an hour's drive north of Lerwick, was spread round the u-shaped beach. The oldest houses were across on my right: the Manse, the former shop (with own pier), the old school, the village hall, several houses that were now B&Bs. Among them were modern Brae, the dark brown council houses and pastel wood of new-builds, the health centre and care home, the school and leisure centre, and several 'Britain's most northerlies': the astroturf pitch, the Indian takeaway, Frankie's fish and chip shop, the Co-op, the fire and police stations.

Behind the main town was the cluster of houses built for oil folk. They were little, square houses, dominated now by the white bulk of the hotel for the newest workers, busy creating a giant gas terminal for Totale. As long as I could remember, people had been prophesying the oil would run out, but the tankers still kept coming. Gas was the new big thing, and Totale had four accommodation barges filled with workers, three in Lerwick and one in Scalloway. The other main effect on islanders, according to my friend Inga, was that you couldn't get a plumber, joiner, brickie, or engineer for love nor money; they were all busy too earning mega-bucks at the terminal to come to the houses of mere locals.

Cat came out while I was looking round, sniffed the air and headed along the pontoon with his plumed tail upright, a cat who was checking out his home turf. His neat white paws stepped disdainfully on the wet wood. He paused at the marina gate, inspecting the sheep in the park above, then slipped beneath the grille, and bounded down to the beach. I went into the boating club for a long, hot shower, laying my clothes on the heated floor to warm up while I washed, then came back to enjoy the last of Gavin's mother's rolls for breakfast, toasted, with raspberry jam. After that, I texted Gavin: *Awake at last. Happy New Year. How is skeleton?*

The reply came within seconds. *I'm least popular person in the force. Big hill walk tomorrow. Forensics on holiday till Monday.*

I'd just finished texting commiserations when the phone rang: Dad.

'Your mother's cooking a wonderful New Year's Day

lunch,' he said. 'Will I come and get you?'

'That'd be great. What time?'

'Don't you be laughing at me, now. *Eugénie, quelle heure déjeuner?*' My mouth fell open. They must be really trying to make this reconciliation work, if Dad was speaking French. He picked up my thought. 'Should have learned it years ago. If I'm going to be visiting France more often, meeting your mother's colleagues, I'd need to be able to say more than just *bonjour*. Hang on.' I tried to imagine my businessman dad at one of Maman's rehearsals, with Greek-robed chorus members chattering like eider ducks in the corridor of some stately home while several highly strung soloists imposed their interpretation of the music on some poor director in the great hall.

'We eat at *une heure*, your mother says. I'll get you at quarter to.'

'See you then,' I agreed.

I'd just coaxed Cat away from a dead fish on the tideline and put him in his basket when the black Range Rover drew up at the marina gate. I scrambled in. 'Hi, Dad. Happy New Year.'

My dad was in his sixties now, but you wouldn't have guessed it. His dark hair had only touches of grey at the ears, his eyes were still blazing Irish blue. I'd got my colouring from him, and the curls, but not, to my sorrow, his commanding height; I was knee-high to a grasshopper, and there were times aboard a tall ship when I could've done with an extra six inches. He had a stubborn chin, a beaky nose, and a voice that bounced round the car. Forty years away from Dublin hadn't eased out any of his accent.

'A good New Year to you too, Cassie. It was a pity you couldn't join us last night.'

'I was out cold. I'd been awake for two and a half days.'

'We thought that would be it.'

39

'Did you and Maman stay up for the New Year?'

He went slightly pink. 'We had a bottle of champagne to toast the bells in France, then in Britain.'

Well, well. It sounded a pretty thorough *entente cordiale.* 'The fireworks woke me, but I couldn't be bothered to get up and party.'

He gave me a sideways look. 'A pity you couldn't have stayed down in Scotland. They take the New Year seriously there.'

'Not a chance,' I said. 'Gavin has a body on his hands,' and explained, which between a description of the skeleton and the work it would generate brought us nicely around the western curve of the voe, above the white bulk of the Jacobean Busta House, the laird's former residence, now a hotel, and across the bridge onto the island of Muckle Roe: the big red island, named by the Vikings. Ours was the second-last house at the end of the road, a square, eighties box, with a path down to the beach where I'd kept *Osprey*, my first dinghy.

We were met by the smell of roast duck. Maman was busy laying the cutlery on each side of her china plates with the pink cupids; I hadn't seen those out of their cupboard for eighteen years. She greeted me with two kisses on each cheek. 'Cassandre! Happy New Year. *Salut*, Cat. Dermot, please open the champagne.'

She looked a most improbable apparition to find out in these wilds, my maman. Her dark hair was swept up in a Callas chignon, her eyes outlined with kohl, her complexion flawless. She wore a black dress with a silver waistband and a rib-length silver jacket, smart enough for the dress circle bar of the Paris Opéra. A jade pendant hung in her curved neckline. She'd stood out like a shalder among seapinks at school functions, which had equally exasperated me and made me proud. I hoped the reconciling would keep working.

She waved us through to the sitting room. A plate of

pastry twists and three champagne glasses stood ready on the low table. Dad had the glasses filled by the time I'd sat down at one end of the couch. Cat inspected the inside of the piano, then installed himself on the Chinese carpet. He liked it here; there was this fire, and there would be a saucer of something more interesting than home-caught tiddlers.

'Eugénie, Cassie, all the best to you for the year to come.' Dad raised his glass to Maman. 'Interesting parts and sympathetic directors.' The glass tilted to me. 'A triumphant graduation and an officer post on your favourite square rigger.'

He must have thought that one through beforehand, for I suspected he really wanted to wish me a happy marriage and a male first-born. I raised my glass, thinking fast. Not even for peace did I think I could drink success to his firm's windfarm. Then I knew the toast I wanted to give, and smiled at them both, sitting together on the couch. 'To the Irish-French alliance.'

The meal was wonderful. There was boar pâté on toast and slices of cured sausage, roast duck, and potatoes, an endive salad tossed in vinaigrette, and Maman's pear tart. The third degree on how I'd got on with Gavin's family was restrained, and we'd just settled back in the sitting room with tiny cups of coffee when a car drew up outside. There was a tap at the door, and a diffident Shetland voice called, 'Is there anybody home?'

Dad rose, and there was a bustle while he ushered the stranger in and along to his study, rather than bringing him into the sitting room. I raised my eyebrows at Maman. 'Business, on New Year's Day?'

She touched a finger to her lips and went into French. 'Have you finished? Then we will do the dishes, like a good mother and daughter. Cat, it is your turn now.'

He leapt up from the fire and trotted before us, tail held high. Maman closed the kitchen door behind him. 'This poor man visited us two nights ago. He worked with your father many years ago. He wanted advice, and couldn't think who else to ask.' She paused to put a bowl of duck trimmings down for Cat, who launched in as if he hadn't seen food for weeks. 'He has a small haulage firm, bringing goods up from south and taking loads down – well, his partner has absconded and he is now in money difficulties. Your father said that if he brought the books round he would look, and see if he could advise him. Though he said to me afterwards that he did not think there was much to be done, except to go bankrupt, or to ask his father to bail him out – his father is the big firm, you have seen the trucks stacked in front of the ferry terminal. Georgeson Removals, and a red and blue logo.'

'Oh, yes, I know. John Georgeson, the councillor.' I scowled. 'Father of Miss Georgeson that we had in primary six.'

Maman laughed. 'I think that she was probably quite a good teacher. You just did not get on well together. You always asked for reasons, when she just wanted you to obey orders.'

'Huh. She had a tongue that would clip cloots.' I brooded darkly for a moment, remembering long-past tussles of will over the sharpness of my pencil, or exactly where I'd laid my satchel. 'So this is her brother whose partner has absconded?'

'He is, I think, the baby of the family, very keen to stand on his own feet, that is why he does not wish his father to bail him out.' She put an arm around my shoulders. 'But children can be very proud.'

'Worst of the seven deadlies,' I agreed. I'd have been proud myself if I'd had to ask a favour of John Georgeson. He was a butting ram of a man, who gave short shrift to alternative views. 'Do I know the absconder?'

'Certainly. He's a sailor at the club.' She filled the basin with hot water and plunged the dishes in. 'Ivor

42

Hughson.'

In Maman's accent it came out as Ifforh Uson, so it took me a moment to work out. 'Who? Oh, him.' He had a yacht in the marina, a beamy flyer with a sugar-scoop stern – that's where some of the money had gone, if I was any judge, for he'd had new sails for her just last year, and distinctive green sailcovers and dodgers, the side panels with the boat's name. The cockpit was bristling with expensive gadgetry: the latest chart plotter, AIS, wireless wind, speed, and depth instruments, all that. He was out in every Saturday or Sunday points race, with a keen, young crew – young, that is, compared to the yacht I crewed on, Jeemie's Starlight, where I was the only one under sixty-five.

I set his boat aside and focused on the man himself as I swirled the sponge around the china. Ivor Hughson wasn't a type I particularly took to: he was too slick, too trendy in his new Henri Lloyds, beside Magnie's ex-trawlerman jacket and Jeemie's ancient green sheep-round-up oilskin. *Thinks himsel nae sma dirt*, Jeemie had commented. He was in his early forties, with chin-length dark hair framing a high forehead, a sideways-tilted smile under a narrow moustache, and designer stubble on his chin. It was all a bit Cap'n Jack Sparrow, that charmer look. I'd nodded at him in passing, but the only time I remembered actually speaking to him was when he'd been stuck at a table with us for the between-races soup and sandwiches. He'd offered me a drink, bright blue eyes crinkling at me, and followed it up with some question about *Khalida*. I'd answered politely, drunk my soup, and taken my corned beef roll to a fellow-instructor, to talk about who we'd trust with the Feva. It didn't surprise me in the least that he'd come up with some business scheme to milk and then abandon. 'When you say absconded …?'

'Completely gone.' Maman dried each plate with meticulous grace, as if a theatre of people was watching. 'I gather this Robert-John Georgeson –' She gestured along the passage. '– became suspicious when he took a phone call intended for Hughson, and so he went to the bank to look at the account and talk to the manager, and realised things were not right. This was back in August, and Hughson was just about to go on holiday, so he said that they would talk about it when he returned.'

'Even I know better than to fall for that one.'

Maman sighed. 'Monsieur Georgeson believes others, because he would cheat nobody himself. So, this Ivor Hughson came back from holiday for only one night, and instead of meeting up with him as they had planned, he left on the next ferry.'

'But surely – has his family not heard from him?'

Maman spread her hands. 'I suppose not, for this Robert-John would have asked them first.' She pulled a face, the goddess Juno being asked to supervise the petty affairs of mortals, then came as quickly back to earth. 'It is very sad. I hope he did not involve his house in the business. He has a family, a very pretty wife, and a little girl, and another child on the way.' She gave me a sideways look from her dark-lashed eyes and changed the subject. 'You enjoyed being down with your Gavin's family?'

Had that last quick kiss on the cheek made me an official girlfriend? 'I felt at home there.'

'You will sort out who lives where,' Maman said serenely. 'You can come and go by water, now you have found the way.'

'Children,' I said. 'They're a handicap to sailing off.'

'I do not see why they should be. If I had been sensible, I would have kept singing, and taken you along to rehearsals, instead of giving up, and withering inside. A month in France, listening to beautiful music, then back to school here.' She smiled. 'Though not during the sailing season, of course.'

44

'Tricky,' I said, 'since your best *son-et-lumieres* are rehearsing in high summer, ready for the autumn season.' I began on the cutlery. 'What's the next one?'

'Oh, one of the Loire castles in February, then my spring tour of Scotland.' Under the smooth make-up, she was blushing. 'Here too, to Belmont House in Unst, then in Lerwick.'

I gave her a sideways glance. 'Since Dad was too proud to come to you …?'

She nodded, a little smile trembling on her scarlet lips. 'But all is well now. And for the summer, I have a first time. Glyndebourne has at last discovered Rameau. *Les Indes Galantes.* A confection of nonsense, but Hébé is amusing to sing.'

'Glyndebourne! Oh, wow!'

'I just hope it will be a traditional production, not some designer whose concept of Rameau is setting the stories in a fridge.' Her dark eyes flashed. 'If only they would understand that all that is needed is some costumes in keeping with the text, to help the imagination, and a stage, and the orchestra and singers. But no, we have to have a concept.' She lifted the pile of dishes and stowed them in the cupboard. 'Your father is investigating how to get tickets – for you too, if you are on this side of the world, and ashore. What is next for you?'

'College. Safety at sea, engines, navigation, handling work rotas, marine waste disposal, buoyage, and all the rest, until I come out with my Deck Officer ticket. I've already sent my CV to all the tall ships I've ever sailed on, starting with the Norwegian fleet.'

'*Sørlandet, Staatsradt Lemkuhl, Christian Radich.*' She smiled. 'You are a child of the north after all.'

'I'll fly back to the UK for Glyndebourne,' I promised.

There were steps in the passage, and Dad's voice: 'I'm vexed I can't be more help.' There was the murmur of goodbyes, the door closing again.

45

Maman and I returned to the sitting room. 'How is it?' Maman asked.

Dad shook his head. 'A mess. Oh, I'll have a go at his books, but the total's clear. He has to find Hughson. He tried an internet firm, but they drew a blank. Hughson owing money like that makes it a police business, but Robert-John would rather try to get out from under by himself. I just don't see how he can, unless he goes back to a single-van outfit with him doing all the driving.'

'The house, does it also make part of the enterprise?'

Dad sighed. 'He put everything he had into it. People like Hughson should be strung up. He's the type who'll go bankrupt without a thought for his creditors, then set up a new company six weeks later.' His fist clenched on his knee. 'I've seen a dozen like him. Enthusiastic, plausible, and with no morals. It's always fine fellows like Robert-John who trust them.' He shook his head. 'Well, I'll do what I can.'

'It's odd that he's disappeared so completely,' I said. 'All his family are up here.'

'Maybe they're ashamed of him.'

'There's not another woman involved?' Maman asked.

'Robert-John didn't mention that.' Dad considered, eyes narrowing. 'Yes, that would explain it. If he's living with her, then he might not show up on the kind of records a tracer firm would use.'

'But he'd need to get money from somewhere,' I pointed out. 'Bank account, credit card, a job. Even I have a national insurance number, and the taxman chases me to argue that I can't really be living on what I'm earning.'

'Perhaps this girlfriend is from another country.' Maman leaned forward. 'He may have gone abroad with her.'

'If that's the way it is, then Robert-John has had it. The sums aren't large enough to warrant the fuss of extradition.'

'Large enough to him, though,' I said, with sympathy. I thought the girlfriend option was entirely plausible. 'I'd better be getting back to the boat.'

'I will drive you,' Maman said. 'No, no, Dermot, you rest there. I will be gone only ten minutes.'

I gathered up Cat and put him into his basket. An indignant miaow came out through the wicker; he'd planned on washing his duck-juiced whiskers in front of the fire, then having a snooze.

'Not that there is any point in saying it to your father,' Maman said, once we were in the car, 'but this is just the day for the police to be out in force, and he is over the limit. Perhaps ...' She stopped. I waited. 'Perhaps you could ask your inspector about Ivor Hughson? Robert-John is an amiable being, and it seems unfair he and his family should suffer for the misdeeds of another. I am sure the police would have surer ways to find Hughson.' Her dark eyes flicked sideways at me. 'But perhaps you are now too tentative. You can no longer ask as a friend, but cannot yet demand as a lover.'

I gave a reluctant grin. 'Mind reader.'

'Then do not ask. *Bonne nuit.*'

She dropped me off at the marina, and I put Cat back aboard, lit the lantern, and sat down on the side-couch. Suddenly it was too solitary, this little world of wood with the lamplight sparking golden grains in the walls, and the curved white ceiling closing me in. I'd got used to people to talk to in the evening ...

There was a brightly wrapped parcel tucked into my bookshelf: the picture-book I'd got for Peerie Charlie, but hadn't managed to get to him before Christmas. The tide lapped at *Khalida*'s sides, the wind tugged my halyards. I went out to fasten them, reached back in for the parcel, and headed out of the marina and up towards the road. I'd go and see what Inga was up to.

Chapter Six

It wasn't quite dark; the sun was just nestling into the hills on the west side of Aith, leaving a bright glow. From time to time, as the clouds shifted, the new moon was visible as a darker shadow. A bonny day tomorrow, the old folk would say: *When the sun gengs sheening tae the hill, the morn geng whaur du will.*

I'd passed the Building Centre, which sold every useful tool known to DIY man or woman, and was almost at the Co-op (Britain's Most Northerly) when I remembered that it was New Year's Day. If Inga didn't have all her in-laws round, she'd be flying every foot to get big Charlie, her husband, ready for going back to sea. As well as having his own smaller boat, he was second in command on one of the pelagic trawlers, the sort with nets so huge that in theory it could catch its whole quota (its permitted weight of herring or mackerel) in one cast. The fish would be bought almost as soon as it hit the ship's hold, and delivered to a processing factory in Shetland, Norway, or Ireland, whichever was nearest. Charlie'd be away for between a fortnight and a month, then the ship would be tied up at the pier until its second outing, in September. There were eight of these huge trawlers, and innumerable smaller whitefish and shellfish boats, as well as all the aquaculture industry of salmon and mussels. Fishing was still Shetland's main source of wealth.

I glanced over my shoulder at the sinking sun. Not quite four o'clock. If Inga had visitors, they'd either be at the tea and coffee stage, or not due till six, and given that the fishing boat had all mod cons, including a kitchen, a cook, and a washing machine and tumble dryer, all that needed done for big Charlie was throwing a few clothes and books into his bag. I kept walking.

Inga and Charlie lived on the old side of Brae, in a square eighties house built by old Charlie, Charlie's father. One look at the drive told me the whole clan was there: Charlie's mother's orange petrol-saver, Charlie's brother's grey 4x4, his other brother's turquoise people carrier. Inga's mother-in-law was known, against stiff competition, as one of the worst gossips in Shetland, so I'd get serious grilling about what I'd been up to down south with that 'policeman ida kilt'. I was about to walk on past when I heard a voice yelling 'Dass, Dass!' and saw Peerie Charlie waving to me from a precarious position at the top of a shiningly new adventure playhouse. I sighed and went in.

'C-C-Cass,' I reminded him.

He gave me that 'humour her' look. 'Cass. I climbing.'

'So I see. Is this what Santy brought you?'

'Come up, Cass.' He pointed round at the back of the fortress. 'You climb here.' His eyes went to the carrier bag in my hand, with the bright wrapping blazing above the plastic. 'Is that a parcel?'

'A Christmas present for you.'

Another two faces peered out from behind him: a boy and girl cousin. The boy had red hair, which made him the people-carrier brother's; the girl was smoothly dark. They were aged around seven. If I stayed in Shetland much longer I'd be getting to the traditional greeting for unken bairns: 'Whaur's du from? Wha's dee midder? Yea, yea, I ken wha du is noo.'

I resisted the temptation, especially when the girl came out with, 'Girls can't climb.'

I looked her straight in the eye. 'How'd you get up there, then?'

She amended it. 'Big girls can't climb.'

50

'D'you mind the tall ships that were in Lerwick harbour, with the fireworks, and the big high masts, going way up there?' I pointed skywards, wondering if she was old enough to remember three years ago.

'I mind,' Peerie Charlie broke in. I took that with a pinch of salt, as he'd been a babe in arms. 'The fireworks went bang. I not scared.'

The girl nodded.

'Well, I climbed right to the top of the masts.'

'Why?' the boy asked.

'To work with the sails, the white cloth things that make the ships go.' It seemed to be an acceptable explanation; the three faces nodded solemnly. 'So anyone any age can climb.' I swung round the fort to join them up in the top storey, and hammered my moral home. 'Girls can do anything they like.'

Charlie opened his parcel, and we read the book. We were just dividing ourselves into Spiderman and baddies when Inga came out of the door. 'Cass, stop winding them up and come in for a cup of tea.'

We'd spent our schooldays as a pair, Inga and I. Her house was the last on the end of our road, so when I'd got on our minibus I'd gone straight to join her and her brothers and sisters on the back seat. Her brother, Martin, had crewed for me in *Osprey*. Inga and I had compared the boys we fancied, and teamed up at discos; we'd swapped moans about our Saturday jobs, done our homework together, and planned our Standard Grades. Then Dad had gone to the Gulf, and I'd been sent to Maman in France. I'd been miserably homesick, had hurled myself on board a tall ship headed for Scotland the moment I was sixteen, and spent the next thirteen years travelling round the world in various damp ways, while Inga had stayed home, married the boy from across the voe, and had three children. I enjoyed baby-sitting Peerie Charlie, but was glad to hand him back, and Inga was already plotting the fun she'd have once the bairns were older. 'When you,' she'd add, with a sideways glint of her dark eyes, 'are just starting with the toddler tantrums.'

I came over to the door, and hesitated. 'You're got the whole clan round.'

'Denner's over, we're just sitting with a cup of tay. Come in.'

They were in the sitting-room, a big square space with a picture window which had a grandstand view of the voe. Old Charlie had been a great sailor, and Martin and I had always made sure we did our best gybes at this window, or we'd hear about it the next time we saw him: 'Whit in the name of the Good Man were you twa doing with those spinnaker sheets on Setterday? I thought you would be swimming for sure. You're no' saying you won? Boy, the opposition mustna have been up to much.'

All three couches in the room were filled. On the right were Charlie, with his people-carrier brother, Harald, and his wife, the redhead. On the left, the 4x4 brother, John-Magnus, and his dark-haired wife; they had a croft to the north of Brae. A toddler and a baby were playing on the rug, one red, one dark.

Beryl, Inga's mother-in-law, was enthroned in the centre of her family. She'd given the house over to Charlie on his father's death with the excuse that 'she was getting an elderly body, and no able, and it was far too big for her to keep up' but her new bungalow a hundred metres along the shore was hoovered within an inch of its life daily, she was the terror of the Co-op check-out workers as she scrutinised each day's reduced price items, and no weed dared raise its head in her symmetrical garden. 'And,' Inga had said, 'until I insisted Charlie had a word with her, she'd give me the run-down on my week's washing every Tuesday, how I could reduce it, what items I was washing away, and what I'd need to replace.'

Beryl was dressed for a party. Her massive shoulders

and bust were squeezed into a maroon frock with a pattern of grey splotches over it, and she wore matching maroon sandals. Going by the photos that marched up the wall, she'd been as fair as Charlie in her youth, and she'd kept her hair blonde, though now it was moving towards that peat-ash colour. Her eyes were narrow, and constantly flicking everywhere. I was suddenly conscious that though my jeans and jumper were clean and untorn, they weren't nearly smart enough. I sidled in with a general hello, and sat uncomfortably on the slope that her bulk made of the rest of the couch.

Her gimlet eyes sized me up. 'Now then, so you got home okay. I saw you dastreen. You were fairly storming up the voe. I thought you'd end up on the beach like the bairns.'

The curved beach at the head of the voe was a magnet for dinghies with any south wind; however much you told the bairns not to get too close to it, they'd drift down and down, then find they couldn't sail away.

'I've had to tow enough of them off it,' I agreed. The problem was that if you went in close enough to get the stranded dinghy off, you usually put the rescue boat on shore instead, or at least lost one propeller blade on the bottom. Even replaceable blades cost more than our shoestring outfit could afford. 'Often the only way to get them off is by swimming them out into deeper water. Or walking them home along the shore, of course.'

'Yea, yea, I'm seen you do that often enough. And how was your holiday south?'

'Very good.' I could either give information, or have it dragged out of me. 'I'd have liked to bide for New Year, but this was my best weather window.'

'And you were biding with the policeman who was up here, the one in the kilt?'

'With his family.' I might as well make that one clear. 'He bides with his mother and brother – it's his brother

53

who keeps the farm.'

The word 'farm' galvanised John-Magnus into speech, and before I knew it, I was getting the third degree on the number of acres, animals, whether the kye were beef or dairy, and what fields were laid down to what crops. I didn't think Kenny would have been impressed by my guesses, but at least I knew the kye were Highland cattle; the horns and long hair were unmistakable, even to me. 'They have horses too, for the stalking. I even went for a ride on one.'

Inga came in with a mug of tea and a plate of Christmas cake and shortbread. John-Magnus took the chance of my mouth being full to launch into a monologue about his plans for trying a new breed of sheep, and Harald stood up for the native Shetland ewes: 'They were bred for the place, they can look after themselves. You get breedy ones and this time next year you'll be too busy in the byre, lambing, to come out for the New Year.' It was all far too crowded and combative, and my brain began to hurt.

'So,' said Inga's mother-in-law, once I'd almost finished my slice of cake, 'what's the news down at the marina?'

'I'm no' been up at the club yet,' I replied, 'but it all looks quiet enough.'

Her eyes narrowed. She heaved herself upright. 'No sign o' that Ivor Hughson's boat up for sale?'

Ivor again. Of course, he and his wife lived just above Beryl, so she'd take a neighbourly interest. I shook my head. 'I'm no' heard anything.'

'If I was his wife, I wouldn't want another year of mooring fees,' John-Magnus put in.

Not that I was going to bother Gavin about it, but since Ivor Hughson's name had come up, I might as well get the story from the horse's mouth. 'What happened to him, anyway?' I spoke casually, and saw Inga's eyes narrow in suspicion.

The couch creaked as Beryl drew a deep breath. 'Well, now, I can tell you all about that, for I was the last one in the place to set eyes on him. He and the wife – do you ken her? Julie Robertson, a bright lass, her folk bide in the council houses here in Brae. I mind her as a peerie lass. She teaches office studies at the Shetland College. Onyroad, they were all booked for a holiday together, south. He took the yacht down, with another of the boys from Brae, Hubert Inkster, you'll ken him, and then a week later she flew down. They had a week cruising, and the idea was the men'd sail home, and she'd fly. Well!' She leant towards me. My hand tightened on the arm of the couch as I felt myself being sucked down against her. 'Whatever happened, he arrived all right, for I wasna sleeping well that night, and then the bang of the door next door woke me, and when I lookit out, there was his pickup, and the lights on in the house, and him in his red overalls taking his bag out of the boot, and the mast back in the marina. The lights were on for a good bit, the kitchen first, as if he was having a bite to eat, then all over the house, one room then another. I thought he must just be checking everything was all right, after the house being left a week, but now I ken he was packing, and flying every foot to be off too, for when I woke up the car was gone already, and when Julie came home the very next day, all she found of him was a note on the table saying he'd gone on the south boat, and nobody's heard a word of him since.'

'Where was it they were sailing?'

'Julie was to meet him in Mallaig. She telt me all about it. They came around to that island with the coloured houses, Balamory, then up through the canal and Loch Ness, most awful bonny scenery, she said. Then he left her in Inverness to fly home, and he sailed up himself, for there'd been some kind o'disagreement with Hubert. Then, when she got home, there was the note on the table.' She lowered her voice to a penetrating sympathy. 'She was that upset about it. I went up to see her, the moment I heard, to check she was all right. Well, I didna ask what had gone wrong atween them.' She paused for breath, her little eyes challenging us all to disagree with that last statement. Inga, behind her back, rolled her eyes ceilingwards. 'But her mother telt me later,' Beryl continued triumphantly. 'Julie wanted to try this IVF for a bairn, and Ivor widna hear of it. They'd left it a bit late, and she was faered they'd no' be able to have one without.' She sat back again, and turned her own question into a statement, in the best gossip-spreading tradition. 'So, she's putting the yacht on the market? Well, that must mean she has heard from him, for she'd no be able to sell it without his permission.'

'There wasn't a "for sale" notice in the window of it,' I said, injecting a note of reality.

'I heard she was thinking of it,' Harald insisted. 'It's near a thousand poond a year to keep a boat in the marina.'

'I doubt there was more to it than that,' John-Magnus said. 'Folk dinna split up like yon just over IVF, not at the first mention of it. I never likit him. It wouldna surprise me if there wasna another lass involved.'

Harald's wife leant forward as if she was about to speak, but Harald shook his head at her, and she sat back again. 'That's all in the past,' he said, 'an' the least said, the shoonest mended.'

Beryl nodded. 'Aye, aye, there's another man in the picture now, so it's no' her he's run off with. But where there's one there'll be others.' She shook her head and went into broader dialect. 'He towt a hantle o' himself, did dat een.'

'Big-headed?' I guessed.

'That's the kind that pulls in the silly lasses. I'll tell you this, Julie's well rid of him.' Her narrow eyes speculated. 'Or of course it coulda been another man, with her.'

John-Magnus's wife shook her head. 'Na, na, she's one

of these career women. She's after the job of vice-principal in the college, and she'll get it too. I dinna believe for one minute that she's that keen on bairns that she'd quarrel with Ivor over it. More likely to be the other way round, that he wanted them and she didna.'

'But if she's really heard nothing,' Inga said, with a quick glance in my direction, 'that's kinda odd, dinna you think? Folk row, I ken that, but they're been married since university, and it's no' the kind of thing to do a moonlight over.'

'If he left his yacht here he meant to come back,' Charlie said. 'He was brawly keen on the sailing.'

'Was he no' in business with the Georgeson Removals man? Him that's on the Council?' Harald made a face, and I remembered that he worked for Serco, and so, presumably, had to deal with Georgeson transporting goods south. 'I widna want to cross him.'

'Na, na.' Predictably, his brother piped up. 'It's his youngest boy, Robert-John – you ken, he was just leaving the school when I went into secondary, then he was a joiner to DITT, while Ivor was with that whisky firm that went bust, then they went into this small haulage business together. I dinna ken how well that's going. You see Robert-John driving the van at all hours, with a long face.'

'Well, that's more likely. He got into a mess financially, and bailed out. If naebody kens where you are, your creditors can't get you.'

'But surely his family's heard from him,' I said.

Beryl shook her head. 'No' a word, not one. I ken that for a fact. His mother Maisie, well, she's head o' the Burra and Trondra SWRI, and I met up wi' her just last month, when our two groups had an evening together. "How's all da faimily?" I asked her, and when she didna mention Ivor, I asked what he was working at now, and if he was coming home for Christmas, and she just puckered up her mooth and said "No' this year" and I kent by that she'd heard nothing from him. He was the only boy, and she was aye that proud of him. If she kent he was working as a joiner she'd be telling us how he was cabinet maker in Buckingham Palace. Na, na, if there was anything to tell, she'd have telt us all.'

It was odd. To me, she sounded like the mother from hell, but for her adored son, surely she was the last person he'd leave in ignorance.

'Besides,' Beryl clinched it, 'I kent by the look of her. She's aged five years since he left, and her eyes were that worried when I mentioned him.'

She dismissed him with a shrug, and returned to the attack. 'Now, then, what's your mother up to? I saw she was home for the New Year ...'

Chapter Seven

Inga saw me out. 'What are you up to now?'

'Really nothing,' I assured her.

'Then what's the sudden interest in Ivor and Julie?'

I could trust Inga to be discreet. 'Robert-John was along, asking Dad for a hand with his books.'

'Our Susan was ages with them, and at Aberdeen Uni at the same time too.'

I considered that. I remembered Susan as being very sensible, and a bit bossy with us younger ones – as she had every need to be, I conceded now, remembering some of our exploits. If a balanced view of Ivor and Julie was needed, she'd give it; but I wasn't sure it was needed. Their marriage break-up was none of my business. I said goodnight, and headed off along the road.

I hadn't expected the club bar to be open that night, with everyone visiting each other for New Year, but prompt at 18.30 the lights flickered, then cast a line of bright squares out over the black gleam of the waves inching up the slipway. I might go up later, and catch up on club gossip. For now I boiled myself an egg for tea and settled down to read a book in the gold gleam of the cabin lantern, with Cat curled up on my lap, purring. I'd only managed a couple of chapters when a car scrunched down to the marina gate, there was a clunk as the lock opened, and the pontoon quivered. I turned my head to look out of *Khalida's* long windows, and saw the blur of a man clambering aboard Ivor Hughson's boat. He went below; a long pause, then a light shone out in the cabin, winking as if it was a moving torch. I set my book aside and picked up my jacket. If it was somebody with legitimate business, well, they could tell me to go away.

I scuffed along the pontoon, making as much noise and rock as I could, and stopped at the boat's bow. *Hi-Jinx*, she was called. 'Hello there?'

There was no answer. The torch light was steady now, and the hatch above the steps had been re-closed. I called again, louder, and knocked on the curve of roof. There was a startled pause, then the hatch slid back, and the person in the cabin came up the steps and looked out at me, shining his torch full in my face for an instant; then the beam fell to the cockpit floor. 'Cass! You gave me a right gluff.'

The torch circle was still dancing in front of my eyes, but I recognised the voice. It was Hubert Inkster, that had gone down with Ivor to the west of Scotland, but not returned with him. He was a third cousin of my friend Magnie on Magnie's Walls grandmother's side, and, like Ivor, in his early forties. He had brown hair, receding a bit, with the sides straggled below his ears and the middle covered with a peaked-brim navy cap. His eyes were the same brown as his hair, set under low, dark brows that gave him a serious look; you could see him as an elder of the Kirk, giving out hymn books, or handing round the plate. He was wearing a navy hooded jacket over an oilskin bib-and-brace, as if he'd come straight from feeding sheep.

He put the washboards back, unhurried. 'I'm just been keeping an eye on the boat for Julie while she's away in Tenerife.' The way he said her name was a give-away, the rough voice smoothing to silk. I wondered how Gavin said "Cass" when I wasn't there to hear. 'She's that busy, and she kens nothing about boats, so I said I'd run the engine from time to time, check the bilges, all that.'

'Yea,' I agreed, 'you can't leave a boat unattended in winter.'

He agreed, and sidled off, head down against more

questions. I went back to call Cat, and close my own boat up properly, then headed up to the bar.

Magnie was on duty, with one customer in front of him. Magnie'd been my teacher when I was a sailing-mad youngster, and he was still senior instructor here at Brae. He'd been a whaling man in his youth, then a fisherman when the last factory in South Georgia closed. He was well through his sixties now, and retired from professional fishing, but no Shetlander ever gave up totally; he had a little boat he took out to 'da eela', and he set the occasional crab pot, lobster creel, or illegal trootie net. He was dressed in his best gansey, a traditional all-over with bands of blue pattern alternated with white The curls of his fair hair were smoothed down with water, his eyes were bright under their heavy lids, and his cheeks rosy with a recent shave.

He looked up as I came in, and nodded. 'Aye, aye, Cass. Happy New Year to you.'

I walked up the line I'd sailed the day before on the lino map of Busta Voe, and propped an elbow against the polished counter. 'The same to you.' I nodded at the bottles of Shetland ale. 'A White Wife, please.'

Magnie indicated the lone customer on one of the high bar stools. 'Do you ken Jeemie o' Grobsness?'

I shook my head. He was in his fifties, with dark hair that was starting to recede, leaving a widow's peak with a plume of white in its centre, and cut in sideburns over the cheeks, Elvis-style. Younger, he might have had something of the King's good looks: the strong nose and cheekbones, the dark-lashed eyes, the confidence in his ability to charm. He was wearing a dark shirt, with a cowboy thong at the neck, and dark trousers. Unmarried, I deduced, or more likely divorced, and joining the lonely hearts club at the boating club bar when everyone else was awash with in-laws.

Jeemie slid off his stool and held out his hand. 'Jeemie

Ridland. An' you're Cass. I'm heard all about your exploits.'

'I'm sorry to hear that,' I said drily. 'They'll have grown arms and legs in the telling.'

He gave me an uncertain look, smoothed quickly over. 'I'll get this, Magnie.'

'No, no, I'm only having the one.' Solo female sailors didn't take drink from strangers. I handed Magnie the coins, and turned back to Jeemie. 'Have you been at Grobsness long?'

I knew Grobsness of course, though from the sea. It was built after the Viking fashion with the house and byre in one line, and a little porch in the middle, all painted dazzling white. It lay above a west-facing beach of white sand at the very end of an asphalt track off a single-track side road. In summer, the fields around were green; in the low sun of winter, the rigs and foundations of a whole community of croft houses showed up as ghosts on the brown hills.

'Two years noo.' He launched into a selling spiel. 'I'm got a peerie antiques business there. I do a bit o' repair work an' all – you ken, second-hand TVs and radios and computers and the like. There's aye folk willing to pick up a second TV for the bairns' room at a reasonable price, and I trained as an electrical engineer, so I ken how to fix them up for sale. Recycling.'

'Jewellery and all, one of the camping van ladies was saying,' Magnie added. He gave me a sideways flutter of one eyelid. 'Boanie rings, she said, for an engagement, maybe.'

Jeemie must have caught my annoyed expression, for he changed the subject quickly. 'Oh, whatever folk want to sell. Now I'm kent, folk ask me if they've a house clearance, or a flitting. No big gear, just peerie tables, ornaments, china, unless it's a right antique I can't bear to pass by.'

'So,' Magnie took up the conversation again, 'Jeemie has a fine business out there at Grobsness, and he has a story I thought would be in your line. You mind how you get to Grobsness, you drive out past the Pierhead pub, in Voe, and then up into the hills, and past the Gonfirth loch, then you turn off to the right, to the Grobsness road. Well, up by the loch – on you go, Jeemie, tell Cass about your njuggle.'

I heard Gavin's soft voice: *one of the best attested kelpie sightings.* I drew a bar stool over and encouraged Cat up onto my lap. 'A njuggle?'

Jeemie flushed, and made a reluctant face. Maybe he'd not had enough drink to try his story on a sober audience. 'A young lass like Cass is no wanting to hear me yarning all night,' he protested to Magnie.

'It sounds a good story,' I said encouragingly.

'Oh, I dinna ken …' Jeemie said, in an unconvincing display of modesty, with a sharp sideways glance at me.

Magnie leaned his elbows on the bar, and took over. 'Well, lass, the police were after Jeemie. You ken how it is sometimes, maybe a neighbour's mentioned that you're driving with a drop ower muckle, or the pub's had a word … but however it came about, Jeemie got word that the police had taken to hanging about in the old quarry at the Pierhead closing time.'

Jeemie nodded gloomily. 'They were after me,' he confirmed. 'So, to get around them, I decided to leave the car in the passing place by the peerie loch next to Gonfirth loch, and walk down the hill to the pub, and back up the hill again at closing time. If there was no sign of them I'd take the car from there, and if I spotted them, I'd just walk all the way home.'

Perfectly reasonable, if the idea of keeping under the limit was dismissed out of hand. It would only be a mile, say, to the loch, or a mile and a half, and another two home, all on good asphalt track. A hour's walk, with the drink to cushion it, and a bonny one on a summer night, through the green hills, or in winter, with the sky blazing with stars above you, and the mirrie dancers shimmering like a luminous archway.

Jeemie settled himself more comfortably on the bar counter. 'So this night I set out from the pub. November, it was, and there shoulda been a full moon, but it was one of these nights of steekit mist, rolling over the hills and filling in along the road, you ken the way.'

I could imagine it: the white mist thick as smoke on the road, swirling away to reveal the hills rumpled with withered heather, ditches bedraggled with autumn rain, then closing over again to blankness.

'I had me blinkie with me, but it was that thick I could only just see the white line along the side of the road, and only the next ten yards of it at that. The warst o' it was the silence. The mist seemed to blot aathing out, except me ain footsteps. I could hear me ain hert beating in me breast.' Jeemie gave me a sheepish look. 'You ken what it's like, you stop being sure of where you are, and I was beginning to think I was lost, when the mist cleared enough that I saw the crash barrier of the loch just on me right hand, and I kent where I was again. Then I began to feel gluffed.' Frightened, he meant. 'I couldna tell you why, but I began to stride along as if me life depended apo' it, without looking behind me. I didna want to look, you ken, I thought there might be something ahint me I'd be better no' to see, though it was like I could feel it breathing down my neck. I just wanted to be in me car and out of there. I could see the water on the other side of the barrier, gleaming like a trap, and I had the feeling that it was unchancy, as if something might come out of it at ony moment.'

He paused to lift his pint with hands that trembled slightly, and took a long drink. I could imagine him, striding faster and faster along the road, torch in one hand,

and the coal-black loch at his side.

'Then I heard something scrabbling on me left hand side, bigger and heavier as a sheep, coming down the hill towards me. I lookit, but there was nowhere for me to hide, unless the mist covered me. I was ready to shite me breeks, I was that faerd. Then I heard hooves like a pony's, and down it came, galloping across the side of the hill above the far side of the loch, right towards me.'

His eyes were turned away from us now, seeing it again. There was a sheen of sweat on his forehead below the dark peak of hair with its plume of white. 'Black it was, but shining moony-way in the mist, like the mareel on the sea in summer, and wi' green weed in its mane, and no white onywye. It was as big as a right Shetland pony, no these miniatures they breed nowadays, but the workhorses we had when I was a bairn. It came up to me, and reared its head, and I saw its face.' He shuddered, and closed his eyes for a moment. 'A great big head it had, on a thick neck like a stallion's, and teeth that snicked white as the mist, and eyes like the bottom of this pint pot. It reared up at me, like it was angry at finding me there, and then it swerved sideways, and I saw the great bush of a tail between its back legs, where the wheel would be.'

That puzzled me for a moment, until I remembered that the Shetland njuggle had a sort of wheel, hidden by its tail, that propelled it through the waters.

'It went capering across the road, and plunged down the hill between the big loch and the peerie one, and clattered over the stones at the water's edge. Then I heard splashing, and in it went, not stopping like a live horse would, it just drove straight into the loch and swam out into the mist. Well, I ran for me car, never looking ahead to see if there was any sign of the police further along the road, I'd a welcomed a patrol of policemen right then, peerie bag or no peerie bag. I scrambled in and locked the door behind me, and my hands were shaking that muckle it took me three goes to get the key in the ignition. I got away from there and drove home as if the fiend of hell was after me, and I'm no' sure that he wasna.'

He finished his pint in a oner, and passed the glass over to Magnie for re-filling. 'An I'm tried ever since to talk mesel out of what I saw, but I ken exactly what it was, and I'll no' be walking by the Loch of Gonfirth on a misty night ever again in me life, na, na, no' even if it means going home sober. And afore you ask, I had four pints, I counted them up in me head that night, four pints and twa nips. It wasn't the drink affecting me eyes or me brain.' He shook his head. 'It was the njuggle of Gonfirth, and I don't mind telling you I hope never to meet him again. And as for fishing on the loch, or even setting a net, which I'll admit I may have done from time to time, I wouldna do that if you paid me a fortune.' He shuddered. 'Go on a boat on that loch? Na, na, no' me.'

He stopped there, and Magnie didn't interrupt the silence, one yarning expert paying tribute to another. It'd been well-told, I gave him that. All the same, as I said to Magnie later, once Jeemie had drunk his pint, wished us a good New Year, and headed off to his car, it was all a bit too *Hound of the Baskervilles.* 'The mist, and the noise, and the great black animal. All we needed was the baying of the hounds.'

'Lass,' Magnie said, shocked, 'you're no' going to say there's no such thing as njuggles.'

'That Njuggleswater on the way to Sumburgh,' I retorted, 'the peerie lochan just before the curve into Quarff. It may look deep enough in winter, but when it dries out in summer you can see it was only two feet deep. How could anything possibly live there?'

'Naebody kens how deep Gonfirth Loch is,' Magnie pointed out.

'Apart from the Ordnance Survey?'

Magnie gave one of his rare smiles. 'It's a good yarn,

and you'll no say you didn't enjoy it.'

'It was a great yarn, and he telt it brawly well, once you'd got him started.' My suspicious mind was still turning possibilities over. 'What's this antiques place of his called?'

Magnie gave me a sideways look, conceding a point. 'He re-named it *The Njuggle's Nest*. It's even got a Facebook page, the man's a great one for his computers.'

'I can just see the signboard. All the same,' I conceded, 'either the man should be on the stage, or something gave him a right gluff up by the Gonfirth Loch.'

Magnie washed Jeemie's glass and set it down foursquare in the middle of the counter. His voice was so casual that I went on the alert straight away. 'Your pal Inga's oldest lass, she's into these horses, isn't she? Why don't you ask her about njuggles?'

His grey-green eyes met mine, giving nothing away. He wasn't going out of his way to help the police, but he thought there was something going on. 'I'll maybe do that,' I said.

Magnie nodded, put his drying cloth away, leaned his elbows on the bar, and went into interrogation mode. 'Now, then, lass, how got you on down south over Christmas?'

Chapter Eight

Three lots of interrogations, I wanted to grumble to Gavin over the phone later, but I didn't want to sound like I was pushing him to declare a relationship. *When will we meet again?* We hadn't even mentioned that. 'How's your murder going?'

'Forensics is still on holiday. Our police doctor says there's no sign of bullets or a bash on the head. He's male, aged between thirty-five and fifty, height just under six foot, medium build, an athletic type. Death could have been between three and six months ago. Unless forensics comes up with something, like his DNA being on the police computer, that's not much to go on. There's nobody like that reported missing for this area, or for the whole Highlands and Islands ... or rather, there is, but we don't chase up adult men who've walked out on their wives.'

I thought of Julie, coming home to an empty house, and a note on the table. Ivor would fit Gavin's description, if he'd not come home first.

'All the same,' Gavin finished, 'he's not obviously one of the ones we know about from round here. We'll start going round dentists on Monday.'

'I was thinking about the clothes. If you'd found him clad, you'd be thinking careless tourist, or climbing accident. So why was it so urgent they had to be removed?'

'According to our doctor, it doubles the speed of decomposition. Whoever left him there didn't want him recognisable. Our artists will do a face reconstruction, of course, but I've never been convinced by the "meet the ancestors" approach. A clothes description would help.'

'But whoever left him there would know you could match his teeth to any name that seemed a possible, from the height and colouring.'

'Agreed.'

I snuggled myself down more comfortably into my berth. 'So the person isn't on any missing list that you have; he's from elsewhere.'

'That might follow,' Gavin agreed, cautiously.

'Suppose his clothes would have been an indicator of where to look for him.' I remembered my thinking as we'd walked downhill from the body. 'If you'd found a woman in a Musto jacket and a Bergen T-shirt, 5'2", with black hair in a plait, then notices around the sailing clubs of Norway would have come up with my name inside a week.'

'You wouldn't necessarily have worn those for a walk up the hill.'

'I would if I'd been on holiday, travelling light. Or a carbine hook in the pocket would have directed you to the climbing clubs.'

'You think the important thing for the perpetrator is that the body should remain unrecognised?'

'Which means that recognition of the body would lead straight to the murderer.'

'A walking partner, a climbing buddy, a fellow sailor.' The phone rattled as he shook his head and launched into dispirited speech. 'Kenny's given me a list of all the cars he remembers, but people often drive down to the head of the loch, so he pays them no attention. Boats come in, more motorboats than yachts, and canoes and kayaks galore. We're already circulating B&Bs and youth hostels, and you know how many of those there are in the Highlands. A tall, dark man, between thirty-five and fifty, travelling with a companion or companions, sometime between July and September. I'm trying not even to think of the number of names we're going to be following up. The whole station's wishing we'd stayed up on the ridge and approached the cave from the other side.'

I wished it myself. That had been our private moment. I could hear in his voice how much he minded sharing it. Now his whole world knew about me. There'd be jokes at the coffee machine, comments about him hoping for a Shetland case. My whole past, Alain's death, would be laid bare. I wondered if his Commander had already called him in: "Not the wife for a promising officer."

Gavin didn't seem to be thinking of that. 'At best we can wait until we've got a list of names, then we can bundle them into areas and pass them on to other police forces.'

'Good luck,' I said, and meant it.

'Without luck,' he said, 'this one will lie in an un-named grave. What else have you been up to?'

'Lunch with Maman and Dad,' I said, and remembered Maman's request. 'I don't suppose you could run a man from here into your police computer? He's done a runner.' I explained about Ivor Hughson, and Robert-John's debts.

'I can, but from the sound of him, finding him won't solve your man's problems. He's probably amassed a new set of debts to add to the old.'

'Dad thought that too. Otherwise, I've been yarning,' I said, and told him Jeemie's njuggle story.

'Interesting,' he commented.

'Unless he ought to be in Hollywood,' I said, 'he really did see something. The sweat was pouring off his brow as he remembered it.'

'*Hound of the Baskervilles*,' Gavin said, just as I'd done. 'A bit of phosphorescent paint, the misty night, a good susceptible witness, and your legend's up and running.'

'Gonfirth,' I retorted, 'is what you'd call a lochan up in the hills, a mile each direction from the nearest house, and

I can't think of any kind of skulduggery anyone would be up to there, that they'd need a phantom horse to divert attention from.' I tried to remember what the purpose of the original hound of the Baskervilles was ... to terrify Sir Charles to death? Well, if someone had been after Jeemie, they'd failed; he looked healthy enough. 'I'm not sure he's that susceptible either. He's using it as publicity for his antiques shop.'

'I don't know where Loch Ness would be without the monster.'

'That's probably libel, in someone who works in Inverness.'

'Slander,' my policeman replied. 'I wouldn't dare write it down. If it's good, clear peaty water, how about an illicit still? Didn't Shetland have a distillery that went bust?'

'Way back,' I said. 'I can't remember the ins and outs of it. Lunna Bridge Whisky, something like that?'

'Hang on,' Gavin said. 'It's coming to me.'

There was a pause, while he teased his memory, and I teased mine: someone had mentioned whisky. Magnie? No. Then it came back: Inga's brother-in-law, John-Magnus: *Ivor was with that whisky firm that went bust.* Ivor again.

'It went missing,' Gavin said. 'The firm was from Manchester, and they got permission to build a distillery, but while it was being built they did the first distilling on a smaller still, two 195-litre casks.'

It was ringing a far-distant bell, from the summer before I'd left Shetland. 'There was a fuss about it. They were calling it Shetland whisky, but the only Shetland ingredient was the water.' John Georgeson, councillor, had led the denunciations: using Shetland's name for publicity, no jobs for the locals. That hadn't been true, if Ivor had been working for them, but it was the kind of thing he would say. 'And there was an idea too that they'd set up to go bust, you know, a profit-losing scheme, for tax.'

'Now who's talking slander? It wasn't a lot of whisky, five hundred standard size bottles, that were pre-sold as collector items, half to locals and half to dealers. Though why anyone would pay fancy prices for something they don't ever plan to drink beats me.'

'They do it with wine too.'

'The firm went bust, but because it was an asset, the casks were kept, maturing away, until the fifteen years were up. The receivers opened them last summer, and one was whisky right enough, but the other one had only water inside.'

I considered that for a moment. 'Had there only ever been water, or had someone swapped it round?'

'They couldn't tell. There was nothing to prove it was the same cask that had been filled with whisky a decade ago. They're handmade, with numbers, but the record of the numbers couldn't be found, and there's been no sign of Lunna Bridge Whisky for sale.'

'This Ivor Hughson, that's done a runner,' I said, 'he worked for the company.'

Gavin went silent. 'Interesting timing,' he said at last. 'The other cask was valued at £10,000. Of course that went to the big creditors. As usual the small people got nothing. I'll tug the grapevine, but don't get too hopeful.' He gave a huge yawn. 'I had to be up at the crack of dawn. *Oidhche mhath, beannachd leat.*'

Good sleep, blessings. 'Night night tae dee,' I replied.

Thursday 2nd January

Low Water at Brae UT	*02.32, 0.6m,*
High Water	*08.45, 1.8m*
Low Water	*15.01, 0.6m*
High Water	*21.23, 1.8m*
Moonrise	*08.25*
Sunrise	*09.15*
Sunset	*15.02*
Moonset	*15.59*

New moon.

You canna judge da deepness o' da grief bi da length o' da crepe veil.
You can't judge what people feel by their outward show.

Chapter Nine

My breath smoked cold in the air, and the cabin floor was icy to my bare feet. I got dressed fast and headed for a hot shower in the boating club, pulling up my hood against the cold easterly wind. I re-dressed in full cold-weather gear (two layers of thermals under my jeans and best gansey, and polar-expedition style socks) before heading out to assess the day properly. The wind had risen again, pushing the tide into the marina entrance and slapping the waves up the boating club slip – a high tide with the black moon, one of the highest of the year, almost touching the road width of tarmac between the slip and the clubhouse.

I tightened my halyards and did the automatic walk round all split-pins and shackles, to check nothing had worked loose overnight, then went for a wander along the pontoon. A winter marina was a strange place; there were gaps in the row of berths like missing teeth, and the yachts looked diminished without their masts. You couldn't believe these little cockleshells had spent the summer going to Orkney, Scotland, Bergen, Iceland. Over on shore, a couple of yachts were laid up, landed whales trailing slim keels, and the forest of masts was stacked into a holder, like tree trunks waiting to be cut up.

Of course my feet took me to Ivor Hughson's yacht. I was becoming intrigued. To just drop everything and run, like that … I'd done it at sixteen, the easiest age, but in your late thirties, to leave a wife, a business, and just get on the ferry with only what would fit in your car, was harder to understand. Unless, of course, he was involved in some dangerously shady business over the missing whisky, I thought, with vague ideas of 1920s prohibition gangsters. £10,000 didn't seem enough to do a runner for. *We don't chase up adult men who've walked out on their wives,* Gavin had said. I wondered if Ivor was relieved now, wherever he was, or regretful at having burnt his boats so thoroughly. On one of the tall ships I'd crewed on, the *Astrid*, there'd been a man who'd put the past behind him as if it had never been. His accent suggested he'd been brought up in the south of England, but when asked where he came from, he replied that he'd been travelling for years, and he never mentioned anything further back than the start of that voyage: not boats he had sailed in, friends he'd made, nor storms he'd experienced. He simply lived in now. Haunted by guilt over my lover Alain's death in the Atlantic, I'd envied him, yet I'd wondered how much effort it took, and what memories he was suppressing.

Looking at Ivor's boat, I could see it had been a sailor who'd stowed her away for the winter. The eye-catching green and white dodgers had been taken off, the blocks that the control ropes ran through were neatly tucked out of the way, the rudder was lashed amidships, and all spare lengths of rope had been removed. The smoked-glass windows kept my prying gaze out. I tried to remember more about Ivor Hughson, but I'd never paid him much attention. *Tricksy*, my instinct had said. A charmer who expected the world to bow down for him. A chancer who had cut his losses and left someone else to pick up the pieces.

I turned away from his boat and went back to *Khalida*. My next term at the North Atlantic Fisheries College would begin soon enough, and one of the items on the syllabus was 'lights and daymarks'. I was pretty good on aids to navigation, but the Med resorts hadn't been frequented by mine-sweepers, tugs towing hazardous material, or anything else an unkind examiner might decide to show us. It wouldn't hurt to begin my revision.

I was just doing settling down with a pack of RYA cards when there was a hail from the marina gate. I peered through the cabin window. It was Kevin Irvine, one of my classmates at the North Atlantic Fisheries College in Scalloway. He was a quiet soul with sandy hair and a sprinkling of freckles. I scrambled out of my hatch just as he was beginning to turn away. 'Come in. What's all doing with you?'

He went slightly pink. 'Well, I was thinking … I heard this boat might be coming up for sale, and I was wondering if you could maybe have a look at it for me.' My eyes went straight to Ivor Hughson's boat, behind him on the pontoon. He turned his head towards it. 'Ivor's boat – that's it, is it no', the white one over there?'

'That one,' I agreed. 'Is it for sale after all, then?'

He nodded. 'I heard it might be, so I phoned Julie, and she's coming down at half ten to let me have a look over it, but I thought if you were here you could maybe tell me more.'

'I can tell you a bit,' I agreed cautiously, 'but you'd have to get a proper survey done. The Malakoff would ken a marine surveyor. What do you want it for?'

'Well, I thought I'd maybe just have a bit of fun with her at first, try the racing and that, and then go further afield. I aye fancied cruising the fjords of Norway in me own boat.'

'She's a competitive racing boat, and her sails are all new. I wouldn't fancy being caught in a real tearer of a North Sea gale in her, but she'd do the fjords fine. Just remember to make a list of the buoys, and cross each off as you pass it.' His finances were none of my business, but I didn't think he had this kind of money. 'She'll be looking at around twenty-five grand for starting negotiations.'

Kevin gave me a sideways grin. 'Yeah, I think I could maybe be a time-waster. I just wanted to get a look at the likely o' her.'

I glanced at my watch; just before ten. 'Come and get a cup of tea, and tell me the news with you from over Christmas.'

We had just finished our tea when the pontoon gate creaked. *One o' those career women,* Harald's wife had said. Julie Hughson wore smartly cut black trousers over glossy boots, and a donkey-brown suede jacket with wide fur lapels, nipped in at the waist. Her hair was dark brown, cut in that curve-around-the-face style. Her cherry-red scarf matched her gloves, and a navy clipboard was tucked under one arm.

We scrambled out of *Khalida* and went along the pontoon to meet her. I didn't recognise her face at first. I'd never seen her in the bar, waiting for the race to be over, or behind the barbecue at club functions, or dancing with Ivor at the prize-giving. Then I realised there was something familiar after all, but I was visualising her in a T-shirt, with her hair scraped back and damp. In another moment I placed her as one of a rowing crew. Her face was tanned. *I've just been keeping an eye on the boat for Julie while she's away,* Hubert had said. Maybe she couldn't bear the Christmas round without Ivor, the sideways glances or the silent sympathy. In her place, I'd have high-tailed it to the Canaries too.

Close to, the business impression persisted. Her skin was smoothed with foundation, her brows perfectly plucked, her lips glossily red. Though her smile was receptionist-friendly, her dark eyes gave nothing away: whether she was raging at her husband having done a moonlight, and was selling his boat by way of revenge, or mortified at him leaving Robert-John in the lurch and making reparation, it didn't show. She could have been a professional saleswoman from a yacht broker's, instead of the default owner selling her husband's pride and joy. I made a mental note to tell Kevin to check her title thoroughly.

She took off her gloves, and held out one hand to Kevin. 'Julie Hughson.' Her nails were manicured and French polished, the tips gleaming white. Then she held out her hand to me, raising her brows in a question.

'Cass Lynch,' I said. 'I live aboard *Khalida* there.'

Her face didn't change, but her hand jerked in mine. I got a feeling of startled wariness, as if she hadn't expected Kevin to bring an expert with him. 'Of course. You were the one teaching the bairns. I saw the pink sails in the voe when I visited me mam.'

'I enjoyed doing it,' I said.

'I ken nothing about boats, so you'll have to excuse me floundering at questions, but come aboard and look.'

She might know nothing, but she went into her spiel as if giving a PowerPoint presentation. 'It's a Kirie Feeling, built in 1993, with only one owner before us. Ivor bought her four years ago for £22,000, and she's been extensively refurbished since. She's 32 foot overall, with a waterline length of 27 foot.' She gestured us into the wide cockpit. 'This is all teak, the benches and floor. There's a sail locker here, and the engine controls on this side – an 18 horse-power Volvo, top speed 6.5 knots. It's been regularly maintained, with a service record. There's a complete sail wardrobe, all new from Kemp Sails last summer, except for the spinnaker, which was original, but had had very little use.' She fumbled with lifting out the washboards. Below, the boat was laid out in the conventional modern 32-footer fashion: a saloon with a U-shape settee that could convert to a double berth on one side, a single settee on the other, a forepeak with double berth, and an aft cabin just big enough to swing a cat, if you were given to such barbarous practices. The upholstery was in cloud-blue plastic, functional and pleasant. There was a nicely enclosed galley on one side, a chart table with seat on the other. The heads (with shower) was small but functional, and there were a couple of hanging lockers. The cabin was lined with cherry wood, and had a good 'ship' feel.

The main drawback to her, from my point of view, was the lift-up centreboard. My *Khalida* had a solid keel with a heavy bulb at the bottom, to keep her upright in a sudden gale. Still, centreboarders these days were made so that if the hoist failed, the centreboard fell down. Her grab rails suggested she was intended for serious sailing, and Ivor had taken her to the Western Isles and back.

There were no signs of that passage now. The berth cushions were bare of sleeping bag, clothes, lifejackets. The chart table and bookshelf were empty, and some of the electronics had been taken away. Julie saw me looking at an empty bracket. 'I was told I'd get more for the plotter and the AIS set if I sold them separately on eBay, so I took them out just before Christmas.'

'Good advice,' I agreed. You couldn't stick an extra five thousand on a yacht price to cover the gadgetry. The multi-function wireless screen for boat speed and direction, depth, and log was still there, and another screen for the wind instruments. They'd cost at least a thousand. I made my voice matter-of-fact. 'The last trip she did was to the Western Isles, wasn't it? What sort of weather did you have, and how did she cope with it?'

'It was as much the west of Scotland.' Her voice was equally businesslike. 'Down to Skye first, Uig, in the north, and round the western side, Dunvegan, the Talisker factory, Loch Eishort and then to Mallaig. Do you know the area?'

I nodded. 'I've just come back from there.'

Her face didn't move, but her body jerked back from me. Her voice continued, silk-smooth. 'I came back with him up the Caledonian Canal.' The white nail-tips glinted as she made a deprecating gesture with one hand. 'I'm sorry not to be able to give more detail. My husband

seemed very pleased with how the long passage had gone.'
She said 'my husband' just as she might have said 'my
mechanic'. 'He'd had some rough weather coming down.'
She gestured towards where the mainsheet would have
been, had the mast been up. 'A pulley on the rope at the
stern broke, and he bought a new one.'

'What sort of weather did you have?'

'Oh, good, I suppose.' Her smile was impersonal as a
doll's. 'Though you sailors seem to have a totally different
scale of weather from us land folk. While I was on board
there were some nice sunbathing days, and no midges on
the water, of course. There was one loch with fierce
downdraughts, because of the height of the hills.' She
faltered and her cheeks flushed, as if that brought up a
memory she'd tried to suppress, but her lipstick-red mouth
continued steadily. 'That was a bit too exciting for me, but
there never seemed to be any worry about whether the boat
could cope.' She closed the subject with a bright smile.
'Like I said, I'm not a sailor.'

I made sure that Kevin saw all the relevant bits, and
had a test raise and lower of the centreboard, then I swung
myself out of the cabin and left them to talk business. It
seemed strange to me that Kevin should waste his time
going over a boat he couldn't afford, but maybe he hoped
to beat Julie down, if she was keen to be rid of the boat.
I'd hear all about it once college started.

Chapter Ten

At midday the sky was leaden, the sea slate purple. The roads were darkened with rain, the rugosa stems in the gardens black, when I walked along to the Co-op to get something for lunch and tea.

The Brae Co-op was small but efficient, especially in the matter of cut-price vegetables. I got a leek, carrots, and parsnips for soup, and then began to think about tea. I hadn't had jambalaya for a while, and it was easily made on my gas ring: a bit of frying, to blend the onion, chorizo, pepper, potato, and rice, then it could simmer all afternoon in the wide-necked flask. A shaft of sunlight as I walked back with my bag lit the flowering currant bushes pale red, and highlighted the pale green buds already visible on the stems. One of the houses had Delft blue hyacinths with glossy green leaves in pots on the windowsill. Now the New Year was past, we could look towards spring.

I'd gone only twenty yards when my phone rang: Inga. 'Cass, are you particularly busy?'

'No,' I said, and waited.

'I have to get Charlie off to the boat, and I've just realised it's Peerie Charlie's friend Orlando's birthday party. He's been looking forward to it for ages, but because it's in the swimming pool, I can't just drop him off and leave him, someone would need to stay with him.'

A toddlers' birthday party in a swimming pool sounded my idea of hell, but I didn't want Peerie Charlie to miss something that he'd been looking forward to. 'No problem,' I said. 'I'm just leaving the Co-op. Shall I come straight to you?'

'That would be great. You and Charlie could have lunch together. It starts at half past two. I can't believe I forgot it. My swimsuit should fit you okay.'

'Be with you in five minutes,' I said. Swimming with a toddler ... a pack of toddlers ... heaven help me. And what sort of name was Orlando? The child must have soothmoother parents, who didn't realise he'd be tormented to death once he got to school among the traditional Johns, Kevins, and Garys.

I started stifling as soon as I stepped into Inga's house, and had to nip into the lavatory to shed a layer before I could join Peerie Charlie for spaghetti rings on toast in the kitchen.

'Now you behave, boy,' Inga said, hauling her jacket on. 'Do what Cass says, and come out of the pool when she tells you.' She handed me a towel roll and clean Charlie clothes, and intercepted his speculative look at me with the ease of long practice. 'Or you'll miss the birthday cake.' She reached into the fridge for an ice-cream tub. 'That's fancies, for the feast.' A package wrapped in green and blue dinosaur paper followed. 'Present. Charlie, did you finish colouring in your card?'

'I finished.' Charlie raced over to his drawing corner and returned waving a dinosaur shape with green crayon scribbles over it. Inga found an envelope, inserted the card, wrote 'Orlando', stuck it to the parcel, and handed them over. The organisation needed to run a family made a tall ship seem child's play.

Big Charlie ruffled his son's hair. 'See you in twartree weeks, peeriebreeks.'

'Come and wave at the door,' I said. We both waved fervently as the car tore off in a spurt of gravel, then returned to the kitchen, where the spaghetti rings were glueing themselves to the pan bottom. I divided them onto toast. Charlie climbed into his chair and tackled his share with determination, if not enthusiasm. 'I eat all this,' he said, 'then birthday cake.' He gave it an ineffectual hack with his child-handled knife. 'Not crusts though.'

I conceded the crusts and allowed a yoghurt in a tube. At quarter past two, I gave his orange-stained face and hands a final wash, and we set off along the road towards the leisure centre. The light was already dimming, and the sun had spread an afterglow over the fields, making them the yellowed colour of old film. The rain had stopped, but there was enough wind for Peerie Charlie to hold my hand as an anchor. As we walked, he babbled about a shark in the pool, specially for birthdays. I could see an alarming number of cars disgorging parents and bairns into the leisure centre car park. It was going to be a noisy afternoon.

The North Mainland leisure centre, like Shetland's other country leisure centres, had been built to provide facilities for the school beside it during the day, and for the community in the evenings and weekends. The warm air and chlorine smell hit me as soon as we went in. There was a white-uniformed lass in the passage. 'Aye, aye, Charlie,' she said. 'Orlando's party's in the pool.'

I handed over the ice-cream tub, and followed Charlie. The changing room was seething with mothers and children. I put my towel roll down beside a stunning Filipina lass whose face I vaguely recognised from church. The noise of mothers controlling their offspring and children shrieking in excitement bounced off the white-tiled ceiling. I tugged Charlie's hand, and mouthed 'Orlando?' at him, but he shook his head. 'We go swimming now.'

Inga's swimsuit was rich purple, and rather curvy for my taste, with a cut-out circle at each side of the waist. I helped Peerie Charlie into his trunks and blew his armbands up to blood-stopping point. We ventured together into the pool area, where the noise was mercifully diluted by roof-height. Charlie gave a triumphant yell.

'See, Dass, shark.'

It was an inflatable run, stretching from one end of the pool to the other. There was a hump-backed bridge, a flat bit, a ship's wheel to wriggle through, a fat ladder with cartoon animals on the side, and, at the point where smaller people could get their feet on the bottom, a shark's head rearing out of the water, its pointed teeth around a flat boat with a treasure chest on it. Charlie charged towards the water, towing me in his wake. 'You walk beside me.'

Inga took him to the pool twice a week, so he was scarily confident. The little girl who'd changed beside us seemed to be his best friend; they held hands crossing the wobbling bridge, and fell in together. She seemed a bit uncertain as she came up, and both her mother and I reached for her, but when Charlie bobbed up, pushing his streaming hair out of the way with both hands and laughing, she laughed too. They scrambled back on the water-wheel, with Charlie on the top rung, boasting about how high up he was. My nerves were stretched watching him, as I went from thigh-deep to waist-deep to shoulder-deep in the warm pool beside him, one hand stretched out to grab; up, down again, out to the toddler pool, with waterfall and bubbles, back to the inflatables – I was relieved when at last a bell rang to tell us it was time to head for the changing rooms. I dried him quickly, ignoring his wriggles, and left him to dress himself. I was just ready when Charlie's little girlfriend emerged, in a party frock of the most traditional sticky-out white, with a velvet sash the exact brown of her eyes. Charlie held his hand out to her as a matter of course and towed her to the door. 'Shall I take them both?' I asked her mother.

'Oh, yes, please,' she said. 'The tea's in the community room. Annemarie, I'll be through in just a minute.'

Charlie led us back towards reception and into a good-sized room with a laden table in the middle: sausage rolls, sandwiches, mini-burgers and pizza squares, crisps, several sorts of fancies, with Inga's chocolate tiffin in among them, and, in the centre, a space for the birthday cake. Now at last I spotted what had to be Orlando (wearing five badges saying 'I am 4'), so I was able to introduce myself, thank his mother for having Charlie, and make Charlie hand over the present and say what fun the swimming had been. Manners satisfied, I stepped back to watch the feeding frenzy.

'Thank you,' Annemarie's mother said, appearing at my side in a party frock herself, the fashionable maxi look that draped gracefully over her six-month pregnant bump, and with her long black hair shiningly dried and put up in a bun with loose strands each side of her face. I didn't need a mirror to know that mine was curling wildly all over my shoulders. 'It's bliss to get a shower in peace. I'm Maya Georgeson. I've seen you at Mass.'

'I'm Cass.' There were a dozen Georgeson families, of course, but I remembered Maman's voice: *He has a family, a little girl, and another on the way.*

'Oh, yes, I know. You live in the boat down at the marina there. We're just up on the hill, the new house.' *I hope he did not involve his house in the business too* ... I turned to face Maya properly. She was show-stoppingly pretty, with perfectly tinted velvety skin, her daughter's huge eyes in the same oval face, and a gleamingly white smile. She was in her early twenties, too young for the worried lines around her eyes, and the faint crease between mouth-corner and nose. She gave a smile that didn't quite reach her eyes. 'Has big Charlie gone off to sea then?'

I nodded. 'Inga had to run him into Lerwick. That inflatable run thing in the pool was amazing.'

'Oh, Charlie loves that. He's so fearless. Annemarie wouldn't go on it without him.'

'It's a wonderful food spread too.'

'We all get together for that. Otherwise a party like this would be so much work. Everyone has their own thing to make.' She pointed to a sort of cinnamon semolina, cut into squares, that I remembered from parish get-togethers as being very good. 'This is my speciality.' She indicated the young woman on her other side, a fair-haired Shetlander with a smiling, rosy face and a baby in her lap. 'Shona always does the butterfly cakes.'

'My favourite,' I said. 'Hi, I'm Cass, temporarily in charge of Peerie Charlie.'

The young woman laughed. 'Good luck.' She rose and set the baby's feet on the floor. 'Shall we help them out with the food mountain?'

'Never refuse a meal' had been the motto of the World War I ambulance girls, and it applied to shipboard life too; you ate while the sea allowed you to. I rose with Maya and Shona, and tried not to be too greedy with the flaky-pastry sausage rolls. It could be midnight before my jambalaya was ready. I was just forbidding myself a fourth when Maya leaned closer to me, in a waft of jasmine scent.

'Your father has been very kind,' she said, 'advising Robert-John.'

'Dad's always glad to be of use.' I gave her a quick glance from out of the corner of my eye. Was she too hoping I'd help trace Ivor Hughson? 'But perhaps Ivor'll come home yet, and take some responsibility.'

Her dark eyes flashed. 'I hope not!' Then she smoothed her face. 'I've taken over the books now, and it won't be easy, but we'll get clear.' Her voice was calm, but her clenching hands bent the coloured paper plate. 'Ivor returning would only start the muddle all over again. Wherever he is, whoever he's with, I hope he never comes back here.' Her eyes met mine and held them. 'I wouldn't want a big search to be made for him either.' Her voice hardened, and her elegant hands came up to curve protectively around the six-month bump as she repeated Gavin's words: 'Wherever he is, all he'll have done is run up more debts. More creditors.'

'I understand,' I said. She held my gaze for a moment longer, then gave a little nod of satisfaction, and turned to take Annemarie's plateful of half-eaten sandwiches from her. Charlie came to tug at me with a chocolate-covered hand.

'Birthday cake next.' He pointed triumphantly down the passage, where a small conflagration was heading towards us. It was shaped like a dinosaur, covered with bilious green icing, and had four sparklers among the four candles. Once we'd sung 'Happy Birthday', Orlando's mother cut it up, and the children fell on it like starving wolves. After that was 'Pass the Parcel', with a sweet between each layer, and a little parcel for every child to open at the final layer, instead of just one (they were going to get a shock when they hit real life, I thought ungenerously), and, in a fanfare of party squeakers, we got to four thirty, and my ordeal was over.

It was pouring when we came out. The neon orange streetlights spotlit a curtain of rain that bounced in puddles at our feet, and the roadside drains gurgled with water. I looked around me with dismay. Charlie's house was only ten minutes' walk away, but the water was being blown like a hose towards us, and even with my Helly Hansen and his oilskin jacket, we'd be soaked to the hide by the time we got there. I hesitated in the doorway, scanning the cars in the parking space. If Inga was back from Lerwick, she'd probably think to come and get us.

'Can we give you a lift?' Maya asked from behind me.

'I was just looking to see if Inga was here.'

Maya gave the tarmac a quick scan. 'No, but Robert-John is. We can easily give you a lift if you don't mind squeezing in the back between the two children.'

'I don't mind in the least,' I said. 'Come on, boy, we're getting a lift with Annemarie, to save us being drookit, like ducks in a thunderstorm.'

'Ducks!' Charlie said, and he and Annemarie quacked

their way to Robert-John's car. It was only ten yards, but the water was running off my jacket and my trousers were sodden by the time I'd got them there and into their seats. I squelched into the space between them and leaned forward to talk to the driver.

'Thanks, Robert-John, this is very kind of you.'

'Na, na, we canna leave you to walk in this doonpour.' His voice was soft, hesitating, as if he could barely manage to string the words together. 'It's no' out of our way at all.'

It's a funny thing, heredity. You'd never have taken Robert-John for a brother of Miss Georgeson's. She'd been dark-haired, high-coloured, and decisive. He was a washed-out, thin creature, with pale skin, pale blue eyes, receding fair hair and eyebrows so light they shone silver in the car park streetlights; *Lik a docken grown under a pail*, Magnie would say. His hands lay irresolutely on the wheel, and he drooped his shoulders like someone who expected nothing but defeat from the world. It was a good thing he'd married someone as go-ahead and competent as Maya.

I dropped Charlie off into Inga's arms, and started to get out myself.

'Na, na,' Robert-John insisted. 'You're no' walking all the way to the marina in this.'

A lift from them would save Inga trailing Peerie Charlie out in the car again to put me home. I got her to bring me the clothes I'd shed, and we set off through the blackness, the slashing rain. 'Thanks to you,' I said.

'Oh, you're welcome.' Maya half-turned her head. 'You're not too cold living aboard this time of year?'

'I just keep adding jumpers, and having hot showers.'

'Your dad was saying you'd been involved with that poor body they found down in the Highlands.' Robert-John paused to let a large truck thunder past on the main road: *Georgeson Removals*, it said, in curlicue letters, with

90

a red and blue logo. Robert-John didn't comment. Beside him, Maya lifted her hand, as if to stop him saying any more. 'Maya's likely asked you all about it – she's a great one for these detective stories.'

'I like English murders,' Maya said. 'Agatha Christie, Agatha Raisin, Midsomer, all retired army colonels and village ladies spying on each other. I'm too squeamish for real-life crime.'

'It was horrid,' I said.

'It got a bit of coverage in the *Press and Journal*,' Robert-John said. 'They don't know who he was, seemingly.'

'I'm sure they'll find out,' I said. 'This modern DNA, and matching teeth, all that.'

We came past the Co-op, dark in its midwinter holiday, past the Brae Building Centre, with a twinkle-lights Christmas tree set up by its door, between the scatter of houses.

'I wasna clear exactly where it was found, from the report.' Robert-John turned down the gravel road to the marina.

'One of the remoter lochs.' I visualised it on the map. 'The long, crooked one opposite the dent in the bottom of Skye.'

The pick-up swerved, and the wheels spurted on the gravel, as if he'd pressed the accelerator instead of the brake. I clambered out, and at the marina gate I paused to wave. Maya responded, but Robert-John wasn't looking at me. He was staring out over the marina, motionless. Maya said something I didn't catch, her voice sharp. Then the engine roared, the pick-up turned in a splash of puddle, and headed off into the rain-black hills.

91

Chapter Eleven

As I came through the marina gate, a grey shape detached himself from the lee of a blue half-barrel for rinsing fish: Cat, his fur ruffled and his yellow eyes round with alarm. I bent down to stroke him. 'You and me both, boy. My nerves are shattered. Let's get indoors.'

The weather side of me was soaked by the time I'd got half-way along the pontoon. Cat slid indoors. I stripped my wet jacket off under the rain-hood shelter, and laid it flat to dry off, then took off my shoes, socks, and jeans as well. There would be enough condensation in the cabin without adding dripping clothing. By the time I'd done that my legs were goose-bumped under my thermal leggings, and my teeth chattering. I stepped onto the top step and pulled the hatch over me.

It was dim inside the cabin, with only the marina bollards shining a silver light. I came down the two steps and my foot touched a soft lump that shouldn't be there: fur. 'Cat, yuck!' A dead rabbit; just what I didn't feel like having to deal with. I stooped to look, and the breath stopped in my throat, for it was Cat, collapsed in the middle of the cabin floor, with the white belly that I wasn't allowed to touch spread long, the white paws and plumed tail limp, his pink mouth open as if he'd tried to mew a cry for help.

I didn't know what to do for a moment. I crouched down beside him. He was too young to have a seizure, and there'd been no sign of injury as he'd dodged along the pontoon before me. I ran a finger down each leg and across his ribs: no blood, no broken bones, as far as I could tell.

Poison? There was no feel of froth round the open mouth, no sign of anything stuck in his throat. I had to suspect the most dangerous aspect of any boat, escaped gas, heavier than air, so that it sank down into the bilges and rested there.

I spat out all the breath in my lungs and picked him up. He was limp in my hands, surprisingly heavy. I retreated up the steps and took a long breath of clear air, then sat down under the sheltering hood, cradling him on my lap, with a hand over his ribs. A rush of relief swept through me as I felt them move. 'Cat, come on ... You can do it, boy.' Then he gave a great shuddering breath, sneezed several times and began to stir again. His eyes opened. He mewed, and wriggled to be free from this unaccustomed cuddle. I turned my jacket dry side upmost, and made him a nest under the rain-hood. 'You stay there,' I told him. 'Stay, just for now. I'll make it safe.'

I went back into the rain, and reached inside the port locker for the gas cylinder cut-off switch. My fingers felt it running parallel to the metal pipe: on. I switched it off, took a deep breath of clean air in the cabin doorway, like a diver, and went in, hand stretching to the cooker. The burner I'd used this morning was in the 'on' position. I switched it off, and dived up through the forrard hatch for another breath, then tied the hatch to the mast, so that a great blast of air would sweep through the cabin. Cat was still huddled in my jacket, breathing steadily, sneezing from time to time, but already looking less dopey. 'Don't laugh,' I told him.

As the butane gas leaked out of the cooker, it had oozed down to the bilges and built up from there, like water rising. While my head was in the cold, wet draught that was filling the forecabin with rain, I'd be safe enough, but I wouldn't dare strike a match or run the engine until it was all gone. If I'd not had Cat as my miner's canary, my first act would have been to light the lamp, and *Khalida* would have blown sky-high. I took the bucket from the hanging locker and made an experimental sweep along the empty cabin floor. The still-empty bucket became heavy. I climbed up the steps and tipped the nothing over the side, and the bucket lightened. I baled emptiness until the bucket stopped increasing in weight. To make absolutely sure, I lifted the floorboards, filled the bilge with water, and baled above it. Then I baled the actual water that had come in the forrard hatch, closed it to a fist-sized slit, wiped off the last drips, and breathed a long sigh of relief. I reckoned we were safe now. I brought the lamp out under the rain-hood to light it, then put the glass chimney over the flame before carrying it back below and hanging it on its hook. Instantly, my cabin came back to life: the gold-grained wood of bulkhead and fiddles that kept my books on their shelves even when *Khalida* was tipped almost to ninety degrees, the blue curtain looped in front of the heads, the gleam of brass on our little fish mascot, the navy cushions along the couch.

'Safe now, I think.' I brought Cat back into the cabin and gave him a soothing stroke. He responded with a purr. I gave my blue-with-cold feet a good rub and put all my layers back on. Then I sat down beside my little table, took Cat on my lap, and considered.

There was no way I'd have left the gas on like that. I had a distinct memory of having paused in the conversation with Kevin to go out and turn the cut-off switch. It was second-nature; a gas build up could kill a crew overnight, or reduce a boat to flaming rubble the moment a match was struck, so you got completely paranoid about switching the cut-off the minute you put out the gas. Of course I'd have turned it off, and I was sure that I had, still listening while Kevin had been telling me about how they'd had Nan round to his house for Christmas lunch.

Someone else had come aboard and turned it on. It

hadn't been on for long either; when Cat had met me, he'd had that alarmed air as if he'd just been disturbed, and his fur wasn't as wet as it would have been if he'd been outside for long. The Georgeson truck had passed us just five minutes before ... Maya's soft voice sounded in my head: *You're not too cold living aboard this time of year?* She hadn't wanted me to investigate Ivor's disappearance. Robert-John had reacted to the name of Gavin's loch. Julie had been startled to see me. And the *Press and Journal* had reported the finding of the skeleton, and the whole place knew I'd been down with Gavin for Christmas. *Links*, Gavin had said. There was no reason why an absconded husband from Shetland should ever be linked up with a skeleton in the west Highlands, except for the coincidence that it was I who'd found it, and come back to Brae, to the marina where Ivor's boat was berthed.

Ivor, who'd left in the early morning, leaving a note on the table, and gone off on the boat. Julie wouldn't chase him after an exit like that, I was sure; she'd be too proud. Robert-John and Maya were left muddling through the books and trying to get back on their feet. I wondered what would happen to the firm if Ivor could be proved dead.

ᚺ

The club was open that evening, but I didn't feel like going up. I was worried about Cat, still lethargic after his poisoning even though he'd only been out for less than two minutes, and I didn't feel it was safe to leave *Khalida*. I'd be securing myself from inside tonight. The person who'd turned the gas tap had a key to the marina, which narrowed it down to about half the population of Brae. Julie certainly had one. Robert-John and Maya probably did. Mr Georgeson senior of *Georgeson Removals* might well have an interest in one of the boats, although murdering a man because he'd cheated your son seemed a bit unlikely.

It was half-way through the evening when I heard the marina gate clang, and felt footsteps on the pontoon. I squirmed on the couch to look through the window. It was Magnie, the hood of his neon-yellow jacket pulled down against the rain.

'I heared you had some trouble,' he said, once he was settled in the corner of the couch. 'Willie saw you baling oot gas.'

Naturally. 'I don't suppose he saw anyone unken at the boat?'

'No' that he mentioned.' Magnie nodded as I lifted the kettle. 'Yea, thanks to you, a cup o' tay would go down well.' He fished in his pocket. 'I brought a fancy to go with it.' He put a margarine tub in the middle of the table. 'So what's going on?'

I lit the gas under the kettle, and sat down opposite him. 'Somebody came aboard and turned the taps. I was lucky not to be blown to smithereens.'

'And for why?'

'I'm the link,' I said. 'That skeleton that Gavin and I found, nothing would ever have connected him with Shetland, if it hadn't been me that found him. Ivor Hughson ran away from his wife, and that was that. His finances were in a mess, there was maybe another woman involved, and he ran. Who'd question it?'

'The lass who's courting with the policeman in charge of the investigation.'

'Yea. Shut me up quick before I mention Ivor's name to Gavin. It would have worked, too, if it hadn't been for Cat.'

'Poor puss,' Magnie said, rubbing Cat's grey head. Cat opened yellow eye slits, acknowledged the sympathy, and curled his plumed tail over his nose once more.

'He ate his supper fine. I think he's okay.'

'So,' Magnie said, getting down to brass tacks, 'Julie Hughson kent you were down in the Highlands, because you telt her. Robert-John and Maya Georgeson did, because they'd read this morning's *P and J.*'

'A lot of folk in Shetland read the *Press and Journal.*'

'Then there was the Georgeson man's truck. John Georgeson, the councillor. His big brother was at the school with me, and a nasty obstreperous object he was an' all. The whole family's the same, what they want, they'll have. Robert-John's the exception. He was the youngest son, and I doubt he got that used to being ordered about by his father an' big brothers that he never developed any personality o' his ain. That foreign wife o' his is the best thing he ever managed.'

I placed his mahogany tea before him, and opened the margarine tub. The fancies turned out to be millionaire shortbread with dates in the lower half. 'You're no' been baking?'

'Left over from the five hundred night at the club.'

Five hundred was a card game, a cross between whist and bridge, and there was a Shetland league who met during the winter. I'd occasionally gone up to find tables laid out, and a crowd of people playing in the kind of silence that you tiptoe through to get to your notes in the teaching room, conscious of every squeak of your slightly damp trainers on the lino floor. The embarrassment was worth it for the fancies which were left as a help-yourself in the fridge. Magnie took a bite of his and shook his head.

'Lass, yon Councillor Georgeson's no' someone you want to fall foul of. There was speak about him paying a secretary from Shetland Transport to give him a copy of every quotation she put out. He'd send one to the client too, but twenty pound cheaper.' He went into proverb mode. '*Da king o' da flukes is as glied as da rest o' dem.*'

'Untrustworthy,' I agreed. 'And he has trucks going up

and down all the time. He could easily transport a body to a nice piece o' wilderness and leave it there. But why should he? What would happen to Robert-John and the firm if Ivor was found dead?'

'They'd have to assess the assets, I suppose.' Magnie drew his brows together. 'Well, I can tell you for a fishing boat, for David Jarmeson died aboard the *Astella*, and he was part-owner. They were allowed to go on trading, sell the fish and land it ashore in Norway, but the books had to be inspected within an inch of their lives, to find out to a farthing what he was worth at the time o' death, and that had to go to his widow.'

That was what I'd thought. 'Maya thinks she can just get them solvent again, with work, so long as Ivor doesn't reappear.'

'What she thinks, Robert-John'll think.'

'Maybe no'. Dad said Robert-John had said he'd set a detective firm on to trace him. Maya wouldna've approved of that. Robert-John's up and down from Scotland all the time too, and on his own, without needing an employed go-between. I bet your Mr Georgeson doesn't drive his own trucks now, or if he did it would be noticed.'

'I think you should leave it all alone,' Magnie said. 'Get your policeman up here as soon as you can to investigate with all the noise he can make, and they'll all ken you're passed on the information you're gotten, an leave you in peace.'

'I'll maybe do that,' I said.

'And if he'll leave his policeman's hat off for an evening, I have a most special dram I think he'd like to try.'

'An illicit fire-water from Norway?' I guessed, remembering past occasions.

'Even better as that. You tell him, now, when you're telling him all about the rest of it.'

I scowled at the cooker taps. 'I'm no' having people

99

coming in and trying to murder Cat and blow *Khalida* to fibreglass splinters. I'll maybe phone tonight.'

He gave me a sceptical look, gathered up his neon oilskin, and headed back out into the streaming night.

I sighed and picked up my mobile.

ᚼ

'So,' Gavin said, when I'd explained, 'you really think this body might be Hughson, and somebody's trying to stop you telling me about him.'

'I can't see any other reason someone would try to silence me. It was a serious attempt at doing just that. If I'd been below, lighting the lamp, there's no way I'd have survived.'

'Specialist knowledge?'

I shook my head. 'No. Anyone who's ever been even an afternoon on a boat would know about turning the gas off. Boat owners are paranoid about it, and the tap being in a cockpit locker usually means someone has to stand up to let you get at it, so it's a visible fuss.'

'Knowledge of your boat?'

'Not even that. Cooker, cylinder. Just a matter of looking.'

'And everyone knows, of course, which boat is yours.'

'The only one with her mast up.'

He was silent for a moment, thinking. 'Question one. Who knows you found the body?'

'Everyone now. It was in the *P&J* – the *Aberdeen Press and Journal.*'

'So it was. And the boat was empty all afternoon?'

'From about twelve right up to five. I was at a children's party.'

His silence was eloquent.

'Peerie Charlie couldn't go without me,' I explained. 'It was fun really – at least, he enjoyed it. Swimming followed by sweeties. Here, that gives Maya Georgeson an alibi – that's Hughson's partner's wife. She was there, with her little girl. *But*, they gave me a lift back, and there was a Georgeson Transport truck at the marina – that's his father. The partner's father, I mean. According to Magnie, he'd bear watching.'

'Isn't he a pillar of the community, councillor and all that?'

'Exactly,' I said darkly.

'Cynic. I didn't get peace to look for Hughson today, but I'll make it a priority tomorrow.'

'Keep me posted, if you're allowed.'

'I'll do that.' His voice changed from policeman to friend. 'Kenny and Mother were asking about your journey, and send their best wishes …'

Friday 3 January

Low Water at Brae UT	*03.32, 0.5m*
High Water	*09.45, 1.9m*
Low Water	*16.01, 0.5m*
High Water	*22.23, 1.9m*
Moonrise	*09.34*
Sunrise	*09.13*
Sunset	*15.07*
Moonset	*18.58*

Waxing gibbous moon

Dem as comes oonbidden sits oonsaired.
Don't expect a welcome if you're a gatecrasher.

Chapter Twelve

I woke to rain drumming on the cabin roof and lashing against the windows. I'd had a restless night, rousing to every little change of sound: the wind backing, the tide turning so that the ripples tapped against *Khalida*'s stern, a car driving down into the marina, waiting with engine running and retreating again. I reached out for my watch, pressed the luminous button, and found I'd slept in. It was eight o'clock, and still black dark, a horrid blashy day. The wind wasn't as cold as yesterday, but it was stronger, snatching my hair loose from its plait and trying to buffet my washing gear from my hand. The tide was flowing like a river, pushed by the exceptionally high tides; there would be a new moon tomorrow night.

I brooded over breakfast. It was all very well for Magnie to say 'Keep out of it'; he wasn't baling gas out of his cabin. If someone had it in for me, I wanted to know who.

I phoned Maman. 'Are you and Dad still going into town today?'

'Yes. You want to come too?'

'Yes, and there's something I want you to do for me, Maman actress. I'll explain on the way.'

'Intriguing. Will I need a costume?'

'Your most imposing black and white chic.'

She laughed. 'Very well. We'll pick you up at ten o'clock.'

I spent the wait on security: double-taping the various split-pins that held the mast up, and adding extra mooring ropes. I secured the washboards and chained Cat's forehatch exit. I'd wondered about sending Cat himself to safety at Magnie's but between Magnie's outsize stripey and the imperious Siamese he'd adopted after she'd saved herself from a sinking yacht, permanently in a state of war with each other, but likely to gang up on outsiders, I didn't think he'd enjoy himself there.

The sky was clearing as the Range Rover bumped down the gravel into the marina. Maman had taken me at my word, and was wearing her white wool coat with a black-flowered corsage, cinched in with a black belt. A jaunty cap with black feathers perched on her head, and her Callas eye-liner and frosted lipstick was as immaculate as if we were heading for La Scala instead of Lerwick.

I scrambled into the back seat. 'Perfect, Maman. You'll have him eating out of your hand.'

'If I thought, now, that either of you girls would be in serious danger,' Dad said, 'I'd be forbidding this caper.'

'You just have to ask for a quote for moving a piano,' I told Maman.

'Ah,' Dad said. 'Robert-John's father?'

'Georgeson Removals,' I agreed, and explained the story as far as I had it, while the long sea-arm of Olnafirth slid by us, pewter-grey turning to silver as the clouds cleared. Behind it was the island of Linga, a symmetrical curve of dark-chocolate heather, and behind that the sun gleamed dully on the wide Atlantic. 'I want to get a look at him,' I finished. 'If he knows me, he knows I wouldn't want a removal van. Maman looks like someone who might, and if he knows Maman, then a piano is just what he'd expect her to be removing.'

'They don't get on, you know,' Dad said. 'Well, Robert-John didn't say that, in so many words. I suggested he could maybe look to his father as collateral for a further loan, and he made it clear he wanted to get himself out of the mess without asking his father for help, and preferably without his father knowing anything about it.'

'He is the odd one out,' Maman said. 'His father, well, we see what a forceful character he is, each week there is something in the papers that he sounds off about.' She made a face. 'Usually it is something some firm from south doing Shetlanders down – you know, the council has given a job to them, like repairing a council house scheme, and they make a mess of it, when local builders would have done better.'

'There's a lot of truth in that,' Dad said. He had begun as a builder. 'We've had a few south firms giving a cut-throat price based on working south, which the council has to accept, as the lowest tender, even though you know it won't be a good job for that money. The firms factor in transport costs afterwards, recoup it on materials, and do a job that won't stand Shetland weather.'

'But,' Maman quibbled, 'if Monsieur Georgeson did not know that his son was in trouble, he had no reason for killing the partner who caused it, even if he would be ruthless enough to do such a thing.'

'He'd know,' I said. 'Magnie knew all about it, from gossip at the club. John Georgeson's one to keep his ear to the ground.'

We came through the village of Voe, and onto the main road between Lerwick and the north isles. The lines of the Long Kames lay each side of us.

'What's the latest with your wind farm?' Dad was a director of a group who planned to create a large wind-farm in central Shetland – over a hundred huge turbines, visible from everywhere, and installed, for the most part, on untouched peat moorland like this, which was already colonised by birds and carbon-absorbing plants. I was trying hard to sit on the fence; like any other Shetlander, I could see what climate change had already done to the seabirds who used to flock the cliffs, but I sympathised with the objectors who said the development was too big and too destructive. We were driving through what would

105

be the centre of it now, between the hills of the East Kame and the Mid Kame, a wilderness dark with wet heather, and with jigsaw pieces of water reflecting the sky.

Dad made an airy gesture with one hand. 'Oh, the objectors are still pushing this judicial review through. They're still on about the birds, and that we don't have an electricity licence, as if any wind farm applications ever do have that. It's just a formality. The council aren't going to revoke their consent, they want the money too much.'

'What if it goes against you?'

'It won't.' His voice was so confident that I gave him a sceptical look. 'If it does, we'll appeal. They want to force the council to hold a planning consent review.'

'I hadn't realised you hadn't had one.'

'Well, girl, we went all round the rural halls with our plan and a scale model, we were absolutely transparent about it. There was no need for the council to waste money on a review. We made sure everyone knew exactly what we planned, and had the chance to ask questions.'

'*A sales talk,*' my pal Inga had called the hall meetings, '*from people you knew stood to make a lot of money from it.*'

'And were many questions asked?'

'Ach, well, Cassie, you know what it's like. The people who speak at these things are the ones who've decided against it already. The ones who are okay with it, or not bothered either way, they don't come.'

In short, as Inga had told me, there had been strongly expressed, near-unanimous local opposition in nearly every village where there would be turbines nearby. I decided to push my luck. 'How's your health paper coming along?'

'Nearly finished – the results, from windfarms all over the world, will be published next month. That'll reassure the worriers.'

I doubted it. I'd read a good number of internet articles

myself, and it seemed to me that people, animals, and local wildlife were demonstrating a number of ill-health effects caused by their proximity to turbines. It would be interesting to see what Dad's tame doctors came up with; but like so many Shetlanders who were keeping quiet, I swallowed my natural daughterly desire to say black to Dad's white.

'There,' Maman said. She passed her iPad back. The internet was open at a picture of a grand piano with solid turn-of-the-century legs and a raised lid. 'Perfect. A Bechstein baby grand, from the Edinburgh Piano Company. 1924, and recently restored.'

The car swerved as Dad tried to see too. '£8,500. If that's what you'd like. We'd have to build an extension to fit it in.'

Maman laughed. 'No, I research my role.' Her voice went honey-sweet. 'I consider to buy this piano, M Georgeson, but I wish to assure myself it can be transported to Shetland.' She took her iPad back. 'Or there is a restored Steinway, £30,000. Of course one would have to hear it.'

She subsided into murmuring to herself, and I sat back and watched the Loch of Girlsta slide past – another deep one, with its own Arctic char, though no njuggle, that I'd ever heard. The ditches at the side of the road were sloping banks carved into the peat, black with rain, and punctuated by spouting waterfalls. The grass of the Tingwall valley was sodden green, the ponies' long coats darkened. Now, in winter, they had fur like a bear's. White patches were dirtied with mud, and the thick manes that fell almost to their sturdy knees were matted with a natural layer of protective grease. Shetland ponies were designed to live outside through the winter, sheltering below peat banks, or in hollows of the hill. I knew that much, but that was about it for my equine lore. I presumed they were intelligent beasts; intelligent enough, for example, to be trained to charge down to the road and into the loch, if there was a bucket of oats for them at the end of it. Gavin had shown me photographs of Luchag and Ribe burdened with dead stags, and talked of one from his childhood that had been trained to take its carcase home by itself, be unloaded, then return for the next one. I'd seen old photos of ponies with a pannier of peats on each side, walking in line down a hill track, without a bridle between them. When I got the chance, I'd go and chat to Inga's oldest lass, as Magnie had suggested. He thought there was something dodgy going on ...

We swooped down the hill around the golf course, up again and down into the industrial end of Lerwick, with, to our left, the blue expanse of Shetland Catch, Europe's largest pelagic fish processing factory. There were no boats sitting beside it, unloading their catch through long black tubes straight into the heart of the factory. I wondered where big Charlie was: off Norway, off Ireland, out at Rockall.

Georgeson Removals was in the new industrial estate opposite the brown bulk of Lerwick's power station. It was a metallic building with a wide glass porch. Dad drew up at the side of the door. 'You go in the front,' he said, 'and I'll go round the back and chat to the lads. You can learn more on the shop floor than in the office.'

He fished a boiler suit out of the back of the car and gave me a sideways grin, the adult masking the child's desire to play spies. His voice broadened so that he sounded like Grandpa Patrick. 'Sure, an' I'm after hearing there might be work for a driver with this outfit, but I'm no' wantin' to be changing me conditions for the worse, now, am I?'

'Go for it, Dad,' I said. I trailed quietly in Maman's magnificent wake to the front door, hanging back enough that I wouldn't be associated with her. My jeans, Hawkshead boots, and worn Musto jacket were far more likely to belong to a delivery courier than to the daughter of Eugénie Delafauve.

'Good morning,' Maman said. 'I would like to speak to Monsieur Georgeson personally, about the removal of a piano.'

The receptionist was a competent-looking woman in her forties, with brown hair clipped back at the nape of her neck, and a no-nonsense top above black trousers. She wore a hands-free headset. 'I can take the details,' she said. 'Where is the piano now, and where's it to come to?'

Maman shook her head. '*Non, madame.* Zat will not do.' Good, Maman, I thought, the 'distinguished foreigner' act. 'It is a piano of value, and I must ensure myself that it can be delivered safely.' She glanced towards the customer chairs and coffee machine. 'If Monsieur Georgeson is busy, I can wait.' Her dark lashes flicked towards the window in the inner wall, showing an office with a grey-suited man behind a large desk, then swept down the receptionist and up again. She added, with polite indifference, 'It is too important for conducting through an intermediary.'

The receptionist eyed up her poise, reached down to her desk, pressed a button, and murmured into her headset. On the other side of the window, the man looked up, then rose. The receptionist nodded, and returned to Maman. 'Mr Georgeson is just coming now, Mrs –?'

'Eugénie Delafauve.' Maman looked at the customer seats, made it clear without a change in her expression that they were not clean enough for her white coat, and simply waited in the centre of the floor. She wasn't much taller than I, but she filled the whole space.

The man came out with hand extended, and a smarmy smile. 'Madame, this is an honour.'

Even without seeing him grinning in the paper each week, I'd have known him for Miss Georgeson's father. He had the same dark colouring, the high cheekbones and ruddy skin, the same air of knowing exactly how this empire was going to be run. Perhaps she'd had qualms under her confidence, being faced with twenty unruly ten-year-olds, but he looked as if he'd never had a qualm in his life. What he decided would be done. Looking at the sharp nose, curved like a hawk's beak, and the harsh lines between the thick brows and around the thin-lipped mouth, I could imagine him deciding that this or that competitor had to be eliminated, and going ahead in a ruthless fashion, even if it wasn't ethical. If there was a secretary to be bribed, he'd have the money ready in the envelope, and maybe, I thought, looking at the narrow, steel-grey eyes, a story from her earlier life ready to threaten her with if she resisted the bribe.

He was all charm now. 'I know your delightful singing of course. I had the pleasure of hearing you in the Town Hall, last summer.'

A concert in Shetland had been Maman's pretext to come to our rescue in the longship affair. She gave a gracious inclination of her head, and let Mr Georgeson usher her into his office, all shark smiles. I was about to follow when I spotted the other person in there: Miss Georgeson herself, with her dark hair coiled up in a bun on the top of her head, and the crisp cotton shirt I remembered. There was zero chance of her not recognising me. I nipped into the corridor behind them, dodged out of sight of the receptionist, went through a varnished wood door, and came out into the working area of the firm.

Dad would be hanging out with the drivers in the glassed cabin by the big roll door. I'd come out in the storage area. There was nobody at this end at the moment, but if I was going to poke around I'd need camouflage. I grabbed the clipboard of forms that someone had abandoned on the top of a pile of cardboard storage boxes. There was a red boiler suit too, hanging over a chair back. I checked it didn't have the Georgeson Removals logo, then hauled it on, tucked my plait down my back neck, straightened my spine, and looked as much like a stupid boy as I could. There was a grey toorie cap; I added that. If anyone challenged me, I was looking for Jeemie, second name unknown, who'd said I was to call today for a package on last night's boat. It was a safe bet that at only – I checked my watch – quarter to eleven – the stuff on last night's ferry wouldn't have made it here yet.

I sauntered into the warehouse centre. Where I'd come in seemed to be a dumping ground for bits and pieces, but as I penetrated further back among the storage bays, it was clear there was organised thinking behind the system. This far end of the warehouse was divided into a dozen bays, each marked with a letter of the alphabet. Every second bay was shelved, and each shelf was numbered. The boxes inside were turned so that the label was outwards, and there was a contents list, with shelf, item and owner, pinned to each bay. Several bays were labelled with destinations: Aberdeen, Inverness, Glasgow, Edinburgh, Birmingham, London. Aberdeen was almost full, as if there would be a truckload ready to go soon; London must have just gone, for the bay was empty. The rest had a variety of parcels and packages: a palette of furniture, wrapped in cling film, a new sofa under plastic, square boxes marked CHINA FRAGILE. Some of the items were clearly newly arrived, and awaiting collection or delivery; others looked as if they were being stored long-term, while the owners changed house. There was a stack of wooden boxes the size of old teachests with Mr Georgeson's own name on them, way back in the corner of one bay, and enough dust on them to suggest they'd been there a while. Beside them were props for the Lerwick Gala: a Bugs Bunny cut-out in sugar blue, and a plump girl in a bonnet in candy-floss pink, several benches and a barrel with a notice still attached: 'Lucky Dip'.

Tucked in beside that was something else I recognised,

from Miss Georgeson's class: a saddle and bridle on a trestle. The reins had yellow cloth festoons on them, and there was a folded cloth over the saddle, one of those long blankets worn by knights' horses. Her big brother had taken part in medieval tournaments, with everyone in costume. He'd been our class pin-up, handsome in his shining breastplate and plumed helmet, astride a smoke-grey horse with this same yellow cloth flung over it. We girls had rather fallen for him, and been thrilled when one day he'd actually come to the school and shown us some of his horse's tricks: rearing up while he whirled his sword around, charging forwards then stopping dead, and jumping sideways out of the way. I was leaning in to see if that glint behind the saddle trestle was armour when footsteps clumped behind me. I turned casually, my mouth falling open, my eyes growing blank, and brandished the clipboard.

'Looking for a box that came off the boat this morning.' I pitched my voice low. 'They said to ask Jeemie.'

If I hadn't just been remembering the photos, I'd never have known Miss Georgeson's brother. The smiling mouth of the photos was set into a sneer; the broad shoulders had a substantial paunch below them. It would take a Shire horse for him to joust now. 'Jeemie wha?'

'They didna say.' I added a whine to my voice. 'Nobody ever explains properly. Just sent me here to say Jeemie would have it.' I squinted at the clipboard. 'I dinna see it on this.'

He was still looking suspicious. I was a bit old for the gormless apprentice I was pretending to be. 'Wha's "nobody"? Wha d'you work to?'

I picked on the largest firm I could think of. 'DITT.' With inspiration, I remembered the classic newie joke. I handed him back the clipboard with a defeated look. 'It's weights,' I said. 'Long weights. Come up from Aberdeen on last night's boat.'

His grin was as much like a shark's as his father's. 'Oh, that's what they sent you for, is it? Come you with me.' He turned on his heel, and I trailed scrape-footed after him down to the strip-lit cabin. 'Bide you there.'

I stood obediently, shoulders slumped against the draught from outside, while he went into the cabin. Dad had made himself at home, I saw, with a mug of tea in one hand, and a caramel wafer in the other. Through the glass, heads turned to look at me. There were guffaws, then Georgeson Junior came out again, still grinning. 'I'll go and have a look for it mesel' for you. The office'll maybe ken.' Then he turned to look at me more closely. 'That's a hell of a mess you're made of your face. What was it, a car accident?'

Mr Tactful. I hung my head. 'Came off a quad. Fucking thing turned right ower on me, split me cheekbone.'

'That'll learn you to be stupid. You'll no' get a girl so easy with yon.' He turned away and strolled off up the warehouse, whistling. Bastard. I watched him open the door I'd come out of and decided it was time to leave.

Chapter Thirteen

'The drivers weren't falling over themselves to recommend the place,' Dad said, once we were safely ensconced in the Peerie Shop Café. The town-centre harbour was bleak and empty, with winter having banished the fleet of visitors which made a guard of honour round the concrete pier: yachts from Scandinavia, Germany, Britain, America. Instead of the white cruise liners, with glassed windows and yellow pod lifeboats, there were two barges for the Totale builders: one red and grey one, a great block of a thing like a sixties student hall of residence, and the other a nightmare zig-zag of black and white, named *Sans Vitesse*.

Once, steamers had come into Lerwick harbour and anchored off, as the largest cruise ships did now, and little flit boats had come out to them from the beaches between the stone-built houses that stood with their foundations in the sea. You could still see how the whole Esplanade had once been when you looked along past the Queen's Hotel: grey stone buildings with the water washing up their walls, and wooden doors and pulleys just above high tide level, for loading goods. The Peerie Shop had once been one of those, gable end on to the sea. Now, it was a shop to go to for an interesting present, with a café above. We'd given in our orders, taken the coloured cube to identify us, and gone upstairs to a corner table, beneath framed prints of peewits by a local artist.

Dad and Maman were flushed and triumphant, as if they'd enjoyed themselves playing detective. They went for coffee with freshly baked scones and home-made jam;

I opted for tea and a slice of strawberry cake that matched even my friend Reidar's best baking.

'Well,' Dad said, 'Georgeson runs a tight ship. "Every time you spit's recorded," one of the drivers said. The pay's not particularly good, given the wages in Shetland right now, with Totale paying Monopoly money. Georgeson doesn't forgive or forget anything, and besides, they said, I'd be lucky if he employed me in the first place, with my accent. The older son, the one who collared you, he's unpopular too, throws his weight around, and has never heard the words please or thank you. "Treats us like he was a laird ordering the peasants." A tough organisation, but I'm not sure how prosperous. I'd like to see their books.'

'I did not like him. He was very oily on top, but underneath there is a ruthless character. His daughter tried to interrupt at one point, when he was giving me prices, and was given a very short answer.'

'Good,' I said.

'I am not sure if he would kill on his son's behalf, how can you tell, but if Robert-John had had an argument with Ivor Hughson that had ended in Hughson's death, I think he would dispose of the body.'

'Did you have any feeling of something dishonest?' I asked Dad.

He shook his head. 'Not in the haulage business. Ruthless cost-cutting at the employee's expense, and I can see them resorting to the kind of dirty tricks you described, but drivers' hours and conditions were adhered to, if only to keep the unions off their backs. I had no feeling of illegal cargo, or none that the drivers knew about. Of course, you'd have to strip the trucks to make sure there wasn't a drugs operation, but at first sight I don't think that's likely.' He leaned towards me. 'The main thing, girl, is to get the police in on this. Don't meddle with them yourself.'

'Yes, Dermot, you are right,' Maman said. 'They are not gentle, *gentil*, not nice people.'

'The son was a bully,' I agreed. 'As for the police, if that poor man we found really was Ivor Hughson, then it can't be a proper investigation until they get the dental results. Naturally there are no dentists open until Monday.'

Dad drained the last of his coffee. 'Why don't you bring your boat round to our jetty? Moor up there, use the house showers and toilet. You'd be less isolated over the weekend.'

Maman's smile said she knew I wouldn't move back to the safety of the parental roof. I shook my head.

'I need to sail back round to Scalloway. Tomorrow's looking good for that.'

'I'll give my contacts a prod,' Dad said. 'Call in a few favours. See if I can find out more about Georgeson Removals.'

'Thanks, Dad.'

We headed out into 'The Street', Lerwick's main shopping road, running parallel to the sea-front.

'I just have a couple of errands,' Maman said. 'Meet you at the car in half an hour, Cass?'

I nodded, and she and Dad headed off, leaving me beside the Market Cross, where the strains of a fiddle swelled around me, from High Level Music. The street ran for a hundred yards southwards and three hundred northwards, until it reached the stone cliff wall and projecting guns of Fort Charlotte, built for the seventeenth-century Dutch wars. I pottered along to the Shetland Times Bookshop and browsed the latest titles, then sauntered back towards the pier carpark. I was just looking in the window of the Shetland Soap Company, and trying to remember how much was left in my bottle of shower gel, when I spotted Miss Georgeson herself striding along the street towards me. She said my name as sharply as if I was still in her classroom. 'Cass Lynch.'

I stuck my chin in the air. I was thirty, and wasn't going to be intimidated. 'Hello.' I took the war right into the enemy camp. 'Maman was saying she'd seen you in your dad's office.'

She looked me up and down, ending with a stare at the scar. 'Well, you've had some very varied experiences since we last met.' Her tone would have curdled milk. 'Including playing the girl detective, I believe.'

Attack was the best form of defence. 'How well do you know Ivor Hughson?'

Her eyes flared in shock. If she'd been less rigidly in control, I suspected she'd have taken a step back from me. She tried for a casual tone. 'Ivor Hughson ... I think I taught him at Bell's Brae. A couple of years younger than you?'

'Ivor Hughson who's in partnership with your little brother.' I suddenly realised that Ivor must be not far off ages with her. 'You were at the Anderson together.'

Her expression didn't change, but the rosy colour drained from her cheeks, leaving them bone white. Her eyes stared dark and round, like a trapped animal's, shifting from the Soap Company's window to the Cross behind my shoulder. 'Oh, that Ivor.' Now she was rattling off words, as if talking could stop me seeing what she was thinking. 'Yes, we were in some of the same classes. He was a great charmer, always laughing and joking.' The off-hand tone didn't stop her voice softening. 'We were at university together too, but I was doing the B.Ed. while he did sciences, so we didn't mix much.'

He was a great charmer ... but the past tense could be because she was remembering. Her gloves prevented me from seeing if she wore a wedding ring now. Hanging round her dad's office didn't feel like a married woman with a home and children of her own. 'What's he doing these days, do you know?'

She gestured with one hand. A little of the colour had

118

crept back into her cheeks, but her chest rose and fell as if she'd been running. 'Oh, you know, you lose touch with people. Once he was a pair with Julie, well ...'

'Your brother's partner?' I reminded her.

She almost managed her old, tart tone. 'I don't discuss his business with my brother.' She looked over my shoulder, gave a start. 'Is that the time? I must rush.'

I turned to watch her go. She bumped into two people before blundering her way out of the shopping crowd and down towards the Esplanade. Naturally, looking in the direction she'd been facing, there wasn't a clock in sight. She wanted to get away from questions about Ivor Hughson.

Gavin could sit her down in an interview and keep asking. I could be nosy, but there was nothing to stop my suspects walking out on me. The shock had been genuine. *Playing the girl detective*, she'd said ... and then, following Maman's visit to Georgeson Removals, the girl detective had thrown the name of Ivor Hughson at her. If the skull staring up from the bracken was Ivor's, did she know it? *He was a great charmer ...*

I was just staring blankly towards her wake when I heard a voice call 'Dass!' It was Inga with Peerie Charlie and his two big sisters, two smaller editions of Inga, with glossy dark hair and brown eyes. Vaila was almost in her teens, and Dawn had just been old enough to join the sailing last summer.

'Hi,' I said. I picked Charlie up and swung him round. 'Hey, peeriebreeks, what're you doing in town?'

He held up one foot, in an eye-hurtingly white trainer. 'I got new shoes, Dass. Boots too.' He hauled at one of the carrier bags Inga was carrying, and opened it enough at the mouth to show me rubber boots with dinosaur eyes at the toes. 'Roarrr.'

'There's snow forecast,' Inga added.

'I'm trying not to think about it,' I said. Life aboard

Khalida might be difficult under a foot of snow; or (I hoped) it might be warmer, with a layer of snow baffling out the wind.

'We have a spare room,' Inga offered. I shook my head.

'Thanks, but no, I'll stick it out. Besides, Cat and your cat would never get on. If it gets really desperate, Reidar would let me sleep in the café.'

'Well, don't be stuck.'

'I won't,' I promised. I crossed the road to the pier car park with them, and while Inga was loading carrier bags into the boot and buckling Peerie Charlie into his seat, I turned to Vaila. 'Vaila, I was talking to Jeemie the other day, and he was yarning about seeing a njuggle.'

Her face stayed straight, but the dancing eyes gave her away.

'I wondered if there might be a particularly good time for me to see one.'

She looked down at the ground, considering. 'A dry night's a good time,' she said at last. 'Njuggles don't like getting wet.'

'It was dusk Jeemie saw it.'

'Yea, dusk is good.' She thought a bit more. 'Dusk, and a bit of a moon. Not too dark and not too bright.'

We were at the blackest time now. 'There'll be a crescent moon soon. Tuesday, say. Dusk is about half past three, four o clock. Where's a good place? Are njuggles no' supposed to like bridges, and mills?'

She shook her head at that. 'No' by the brig. Up by the loch is better.'

'Gonfirth loch, at dusk of Tuesday.'

'I canna promise you'll see een, mind,' she said quickly. 'Njuggles is particular beasts. They dinna aye want to come out.'

'I'll chance it,' I said.

'And you mustna photograph him. The flash'd gluff him something awful.'

'I won't,' I promised.

Inga gave us a suspicious glance. 'What are you twa plotting?'

'I was asking about njuggles,' I said.

She gave me a fierce stare. 'No trouble, Cass. Whatever you're up to, you'll no' drag my bairns into it.'

'This isn't trouble,' I assured her. 'At least, I'm pretty sure it isn't anything to do with what may be trouble.'

'Njuggles?'

'Jeemie o' Grobsness saw one by Gonfirth Loch.'

'Oh, him. How many nips had he had at the Pierhead beforehand?' She turned on Vaila. 'And since when were you a njuggle expert, young lady?'

'Since the play,' Vaila retorted. 'Remember, you brought Peerie Charlie to it, with the playgroup. *Kirsty and the Snarraness Njuggle.* Izzy did it, our drama teacher, and she took it around the schools. We did all sorts of stuff about Shetland creatures in the school as a project to go with it.' She threw in a diversion. 'We did trows an' all, an' Finns, an' selkies. I could tell you about those too, Cass, if you like. Did you ken that the real selkies were mebbe Inuit, come from Greenland?'

'I'd like to ken about Finns,' I said.

'Another time,' Inga said, and bundled her brood into the car. She paused by the door. 'No trouble, Cass.'

I nodded, and watched them drive off. I was pretty certain that me seeing the njuggle for myself wouldn't bring trouble. Whatever Vaila was up to, I didn't believe for a moment she was doing anything dishonest. But I did suspect Jeemie was making use of it.

It was time I visited 'The Njuggle's Nest.'

Chapter Fourteen

When Dad deposited me at the marina gate, I gave Magnie a ring. 'I was wondering if you'd run me over to have a look at Jeemie's shop.'

'That will I, lass. Will I give him a ring to say we're coming?'

'No, if you dinna mind a wasted journey if he's no' there.'

'I'm doing nothing this afternoon, lass. A peerie drive into the country'll suit me fine. I'll be with you in half an hour.'

I gave *Khalida* a thorough check over before getting aboard, and another once I was inside. Cat was sleeping in my berth, plumed tail curled over his nose and white paws. He stretched and rose to greet me with his silent miaow. I brushed and fed him, and locked up thoroughly again before heading out to wait on the pontoon. Above me, the sky was mottled with racing clouds, and the voe turned from silver to pewter and back as they scudded over the face of the sun.

Magnie still had the mustard-coloured Fiesta that he'd driven as long as I'd known him. He cleared his oilskin jacket, a pail, a rushy bag for the whelk ebb, and a thermos flask off the passenger seat for me, and I clambered in. 'Thanks for this.'

He gave a 'no bother' grunt. We headed off along the road and turned downhill into old Voe: the waterfront, with a mini marina, the old sail loft, now a camping bod, opposite what were once the weaving sheds of Adie & Co. The jumpers Tenzing and Hillary had worn on the top of

Everest had come from here. The road narrowed to single track between the buildings, then widened again at the Pierhead restaurant; the proprietor also owned a mussel farm, salmon cages and a fishing boat, so the fish served there was meltingly fresh. Magnie swerved round the grassy bank beyond it, bumped over the little bridge and nodded at the house above it. 'John Georgeson's house.'

It was a traditional two-storey crofthouse, refurbished with double-glazed windows and a glass sunlounge looking out over the voe. A ride-on tractor peeked out from the open garage door, and the garden was a sweep of green lawn.

Magnie changed down a gear to climb the steep hill. Now there was springy heather on each side of the road, and damp-looking sheep grazing. We came around the last bend and the Loch of Gonfirth lay before us.

It was about a mile across, a rough heart-shape indented by little headlands, with an island across at the far side, and a jetty by the road. The steep hills gave you an idea of how quickly you'd lose your footing. I had a vague memory that bodies were never recovered. There was a fluorescent ball like a lobster pot marker two hundred metres out. 'What's that mooring buoy doing?'

'Floating,' Magnie said, straight-faced. He pulled into the side of the road to let me look at it: a normal orange buoy, with a ring in the top. 'Fishermen moor their boats to it.'

'Are there any fish in the loch?'

'Brown troots,' Magnie said. 'I'm caught a good few here myself.'

It was talking about the loch that had got Gavin and I speaking of whisky. I wondered if you could sink a cask of whisky, the way you could sink a lobster pot. The wood that kept liquor in would keep liquid out; maybe. Could Ivor and Jeemie have been in cahoots in some way, with Ivor stealing the missing whisky, and Jeemie hiding it here, then using the njuggle legend to keep people away from the loch?

Magnie started the car again. 'So Jeemie was walking along here,' I said, looking at the barrier between us and the loch, 'and he'd almost got to the end of the barrier when he heard the njuggle.'

The car came up the short hill. At this end of the loch, there was only sky above the hills surrounding it, as if it was perched on the height of the world. A bank of wiry moor grass led down to a narrow shingle beach. I craned across Magnie to see if there were any hoofprints in the soft turf, then leaned back, shaking my head. 'No pony tracks. It would be the only place a real pony could go into the loch. Otherwise it would have to jump the barrier and either land on those large stones or leap straight into the loch.'

'A pony could scrabble down here, right enough.' Magnie put the car back into gear and drove on, past the miniature loch where the grey-throated divers nested in summer, and around the bend to face out over Swarback's Minn once more. Already the sun was dipping towards the horizon in a glory of soft apricot light.

Jeemie had left his car by the peerie loch. The Grobsness turn off was a mile further. It had a sign beside it, a rearing black horse with a weed-festooned mane, holding a shield with the words *Njuggle's Nest, Antiques* beneath its raised front hooves. A bend and we were running parallel to the sea again, above a dizzyingly steep bank, with the Pierhead salmon cages below us, and a glimpse through headlands to Papa Little and out to the wide Atlantic, then the view was closed in by the dark curve of Linga, and the sandy beach below the road, with the roofless walls of the Old Hall above it. The pair of ruined crofthouses had perhaps been a haaf station, for the long stone beach below them would have been perfect for drying fish.

Jeemie's house was through a gate and along a gravel track. It was an oddly converted crofthouse, with a front extension and a little jutting afterthought at the ben end, smaller than the main house. The byre been given windows, and the whole thing was glossily whitewashed. There was a duplicate njuggle notice outside, with an arrow pointing to the sky-blue door of the byre. It looked a prosperous outfit, run by someone who understood the importance of show: the paint was gleaming, and even in this depths of winter, when he wouldn't expect tourist trade, there were scrubbed flagstones on each side of the door, and blue plastic pots with velvety dark pansies flowering in them, and the first fringed spikes of crocus showing. A Berlingo van was parked at the end of the yard, silvery-blue, with the njuggle logo on the side, and a little navy runabout sat beside it. There was an Edwardian brass bell beside the door, with an oval handle dangling from a pull-chain. Magnie gave it a yank. There was a pause, then a twitch of curtains in the house window, a rattle as the door opened, and Jeemie came out.

He still had that air of auditioning for an Elvis movie, with his dark hair sleeked back and standing in a quiff, but he was dressed in an old brown jumper and shabby breeks. I got the feeling that he wasn't over-pleased to see us, but he covered that with smarmy bonhomie, unlocked the byre door, and ushered us in.

The first thing I noticed was the warmth. I recognised the brass polish smell straight away too. I'd cleaned a lot of binnacles and ship's lanterns in my tall ships days. Then Jeemie moved out of the doorway, and I got a look inside.

It was a room to give me nightmares. The last rays of the sun slanted across from the windows to dazzle off shelves of brass: plates, kettles, candlesticks, ornaments. The next row of shelving was little china ornaments, gleamingly clean, and arranged by colour: blue and white at waist-level, green above, pinks above that and multi-brights on the top shelf. That was followed by dolls and figurines: replica wax dolls on the bottom shelf, moving up through doll's house land to china shepherdesses. Next came chinoiserie and oriental, then individual plates standing up on holders, then soft toys. I would never have believed you could cram so much stuff into one ex-byre. He'd spoken of furniture, but there wasn't much – a couple of chairs with elegant backs, and several little tables, also littered with ornaments. It made me wonder if the fish horse-brass that was *Khalida*'s only passenger was one ornament too many.

I suspected Magnie was thinking the same thing. He shook his head in what Jeemie could take as admiration, if he was so minded. 'Boy, you're gathered a braw twartree bits and pieces here.'

I looked round again, and began to see method behind the obvious ordering. 'It's mostly peerie stuff, portable – for the tourist market?'

Jeemie nodded, as if I was a bright pupil. 'Yea. Folk don't want to carry great lumps of lem home with them, though I'm had folk up with cars taking bigger stuff, or there's more and more motor homes passing these days. That plate there, for example.' He nodded to a green and white ashet as big as *Khalida*'s little table. 'That's as big as I'd go, and that's more likely to be bought by someone from Shetland, wantin' something bonny for serving up their Christmas turkey.' He moved to one of the 'china' shelves. 'Here, see, there're a few things labelled with 'Shetland', but most of it is just bonny peerie things that might take someone's fancy as a souvenir to take home.'

I moved to the shelf opposite the door and began to look more closely. This one was china animals: a little dog, a cow, several cats, several birds, a giraffe and zebra. The cheapest (a nauseating cat with smirking whiskers) was £4.25. They were all in good condition, as far as I could tell, with no missing tails or ears. I lifted the cow carefully (£14.50) and looked underneath. Delft, it said, in curly writing. The hand-height giraffe was £37.50, and nothing on earth would have induced me to risk picking it up. 'Where do you find all these things?'

Jeemie made an airy gesture with his hands. 'Here and there. Auctions are good. Harry Hay has job-lots of boxes, you just buy them cheaply and hope there's treasure trove inside. Charity shops like Aith and Whalsay. Not so much the town ones as there's all chains now, and anything out of the ordinary gets sent south to specialist auctions.'

I'd been to the Aith charity shop, whose prices were minimal. If he'd picked up the giraffe there, he'd make around £35 profit.

'House sales, that kind of thing.' He gave me a swift sideways look and took the wind out of my sails. 'Ivor Hughson, you ken him, he has a boat in the marina. Well, he used to give me a hint if someone was flitting, when they booked him for the removal, and he'd give the folk my card too, so that they could get me to look over stuff they weren't wanting to take. If someone would give a pound or two for an auld table you were just going to ball on the bonfire, so much the better.'

Well, well. It seemed a bit unethical on Ivor's part to be passing on details of his clients. I wondered if Robert-John knew that was what Ivor'd been up to. Furthermore, I could just see Jeemie assuring some peerie crofter wife who was moving to a sheltered house that the plate she'd always been told was real old china brought back by an ancestor was actually made in Birmingham.

'A course, it's taken a good few years to build up this much stock. Folk are aye impressed when they walk in.'

'It's a fair eyeful that greets you,' I agreed. I wandered past the gold dazzle of brass and the blank-eyed dolls to inspect the books behind the mahogany desk. I hadn't managed to finish *Waverley*. I could feel Jeemie's gaze on my back. That sideways look he'd given me as he'd talked

128

about Ivor had reminded me of something. I puzzled over it as I looked. The authors were alphabetical, with nearly a full shelf of Dickens. I crouched down and found Scott. Then the waft of brass polish brought it back to me; some trainee telling me about how he'd dropped the ship's compass while he was polishing its brass case, and busily pointing out the small dent on the deck, hoping to divert me from the crack in the compass glass.

What was Jeemie trying to divert me from? I didn't see anything untoward about all these shelves of expensive bric-a-brac. There was no *Waverley* among the gold-bound books, but I found a plain green copy at an affordable £2. I brought it to the counter, which gave me a view into what would have been the feed store. It was filled with TVs and computers; there was a soldering iron and a pair of crimping tongs lying on a workbench in the middle of the tiny space, along with a blow-torch and a row of small files. The metal-working tools reminded me. 'Did you say you had jewellery too?'

He gave me a sceptical look, as well he might, for one glance would write me off as a necklace sales potential, but answered readily enough, 'Oh, yea, I have twartree bits and pieces. There's not a lot of call for it, but some folk prefer antique to modern.' He went over to the big desk, unlocked the wide central drawer, and brought out a tray lined with shiny white material and glittering like a magpie's nest. 'Last summer there was a fashion for diamanté brooches, the fancier the better, so I had a run on them.'

I bent over the rings, looking. I'd thought, when Magnie had mentioned them in the bar, that Jeemie had changed the subject out of deference to my feelings, when Magnie had mentioned 'engagement rings', but now, although his professional smile was still firmly pinned on, uneasiness came off him like ripples from a boat's propeller swelling up around you before you put her in gear. He was happy enough about the girl detective looking around the shelves, but not so keen on her checking out the jewellery. I wondered if it was always kept in a locked drawer like this, when everything else was displayed. I'd have expected a glass case to show it off; but maybe it was just put away because we were out of season. I scanned along the lines of rings and picked out one at random, a design of two clasped hands in what looked like the original leather-covered box. 'This looks a good age.'

'Around 1880. A gimmel ring, it's called. The hands come apart, see.' His pudgy fingers were surprisingly delicate, sliding the two hands back to reveal a heart-shaped stone. 'A garnet heart in the centre, and the gold is 18-carat. An expensive item for a Shetland fisherman to give his girl. The box is original too. I'll try it on eBay in the run-up to St Valentine's Day. I should get the price from a Shetland descendent in Canada or the US, if I advertise it right.' He picked out a little brooch. 'Have you seen one of these before?'

He set it in my hands, a pair of joined silver hearts. One had a diagonal bar with a name, *Mizpah*, and a flourish of flowers. The other heart had tiny writing on it: *The LORD Watch Between Me & Thee When We Are Absent One From Another.* I shook my head.

'A token between sweethearts or a husband and wife. It's a seaman's thing. A Mizpah brooch, it's called, and the writing's from Genesis. It was thought of as a kind of protection, very popular in Victorian times. This one's quite early, from about 1850.' He turned away from the jewellery and reached into the window embrasure. I felt the wave of relief come from him. 'Now here's something you'll like, a real ship's chronometer, from a tea clipper called the *Charlotte Rose* ...'

ᛚ

I brooded over it as I made my tea that evening. On the
face of it, there was nothing wrong in the set-up: a retired
man (he'd been invalided out, he'd told us over a cup of
tea in the sun room), who fancied setting up a little
business. He'd aye been interested in antiques, his mother
had collected china, and it gave him something to do. I
could see that the items he had for sale were a mixed bag
of junk shop bric-a-brac and (taking his word for it)
genuine antiques which he could easily have picked up in
charity shops and at displenishment sales, just as he'd said.
The bric-a-brac could go to passing trade, and the dearer
stuff was more likely to sell on eBay than to passing
tourists. The clasped-hand ring had been £725, the Mizpah
brooch £545. I opened my lap-top and had a quick look at
eBay. A gimmel ring, he'd called it; there were plenty of
examples, at that kind of price for the gold ones. There
wasn't a Mizpah brooch, but there were other Mizpah
items, and again the prices were similar. It still sounded a
lot to me, but then the new sails I craved would set me
back over £1500.

It all ought to be above-board; except for that odd
mention of Ivor passing on information. There had been no
need for Jeemie to speak of that, unless it was going round
that I was interested in Ivor. Beryl had probably seen
Robert-John give me a lift, that day of the party, and put
two and two together. I could just see her leaning over to
her far-out cousin, my dad's cleaner Jessie: 'And sho was
axing a lock o' questions about Ivor Hughson, him that
was married to Julie and went off south ...' Jessie might
reply that Robert-John had been round talking to Dad, and
before an hour was past they'd both be spreading a highly
coloured version round all their friends. Jeemie looked to

me like one who'd be well up in the gossip chain. Had he thrown me that connection with Ivor as a tub to distract a whale?

But distract me from what? I remembered his uneasiness as I'd looked at the jewellery, palpable as a cold wind. Was it possible, I wondered, that Ivor had been nicking stuff from boxes as he transported them from place to place? *Whaar der truss, der buss.* Ivor would warn Jeemie of the person moving, Jeemie would have a look around and suggest items to Ivor, and Ivor would take them. A grandmother's engagement ring, kept safely but never worn, wouldn't be missed like an ornament that took up pride of place on the mantelpiece. £725 clear profit to share between them ... but was Ivor, was Jeemie, really so unpleasant a person as to run a racket like that? I could see Jeemie doing it. There was a slyness about him that made my back neck creep. Ivor, though, no. It wasn't just reluctance to think ill of a fellow-sailor. He'd been brash, Ivor, a charmer, too ... too big for a scheme like that. I gestured with my hands, trying to articulate it to myself. Ivor was a bolder character than that. I could see him getting involved in some daft quixotic big scam – stealing the Stone of Destiny would have been right up his street – but not in this petty thievery. Jeemie, though, Jeemie could easily pocket a ring here, a brooch there, as he looked through a jewellery box, especially as folk in Shetland wouldn't be suspiciously standing over him. But he'd be known as the last person to have howked about in the box, when the item was found to be missing ... I shook my head and got on with my tea.

Chapter Fifteen

I was just at the cup of tea stage, with a blanket wrapped round my legs, Cat purring in my lap, and both of us drawing warmth from each other, when I heard the gate clang. It was Julie Hughson in her businesswoman jacket, face shadowed by the fur-lined hood. I expected her to go to Ivor's boat, but she continued along the pontoon, and paused by the finger leading out to *Khalida*, her face uncertain. I untangled my legs, still watching her. A step backwards and a deep breath, then she tapped on the roof of my cabin. I clambered into the cockpit, gesturing her in. 'Come aboard.'

I waved her into the corner seat which I still thought of as my friend Anders' place, and re-lit the gas under the kettle. The lamplight gave her tanned face a gold colour, but her eyes looked haunted, with dark shadows under them, and a blotched look as if she'd been crying. Her fingers were restless, plucking at her fur collar, running along the edge of the table. Cat put out a paw to tap them, thinking she wanted to play, and she jumped, and laid them in her lap. 'This is right boanie, with all the older wood. There's a lot of wood in Ivor's one, but it's all new. This is like a real old boat.' She tried to suppress a shiver. 'You don't find it cold, living aboard in winter?'

'Yes,' I said frankly. 'You should see Cat and I at night, huddled together under two downies. Tea, or drinking chocolate? It's sweet, but warming.'

She shook her head. 'I'm no' keen on sweet things. A cup of tea would be fine.' She had a good teaching voice, low-pitched, and pleasant to listen to. I made the tea, and waited for her to tell me what she'd come about.

She clasped her hands around the mug, hesitated, then plunged in. 'I had a visit from Robert-John on his way home from his work. He thought I ought to know – he'd had a phone call from his sister ...' She'd got tangled in her sentence. She took a deep breath and came to the point. 'Is there any truth in the rumour that the skeleton you found down south is Ivor?'

I looked her straight in the face. 'I don't know. I couldn't ken him. It's a possibility, that's all.' Made the more possible by the speed my questions had been passed round the Georgeson clan. 'Someone from Inverness HQ will likely be contacting you soon, to ask about dental records.'

She shook her head, wondering. 'But how did they connect a skeleton down in the Highlands with Ivor? He was *here*, he brought the boat back.'

'I suppose the connection was me.' I jerked my chin at the gas tap. 'Someone tried blowing me up. Of course I wondered why, and that was all I could think of – that I was joining the two ends of the puzzle, the unidentified skeleton there and the man who'd disappeared here.'

'I never thought of him as having disappeared,' Julie said. 'He left a "Dear Julie" note on the kitchen table and went south on the boat.' She grimaced. 'I expected him back, once he'd got it out of his system. His boat was here, his stuff. I didn't realise until Robert-John told me that he'd screwed up the business as well.'

Curiouser and curiouser. 'You mean he didn't take much with him?'

Julie shook her head. 'Hardly anything. His car and a bag of clothes, as far as I could see.' She flushed. 'I was that angry, I fired all he'd left in the drawers into black bags and shoved it into the bottom of his wardrobe. Then, when it had been three months without a word, I decided that was that.' Her dark eyes were stone-hard. 'No phone call, no' even a lawyer's letter. So I packed up every last thing that had belonged to him, from his teddy bear to his business suit, and took it to Save the Children. I changed the locks, cleaned the house from top to bottom, re-organised the furniture, and took off for Christmas in Tenerife.'

'A clean sweep.'

She nodded. 'Yea, that was it. He'd gone out of my life after all these years, so I decided I'd have done with him. If he came back, there'd be nothing left there he could return to.' Her thin hands clutched the fur at her throat. 'Nothing inside me either.' One hand made a chopping gesture. 'Finish.' Her face crumpled. 'And now it seems ...' She lifted her hands to her face; her shoulders shook. I sat stroking Cat, understanding. She'd made herself hate him because he'd left her without a word, and now it seemed he hadn't done that. If he'd not been killed, the word might have come.

Julie lifted her head again. Her eyes were bright with tears, but her mouth was set in a determined line. 'I'm fed up of the lying. I'll tell you. It wasn't just about having a baby, though I suppose that was part of it. Ivor didn't see himself as ever being grown up. He didn't want a family. He didn't want to believe he was forty.' Her cheeks flushed, under the tan. 'I said we'd come home through the Caledonian canal, up through Loch Ness, because that was the plan, but it wasn't that way at all. I'd been aboard just one night when I found a pair of knickers that werena mine. Well, of course there was a row. I was that mad that I stormed out and I thought about coming home, but you see aabody kent how long we were going for, and I didna want to come home early and face all the questions. So I did the same as Hubert, sight-seed round the Highlands for those four days, until my Inverness booking. Ivor tried to phone me several times, but I just snicked the phone off. Then ... when I came home ...'

She drew a long, shuddering breath. 'I wondered at the time about the odd way he'd taken his clothes. It was like he'd just taken half of each drawer: socks, underwear, T-shirts, shirts. His suit, too, he'd left the new one and taken the old.' Her brows drew together. 'Of course, it wasn't him who packed it at all. She was watching for him to come in.' Her voice hardened. 'In my house, while I was down south. And then …' She began twisting the fur collar in her hands again. 'Me going like that, I think it made him realise. When he came home to her, he told her it was over, and she killed him. But why should she have taken his body down to this loch south?'

'Hang on,' I said. 'Who's she?'

Julie's voice was venomous. 'I hadn't found out her name. I was too proud to go following him, but I knew she existed. He was pretty obvious about it. Late meetings, working overtime, an "overnight down south" with the van parked in Lerwick for all to see.'

My head was spinning. 'But why should she kill him?'

'Because of the holiday.' Julie shook her head in impatience at my slowness. 'We'd booked this holiday together, to make time to re-discover each other. I wasn't keen on the sailing, but I knew I had to make an effort, or we'd be over. And it worked, for that first night.' She went a delicate pink under the tan. 'We talked about what had gone wrong, and how we could fix it. Oh, I was angry about the girl, but I thought, I thought that he'd be waiting when I came home, with bubbly in the fridge, to coax me round, the way he always had. Then, when I arrived …' Her hand clenched into a fist. 'Don't you see, he told the girlfriend it was over, and she killed him.' She bit her lip. 'I carried the note everywhere for a week. Just having it in my pocket reminded me it was true. It was his handwriting, I'm sure it was.' Her eyes opened wide, her jaw fell. 'It *was*,' she repeated. 'But it wasn't to me.' She turned to face me, vehement, eyes flashing. 'It was to her, don't you see? *Darling, I can't go on any more. It's just not fair. I love you, but this has to be the end. Ivor.*'

As a finish to twenty years of marriage, it left a lot to be desired. Even I could see that. As an end to an affair, it was only marginally better.

'She killed him, and left it on my table. It was her revenge, because in the end he'd loved me better.'

Only she knew their history. If re-writing it made her feel better, then I supposed it was a good thing. Nothing she'd said had made me feel Ivor was capable of loving anyone better than he loved himself, but what did I know about love? My last attempt at it had ended in the middle of the Atlantic, with Alain's death.

'And she killed him, and took the body where she hoped nobody would ever find it, because if it was found here, if I came home to find him lying here, dead two days ago, when I'd been miles away, then *she'd* be the prime suspect.'

I didn't see why the girlfriend would've taken the body to Scotland to dispose of it, when there were perfectly good cliffs and bogs in Shetland. Julie stood up. 'It was *her*. I know it.' She handed me her cup and smoothed her collar. 'I'll wait for the Inverness police to contact me, then.' Her face twisted again. 'You know what I can't forgive him? Even if he's dead. He gave her my great-grandmother's engagement ring. If the police find her, I want it back.' Her mouth turned down. 'No' that I could bear to wear it, after her having had it, but it was *mine*. He had no right.'

'No,' I agreed.

Julie spread her hands. There was no wedding ring mark on the smooth tan. She touched one middle finger with the other hand, as if drawing off a ring. 'It was that pretty. I was afraid to wear it, because it was so old, and the stone was loose, and people always wanted to see how the hands unclasped, so I didn't wear it to work, but

137

there's to be a college do next Friday, so I thought, instead of my wedding ring – and then I looked for it, and it was gone. Her voice hardened. 'I'd know it anywhere. If she still has it, that'll be proof it was her, won't it?'

'Unless she got rid of it, in a fright,' I agreed. An old ring with clasping hands over a stone ... Maybe I'd been doing Jeemie an injustice. Maybe his uneasiness was because he'd recognised Ivor's girlfriend, trying to get rid of the ring he'd given her. I wondered how well Jeemie kept his records of who'd sold him each object.

ᚺ

I told Gavin about it when he phoned. 'Julie's convinced herself that the note was to the girlfriend, not to her, and that the girlfriend then killed him, for revenge.'

'If the skeleton is him, if he was having an affair, we'll find out who with soon enough.'

'I think Inga's brother-in-law knows.' I remembered the conversation on New Year's Day. Beryl had said, *Another woman*, and Harald's wife had leaned forward as if she was going to speak, then Harald had shaken his head at her. *That's in the past, and the least said, the shoonest mended.* 'Or it may be in Jeemie's records, the antiques dealer. Doesn't he have to keep a record of who he buys things from?'

'It would be usual,' Gavin said cautiously, 'but I've never had the impression that Shetlanders are obsessed with book-keeping. Explain to me the chain between our skeleton and Julie visiting you. I'm finding that a bit suspicious.'

'I think it's okay. When Maman went in to see Mr Georgeson senior, the owner of Georgeson Removals –'

He cut in, very gently. 'Had she a particular reason for

visiting him?'

'Fair cop,' I conceded. 'She was asking about a piano removal.'

'I haven't met your mother, but your father seemed a sensible man.' It was still gently said, but I could tell he wasn't happy, his smooth voice rougher, like a stream running over pebbles. 'What was he saying about this?'

I chuckled. 'He was in the back shop, in a boiler suit and toorie cap, with his best Dublin accent, asking about work there.' I left a pause for Gavin to object, if he was so minded.

'You know this isn't a game.' Now his voice was grave. 'My ship, Cass.'

'I know,' I agreed. I felt a brief spasm of contrition. I was interfering with his investigation, losing him the element of surprise by meddling, making it harder for him to do his job. 'I should have thought it through.' I took a deep breath. 'I'm sorry if I've made your life harder by warning them. But they had a good shot at blowing us up, and nearly poisoned Cat. I thought he was dead. And Maman enquiring about a piano, what could be more innocent?'

'It obviously wasn't, if you've stirred a hornet's nest up about your ears.'

'You'd lost the element of surprise anyway,' I pointed out. 'Ironic, isn't it? I wouldn't have connected the skeleton with Ivor if – I presume – the person who killed him hadn't tried to kill me with my own gas.'

'The engineer hoist with his own petard. Go on, then. Your mother saw Mr Georgeson senior about a piano.'

I began laughing. 'You should have seen her. She treated the receptionist as if she was invisible. But in came Miss Georgeson, the nastiest teacher I ever had. We hated each other with a passion right through my primary 6. I dived backstage before she could see me, but of course she'd have known Maman straight away, from parents' nights.'

'Primary 6 was twenty years ago.'

I shook my head. 'You don't forget Maman. Anyway, I met her – Miss Georgeson – again in Da Street, and she stopped me. She was being sarcastic, and I suddenly thought she'd be ages with Ivor Hughson, so I tried the name on her.'

'How did she react?'

'She'd been keen on him at school. You could hear it in her voice when she said his name. She said what a charmer he was.'

'Was?'

'Yes, she used the past tense, but it could have been for the schooldays, rather than Ivor. Me mentioning him was a shock, that was clear. She went sheet-white, then she looked behind me at an imaginary clock, muttered something about the time, and rushed off.'

'To phone her brother, Ivor's former partner; and he phoned Julie Hughson.' He was silent for a moment. 'Write me down an account of your meeting with each of them, as detailed as you can remember, and as soon as you can. Tonight, tomorrow morning. Re-live it, every look, every gesture. Will you?'

'No problem. Gavin ...' I was still tentative about using his name. 'If the word is out that Ivor's being linked with the skeleton, should I be safe now?'

'That depends what sort of a hornet's nest you stirred up this morning. If the murderer's only worry was that you were the link between the skeleton down here and Ivor's disappearance up there, well, they're linked now. But if the Georgeson clan are involved, well ...' He was teasing me now. '... there's a mild possibility, don't you think, that they'll think you want to play detective?'

Playing the girl detective ... 'In which case they might prefer to warn me off?'

'What did you see backstage?'

140

'A barrel. You spoke about casks of whisky, but it's barrels it's matured in, isn't it?'

'It would be. Where did you see this barrel?'

'In a dusty corner, labelled 'Lucky Dip', and with cut-out cartoon figures in front of it. The Lerwick Gala stuff. Oh, and the oldest son's harness and armour, from his re-enactment days. It was pretty well hidden.'

'Re-enactment? You mean horse harness?'

'Yes. Miss Georgeson told us all about it, and we had one of those poster-size photos of him as our classroom pin-up. You know, knights in armour stuff. He came and gave us a display. He was jolly good.'

'Interesting,' Gavin said, and went silent again.

'And the barrel was behind this,' I said, when it was obvious he wasn't going to share his thoughts with me, 'and covered with far more dust than would be natural since last summer's Gala. Do you think that Ivor Hughson and John Georgeson might have conspired together to steal the whisky?' I could see Ivor doing that; it was a victimless crime, for nobody counts insurance companies, and a fun, breaking into a locked warehouse to swap two barrels. 'He'd have seen it as a lark.'

'A street value of ten thousand isn't just a lark. Where are you moored?'

'Brae tonight, right under the clubhouse windows.'

'Until the club-goers go home, and there's nobody to hear you scream.'

'Dad suggested I might go along to the jetty below our house, and give myself an earlier start for tomorrow.'

'But you haven't done that, and if your night is anything like ours, it's too dark now.'

'Black as pitch. But I set off for Scalloway tomorrow. Whoever it was had a key for this marina. It wouldn't be likely they'd have a Scalloway key too.'

'Another marina gate designed to keep honest folk out.' He paused, thinking. 'I had a quick trawl through the usual places, and there's no sign of Hughson. He hasn't used his credit card or his bank account since the morning of Monday 12th August, when he drew out £200, the maximum, at a cashpoint in Mallaig.'

'Nothing from Aberdeen?'

'No proof that he ever got there.'

I thought of Georgeson Removals. 'You could put a car with a body inside into one of those big trucks. But why take it clean across the country like that?'

'Maybe the person who left the body knew the loch, and knew how remote it is. Even if you knew someone was missing here, you still might not find them. The other possibility, if Julie's right that the girlfriend killed him, is that she shifted the body here to put the blame on Julie. If it didn't turn up, she still had the stigma of being the deserted wife, and if it did, well, our loch is in the area where they were. If your friend's mother hadn't seen him, then there'd be no proof he ever made it home.'

'And how did they get it to where it was found? They couldn't have carried it.' It still sounded too rigged, somehow. 'How would they get it into a boat at the head of the loch without someone seeing?'

'I've been wondering that too. But if it is him, and we're talking late August, the answer is the Argyllshire Highland Gathering. It's on the fourth Thursday of the month, in Oban. Last year was Thursday 22nd August. We left the farm the moment the cows had been milked and only returned at seven in the evening. It's a two and a half hour drive, but Mother loves it. She would never miss it, nor would anyone else in the area. It's like your Up Helly Aa, it's our local celebration, and anyone who knew the Highlands would know they'd have a good chance of doing anything unobserved on the area's Gathering day.'

It still seemed hard work. 'And then they'd have to carry him from the boat to up to where we found him.'

'There's an easier way of doing it, on that day, when

there would only be the animals and machinery left at the farm.' I heard the laugh in his voice, and was warmed inside. 'It may not have occurred to a sailor like you. I'll leave you to think it out.'

I thought. 'You have a quad, don't you?'

'We do.'

I wouldn't fancy taking a quad along the track we'd walked, but Gavin had mentioned a path over the top of the hill, and Shetlanders were well used to going over heather on a quad, to round up sheep. 'Is there any movement on the dental records front?'

'Our own dentist is on standby to compare the records with the body's teeth as soon as he gets them. If we've got a match, I'll be sent up. Can you keep yourself safe until Monday or Tuesday?'

'I'll be fine in Scalloway,' I assured him. 'Reidar's there, setting up his café, remember, so I'd have help on call if I needed it.'

'Don't overdose on his hot chocolate. Have a good sail tomorrow. I'll be envying you as I'm dealing with paperwork. *Oidhche mhath, beannachd leat.*'

'A fine night tae dee an all.'

Saturday 4th January

Low Water at Brae UT	*04.30, 0.6 m*
High Water	*10.51, 2.0 m*
Low Water	*17.03, 0.5 m*
High Water	*23.35, 1.8 m*

Sunrise	*09.06*
Moonrise	*09.54*
Sunset	*15.08*
Moonset	*20.30*

Moon waxing crescent

Sunday 5th January

Low Water at Scalloway UT	*05.06, 0.6m*
High Water	*11.30, 1.8m*
Low Water	*17.41, 0.6m*
High Water	*00.23, 1.8m*

Sunrise	*09.06*
Moonrise	*10.15*
Sunset	*15.15*
Moonset	*21.59*

Moon waxing crescent.

Da aalie lamb is ethkent.
The lamb which has been hand-reared is easily recognised; used of spoiled or petted children.

Chapter Sixteen

I'd set the alarm clock for seven, but I had a fitful night, hearing every car that went past, every herring gull scraiching on the pontoon. At half past six I gave up on sleep, and put the kettle on. It was still black dark and I felt as though the chill damp had crept into my bones. I had a shower, as hot as I could bear it, keeping my hair dry, and dressed in all my layers. By the time I'd wriggled into my black Musto teddy-bear suit and hauled my red oilskins over it, I was warm again, and my heart was singing. I was sailing today.

I filled up the flask and made rolls, then started the engine and threw off the ropes that bound *Khalida* to the pontoon. We backed out, the engine putt-putting softly in the early morning silence. There was a purr of north wind, just enough to blow me to Scalloway. I hauled my light-airs foresail up to the masthead, then went back to the cockpit and hauled on its sheet. The sausage unrolled and filled, a great half-balloon of red, white, blue, and I felt *Khalida* surge forwards, leaving a broadening V behind her.

Around me, the world slept in the grey dawn. The houses of Ladies' Mire were darker rectangles against the green hill; Busta House was a ghost-blur among its trees. The Burgastoo, the little island that guarded the Muckle Roe bridge, was separated from its reflection by a line of foam. I kept well out in the middle of the voe, to stop myself being entangled in the mussel lines; the only indication of their presence in this half-light was the flashing yellow buoy that marked their furthest corner.

It took three-quarters of an hour to get out of Busta Voe and around the corner. The still air was broken by showers that brought more wind with them, so that the bright geneker strained from its sheets, and *Khalida* leaned her shoulder to her whispering wake. We came around Muckle Roe, where Dad's kitchen window glowed orange: Maman making her first coffee. We passed Vementry Isle, the cliffs of West Burrafirth and Melby, and came through Papa Sound with the tide. As I came across to the landward shore, I heard birds singing in the trees around a house in a little bay, chuckling like running water, the first sign of spring.

By ten o'clock, it was mostly light, and the showers had settled into steady rain. Cat stayed in the cockpit for five minutes, then went below, shaking his paws in disdain. The green fields of Sandness were sodden, water glinting over the grass, and two ponies stood in a corner of a grey stone dyke, noses down, hair in dark points. Water dripped from the mainsail and ran down the cockpit seats, onto the floor, and out through the drains; below, the toilet paper was damp from condensation, and the port window dripped on my barometer. The hills above the shore were as grey as their reflections. Then the rain eased, and a shaft of sun crept from below the clouds to light the water to pale blue, then, as it strengthened, to straw gold. The streetlights were still on as we caught a glimpse of the village of Walls, its grey and fawn houses faded into the hill. To starboard, Foula lay in a wreath of mist on smoke-grey water.

At last, as we came past Grutness Voe, the colours came clear once more: the deep pinkish rust of the heather, the lichened grey of stone, the soft green of sheep-cropped grass, the olive of bog grass. Within the voe, two mussel lines were magnified by stillness, and four ducks sailed by, trailing their V wakes. A white froth on the shoreline marked where a burn met the sea; a solitary hooded crow flapped up with a derisive caw as we passed.

Khalida lifted and fell to the ocean swell. Her sails were still filled in a perfect curve, and even in this slight breeze she was going as fast as the engine would have propelled her. Cat came out again and settled in his corner, head up, paws braced. I ate lunch as the red cliffs of Skeld slipped past, then we were among the little islands that guarded the entrance to Scalloway, Shetland's ancient capital, the port for the Viking parliament. I dodged between the rocks, circled round the north cardinal, and entered the buoyed channel just after 15.00. Already, the sky was whisky gold to the west, with a sliver of crescent moon against the dimming blue in the east

From the sea, Scalloway looked like an east coast fishing village, with sycamore trees thick between the grey houses, front doors opening straight onto the pavement, and narrow lanes running up from the waterfront. The tide was near as low as it went, leaving a swathe of pebble shore below the low retaining wall. To my left was the marine college, with the Scalloway Boating Club's pontoon beside it. Cat stretched his neck, whiskers twitching. He'd spent more time here than in Brae, and he knew it as a haven of peace and plenty, particularly the college restaurant, where the chef, Antoine, thundered French denunciations of all cats while feeding him trimmings of best plaice.

The long stretch of Port Arthur Road led round the bay to the village. First came the jumble of sheds where the men of the Shetland Bus had repaired the fishing boats they'd used to run arms and radio parts into occupied Norway, with the last rays of sun making fire-red of the wooden building they'd lodged in. Next was the old folks' home, the nineteenth-century kirk and Dinapore, the doctor's house, which the Bus men had used as their operations centre. The two-storey cottages with Georgian sash windows that followed were half-hidden by fish processing stations now turned to the youth centre, shops, businesses. Main Street ended with Mary Ruisland's garden, bare and brown for this month, and the pink-painted height of the seventeenth-century Old Hall. After the Hall came the 'coloured street': the white former inn where Sir Walter Scott stayed, the blue house, the ochre, pale green, white again. The shore ended in the tyre-hung wall of Blackness Pier. Behind it, Earl Patrick's ruined castle lifted its bare gables towards the sky.

I hadn't phoned Reidar, but he must have spotted my sails coming through the lines of red cans and green cones, for as I curved into the marina he was waiting on the pontoon, ready to take my lines.

I'd met Reidar last autumn. He and my friend Anders had come over from Bergen in his high-bridged fishing motorboat, *Sule*. He was a great, untidy bear of a man, Danish, well over six foot tall, with tawny hair and a tousled beard. He was completely unflappable, and dealt with any emergencies by producing drinking chocolate with marmalade cream on top – the man was a genius, and if ever he wanted to run for Prime Minister of Denmark, I'd go round doors with his leaflets. Best of all, he'd been so horrified by the lack of continental coffee and accompanying pastries in Scalloway that he'd leased the former Museum to turn into a café. He was basing the decor on the Long Room at Busta House, where you sat down in comfortable armchairs, as if you were a visitor, and had tea brought to you. We'd scrubbed, painted, refurbished armchairs and little tables, and starched and ironed embroidered tablecloths found in the charity shops. John Lewis had supplied silk festoon blinds that cost as much as a new mainsail, and Reidar had negotiated with a local drama group for mid-Victorian costumes for the waitresses. I was resigned to the prospect of a long grey dress with pinnie and lace cap for the sake of continuing to fund my college year. 'But you wait,' I told him, 'until I get a job on a tall ship. No more waitressing, ever.'

'The lace cap will look smart against your dark hair,' Reidar said, consolingly.

The grand opening was Friday, the day of Scalloway Fire Festival.

'Now, Cass,' Reidar rumbled, reached over *Khalida*'s bow for her mooring line, and tweaked it around the cleat. I jumped ashore and was greeted with a large hug, my cheek pressed to his chest. He smelt of oiled wool and spices. 'The wanderer has returned. Come and have some chocolate and tell me how you enjoyed your Christmas.'

ᚺ

Reidar took me out for a meal in Lerwick, at the Bengal Tiger, just opposite where the Co-op had been all my childhood, and where Frank Williamson's was now, on the main North Road out of town. It was warm and welcoming, with red-flocked wallpaper, and buffet dishes laid out on a long table, and Saturday-night-busy, with only a couple of tables left. The waiter was about to put us beside a ten-person works do, but I shook my head and indicated the other free table, in a quiet corner beside two lasses. Work doos tended to spill over every table within earshot, and were no fun for outsiders.

Brae had an excellent Indian takeaway, but it was a mile walk from the marina, so it was a treat for bonny summer nights. The Bengal Tiger had the same starters range of brown spicy balls served with lettuce strips, and sweetly sticky red-coated ribs. It was while I was negotiating one of these that I became aware of the way one girl at the next table was staring at me.

I hadn't paid them any attention as we'd sat down. They were well through their main course and obviously enjoying their dinner, chattering like nesting gannets and trying each other's food. Now, though, the dark girl's laughter was forced, and her eyes kept returning to my face – to the long, straight scar across my right cheek. I did what I usually did in these circumstances: caught her eye, stared back for a moment, then looked back to my plate.

I was sure I'd never seen her before. She was much younger than me, twenty at a guess, with dark hair cut in that fashionable style that left feathery ends sticking out, as if it'd been hacked off by nail scissors. She had level brows under the ragged hair, dark eyes fringed by thick lashes, a long nose and a tilted smile. It was the pixie look, Julia Roberts playing Tinkerbell, with something very vulnerable about the eyes, the soft mouth. *An aalie lamb ...* The youngest of her family, I'd have betted, and never been permitted to lift a finger since her birth. The Tinkerbell resemblance was heightened by her sage green blouse, with a curved neckline. Her voice was Aberdeen.

The other lass was Shetland, and she was well launched into the saga of what her peerie sister had done over New Year, and what Mam would say when she found out. The pixie girl was laughing until she looked back at me, and saw that I was listening. Her eyes dilated in fright. For a moment, she was a young guillemot watching the boat approach, mesmerised, unable to decide whether to dive or swim away. The other lass leaned over to her. 'Donna, are you okay?'

Donna ... I definitely didn't know a Donna. She shook her head.

'I'm fine.' The colour had drained from her cheeks, leaving the pink blusher standing out. 'I feel a bit sick, like.' She began to gather her stuff together, hands shaking. 'I'd maybe better geng hame. I'm really sorry.'

'Here.' The blonde lass poured her a glass of water. 'Drink this.' The glass rattled against Donna's teeth. She didn't look at me. 'I'll get the bill.' She went off, and

Donna remained standing there, her coat huddled about her, her little face tight with misery. I wanted to lean over and reassure her, but I didn't know what I could say.

The other girl came back. 'You okay to drive?'

Donna nodded, and the door closed softly behind them. A pause, then a car started up around the corner. I got a glimpse of a small red car going past.

'You were listening,' Reidar said.

I grimaced, and agreed. 'She seemed frightened of me, yet I'm sure I've never seen her before, and I don't know a Donna.'

'Perhaps she has heard of detective Cass, who works with the police.' Reidar ate his last samosa and laid down his fork with regret. 'There is something that she is afraid you will find out.'

'I'm not a detective,' I insisted. Yet when we went up for our next course, I approached the young girl behind the counter. She looked ages with Donna; she'd know her.

''Scuse me,' I said, 'but you don't ken who that was, the dark lass at the table next to us, who just left? She was looking at me as if she kent me, an' her face was familiar, so I said "Aye aye", but it's going to bug me now the whole night, trying to mind where I ken her from.'

The girl smiled. 'It's aye the way, isn't it? You ken someone fine if you're used to seeing them in that place, then you see them somewye else, and you feel that stupid for kenning you should mind who they are. You'll have seen her at the north boats, she works to Serco. She's on the counter, so when you were getting your ticket, it'd be her handing it to you.'

'Of course, I ken her now. Donna something.'

'Donna Fraser, that's right. She's a bit shaken ee noo.' She leaned forward. 'There's a rumour going round that they found Ivor Hughson's body south, somewye near Inverness. So least said, shoonest mended. There's no need for her to be mixed up in that.'

151

'Best forgotten,' I agreed, and headed to the table to re-fill my plate, my brain buzzing. It had been Harald, Inga's brother-in-law, the one who worked to Serco, who had shaken his head at his wife when Inga's mother had mentioned Ivor Hughson having a girlfriend. *Least said, shunest mended.* This, then, was the girlfriend, and ten years younger than me, when Ivor had been a dozen years older. Vulnerable, naïve – had she known, I wondered, that he was a married man? It seemed word had come back to her, maybe through Harald, that Cass Lynch, you ken, her that does the sailing, with the scar apo' one cheek, had been asking questions about Ivor Hughson. Then she'd seen me asking for a table next to her, listening in …

When Reidar and I got out at the marina, the wind had backed still more, to almost due southerly, and it was rising. The cold air tugged at my plait and stung my nose and cheeks. Across at the sea wall, the water was not far off as high as it would go, the wind pushing in the flowing tide of a new moon. The stars above us were hazy, and the returning moon was tipped on her back, with the black disc of the new moon caught in her arm. There was a storm coming.

Chapter Sixteen

It was the movement that woke me, my boat suddenly come alive, and the sound of water knocking on the hull. I'd gone to bed dog-tired, after the night's watch and day's sail, conked out like a doused lantern, and while I was dead to the world something had gone wrong, for *Khalida* was moving.

I was out of my berth and hauling on my teddy-bear suit and boots faster than it takes to say it. I could see the shore slipping past through the window, the black water at the sea wall. I caught up my jacket and pulled it on. This high tide would give us valuable extra metres of sea room. I snatched the washboards out of the companionway slot and scrambled into the cockpit.

Yes, *Khalida* was loose. The loops of mooring lines had been quietly, gently lifted from her cleats.

The wind had risen, as the moon had forecast. The rigging whistled, and there was a tumbling waste of black waters around me, their white crests burnished by the thin crescent of moon. We were moving fast towards the shore below Main Street. I put the engine in gear and reached in to the start battery, then, with a quick prayer, turned the key. My ancient Volvo Penta coughed, and started. I watched the shore coming closer and counted a nerve-stretching ten before putting it into forward. There was a horrible grinding noise, and *Khalida* shuddered and stopped dead. The tiller bucked under my hands. I'd made a stupid mistake: the mooring ropes aft had been lifted off, so I'd assumed they all had been, but the front spring, wound around the cleat on the bow of the boat, where the person would have had to climb aboard to undo it, must have been cut. Left trailing under the boat, it had wound around the propeller.

There were ways of dealing with that, but not right now, with the wind and waves pushing *Khalida* shorewards. I uncleated the jib furling line and let out half the sail. It steadied her, but she was still being driven sideways as well as the forwards her nose was pointing. Sideways would take me to the Blackness pier. I could lie there until morning. I looked at the tyre-hung wall, assessing. Yes, with luck I could get her in there until I'd sorted the prop out.

Then I saw the car on the pier, sitting with its lights off in the shadow of the little stair running down from New Street. There wasn't usually anyone parked there. The streetlight glow meant I couldn't tell what colour it was; brown, perhaps, or red, maybe even navy, anything other than white. Looking through the hissing dark to the orange streetlights on the pier, I thought I could see the shadow of one person sitting in the driving seat, watching as I fought to save my boat.

I wasn't going in there. I turned *Khalida*'s nose away, tightening the jib as I pushed the tiller, and the deck tilted under my feet. To get her to go upwind, away from the shore, I needed the mainsail, and to get that up I had to go forrard to the mast. I'd need my lifejacket and harness. If she'd heave-to under jib alone it would buy me breathing time. I pulled the jib as tight as it would go, shoved the helm from me, then, as her nose went across the howling wind, pulled it up and looped a line around it. Now her sail was steering her one way, and the rudder the other, and if she'd had her mainsail she'd sit safely like that for days. I leapt down into the cabin, grabbed my lifejacket, harness, and gloves and was back up before she'd pirouetted her first circle. 'Come on, lass,' I told her. 'We can get out of this, just help me.'

The mainsail was secured for shore. I clipped on and went forwards to roll the canvas cover off and drop it into the cockpit, fingers working frantically on the velcro. The wind pulled at me, trying to wrench me from my rocking hold on the cabin roof. My face was frozen with cold; I hauled my hood up and continued working at the sail, one arm looped round the mast, so that I could use both hands. *Khalida* yawed over and back with the waves, and the jib strained, flapped, strained again. Now the shore was less than a hundred metres away. Even with this high tide, her keel would touch the bottom in half of that. I tied the third reef in the mainsail, secured the reefing line at the sail's clew, then hauled up the first quarter of her mainsail. In this wind, the less sail I had up, the safer I'd be. I winched it bar tight, scrambled back to the cockpit, and grabbed the tiller. 'Come on, lass. Let's get out of here.'

Now she responded properly to her helm. With both sails up, she'd fight her way out of any corner. I hauled the mainsail in and set her nose as close to the wind as she'd go. I was heading out to sea.

The wind was a good six, gusting seven; not quite storm force, just a yachtman's gale. Even with these scraps of sail, *Khalida* was tilted so far over that the waves were washing her lee windows. Every so often there was a soft thump from below as something slid over onto the floor, but I had no time to go and look right now. Cat would be tucked into my berth, tail over nose, ignoring the angle, and nothing else mattered but getting us out of the Scalloway channel and into safety.

We tacked in a flapping of jib just short of the accommodation barge at the pier. I looked up and saw an astonished face at one square window. Damn! Now there'd be a lifeboat call-out. I got *Khalida* on course, then looked back and gave a cheery wave, hoping he'd interpret it as an 'I'm okay' sign. Once I was out of here I'd radio the Coastguard. I didn't want to spark off a rescue. We forged across, almost back to the marina breakwater, tacked again. Out of the streetlight glow, the water was a shifting coal-black mass between the red and green lights of the buoyed channel. It wasn't often I wished I had the latest chart plotter, but I could have done with it here. I rolled away more jib, and her lee side came out of the waves. I looped the chain over the tiller and left her forging ahead while I reached into the cabin for the chart, the guide book and my head torch. Once we were on a longer tack, I'd go below and put a jumper on too, and a scarf; cold was responsible for as many mistakes as stupidity.

A quick look at the chart showed me that my fastest way out was the way I'd come in yesterday. It'd be a beat out of the Scalloway channel, then a reach through the islands into the clear water below Skelda Ness. After that, I'd be two miles from the lee shore; I could keep going west for a bit, then heave-to until morning, and come back in daylight, with the engine free of rope, and Reidar warned to watch out for any reception committees.

I tacked again, then ducked below and picked up the radio. 'Shetland Coastguard, this is yacht *Khalida,* yacht *Khalida,* over.'

A crackle, and Ian's voice came through the speakers. 'Yacht *Khalida,* channel sixty-seven, over.'

I changed channels and explained myself. 'Just in case you get a report of a sailing boat in trouble. I've been cut loose from the marina. I'm now safely heading for open water.'

'Okay, Cass. Let us know when you get back in.'

'Will do.'

I checked through the window, went up and tacked again, then went below for warmer clothes. By the time I'd done that we were almost between the last set of buoys, and in another hundred metres I could free her off and let her surge towards the open sea. It wasn't a route I'd have chosen for night sailing in a gale, with the little islands each side of the channel, one dead in the middle of the next channel, and a submerged reef between the two, but between human enemies and the sea, I'd take my chance with the sea any day.

Now we were away from Scalloway my eyes had adjusted to the dark. Even this sliver of moon cast a pale glow on the sea, shifting silver between the dark islands. I sighted ahead and noted my compass bearing on my route to safety. The submerged rock was a mile and a half away, twenty minutes at this speed, and – another squint through the compass – I reckoned our leeway was five degrees. I did the arithmetic, and got my course to steer. If one of these scudding clouds came over the moon, I just had to hold this course and listen for breakers for all I was worth, and we'd be safe.

All the same, it was one of the most dangerous things I'd done recently. My heart was thudding as I heard the waves hiss on the islands not fifty metres from me, and saw the gleam of white foam among the long rocks that seemed to stretch out bony fingers towards us, my tough little boat and I, alone in this wilderness of water. We came between the first pair of islands, Green Holm and its satellite, and forged on to Langa. The wind was blowing the waves onto the rocks, and the back eddy shoved at *Khalida,* knocking the wind from her sails. The rock in the middle of the channel was bang on my nose; I adjusted my course towards the Cheynies. *Khalida* was making nearly six knots through the water. As soon as I'd passed the little rock I brought her up and away from there, came round the last corner, and we were free, with the sea open before us, and the wind blowing us out into it.

It could be a long night. I hooked up the steering chain that kept *Khalida* on course and nipped below to put the kettle on, add another jumper, and check the forecast. This wind looked set to blow itself out overnight, and back westerly, which would give me an easy ride home.

157

I huddled myself into the corner of the cockpit that gave most protection from the bitter wind and flying spray, and clasped my mug of hot chocolate in both hands. Out here at sea, the waves were twice the size, above the height of *Khalida*'s cabin roof, shrugging us from one side to the other. One moment we'd be on the crest, with the waste of water shimmering around us, and the next we'd be enclosed in black water. As the wind rose, the crests stopped breaking; the wave would build, and build, then implode from inside in a rush of foam, and the foam itself was building up into lumps; at one point I thought I glimpsed a white motorboat, just fifty yards away, then, as we rose on a wave, realised it was a great block of foam the length of *Khalida*.

Frightened? Yes, I was. It would take only one split-pin on the straining rig to work loose, one shackle to undo, and we'd be caught up in disaster: a split sail, a fallen mast, *Khalida* tossing loose on this sea with no steerage to keep these waves rolling harmlessly to her bow. I started doing what ifs: I could cut the mast free and we could lie a-hull until morning, I could deploy the sea-anchor in the aft locker to keep her nose to the wind. When you're out at sea, when there's nobody to rely on but yourself, panic doesn't help you. I'd learned that in those bleak days after Alain went overboard in the middle of the Atlantic. At first I'd circled, looking, and called for help on the radio, but the help never came. In the end I had to accept he was gone and resume the sail home. A thousand miles from Scotland, I had to do everything alone in a grey wilderness of water: log-keeping, boat checks, sail changes. The ship's routine helped keep me focused, and when I felt that dangerous bubble of panic rising in me I'd walk round the rigging again, or take sextant readings, or mess about with the sails until they were in perfect racing trim.

Now I looked out at these waves, and reminded myself I was only a handful of miles from port. The engine was disabled, true, but the sails were working, driving my tough little boat through the water. Cat was safe below. I was well away from deadly rocks. I'd been in far tighter situations. I reached into the cabin for the fleece blanket, wrapped it around me, put my left hand on the tiller, and prepared to sit the night out.

ᚻ

'Absolutely deliberate,' I assured Gavin. It was just after nine, and the start of a golden morning, with the wind soft on the water, the sky summer-blue, and the grass hills the soft green of August. Cat had come out into the cockpit and was washing his whiskers after eating my crisped bacon rinds. A cormorant surfaced alongside, the sun glistening on its iridescent green back, tilted its grey beak at me, then ducked back under the water. 'Someone lifted off the ropes they could reach easily, and cut the fore ropes that were up on the bow. A knife sawing would have woken me, so I'd guess they used scissors, the sort you'd have in a kitchen for cutting meat.'

'You couldn't ID the car?'

'No. It was a car, not a pick-up or 4x4 or Berlingo, but that's the best I can do. Small, maybe a hatchback, not a long estate. Something like a Fiesta, that shape.' I could see it still in my mind's eye, with that faceless shadow watching. 'The colour was distorted by the streetlights, but it was a colour, mid-shade, not white.'

'And no doubt the entire place knew you were in Scalloway.'

'No doubt at all,' I agreed.

The low sun danced on the water, turning it to whisky gold. On the island of Hildasay, it lit up the ghosts of long-gone crofts, the oblong ruin of house in its square of yaird, the long rigs running down to the sea. The sea kissed the grass of the nibbled banks, hiding the beaches; torpedo-shaped seals were hauled up on headlands, heads lifted to the light. On the east side of Scalloway, the houses were silhouetted by the rising sun, the black hills broken by silver twists of water; the western hills were dusted with light, the longer grass pale gold, the heather chocolate rust. A flock of greylag geese passed overhead and skated down onto the water.

'Gavin, do you think the skeleton we found really might be Ivor?'

'You haven't uncovered anything else that could make someone want to get you out of the way?'

'Something I know that I don't know I know?' I shook my head. 'That odd business of the njuggle and the ring.' I tried to remember what Jeemie's car had been. Average shape, navy. 'It could have been Jeemie's car.'

'I'll ask the local officers if they can look into the ring as soon as possible. That connects back to Ivor Hughson too, if it was the girlfriend who sold it to Jeemie. Confusion take all these holidays! The dentists will surely be back to work tomorrow.'

'And if it's him?'

'Then it's a case, and we'll interview you in form, with as many police cars as Lerwick will allow me.'

'Word will just go round that I've been arrested.'

'All the more likely that you'll have told all you know. For the moment –'

'Believe me, I'll be checking all systems and ropes within an inch of their lives. I'm not having the mast falling on me.'

'Yes, I think you'll keep yourself safe from hands-off long-shots like the gas and the cut mooring ropes. What I'm more concerned about –' his voice flattened to impersonal, as if he was talking in an interview room, 'is that the perp may proceed to direct violence, since you

160

have as many lives as a cat for maritime disasters.'

'I'll be too busy in Reidar's café to tempt murderers by lonely walks at night. We open on Friday. Listen, I'll need to get back in, Maman and Dad are picking me up for Mass. Speak to you later, *beannachd leat.*'

'*Madainn mhath.*' Have a good morning.

The first thing I'd done in the half-light of dawn was ease the mercifully short end of bow rope from around the propeller. Now I started the engine and set *Khalida* chugging forward under engine and jib as I stowed the mainsail. We'd be back in Scalloway in less than half an hour.

Reidar came out to take my lines. 'A fine day for a very early sail.'

'I was cut adrift in the night.' I swung myself onto the pontoon. 'I'll tell you all about it later – are you working in the café this afternoon?'

He nodded. 'All afternoon. Come along. I have a new biscuit recipe also that I wish to try out on you.'

'Any time,' I assured him, and headed below to change my sailing suit for jeans and a jumper. I'd just finished lacing up my winter boots when I heard a beep from the shore. I scrambled out, secured the washboards behind me, and headed to the car.

Chapter Eighteen

It was a most beautiful winter's day for a drive. There were parties out at the golf course, dark-clad figures against summer-bright grass. The few still-worked Lerwick peat banks were black gashes in the rust-rose heather, with weather-faded palettes lying in the greff, ready for next year. Three fishing boats were tied by the blue Shetland Catch factory, offloading their harvest. I wondered if Charlie's was among them. Peerie Charlie would be blyde to get his dad home so quickly. The Northlink-Serco ferry was in, with its newly painted Viking pointing the vessel forwards. The coloured lights and picture of Santa in his sleigh that used to brighten the town from the start of December until Up Helly Aa had been discontinued this year, along with the Christmas tree at the King Harald Street junction. I hoped the money saved had gone to something worthwhile, like meals for the elderly, or care for special needs children.

The church was still in festival mode, even if everyone else had thrown out their Christmas trees long before Twelfth Night. The wreath by the lectern was made of prickly holly and scarlet chrysanthemums, with the great Easter candle in the middle of it. We had a satin shimmer of white lilies at the altar, and before it, surrounded by hay, was the crib, its roof fret-worked by two of the Polish community. There was a scarlet-leaved poinsettia on each side, the pots sprayed gold and wreathed with tinsel. The metre-high figures went way back to my childhood: Mary, hands folded in prayer, Joseph standing behind her, the ox and ass, the shepherds led by a grey-headed man carrying a lamb, the little boy bringing up the rear. Today was the feast of the Epiphany, so the wise men had been added: a tonsured English king in scarlet robes trimmed with ermine, an African in royal purple over silvery-blue, a Persian whose green cloak was flung back to show the gold underneath. I remembered when I'd come to my very first Midnight Mass, aged seven; I'd been thrilled to be given the task of carrying the baby Jesus forward from the back of the church. There he lay in his basket, a little Victorian boy with milk-white skin and golden curls, arms outstretched.

Maman wore her white wool coat with a black fur pillbox hat, and Dad had a white polo-neck jumper under his jacket. They could have come straight off the set of a Russian episode from a James Bond. Maman led us to the pew we'd occupied when I was a child, and Dad motioned me in before him, and there I was, sandwiched between two parents. I was far too old, I told myself, to feel this daft sense of security, of the world suddenly being right way up again. We'd got on fine after Maman had left, Dad and I – then the memory rose up of going into their bedroom when Dad was out, to open the wardrobe door, smell her perfume on her dresses, and promise myself that while her clothes were there, she'd surely return. She'd meant to, I thought, but she'd lost my baby brother, and the distance between them had stretched too far to cross. I said a prayer for him. Patrick, he would have been called. He'd have been twenty-six now, maybe married, with his first child …

The keyboard struck up, the guitars joined in, and we were launched into 'Bethlehem of Noblest Cities'. I listened to Maman sending her clear notes across the crib to the saints at the altar, and imagined the chirping sparrows in the bushes outside pausing to listen. Then we had the reading: the wise men and Herod's trickery and slaughter. At communion one of the singers did a solo of a carol I hadn't heard before, a lament for the slaughter of the innocents: *Lully, lullay, thou little tiny child.* Genocide, we'd call it now; I thought of villages in war-torn Syria, of the schoolgirls who'd been kidnapped in Nigeria, and wondered where we'd ever got this belief that two thousand years of civilisation had made us better.

As we came out of Mass, Father Mikhail bowed over Maman's hand. 'Happy New Year, madame.' He turned to me. 'What is it you are mixed up in now, Cass? I hear rumours of another death.'

I shook my head. 'I just found the body. The police are establishing identity, then they'll take over.'

His eyes were worried. 'You take care, now.'

We went for a cup of tea in the parish house, then Dad and Maman drove me back to Scalloway. I ate Sunday lunch (stew maison with pasta twists, cooked in the flask), and was just about to head for the café when I heard my name being called. Hubert Inkster was at the marina gate.

He was wearing church-going clothes, a dark suit, with his navy jacket over the top, and black shoes. He raised a hand. *The perp may proceed to direct violence,* Gavin had said. I considered Hubert as a perp, as I headed along the pontoon towards him. He'd been with Ivor on the trip to the west of Scotland in August, and there had been some kind of quarrel, severe enough that he'd left Ivor to sail short-handed round Ardnamurchan and through the Caledonian Canal, then alone through the tricksy tides around Orkney and up the wastes of the North Sea. He was in love with Julie, but that wasn't a reason for murder, unless his own religious convictions meant he didn't believe in divorce. I contemplated a Christianity that would prefer killing the husband to marrying the divorced wife, and didn't believe in it. I opened the gate. 'Aye aye.'

'Now then, Cass. I was just wondering if I might have a word with you.'

'Come in,' I said, and motioned him before me along

the pontoon. 'Would you take a cup of tea?'

He sat in silence until I'd filled the tea-pot and set it to stew on the ring, and set the mugs in front of us. 'Milk? Sugar?'

'Just milk. Thanks to you.'

I put the biscuit jar between us, and he helped himself to a couple of Rich Teas, then at last he looked at me, shyly, sideways. 'I was hearing that maybe Ivor was dead.' His voice was uneven with bewilderment. 'I wondered that he took off like that, without a word, but I thought –' He lifted his cup and drank a couple of mouthfuls, set it down again. I waited. Hurrying him would make him more tongue-tied.

His fingers relaxed on the cup. He drank another few mouthfuls, then lifted his head. 'I wanted to tell you about the time I was down there with him. To be sure you kent that Julie wasn't involved.'

'Julie was still south when he came home,' I said. His heavy face brightened at that. 'But tell me about the voyage.'

'Well, we set off from Brae on Friday the second of August.' He was obviously one of those people that have an exact memory for dates. 'It took us twa days and a half to sail down there. Boanie, boanie weather it was, all the way, though the wind a bit light at time, so we did a bit of motoring once we were level with Scotland. We arrived in Uig, on Skye, and had our first night there.'

'Hang on,' I said, and fished out an old envelope. 'Let me write this down. Left on the second, so you were in Uig on the fifth?'

'All day Friday, all day Saturday, Sunday taytime. The fourth, Sunday the fourth. Then we went round the back of Skye, and had a night in Loch Snizort, and a night in the shadow of Dunvegan Castle, that was most special boanie, and then Loch Harport. Have you been there?'

'Under the Cuilleans,' I said, and he nodded.

'Yea, this great mountains of rock. I coulda lookit at them all day. Then – where are we now? Yea, we came out again, and had a beat down the back of Skye, with the wind dead on the nose, a force six with some vicious gusts.'

'How did the boat handle that?' I asked, getting diverted into technical. 'With the centreboard, rather than the fixed keel?'

'She was good. I was dubious about it as well, but she pointed fine, without too much leeway, a bit more as a fixed keel, maybe, and she didna slam into the waves more than any other would a done. She went well altogether.'

'What day are we on now?'

He counted the days on his fingers, muttering the names. 'Thursday. It was Thursday we were going into the wind, and that night we were in Loch Eishort.' He took off his cap, and began turning it round in his hands. His voice became hesitant, as if this was what he really wanted to tell me, yet wasn't sure that he should. 'See, Ivor had been getting these texts. I kent him and Julie had had their differences. We were aye friends, Julie and I. His phone would bleep, and he'd take it away from me to read, and I kent by the smile o' him that it wasna from Julie. He was high way, as if, as if he'd got a ticket he kent was a lottery winner. Excited. Then she turned up. Donna.' I couldn't read his voice as he said the name. For the first time I wondered about his friendship with Ivor. Suddenly I could see them as teenagers, Hubert with spots or greasy hair, two steps behind and envying Ivor his charm, coveting his girlfriends.

'At Loch Eishort?'

'Na, na, the following day. The Friday. We went across to Mallaig, and then in the afternoon this young lass arrived.' He spread his hands. 'A *young* lass. Ivor could a been her father. She had a bag with her, and waterproofs, and she was riggit all ready for coming aboard, with jeans and a warm jumper. I was that taken aback to see her, and she was the same to see me. For a moment neither of us kent what to say. Ivor telt me she was called Donna.' His voice softened. 'She was a right boanie peerie thing, with dark hair, and that kind o' open look, and I thought black shame of Ivor to have taken up wi' her, for you could see she wasna a bad lass, and I wondered if she even kent he was married at all.' He fell silent, lips tight.

'So she arrived in Mallaig on the Friday,' I prompted.

'Yea. Well, we had a cup of tea with her, then she said she'd forgotten suntan lotion, and she'd just need to go and get some, and off she went. Ivor and I had words then. I telt him he had no right to be doing this to Julie, and if Donna was biding aboard with him then I most certainly was not, and he tried to talk me out of it, and it ended with me firing me gear into my bag and walking out.'

His brown eyes lifted to mine. 'That's why I thought, when Ivor went off, I thought that was it. He'd gone off with this Donna. He was most awful keen on her.'

'But,' I said, trying to get my head around the timetable, 'surely Julie was coming down to join him?'

'Well, it was kinda off and on. When we first spak, back at Easter, she wisna coming – well, she never did. Then come June Ivor began to speak as if she might be, after all, and she telt me she'd decided she should gie it a go.'

I thought of Maman, organising her tour to include Shetland, just to meet up with Dad. 'But then, if they were trying to get together again –'

Hubert's voice was harsh. 'He was planning the weekend with this lass, she had to be back for her work on the Monday, and then Julie was coming on that same Monday. I could hardly believe it, but he was in one of those moods where there was no reasoning with him.'

'So what did you do next?'

'I walkit out and found a B&B in the village. When I

168

went for a walk that evening, then the boat had gone. I wasna going to wait around till them coming back on Monday.' His brown eyes lifted to mine, and I saw the worry he'd felt. 'Except I wondered if I maybe should, you ken, stick around to meet Julie, not have her walking into the situation unprepared, but then I thought no good ever came from interfering atween man and wife.' He paused, then added, bleakly, 'They'd likely both join together to shoot the messenger.' His fist thudded on the table; the words burst out of him. 'I'm kent Julie from we were in primary school together, and there's never been anyone else for me. If she'd a chosen me I'd a loved and cherished her all her days.' His voice sank to a murmur. 'I'd a died for her. But it was Ivor right from primary 1. Always Ivor.'

There was a long silence. Then he sat up straighter. 'I got the bus to Inverness and hired an estate car, long enough to sleep in, and I spent the week exploring the Highlands.' His slow speech speeded up, as if he was rattling off something he'd learned before he had the chance to forget it. 'I was in Strathpeffer the next night, and then Loch Broom, I kinda went across the middle of the top section of Scotland, and boanie country it was too, then on the Monday I took the ferry to Stornoway, then to Uig from there, and went climbing – well, scrambling, I suppose you'd call it, on the lower slopes o' the mountains for twa days, that was the Tuesday and Wednesday, then on Thursday morning I crossed the Skye Bridge again, and just daandered up the west coast and along the north coast, and then on Setturday I got the Wick boat to Orkney, had twa days there, got on the Sunday night boat, and I was home for me work on the Monday.' He looked at the teapot. 'Is there another cup of tay in there?'

'It'll be a bit cold, but go ahead.'

He poured, drank, then looked at me again. 'Do you really think it was Ivor that you found?'

The empty eye sockets stared at me again. For a moment I felt sick. 'I couldna tell, but they'll be comparing the dental records.'

'And where was he, exactly?'

I explained. He drew his lips together, frowning, then took a deep breath. 'I dinna want to get her into trouble, but he was going to take Donna there. They spak about it over tay. I mind that. She said it was one of the most romantic of the lochs, with Prince Charlie's cave an' all, and she'd like to see it, and he said, well, they could easy go there in the weekend.'

'If it was Ivor, we'll ken soon.'

'Wid you phone me?' He fumbled in his pocket and brought out his phone. 'Or could I mebbe phone you? If it is him, if he's dead like that, I'd like to ken, in case Julie needed me.'

She hadn't needed him as a deserted wife, except to check up on the boat; but I wouldn't say that. I got him to phone me, and entered his number into my address book. 'If I hear, I'll let you know, so long as I'm allowed to.' The words echoed the suggestion that I'd have information the police weren't releasing; I amended them hastily. 'But I won't be told anything that's not in the public domain, so you might see it on the Shetland News website before I hear. But I'll call if I can.'

'Thanks, Cass.' At last, he rose to go. 'Were you going out? Can I give you a life somewhere?'

Accepting lifts from someone who had every reason to have killed Ivor didn't come under the heading 'Keeping myself safe'. I shook my head. 'Thanks, but no, I'll be a minute sorting out here.'

He hesitated in the doorway for a moment, as if there was something more he wanted to say. Suddenly I remembered what I'd wanted to ask. 'Was it you who took the boat's heather off, when you tidied her away for the winter?'

He looked blank. 'Heather?'

'From going round Ardnamurchan.'

His eyes cleared. 'Oh, the sprig of heather, aye.' He was silent for a long moment, as if he was thinking what to say. I wondered if Julie had told him she'd not been there, but he didn't know she'd also told me, and didn't want to give her away. 'Right enough, they came home round the point and up Loch Ness. Julie told me that. Likely she threw it away, it would be all withered. There was no sense in keeping it.' His smile didn't reach his eyes. 'But you, now, I can see you letting your boat keep her prize until it fell off her. I'll hear from you, then.'

His footsteps clacked along the pontoon; there was the clang of the gate, his car starting up, then the silence flowed back.

Chapter Nineteen

Cat and I strolled along the seafront and past the village shops to the grey granite of the old museum, Reidar's café. The sky was an arch of pale blue, with the sea disappearing into a misty haze. The long, grey cumulus to the north threatened a colder night.

I thought as I walked. Hubert had come out pat with what he'd done in that week, yet everything else he'd said had shown his motive for murder. Ivor had betrayed Julie with Donna. There had been a quarrel. How easy it would have been for Hubert to have phoned Ivor, and offered to join him in Inverness. He could have staged an accident at sea, but then there would have been an inquest, and questions. It had been hard enough, after Alain's death, when they'd pressed for details I couldn't remember; I couldn't have sustained a lie. Maybe Hubert hadn't dared risk it.

No, easier to wait for him here. They'd planned the trip together, so Hubert knew when Ivor was expected home. He could have waited for the boat to reach the marina, then gone into the house via a back door or unlocked window. A crofter who was used to hauling sheep around would have had no difficulty in hefting Ivor over his shoulders and dumping him in the boot of his own car. Then the packing Beryl had seen, with the lights going on in the rooms, the grabbing of clothing as if he'd left by himself.

Then what? ... *one of the most romantic o' the lochs* ... He'd made it clear that the loch was Donna's choice. Maybe he'd heard talk in his B&B about the Argyll Gathering, and how everyone went to it. He went down on the boat, with Ivor's car, left it in Aberdeen, and got the Sunday boat home. Then, on the Wednesday, he went down and took the body to the loch, where it would link up with Donna, who'd stolen Julie's man. He'd have no bother handling a quad. Then he took the car back to Aberdeen and left it, and came home to Shetland. I wondered what traces had been found in Ivor's car.

Gavin would find that out. *My ship, Cass.* I knocked at the freshly painted door of the old museum, and went inside. The stove was glowing in one corner; Cat went straight to the hearth and began washing his paws. I followed the cinnamon smell to the kitchen, and found Reidar busy with boxes of old china. 'I got these at the last auction. We must look at them, and arrange them ready to use. But first, I want you to try these.'

He produced a plate of rolled biscuits, like brandy snaps, but flavoured with cinnamon instead of ginger, and oozing with softly whipped cream. 'Delicious,' I assured him, licking the last crumbs off my fingers.

'You must not do that when you are waitressing,' he warned me.

I wiped my hands on my jeans. 'Ready for work, sir.'

We began washing tea sets and stacking them in the shelves behind the counter. I felt a sense of the past as I looked at the patterns: a navy swallow with forked tail and red head, a sprig of pinks with a gold embossed edge to cup and saucer, a green spray of flowers around the nibbled rim. These had been wedding presents, or bought with her knitting by some crofter's lass for her bottom drawer; this single plate with a Chinese pheasant might have been brought back by a seaman grandfather and cherished in the middle shelf of the dresser until its old-lady owner died, leaving nobody to remember the bringer.

'You are dreaming,' Reidar observed, taking the Chinese plate from me.

I shook my head. 'Just wondering who owned these,

and what stories they would have to tell.'

'Do not forget to examine each one. No chips or cracks. We wish the customers to wonder on the history, not worry about the germs.'

We were almost finished when there was a rap at the door, a male voice calling. Reidar and I looked at each other, startled, then the door jangled open and Mr Georgeson strode in, his shark grin puckered to sourness, as if he'd just sucked on a lemon. He took up the centre of the room, and looked around him.

'Can I help you?' Reidar asked.

John Georgeson's gaze scorched me, then moved to Reidar. 'Councillor Georgeson. A good idea this, to use the old museum for a café. I hope you'll no' be over much in competition with the local folk at the hotel and the college.'

Given that the hotel owners were from Plymouth, and the college café presided over by Antoine, 'local folk' wasn't really relevant, but I kept my mouth shut.

'I hope not too,' Reidar replied smoothly. 'We are concentrating on tea, coffee, pastries, and a snack lunch menu, not evening meals.'

Georgeson turned to scowl at me. 'You're working here?'

'Reidar's keen to employ locals.'

He didn't like that. 'I'm sure there are Scalloway youngsters who'd be glad of the work. Aren't you supposed to be at college?'

'I'm paying my way through it.' I looked him straight in the eye. 'I was born in Shetland, you ken that, and I went to school in Brae. If I dinna belong here, then I dinna belong anywhere.'

He scowled and turned back to Reidar. 'I'm sure you have all the proper permits. It'd be a right shame if there was bother with that.'

He was a tall man, Mr Georgeson, but Reidar seemed

to grow until he was a head taller. 'I have all the permissions I need, Councillor Georgeson, granted by your own departments. Now, if that is all, we have work to do.' He went over to the door and opened it. 'We open on Friday, as I am sure you know.'

The look Georgeson gave him would have burnt a hole through metal. He gave me a last glare. 'And you, keep your nose out o' what doesna concern you.' He turned on his heel and marched out of the shop. Reidar closed the door behind him.

'You are making enemies, Cass.'

'Maybe I should make myself scarce. I don't want them to rescind your change of use permit or whatever he's likely to do.'

Reidar's chest swelled. 'I am not being dictated to by that bully. I wish you to work for me. But I also wish to know why he is so keen to put pressure on you.'

'I'd like to know too.' I didn't feel as if I'd learned enough to be a threat to anyone. *Making links* ... but what link had I made between Ivor's death and John Georgeson?

We worked until the shelves were full of tea sets arranged in order of how many there had been: a pair of cups, saucers and plates, three, four, five, and just one complete set from all five boxes, guarded carefully from new, and used only at Christmas and New Year at home, and taken down to the local hall for weddings and funeral teas.

It was dark when we came out. The sky was ringed round with cloud still, but the stars shone bright around the moon: the W of Cassiopeia, the square of Pegasus, the misty ribbon of the Milky Way. The air was cold, the tide as far out as it could go, leaving a dark width of pebbles and the iodine smell of seaweed. There was a red car waiting by the boating club, and as we came towards it the driver's door opened, and someone got out and stood there, silent, watching us.

It was Donna.

Even in this light I could see that she'd been crying, and her breath still caught in her throat, as if it would take only a word to set her off again. I was tired of people making me the repository for their problems. I wanted to curl up in my bunk with a hot water bottle, and Cat purring at my neck, to read my book by candle-light until I was ready to sleep ... but she was standing there, shoulders drooping, and I couldn't turn her away.

'Hi, Donna.' I smiled at her. 'How can I help you?'

'I wanted to talk to you.' She hauled a crumpled paper handkie from her pocket and plunged her face into it. Standing beside her, I found the pixie face gave a false impression; she was a good four inches taller than I.

Reidar glanced at her, then shepherded us both along the pontoon and onto his motorboat, as if he regularly had strange young women coming to burst into tears on him. 'I am Reidar. Come, I have a heater, and I will make hot chocolate for you.' He motioned Donna into the U-shaped settee around the table. 'Do not try to talk until you are warm again.'

She watched, round-eyed, as he heated the milk and chocolate together, looking uncertainly at me from time to time.

'He's right,' I assured her. 'Whatever's wrong, one of his hot chocolates will make you feel much better.'

Reidar whipped some cream, added a tablespoonful of marmalade, divided the chocolate mix between two coffee cups, added a layer of the cream, and placed the result in front of us.

Donna clasped her hands around the cup and gave a long sigh. She'd brought a waft of sickly, floral scent into the cabin. Her fingers were blue with cold, as if she'd waited in her car for a good while. She was as pretty and vulnerable as I'd remembered, and I felt a flash of anger at Ivor Hughson. She bent her head to the cup and sipped. Her eyes widened; she looked across at Reidar, and gave him a tentative smile.

Once I'd savoured the last soft marmalade chunk and eaten the last crumb of cinnamon biscuit, I looked across at Donna. The colour had returned to her cheeks, the tension washed from her shoulders, but her face was strung up, as if she was bracing herself for confession. She set the cup to one side, and raised her dark-lashed eyes to mine. 'Cass, I wanted to come and ask you – to *tell* you.' The tears welled up again. 'I saw you watching me last night. When you came into the restaurant, I thought you'd followed me, and I was so afraid I couldn't bear it. Everything was all so awful, and then when I met –' She crimsoned, and didn't say the name. 'Everything was all right again, and I couldn't bear for him to know how stupid I was.'

I picked on what made sense. 'You don't want your new bloke to find out about Ivor Hughson.'

She wailed into her handkerchief. Reidar leaned forward and covered her hand with his gentle paw. 'Now, now, you are not to mind Cass. She likes to make things clear. Tell us your history at the beginning, and we will see what we can do to help. It will make you feel better also.'

His soothing rumble did the trick. She hiccupped a bit, then began. She was from Aberdeen, as I'd heard, and the youngest of three. 'My older brother Jamie, he drives to the Co-op, a delivery van, like, and he works with the horses.'

We looked blankly at her. 'The Clydesdales,' she explained. 'They still keep them for the Highland Show, the Braemar Gathering, that kind of thing. You ken, the big horses with the hairy hooves. I used to help him groom them, and we'd brush out their feathers till they shone like silk, and plait red ribbons in their manes, and I'd dress as a boy to sit up beside him on the box. Me sister Shivonne, she's just graduated as a nurse. I wasna that good at the school, I hadn't any particular ambition for anything. I thought about a hairdresser, or a beautician, or something to do with children, like, but in the end I didna train for anything. Me ma works in a care home, and I worked with her for a bittie. Then Jamie heard about this job in the Serco Northlink office. It said it was general office duties, and I'd be trained on the job. I went along for an interview and I got it. I was on the desk, checking folk's bookings, and issuing the cabin cards.' Her face had brightened while she was talking about her family; now it puckered again. 'That was where I met Ivor.' It hurt even to say his name. 'He was aye friendly when he got his card, and then one day he asked me about the night life in Aberdeen, and what pub I would recommend. He asked if I'd meet up with him there.' She stopped short, then burst out, 'Me dad woulda killed me if he'd kent, with Ivor being that much older. I'd say I was going out with me pals, and he'd come and join us in the pub. Then, to celebrate me eighteenth birthday, he took me to a hotel, and we had champagne.' She dabbed at her eyes again. 'After that, we kept meeting up, and he said he loved me, and wanted us to be together. I didna ken he was married, he never said anything about that. I wanted to take him to meet my folk, but he wasna keen, because he was so much older. He didna want them to think he was dodgy.'

Dodgy as hell. Gavin would have to follow up Ivor's love life. When he had a van to drive, and several nights a week on the mainland, Donna, the supervised baby of her family, wouldn't be the only girl.

'But he did ask me if I'd go on holiday with him. He

179

was keen on the sailing – well, you'd ken that. He was planning on taking his boat around Skye, so he asked me if I'd come, spend a whole two weeks together, just him and me.' She flushed. 'It meant lying to my folk, because if he widna meet them there was no way I'd be allowed to go off with him like that. It was the first time, and I could tell Mam didna believe me when I said I was going with one of the lasses from work. Then, in May, this job came up in the Shetland office.' She shook her head at herself, her face adult at last. 'I thought he'd be pleased. I didna want to be over eager to move in with him, so I got a flat, and put all me stuff in me car, and drove onto the ferry. He came to meet me, and we went into the flat together, and I was so happy.' The tears ran like glass over her porcelain cheeks. 'I canna believe I was that stupid. Of course I found out the truth straight away, from the other girls in the office talking, the next time he needed a ticket. All about his wife, how they'd been childhood sweethearts, and at university together, and she was a lecturer in the college, and that they were trying for bairns.' Her fair skin flushed scarlet. 'I even went to the college and sat in my car, waiting for her to come out. I just wanted to see her. She was Ivor's age, and smart. Stylish.'

'Did you tell Ivor you'd found him out?'

She nodded. 'He said they'd grown apart long ago, she was wrapped up in her teaching and she kind of looked down on him for not having a prestigious job. He said he loved me more than he'd ever loved anyone, and he wanted us to be together and have a family.' She blew her nose, then sat up straighter, suddenly resolute. 'I couldn't have my whole holiday, with changing jobs like that, but I had a weekend, and I said I'd go down and meet him in Mallaig. He said he'd tell his wife about us, and then when he came back he'd move into my flat with me.'

I wondered how Ivor thought he could keep up this kind of juggling between women. Was he so conceited that he thought they'd forgive him anything?

'But it wasn't true!' Donna burst out. 'When I got there, there was this other man, Hubert something, and he and Ivor quarrelled about me. That's how it came out that Ivor hadn't told Julie. He hadn't said anything to her at all. She was arriving the very day after I went back to Shetland.' The tears came back to her eyes, but she blinked them away, vulnerable mouth set in a hard line. 'I was stupid to believe any of his lies, it was all straight from a problem page letter where the answer begins "Ditch him". I was so ashamed of myself. I went back to Shetland and tried to act just as normal, but inside I was devastated. I'd go down to the pier at night, after dark, and look at that black water and think about chucking myself in, and I might have done it if it hadn't been for –' She stopped on the name again. 'My new bloke – I don't want him mixed up in this. He's that good to me, he kens, and he doesn't hold Ivor against me, but his family, they're the kind of folk me mam and dad would like. His sister's a teacher, and his brother runs his own business, and I'd just die if they found out how stupid I'd been.'

She was back where she belonged, being protected in the middle of a big family. This new man would spoil her and love her and look after her. Her family would approve of him, and she'd have a traditional white wedding, with her old aunties crying, and all her littlest cousins as bridesmaids.

'He's coming with me to meet my parents the next time I go down. I ken they'll like him.' Her delicate hands spread in in the air. 'Then I heard about you.' Her eyes rested briefly on my scar. 'How you'd found Ivor's body down in Scotland, and were asking questions. You'd worked with the police before, they said, and were courting with a policeman down south. And there you were, right at the next table, listening.'

I looked steadily at her. 'I really wasn't. It was pure

chance, and if you hadn't reacted to me, I'd never have noticed you. I knew he had a girlfriend, and that was all.'

The hands spread towards me. She fixed me with those dark-fringed eyes. 'What I'm asking – I'm begging – please, please keep me out of it. His family are all church-goers, and they'd think the less of me for having an affair with a married man.' *I canna be a Sathin i Papa*, the old folk would have said: I can't be a bad person among good ones. She flushed. 'I think the less of myself for keeping on with him, once I learnt. Please, can't you just forget about me, so they never find out?'

So that she could have her happy ending after all. Something in me was envious. I'd flung myself into the world at sixteen, with nobody to shelter me from nasty reality. If ever I'd had a hankering for a white satin dress and veil, I'd suppressed it. But Donna too had hit nasty reality; Ivor had conned her, having his cake and eating it, and the Lord knew how long he'd have kept stringing her along in ignorance, if she hadn't come up to Shetland. I remembered Julie's angry voice: *He told the girlfriend it was over, and she killed him.* Had the note been left for Donna, as a last-minute attempt to stop her joining him?

'Did Ivor have a key for your flat?'

She jerked her head back. 'A key to my flat?' Her eyes moved round the cabin, as if she was thinking what to say. She bit her lip. 'Yes, but I asked for it back, when we quarrelled.'

'When did you quarrel?' Reidar asked. 'Was it you who ended the affair?'

She turned towards him eagerly. 'Yes. In Mallaig. I got on the bus and left him there on the pavement. I didn't want to ever see him again. It hurt more than I could have believed it would, like stripping my skin off, but at the same time it was such a relief. It felt like I'd been trying to con myself into believing he loved me when deep down I knew he didn't.'

Her story or Julie's … which did I believe? Then I remembered that judgement was Gavin's problem. 'Was it you,' I asked, 'who set my boat adrift?'

She burst into tears again. I understood her to say, between sobs, that she'd been so afraid I was after her, and I was such a good sailor that she knew I wouldn't come to any harm, but when she'd seen my boat in the storm she'd been so scared, and she was really sorry, and that's why she'd come to talk to me. 'I just wanted you not to investigate me,' she finished. 'Please, please, don't tell on me.'

'It's up to the investigating officer.' I leaned over the table towards her, hands spread. 'If I keep quiet, they'll hear about Ivor having a girlfriend from someone else, then they'll have to ask about you in the office at Serco. That'll make far more talk, don't you think?'

She was silent, considering that.

'Wait and see if it is Ivor's body,' I coaxed. 'Then, if it is, you should go to the officer in charge and tell them all you've told me. If you do that, I won't need to say anything, and nobody else will know anything about it.'

'Promise?'

'Don't you think,' I asked, tentatively, 'that you might be better letting your new man tell his family the truth?'

She shook her head so hard that her hair flew out like spikes around her head. 'No, no, I couldna.' She rose from behind the table. 'I must go. Now mind, you promised.' She gave Reidar a last smile. 'Thanks for the drink, it was fabby.'

I put out a hand to stop her. 'Donna, did Ivor give you a ring? Two gold hands clasping a heart?'

She froze, face defensive. 'No. No, I never had a ring like that.' She snatched up her bag, and bolted up the companionway, clattering the two doors open and slamming them behind her. Her boots clacked along the pontoon, the gate clanged, the car revved up and drove away, until its sound was drowned by the waves on the shore.

'Well,' I asked, 'what do you make of that?'

Reidar shook his head. 'She talks like a ladies' hairdresser magazine, but you can see she was hurt by this Ivor.'

'Hurt enough to kill him?' I mused on that one for a bit. 'If she really did finish with him in Mallaig, that lets her out. But suppose, just suppose that he phoned her from south, and smoothed things over. He came back from the trip, and went round to see her. Suppose she killed him then. If anyone could get on the ferry with a car at the last minute, a Serco employee could.'

'That little girl, move a grown man?'

'She's a good bit taller than me,' I retorted, 'and she looks as if she does aerobics, or plays hockey. *And* she was strong enough to come out here in a gale and cut my mooring ropes.'

'And then she drove his body to the loch, and moved it to halfway up the hillside?'

'Okay,' I conceded. 'I don't quite see that one.'

'She has a brother who is a van driver,' Reidar said. 'She told us so. A driver to the Co-op. A man who spends his days lifting packages of groceries would be able to lift a body. If she talked to him as she talked to us, and begged him to help her, do you think he would not?'

'Plenty of cliffs near Aberdeen,' I pointed out. 'Why not just drive to one and throw the body over?'

'Because it might be found and identified. The whole point was to keep her out of it.'

'He should have known she'd be hopeless at keeping herself out.'

'Only because there are rumours that the body is Ivor. If it had been anyone else who found it, it would have remained an unidentified body. Providence. *There is a special providence in the fall of a sparrow.*'

I was silent for a moment, contemplating the vast jigsaw of little pieces that God would have moved to make sure that Gavin and I had walked that path, to give Ivor justice: the defeat on Culloden moor and the Bonnie Prince's flight through the heather, Gavin's ancestor guiding him to that cave, and then, centuries later, the longship murder, and the carelessly taken message that had brought a country DI up to Shetland instead of the top brass; even the rain drying up on that day, to give us a longer walk. 'Do you really think the universe is such a pattern?'

'I am sure it is. We cannot see it, any more than the red tuft of wool in a carpet knows that it is part of a flower, but the pattern is there, all the same. Will you tell Gavin about her?'

I shook my head. I would give her a chance to tell the story first, in her own way.

Monday 6th January: Epiphany

High Water at Scalloway UT	*00.13, 1.7m*
Low Water	*05.53, 0.7m*
High Water	*12.19, 1.7m*
Low Water	*18.32, 0.7m*

Sunrise	*09.05*
Moonrise	*10.31*
Sunset	*15.16*
Moonset	*23.24*

Moon waxing crescent.

Tuesday 7th January

High Water at Scalloway UT	*01.02, 1.5m*
Low Water	*06.43, 0.8 m*
High Water	*13.10, 1.6m*
Low Water	*19.28, 0.7m*

Sunrise	*09.04*
Moonrise	*10.47*
Sunset	*15.18*
Moonset	*00.34*

Moon waxing crescent

Du could as weel aet aa du sees as believe aa du hears.
A warning to the credulous: you could as well eat all you see as believe all you hear.

Chapter Twenty

I slept badly, waking at each bump on the pontoon. When I went out, just after nine, the sky was misted over with cirrus clouds, coloured a soft pink that intensified the nearer you turned to the east, where the sun turned them to a dazzling deep rose. To the north, there was a bank of lenticular clouds: wind coming, and cold. Red sky in the morning ... even as I watched, the rose turned to gold, then began to fade.

The North Atlantic Fisheries College didn't give students the long holidays that taxpayers complained about. Today was back to work until the end of March. We gathered together for a welcome from the principal, then it was business as usual. Cat disappeared off to the canteen to talk to Antoine, who had given him a box in a warm corner of the kitchen, and I headed for the workshop. My odd mixture of courses would, I hoped, end up in a Deck Officer of the Watch (Unlimited) qualification with the option of moving on to Chief Mate (Unlimited) once I'd done eighteen months of service at sea. The courses were more geared towards fishing or merchant service more than tall ships, but I was generously overlooking that.

'Did you ever do anything more about Ivor's yacht?' I asked Kevin, once we were ensconced beside 'our' engine. He shook his head.

'No' yet, but there're twartree of us who'd fancy a yacht like that, so we're thinking to join together, maybe. Right now it's hard to get anyone to think of anything but the Fire Festival. We're all in the same squad, so I'm mentioning it as we practise.'

The Lerwick Up Helly Aa was Shetland's best known fire festival, but there was a smaller version of the Viking-inspired procession in every district. Scalloway's was held on the second Friday in January. The procession and galley burning was followed by a long night of drinking, feasting, and dancing in various venues through the village. The 'squad' that Kevin belonged to was one of the groups of guizers who made up the procession, and they'd come round the venues to entertain the revellers. Kevin's squad's act must be pretty racy, judging by the way his cheeks had reddened.

'I've got a ticket for the boating club.'

The scarlet reached his neck. 'You'll mind it's just a fun, and no' take offence. I wouldna like you to be vexed.'

That intrigued me, but it wasn't done to ask, so we went back to taking our engine apart. We'd graduated from the fuel system to the pistons and cylinder head. Naturally, *Khalida*'s Volvo had only one piston, and while it still clanked up and down I was leaving the cylinder head strictly alone. Still, you never knew when the knowledge might come in useful.

It was a good day when we came outside: not too cold, with the wind blowing softly from the west, then falling altogether to give a puff from the north, and backing west again. The lenticular clouds had lengthened to ominous lines of black, filling half of the sky, and every so often a stronger gust rattled the halyards as I drank my soup at *Khalida*'s little table. I was just rising to head for the café when my mobile rang: Gavin.

'The skeleton was Hughson. Our dentist says there's no question about it. I'm booked on the 17.30 this evening. I'll have to spend a bit of time liaising when I arrive, but can I come round after that?'

My heart gave a nervous jump. He wouldn't expect to stay on board *Khalida*, of course not – *It will work out,* Maman had said. 'What sort of time?'

188

He'd heard my hesitation. 'Not too late, or the Glenorchy landlady will lock me out. Nine o'clock?'

'Yea. Will you have eaten?'

'I hope so! Surely Lerwick can run to a visit to the chippy, between files. See you later.'

ᚺ

By half past eight, I was like a cat on hot bricks. I would read a page of engine manual, look out of the window for a car drawing up at the marina gate, sit again for two minutes. Get a *grip*, Cass, I told myself. You're not doing this for any man. I went along the pontoon to unlock the gate, then began a drawing of all the pieces that made up an engine. He'd be here when he arrived.

The rattle at the gate alerted me. Should I stay at the table, showing I wasn't waiting for him, or come out and meet him? Damn it, he'd rumble me whatever I did. I compromised with putting the kettle on, so that when his steps came along the pontoon I was ready to open the washboards and come up on deck. 'Welcome back.'

He came past me and went below, hung his heavy jacket up on the rail. I followed him and put the washboards back. Now we were enclosed in this little space. He sat down aft of the table, with room enough for me to sit beside him, if I wished, and considered my drawing. 'A two-cylinder Yanmar?'

'I thought you only had outboards on your boat.'

'We have a generator in the byre, for power cuts. Kenny and I have a division-of-labour agreement: he does the animals, I do the machines, which don't mind waiting for police work to finish. One of my summer jobs is servicing it, but so far I've managed to avoid taking the cylinder head off.'

'Worth avoiding,' I agreed. I set the mugs between us and sat down on the other side of the table. Now we could look at each other directly. His grey eyes were smiling at me, crinkling the tanned skin at their corners. I looked down at my mug, suddenly shy.

'Your Lerwick police are on the ball,' he said briskly. 'They had all the official stuff about everyone involved on the table, backed by a sheaf of gossip notes and passenger information for the days we're interested in, from both ferries and planes.'

'What days?'

'We started with the assumption that the goodbye note was genuine. He left Shetland under his own steam, went to the loch, and was killed there. His car was booked on the Saturday night boat, with him as accompanying driver, and there's no return journey.'

'But why would he go back to the loch?'

'He did have one far-off link with it. He was a member of the university climbing club, and our loch was one of their camp-out spots; his favourite, according to a fellow-member who's now a lecturer there. If there had been someone important to him, he might have taken her there.'

Donna said something about them going there ... Gavin was quick. 'You've thought of something.'

'I can't tell you about it yet. It was someone I met, but I've told them they need to come to you, and I hope they will.'

'I've already talked to the folk who run the new marina in Mallaig. They have so many visiting yachts that of course they can't remember all of them, especially four months later, but the young man who took the lines remembered Ivor's face, when I sent him a photo, and he described the pretty girl that came off the bus to join him for the weekend.'

'I did my best to persuade her that it will make far more stir if you have to look for her.'

'Give her my number, and she can phone me directly without having to appear at the police station.'

'I'll do that.'

Gavin nodded, satisfied. 'Second possibility, he was killed at home and brought to our loch. Maybe he even described it to his killer as "a remote wilderness, if you got lost there nobody would find you". The killer hoped he wouldn't be found at all, or, if he was, that he wouldn't be identified. It was the worst of luck for them that you should have found the body.'

'Providence, Reidar reckons.'

'"For nothing is hidden that will not be revealed." If that's how it was, then someone bundled him into the boot of his own car and brought him to the head of the loch on the day of the Gathering, to transport to where we found him.'

'By quad,' I agreed.

Gavin smiled. 'It's such a help to the police, you being an island. Flights and ferries leave a trail. If Hughson was killed in the early hours of Saturday morning, then anyone who was off the island on a Friday ferry or flight is automatically excluded. Equally, if his body was disposed of on the day of the Gathering, Thursday the twenty-second, then anyone who was here on Shetland from after the boat left on Wednesday is out of that part of it.' He took out his notebook. 'His wife Julie first. She flew back from Inverness on the Sunday. She'd booked into the Inverness Youth Hostel for two nights, paying in advance, and there's nothing to prove or disprove that, six months ago. She could have sailed home with Ivor, killed him here and taken his body back, and she could just have returned to the loch, dumped the body, and driven the car to Inverness in time for her flight. The timing's tight, but possible – except that so far his car hasn't turned up in Inverness. And of course it was the weekend – we were all about. She couldn't have transported the body without one of us seeing her.'

'What about the Thursday, the Gathering day?'

He shook his head. 'In college all week, teaching, in front of twenty students. Next, Hubert Inkster. He was on the ferry as he said, that Sunday, from Orkney. He has no alibi at all for his time in Scotland, so he could have met Ivor in Inverness, sailed home with him, killed him, returned with the car and body, come back to Shetland via Orkney, and gone back down on the Wednesday to dispose of the body. He only works part-time, and Thursday is one of his crofting days. We don't accept alibis from sheep.'

'It's all so complicated,' I complained. 'Jumping on this ferry to get home, on that one with Ivor's car, back home, back on the Gathering day to dispose of the body, back home again. What about Robert-John Georgeson?'

'His business partner.' He drank the last of his tea and rose to wash the mug. 'How am I doing for time? Twenty to ten.' He had an old-fashioned round wrist-watch. He sat down again, but on the edge of the seat, as if to remind himself that he had a waiting landlady in his B&B. 'Robert-John. At that point, he was worried sick about money. As soon as Hughson went off on holiday he got rid of the firm's secretary, to save money, and did the paperwork himself. From mid-August till mid-September, when his wife took over the books, the paper trail is … scanty.'

'Non-existent?'

'No, no, there are at least a dozen invoices which look as though his wife found them in a pocket, smoothed them out, and put them in the system. Where the rest are, goodness knows. Robert-John himself thinks he was doing a house move that weekend, someone going to Dundee, and bringing another houseful back, but that could have been the following weekend, in which case he was at home in the week that interests us. Lerwick are following those up.'

'What did Maya say?'

'His wife would have said whatever would have given him an alibi, except that I carefully didn't tell her what that was. Her own alibi for Friday night was the child being in bed. I don't think she'd have left her.'

I jerked my head round to him, surprised. 'You think she might have killed Ivor Hughson?'

'As far as motivation goes, she's the strongest. Her whole world is her husband, her children, her house, and Hughson threatened all that. Robert-John says he didn't tell her about the difficulties until Hughson didn't return from his holiday, but she's an intelligent woman. She knew fine that he was worried. One look in his papers would have told her the whole story.'

'And,' I added thoughtfully, 'Robert-John and Maya knew when Ivor was due home. He was going to meet Robert-John on Sunday evening.'

'There's no reason why Robert-John should have told the rest of the Georgeson clan – particularly if he was keeping his difficulties quiet.'

'Robert-John has a croft,' I said. 'He could ride a quad.'

'There's a better form of transport for bodies in the Highlands. We use it all the time.' He smiled. 'Think four legs.'

The penny clanked home. 'Ponies?'

'Transport without sails, oars, or a motor.' I didn't try to resist the charm of Gavin's smile any more, but laughed ruefully back at him. 'Our ponies are used to strangers, and easy to catch. More importantly, you couldn't dump something dead on the back of just any horse, horses are very sensitive about blood and death, but these ones are used for the stalking, and trained to carry a dead stag. You don't need to go looking for bridles or saddles, just bring a halter and a rope to secure your body.'

I could have kicked myself. 'No wonder you were so

interested in the contents of Mr Georgeson's warehouse. Mr Georgeson junior may not ride any more, but he could lead one of your horses.'

'Yes, anyone who's taken part in one of those re-enactments is well able to handle a horse.' He added, kindly, 'Don't feel too bad about not thinking of horses as transport. They're not that good on water.'

'Unless it's a njuggle.' I imagined Donna catching a pony, dragging the heavy body onto its back, and leading it through the hills. The Little Folk were tricksier than their innocent faces suggested, and she'd helped her brother with the Co-op horses. 'If it was tied to a fence, say, would your pony stand patiently while someone levered a body over its back?'

'Yes. Well, provided they didn't take too long about it. It wouldn't be an easy job. You'd have to lift the body until it was over the pony's back, then tie the dangling arms and legs together under the pony's belly.'

'Definitely someone who was used to horses. You wouldn't catch me fooling about among those hooves.' Clydesdales had great hairy feet the size of tea-plates. If Donna was used to those, she wouldn't be daunted by Gavin's quiet garrons.

'As for Hughson's car, I expect to find it in Aberdeen somewhere, parked in a quiet street, if it's not in the records of cars towed away.' He stretched and rose. 'I'm staying in the odour of sanctity.'

'The Glenorchy Hotel?'

'It was built as a convent for Anglican nuns. Have a look at the gable end the next time you pass. You can still see the shape of the chapel windows. Mrs Howarth said the actual windows are in the Episcopalian church. I must go and look.'

'Oh, yes, St Magnus.' I'd never been inside it, but our congregation and theirs got together for dances and quiz nights, so I knew a few of the people. I rose too, and came behind him up the steps into the orange-lit night. The cold wind sluiced my skin, after the warmth of the cabin. 'I didn't know there had ever been a convent in Shetland, apart from the nuns on Fetlar.'

'There were Catholic nuns too, in a place called the White Rest. It was a seasonal hostel and first-aid post combined for Irish fisher girls in the twenties.' Gavin swung over the guard rail and dropped lightly onto the pontoon. 'Founded by an artist's model turned suffragette. Shall I bring round a Chinese tomorrow, work permitting?'

'Wouldn't say no.' Now I was faced with more calculations; whether I waved goodbye here or walked with him to the marina gate, as if I was expecting a kiss. Oh, but I would have to, to lock it behind him. I caught up my jacket and joined him on the wooden walkway. We swung along in silence, side by side, as we'd walked along the pebble shore of the loch. It wasn't cold enough for our breath to smoke, but I was conscious of the sound of his breathing, soft as the water rippling under our feet.

'I was wondering,' Gavin said, as we reached the gate, 'if we could do an excursion to this njuggle loch of yours. I'd like to look at the terrain for myself.'

'I think I might even be able to do better than that.' I grinned in the darkness. 'I might have set up an encounter with the njuggle, at sunset tomorrow, if it's fine. Njuggles don't like rain.'

'Ah, insider information.'

'If you picked me up here at three, say?'

He snicked his car lock open. 'It'll have to depend on how I get on. I'll phone you. I could combine it with an interview with your antiques dealer.' He swung himself inside, turned the key, and wound down the window. 'If you don't mind sitting in the car while I do that.'

'Sherlock always took Watson into the villain's lair.'

He shook his head. 'He didn't take Mycroft. Good night.'

I watched his lights dwindle along the shore road. Mycroft ... Holmes's brilliant elder brother, a quirky original thinker who pursued his own investigations and acted as a consultant when Holmes was stuck. An independent force to be reckoned with. I liked Gavin thinking of me like that.

Chapter Twenty

Tuesday 7th January

It had been a bonny day, what my Irish granny would have called a soft day, the sky clouded, but with glints of sun coming through to light up the hills and turn the wind-scoured water to polished pewter. I didn't trust it though; there was a bank of low, yellow cloud to the west, which built and built, until by midday the sky was covered, and the faint tinny smell in the air as I walked to *Khalida* for lunch meant snow. I had my soup, threw silver paper for Cat to retrieve until he got fed up, and settled in my berth for the afternoon, then put on my jacket and did a rigging inspection while I waited for Gavin. I hadn't noticed what he was driving, but it turned out to be a small red Fiesta from Bolt's Car Hire, with the warning sticker on the back window, for the benefit of natives. It had that 'new car' smell, and the plastic dashboard was spotlessly black.

It was strange to be sitting side-by-side like this. Going to Midnight Mass, we'd taken his car rather than the farm Land Rover, and his mother had sat in the front, while Kenny and I dozed behind. Last summer, Gavin had driven me back to Voe from Lerwick, up the long Kames, but we'd been on more formal terms then. Now I found myself suddenly shy, shut with him in this enclosed space. His profile was remote, a policeman's face; his brown hands on the steering wheel were square countryman's hands, made for use, not beauty, yet delicate as a seabird hovering with the wind when he was tying intricate knots in near-invisible nylon fishing line, or winding thread around wool

197

and feathers. Then he turned his head to smile, and the illusion of distance was gone. The silence became easy again.

'We've found Hughson's car. It was left in an Aberdeen sidestreet, not too far from the train station.'

'So he did mean to do a runner after all.'

'That's what we're meant to think, a second line of defence if anyone ever looked for him. The car was booked on the ferry on Saturday the seventeenth, with him as sole driver.'

'If the car was in Aberdeen, does that mean both Julie and Hubert are out of it? Neither of them would have had time to drive it there then come back for the Inverness flight, for Julie, or the ferry in Orkney, for Hubert.'

'Julie wouldn't have; Hubert might. I'm not eliminating them, but I spent the day on the Georgeson clan. John Georgeson was at home all the weekend Ivor died; alibi, his wife. However the Lerwick officer got a look at John Georgeson's last year's diary, and he was at a council meeting on the Thursday of the Gathering. The secretary even produced the minutes of it. He couldn't have disposed of the body – though that doesn't mean one of the sons didn't do it for him.'

'Or the daughter.'

'Children know their teachers. Do you think she would have?'

I made a doubtful face. 'She was tough and determined, but she was principled too. We trusted her to be fair. I think she could have done it, if it was important enough to her. I don't know how she got on with Robert John, but she talked a lot about her big brother, Laurence, the re-enactments one.'

'Laurence wasn't here the weekend Ivor was killed. He was on the mainland that whole week, going down on Friday night, with deliveries for Inverness and pick-ups in the area.'

'Which puts him right on the spot. Don't they have a drivers' log, or a spy-in-the-cab?'

'The drivers keep a diary, but the secretary couldn't find Laurence's in among last year's. That's not particularly sinister. There were several drivers who hadn't turned theirs in yet. However Serco-Northlink confirmed that a Georgeson truck whose driver was named as L. Georgeson went down on the Friday night boat, and returned from Aberdeen on the Sunday week.'

'What about brother 2?'

'Peter. The one with the office supplies business. He was down at a trade fair in Glasgow that weekend. His hotel confirmed he checked in on Friday afternoon, and ate Saturday and Sunday breakfast. We need to interview the trade fair stall holders with his photo. He had various meetings with suppliers in the central belt during the first half of the week, and he came home on Thursday's boat.'

'On the spot for disposing of the body.'

'But not here for Ivor's death, unless he did a Freeman Wills Croft alibi-creation involving rapid flights up and down again, or bribing someone else to eat his breakfast.'

'And Miss Georgeson?'

'The schools had just gone back, so she was teaching all that week. She could have gone down to the mainland on Saturday night with the car and the body, returned on the Sunday night ferry, and gone straight into school on Monday morning.'

I made a face. 'A double night on the boat.'

'The school secretary said she looked a bit under the weather.'

'So,' I said, processing this, 'she and her father could have done the murder, but not disposed of the body. Laurence and Peter couldn't have done the murder, but they were on the spot to help dispose of the body, if Miss Georgeson had brought it to them in Inverness.'

'You make it sound like a family party.'

I remembered the way Miss Georgeson'd flushed at the mention of Ivor's name. 'I don't know if she'd have killed him.'

'But would she have helped cover up for her father, if he'd killed him?'

'Oh, yes, for sure.' I had no doubt about that. It was a family which stuck together, except for Robert-John, the break-away.

'It took two officers all day on the phone, but we've finally checked up on every passenger on board the ferry back to Shetland on the Sunday and Monday. The bairns were back at school, praise be, and the main tourist season over, so there were fewer than we feared, only about a hundred and thirty.' He sighed. 'Not one is unaccounted for. Every one of them was who they said, living where they said. If someone else took Ivor's car down to the mainland, that person didn't come back by ferry.'

The clock on the dashboard read 15.20. Already the light outside was beginning to thicken, the hills in the distance turning from olive to grey. We'd come past the ruffled silver of the Loch of Girlsta, where the drowned Viking princess slept on her green island, past Sandwater Loch and the Half-way House, past Petta Water, pressed in the shape of the Giant Petta's two-toed foot. As we came up to the Whalsay ferry turnoff, Gavin made an exasperated noise. 'I'll need to stop at the Voe shop. Two minutes.'

He pulled in around the pump and went quickly through the glass door, then came out with a packet of XXXX mints in his hand. 'Njuggle bribery. You'll see.' He stuffed them into the misshapen pocket of his tweed jacket. 'Now for this loch of yours.'

We came past the Pierhead and up the hill between the houses, built when the road was a foot-worn path, so that now the asphalt track had to snake round on itself to avoid them. John Georgeson's picture windows were gold rectangles in the dusk above the hump-backed bridge. As the road climbed, we were looking down on the two substantial farmhouses in the river valley, houses like a child's drawing: a square front with two windows and a porch below, three windows above, a thread of smoke from one chimney. There was a large byre, and a scatter of Shetland ponies coralled in one corner of a field: two black, two red-and-white and one grey. Two small figures in dark jackets were working among them.

Around a bend, another, and the loch lay grey before us. Gavin pulled over to the gravel path beside the road, tucking the car in under the bank of the hill, and we got out.

The wind had fallen away completely. The loch lay mirror-still between the cradling hills. The western horizon was bathed in deep rose, and the sun's last rays spilled over the hills, dusting them with neon-pink light, and turning the water to whisky-amber. We walked briskly alongside the crash barrier that separated the single-track road from the loch, with just a metre of steep bank and pebble shore between. Gavin paused at the centre of the loch, looking out. 'I'd like to try this loch with a trout rod.'

'Brown troots,' I told him.

'Aye. And that buoy there, I'd think it's for mooring a boat just off shore for that very purpose. What's in the shed?' He nodded over at a square shed ten metres from the road, with a little jetty leading out into the water.

I shrugged. 'I'd always thought it was water works. I suppose this loch supplies Voe. I've never seen a boat at the jetty.'

Gavin looked critically at the crash barrier and shook his head. 'You'd never ask a horse to jump over that, with the drop behind it.'

'Jeemie said it came down here.'

'That's more like it,' Gavin said. He came around the end of the crash barrier and walked down to the pebble shore, stopping every two or three strides to examine the ground, looking first, then reaching a hand down. 'Here we are.'

I joined him. His finger touched a round indentation in the grass. 'A hoofprint?'

He nodded. 'And another. A small, heavy pony with a well-bred hoof, charging its way down the hill. Where will we wait until dark?'

We strolled slowly up and down the road, watching the rose light fade from the sky, until the moon came up over the north-east hill, almost a full quarter, and turned the water to molten silver. It was eerily still.

It felt an age that we waited there. I was just about to suggest we gave up when there was a clatter of stones, and then a black shape sliding and stepping down the hill towards us, head up, mane tossing. The moonlight glinted in his wild eyes. His coat sparked light, like the sea's phosphorescence on a dark night, and I could have sworn there was water weed entangled in his thick mane. He was all fire and muscle, with a broad chest and rounded quarters, heading straight at the section of road we were on, as if he was all set to mow us down. I took a step back, but Gavin stayed put, and half-spread his arms. For a moment my heart was in my mouth as I saw him being trampled under the creature's feet, and without thinking I came back to stand with him. Maybe it would think twice before attacking two of us. It was coming fast, fast, head turning from Gavin to me, as if unsure, then it jumped down over the last piece of hill and landed on the road with a clack of hooves, snorting and flinging its head up.

'Whoa there,' Gavin said, as calmly as he was on the back of one of his own garrons, and the creature jumped sideways, wheeling its quarters round, as if preparing to kick out. Gavin stood his ground, and I stood with him. It could probably smell my fear, but I was damned if it was going to see it. 'You're not fooling us, boy. Steady then.'

The dark head tossed, the eyes rolled. I could have sworn there was a spark of annoyance that we hadn't run like everyone else. It flattened its ears and bared its teeth. Gavin stepped forward. 'You don't expect us to be taken in by that, do you? Come on now.'

I'd never heard his voice coax like this. I'd defied the no-nonsense investigator and been teased by my sort-of lover. I remembered the wildcat spread along his shoulders in the wood-lined sitting room.

The creature lowered its head, sidled backwards and stood at the verge, waiting. Gavin held his hand forward, palm-up. The creature snorted again, and the wildness went out of it. It stepped forward, feet picked up as daintily as if it was in a show ring, and accepted the offered mint, tossing its head as it tried to crunch it. Gavin produced a cord from his pocket and looped it around the creature's neck, fashioning a halter out of it, and suddenly he was holding a Shetland pony, taller than most, with a thick mane and a bush of a tail, just as Jeemie had described. I advanced cautiously. The pony flung its head up again, and Gavin shooshed it, voice gentle as a lover's. 'Come on, then, this is Cass. She's no' going to hurt you. Have another mint.'

The beast gave me a sideways look and stamped one forefoot on the road with a clatter. 'We'll no keep you long,' Gavin assured it. He ran one hand down its shoulder. 'There you are, Cass, a very bonny Shetland stallion who's well used to being handled.' He put his hand to the green streamers in its mane. 'Wool, fastened with those little clips girls use for hair extensions.'

'Hello, njuggle,' I said warily. He blew a warm stream of mint-smelling breath into my face. I patted his broad neck, and felt the muscle beneath the thick coat.

'He must be only just within the breed standard,' Gavin said. 'They have to be below a certain height to be allowed in the Stud Book.' He stepped back and admired. 'Solid muscle. He'd be as strong as one of our garrons. Look at the length of that mane.' It fell to below the pony's thick neck, twisting like flowing water. The pony suddenly lifted its head, as if it could hear something, although to me the night was still graveyard silent. 'Shall we let him loose and see what he's been trained to do?' He untwisted the halter. The beast shouldered between us, charged down the little hill, splashed into the loch, picked its way confidently in the water by the shore for some fifty metres, to the next break in the hills, then scrambled out again, charged up over the hill and was out of sight.

'Did you see the way he heard something we couldn't? That's a dog whistle been used to train him, I'd say. Let's go around the hill and meet the owner.'

He strode round the bend in the road. Now the whole west side was spread before us in black and silver. Gavin pointed silently to the hill on our right and began working his way around the side of it. I knew I wouldn't be able to match his stealth on the hill, so I stayed put, listening. Thirty seconds later there was a whinny from the pony, as if it was recognising him and demanding another four-X, and giggles from a couple of girls. I followed, and found them in a little gully, hidden from the loch by the headland and from the road by the hill.

It was Inga's Vaila, of course, and her pal Rainbow, unfortunately named daughter of a family who'd taken the retro sixties fashions a bit too seriously. Now I thought about it, she lived in one of the farms in the valley, so they must have been the two figures we'd seen among the ponies.

'Were you scared, Cass?' Vaila asked.

'When I heard him coming.' I didn't want to spoil their fun by macho pretending. 'When he appeared out of the shadows on the top of the hill, he looked really eerie in the moonlight, and I was definitely scared when he came charging towards us.'

'You didn't look scared.'

'You couldn't see me shaking.' Close up, his coat still glinted in the moonlight. 'Have you put glitter on him?'

'Glitter hair gel. It doesn't hurt him.'

'What's his name?' Gavin asked Rainbow.

'Redsand Yahbini. It means star. He's five, and he was passed for a stallion last summer.'

'It's good to see a Shetland this tall with strong bone. We have a couple of Highlands.'

She began bombarding him with questions. I turned to Vaila. 'How often have you done this?'

She giggled again. 'No' very often, for fear he'd get hurt on the road. Just when we ken there's someone coming along on foot.'

'How did you train him?'

'It started with them being on the hill.' The herd running loose, she meant, bounded only by the fences of the whole scattald, which meant in this case that they could be up to seven miles away. 'It was a right pain when we wanted to go riding. They'd come when they heard us call, but we had to get sight of them for them to hear us. So we thought of a dog whistle. We'd find them and whistle, and when they came we'd feed them. Soon all we had to do was blow the whistle and they charged across the hill like a wild west stampede.'

I could imagine it, the summer hills pine-green with heather, the piston hooves thudding, the manes tossing as the ponies charged towards them.

'Then Izzy, she's the drama teacher that visits all the schools, well, she came with this play, *Kirsty and da Snarravoe Njuggle*. Rainbow said she could train one of her horses to be a njuggle and charge into the water, and we thought what fun it would be to gluff Jeemie when he was staggering home from the pub. Yab's the biggest, and he's black, so we worked with him. Njuggles are supposed to like mills, so we tried at first by the brig, you ken, at

Mill House, but then Councillor Georgeson cleared us, so we came up to the loch. I'd stand behind the hill here and whistle, and Rainbow rode Yab down and along the water edge. Once he'd got that idea we tried him on his own. He learned really quickly. Then we had a sleepover one Friday night, and we gluffed Jeemie.' She was laughing so much at the memory that she could hardly speak. 'Honest, Cass, you shoulda seen his face. He ran for his car as if a demon was after him.'

'The Njuggle's Nest,' I said. 'He's using you as publicity.'

Vaila giggled. 'The funniest thing was, he painted the sign himself, and he asked Rainbow if he could come and draw her stallion, as that looked the most like what he saw. I wasn't sure if he was being stupid, or if he was laughing at us.'

Laughing, I suspected, but I didn't say so. 'Has anyone else seen him?'

'A group of boys from the school, when they were out kale-casting. They were boasting in the playground of coming to look.' She grinned, white teeth glinting in the moonlight. 'One of them was Drew, you ken, that comes to the sailing, and he was that scared when Yab came over the hill that he musta been back at Voe by the time Yab got to the loch. They all ran like rabbits.' Her voice was joyous with satisfaction. 'There was a lot less big talk in the playground for a month after that.'

Yahbini had his proper halter on now and was looking round and fidgeting his feet like a bored Peerie Charlie. Gavin swung onto his back and led the way back to the road where we'd left the car. His feet couldn't be far off the ground, but the pony didn't seem in the least worried by an adult's weight.

'Shetland ponies are stronger than any other breed, for their size,' Rainbow told me. 'They used them to pull carts in mines, after Parliament made a law to stop them using children. That's when the ponies became valuable, up here.' I suspected that she'd become a horsey encyclopaedia with any encouragement; but she changed tack. 'The policeman said we weren't breaking any laws. We ken no' to do this when there are cars about.'

We said goodbye to the lasses and Yahbini at the car. Gavin dismounted reluctantly. 'Let me know when you have his first foals.'

They scrambled up on his back, Vaila behind Rainbow, and clattered off down the road. We sat in the car for a bit, windows open, letting them get home before we came past them with noise and sight-spoiling light.

'Well done,' Gavin said, as the knock of hooves had died away.

'I'd have run if you hadn't looked so sure that he'd stop.'

'The hoofprints proved it was a real pony, trained by someone, which meant it would probably respond to commands. I was pretty sure it would swerve rather than knock me down.' He turned his head to smile at me. 'Don't go trying that with a real wild horse.'

'No fear. Did you think Jeemie was behind it? I did.'

'From what you said, I thought he'd had a genuine fright, but was cashing in on it with the shop's name, and the sign board, and telling the story ... ergo, he doesn't have anything hidden in or near the loch, because he'd be trying to scare people away from it, and njuggles are just too intriguing to be scary. The girl – is she really called Rainbow?'

I nodded gloomily. 'In France, you're only allowed to call children by a name from an approved list.'

'She said a few people had come to look, but she didn't want to release the stallion if there was any chance of a car coming along, so not many have seen him. A pity. He was spectacular in the moonlight, with his coat glinting like that, and his mane and tail flying. A real beauty.'

'But it was just a fun. Nobody put them up to it. It was a challenge to see if he'd do it, and to scare the boys in their class. So the loch and the njuggle are just red herrings. Red ponies.'

'They are, but I still agree with you that there's something funny about Jeemie's business. It may just be delicacy on his part, of course, showing his rings only to tourists.'

'He showed them to me.'

'Because you asked. Magnie only knew he had them because he'd seen him showing them to a tourist.'

'Delicacy, because they've been sold by someone local, and other people would recognise the ring and gossip?'

'It could be that.' He turned the key and put the car into gear. 'Let's go and ask.'

Chapter Twenty-two

'Your girl came to talk to me,' Gavin said. He pulled out into the road and we drove on. 'Just after one, so I suppose it was her lunch hour. Very tearful and repentant. I said I wouldn't tell her new boyfriend if she hadn't killed Ivor, and she assured me that she hadn't.'

'Did you believe her?'

'I don't see her hauling a body about, but she could well have been a horsey little girl.'

'Her brother works with Co-op dray horses.'

'Does he, now.' He was silent for a moment, negotiating the turn onto the single-track road leading to The Njuggle's Nest. The road was dark on each side of us; far below, the moon glinted on the water. 'She didn't say who the boyfriend was?'

He didn't answer, which I took as 'Yes, but I can't tell you.' Fair enough. I was sorry for Donna, though; I knew what it was like being afraid of your past returning to haunt you.

'Now she's going to spend the rest of her life in fear somebody else'll tell the new man's family about her affair with Ivor – and in the end somebody will.' I looked straight ahead, into the darkness, where the headlands of Voxter and Cole, the dark bulk of Linga, were black against the silver water, and was glad Gavin knew about Alain's death. The headlights caught the bars of the gate; I nipped out to open it, and we bumped down the gravelly drive to the house.

Jeemie was in. The lights shone gold from each side of the porch, and I could hear the murmur of Radio Shetland

209

in the kitchen. Gavin knocked on the door; a moment's pause, then the radio was turned down, and a shadow crossed the window. I tried not to listen as Gavin explained who he was, and was beckoned in, but my window had been down, and this was one of these cars which needed the engine running before I could put it up again. I snuggled down in my seat and prepared to hear.

The lights went on in the shop. I could see Gavin in front of the counter and Jeemie behind. He got out the tray of rings, and Gavin indicated the clasped hands of Julie's grandmother's ring. 'Can you remember anything about the person who sold it to you?'

'Well.' Jeemie fished in his desk for a blue-bound book. 'I've not had that one long.'

I sat up, frowning. If Ivor had given Donna the ring, it was way back before August. Why had she waited to get rid of it? Answer: she heard a rumour of Ivor's death, and saw 'the girl detective' in the restaurant, looking at her.

'The gimmel ring ... yes, here it is. Victorian gimmel ring, gold with garnet heart. The name I have is a Caroline Kingsley, at 34, King Harald Street. She brought in several things. This gold chain, and a bracelet, and a few trinkets.' He bent forward to lift up items. 'This one, and this.'

Gavin fished in his sporran for his black notebook. 'Caroline Kingsley, 34, King Harald Street. Do you remember what she looked like?'

'She was a south-spoken lass, dark haired, and bonny the way they all are now, with a face made-up like one of these porcelain dolls.'

'South spoken? English?'

Jeemie shook his head. 'Oh, I'm no good at accents. Scottish, I think, but I couldna be more particular.'

'What height and build?'

Jeemie shook his head. 'Medium height, I think, and skinny.'

'Clothes?'

'Oh, I don't remember. A black jacket, jeans. Fashionable looking.'

'And when was this?'

'Oh, I mind that fine, for I was only open a couple of days between Christmas and New Year. It was last Wednesday.'

'The day I arrived home,' I reminded Gavin. '*Before* she saw me in the restaurant. And the next day someone tried to gas me.'

'But then she could be like Hughson's wife, Julie. Christmas is a time for wiping the slate clean. Throw out the letters, get rid of the reminders.'

'Then why not do it before Christmas?'

'Work, maybe. It's too far to do in her lunch hour, and he'd be closed by the end of her day.' He was silent for a moment, frowning in the green lights of the dashboard. 'The description was very vague.'

'It fitted Donna.'

'Not in any meaningful way. Dark, made-up, medium height, skinny, Scottish accent, fashionable black jacket and jeans. Shall we stand on Commercial Street one Saturday morning and see if we can pick her out from that?' I saw what he meant. 'And what's striking about Donna, if it was her, is that fragile air. She was invented for knights in armour. No man would miss that.'

'So you think he was making up a description?'

'It's possible that this Caroline Kingsley found herself short of money at Christmas, and sold an old ring she didn't wear, and other bits and pieces. He's the obvious place in Shetland to buy it. But there're two minor snags.' Gavin rolled smoothly to a halt in the middle of the T-

211

junction onto the main road. 'Brae and Frankie's, or back to the town?'

'Oh, Frankie's. What're your difficulties?'

'Well, I stayed at 34, King Harald Street, on my first visit. It's a very comfortable B&B.'

'Maybe she was here on holiday.'

'You don't take your family jewellery with you on holiday, on the off chance you might want to sell it.'

I had to agree. 'Difficulty two?'

'I don't like her name. Did you read *The Water Babies* when you were little?'

I shook my head. 'We had a cartoon video. What has that to do with Caroline Kingsley?'

'It was written by Charles Kingsley. Earlier on the page there was a Sam Boulter who'd sold a Victorian fob watch. Samuel Butler was a writer too – *Erewhon* and *The Way of All Flesh*.'

'Ohhh,' I said, enlightened. I remembered the shelves of old books, with their dark red leather covers and ornate gold decorations. 'You think Jeemie is pulling a fast one?'

'The page before had a Madge L. Feint. Margaret Oliphant was one of the most popular rivals to Dickens.' He added, apologetically, 'The Inverness library has a lunchtime readers' group that specialises in Victorian literature.'

'So he's getting this stuff from a provenance he doesn't want to reveal.'

'Did I see in the paper that you've had a rise in burglaries recently?' He pulled in to the red-gravel verge. 'This won't take a moment.' He got out his mobile and turned away slightly. 'Freya – good. I've had a look at The Njuggle's Nest, and I wonder if we're looking at receiving stolen goods. The names and addresses in his books are suspect ... yes. See what you can dig up. Small pieces of jewellery thought to be lost somewhere, and reported a while after they went missing. Thanks.'

He snicked the phone off, and put the car back into gear. The mussel floats of Olna Firth bobbed like serpent humps on the silver water, then we were between the banks that enclosed the double road. In spring they'd be yellow with daffodils planted by Community Service folk, but now the headlights spotlit bedraggled tussocks of fawn grass.

'Well?' I said at last.

'What would you say security is like in Shetland houses?'

I looked blankly at him. 'Security?

'Burglar alarms, double locks, catches on windows?'

'Good gracious!'

'Your dad's, for example.'

'Definitely no burglar alarms. The front door might have a mortice lock as well as the Yale. The window catches – well, just the usual sort, the long bar with the holes in it.'

'So it would be easy for anyone to come into the house, if they knew, say, that your dad was off on business for a fortnight.'

'Any house in Shetland, if you could avoid the neighbours seeing you. And anyone in the gossip chain would know who was away.'

We came out into the open again. The lights at Busta shone over to us as we came past the little bay at Sparl, then winked out again as the houses surrounded us. We came through the first half of Brae and turned smoothly into Frankie's Fish and Chip shop. A comforting odour of frying filled the air.

It was only half a dozen miles further to Muckle Roe. I closed the door and looked at him over the roof of the car. 'Shall I phone Dad and Maman and see if they've eaten yet?'

It was the first time I'd seen him look dismayed. He gave a quick glance down at his comfortable jacket and green kilt.

'Better still, let's not give them notice, let's just turn up. Otherwise Maman will terrify you with full Callas make-up and her best jewellery, and the sitting room will be so immaculate we'll be scared to sit down.'

He didn't answer, just stood there looking out across the glimmering water, face downcast, as if he'd wanted his scarlet dress kilt and the black jacket with Prince Charlie's button to meet my parents. I struggled to express the vague feeling in my mind.

'I want them to meet you. This you.' Damn it, I wasn't good at this kind of words. I kept making the effort. 'You were being DI Macrae when you met Dad, and you haven't met Maman at all. I want them to see the you that just blandished a njuggle, the countryman who can handle a boat.' I was running out of words. I finished in a burst: 'If they see you in full Highland dress they'll never believe you want me.'

The words hung in the air. I could have bitten my tongue off, asking him to sacrifice his pride to save mine. My cheeks flushed scarlet; and then his hand came over the roof of the car, his fingers curled around mine, gentle as a ripple touching the shore.

'Phone away.' Now he was smiling again. 'We'll turn up scruffily together, and whatever scolding you get will be on your own terms.'

I considered that as he waved me in front of him into the chippy. I had to concede he was right. If he'd been in full dress, Maman would have expected me to live up to his magnificent swirl of scarlet pleats, the stocking dagger with the winking gold Cairngorm in the handle. Here, now, we matched. I'd get told off for arriving without warning, or not inviting ourselves to tea, but the long-running battle of clothes would be left at truce. I fished out my mobile and called Maman.

'*Salut.* Gavin and I are just at Frankie's. We're going to

get a fish supper, shall we get for you and Dad too, and bring it round?'

There was a half-beat pause, then a wail. 'Oh, Cassandre, you must do everything the wrong way round! No, no, do not get fish and chips. I have a casserole in the oven. You will have to wait until it is cooked. Dessert, I have a tarte tatin in the freezer. Stop at the Co-op and buy some cream.'

'We can't stay all evening,' I warned. 'I left Cat alone on *Khalida*.'

'The casserole will be ready in not less than an hour.'

'And we're not dressed for a formal meal.'

'I think that what you are saying,' said Maman severely, 'is that you wish me to meet your young man over a paper of greasy chips and fish in batter eaten with the fingers. Will you permit at least that I offer him a cup of tea?'

Greasy was a libel on Frankie's. 'He'd prefer a cup of your best French coffee.'

'Then your father will have a steak pie supper, and I will have mussels without chips, and once this ice is broken you will bring him for a proper French lunch on Sunday.'

I turned to Gavin in English. From the quirk at the corner of his mouth he had a working knowledge of French. 'Would you be available for a proper French lunch on Sunday?'

'I would be delighted, if work permits.'

'He's a policeman, his hours are worse than a sailor's,' I relayed to Maman, 'but he would be delighted, if his work permits. See you in twenty minutes.'

The fleas jumped in my belly as we waited in Frankie's for our fish to be cooked. Twenty minutes was time for Maman to get on full dress. I didn't trust her not to give Gavin the third degree on his family background and promotion prospects, and if she didn't, then Dad might. It

215

could all be horribly embarrassing.

Gavin put a hand on my shoulder. 'It can't be worse than Kenny cross-questioning you about Shetland cattle.'

My ignorance of the native cow had been exposed most horribly. They were black and white, smaller than normal cows, and there was a stuffed one in the museum; that was my limit. 'It'll do you good,' I retorted, 'to be on the wrong end of the interrogation, for once, and without even being able to tie trout flies.'

He tapped the tin in his pocket. 'Your father might be delighted to talk about something so uncontroversial.'

I gave him a glum look. 'I've never taken anyone home before. I don't know how they'll behave.'

His grey eyes were smiling reassurance. 'I'd never taken anyone home before either, and you fitted in straight away.'

'But you fit in your home. I'm not sure I fit in mine.'

'Then we can not fit together. Anyway, I want to meet your Maman. There was a know-it-all officer on the longship case who came back from a session with her looking as if he'd been put through a mangle.' He grinned. 'There was coffee-break talk of sending her an anonymous bouquet.'

We drove past the marina and onto the Muckle Roe road, with me clasping the four warm blue and white boxes in a wonderful smell of batter and vinegar; past the white crowstepped gables of Busta House, over the bridge, along the single-track road, the headlights picking out the white lines on each side, and into the gravel space before our house. Gavin turned off the engine. 'Well, are you all set?'

'*A la lanterne,*' I said heroically, and got out just as the front door opened in a flood of golden light.

Twenty minutes was all Maman had needed. She'd put on dressed-down wide-legged trousers and a polo-neck pullover in her trademark black and white. There were pearl studs in her ears. She held out her hand to Gavin. 'Lieutenant Macrae, I am enchanted.'

'I'm honoured to meet you.' Gavin managed a little continental bow over her hand. 'I have several of your recordings.'

She gave a deprecating flutter of one slim hand, and ushered us into the kitchen, where the table had already been laid with mats and cutlery, to make sure that the despised chips were at least eaten with knives and forks. *Les Anglais do not take food seriously* ... 'You know my husband, of course. Dermot, this is Gavin.'

Dad was wearing a visibly just-ironed shirt. While he and Gavin shook hands, I dumped the stack of blue and white boxes on the table. 'Mussels, Maman – steak pie – muckle fish – peerie fish.'

Maman whisked a stack of china from the oven, indicated Gavin and I to opposite sides of the table, and dealt the plates out. There was merciful silence for a few minutes while we sorted out whose box was which, and Dad opened a bottle of wine. 'A nice Loire white this. I got a case of it when I was over at one of your mother's concerts during the summer.'

'Chenonceau,' Maman said. '*Hippolyte et Aricie.* I played Diana, a good role to sing, but the costumier's head-dress –' She lifted her hands to above-head level, and spread them out like a stag's antlers. 'It was as big as this, a crescent moon with stars dangling from it. One would have said Turandot, or something from a children's show.'

It felt odd to be eating fish and chips with a knife and fork, here in the house, rather than aboard *Khalida,* with Cat wolfing his share at my feet. 'I hope Cat's okay for this long on his own,' I said.

Dad made a visible effort. 'You'll be used to animals, Gavin, from what Cass was telling us.'

'Yes, sir, we have a farm.' He managed to make the 'sir' sound like respect, rather than police. 'Though it's my brother Kenny who is the animals man. I'm not home enough; I have a flat in Inverness through the week. I do a bit with the stalking ponies.'

'Do you have a lot of stalking?'

Gavin spread his hands. 'Nothing compared to what there was in my grandfather's day. The owner of the estate comes up for a fortnight and culls the number required, but he's not really keen.'

'But you get the venison.'

'Oh, yes, there's never any shortage of that.'

It was stilted, but at least everyone was trying. I could see by the approving glances Maman cast his way from under her mascara-dark lashes that she liked him; I wasn't sure about Dad, who had a Catholic Irishman's distrust of the police.

'My mother grew up on a farm,' he said now, 'before she married my father and he took her to Dublin. She always missed it. We'd go back there every summer sure as fate and help with the harvest.'

'It's a lot of work. We have hay, just enough for the animals, silage, and the vegetable garden. That's my mother's side of the farm, and the poultry of course.'

'It was lovely,' I told Maman. 'Fresh milk every morning, and bottled raspberries, just like Mamy's in France.' I turned to Gavin. 'We used to go to Maman's parents for Easter and October. They had a farm near Poitiers, well, a smallholding, with a cow, and chickens, and being France, they could grow just about anything, pumpkins, courgettes, even tomatoes outdoors.'

That seemed about it for the farming topic. There was another silence, broken only by the scrape of knife on china. I was just trying to think of an innocuous topic when Maman dived in, graceful as a swooping tern, and with as much of a splash on the water. 'Did Cass tell you that Dermot and I rendered a visit to Monsieur Georgeson with her?'

I choked. Before I'd recovered enough to say that Gavin didn't appreciate our efforts to get in his way of catching a murderer, he'd replied, very smoothly, 'She did. What did you make of him, madame?'

'Ambitious. He would play Macbeth. He has built up his business from almost nothing and now it is the largest haulage firm in Shetland. He has done well, and now he expects that all his children should do well too. His daughter is adjunct director of the Anderson High School.'

'Vice-principal,' I translated helpfully.

'Expected, it seems, to take over should the director take early retirement.'

'Not much chance of that right now,' Dad said. 'The authority's cutting its expenses right down. Once the windfarm's built, of course, it'll be different. We'll be able to expand again, with that money flowing in.'

Gavin had told me that the tide of opinion was turning against windfarms on the mainland. I saw him thinking it again, but his long mouth remained shut.

'The oldest son is a part of his firm,' Maman continued, 'and the second son has a building supplies business, also very successful, according to Monsieur Georgeson. I think he would not be content if the business of a son of his was declared to the receivers.'

'There's a difference,' Dad insisted, 'between being not content and going on to murder his partner.'

Maman spent too much time in the world of ancient Greece to be convinced by that. 'It was his youngest son, and that was the man who has brought him to ruin.'

'He should declare bankruptcy and start again. That's the businesslike option.'

Maman shook her head. 'He will not do it. It is businesslike, but he is not that sort of a businessman. Now, does that make his father's motive more plausible or less?'

'More,' I said. 'If Ivor Hughson ran off, leaving Robert John in charge, it could all be hushed up quietly. As you said, Dad, he can get out of it himself, and nobody much the wiser.' Except, of course, the whole community; John Georgeson ought to know that. 'That is, assuming he can be made to disappear in a way that he never turns up again, and there's no hue and cry after him. An injection of cash into the firm –'

'Robert-John wouldn't take it,' Dad said. 'I'm certain of that. He feels he's the family failure.'

'I think that could make Georgeson senior's motive stronger. His son won't take his help, so he has to act in some other way.'

Dad gave me that parental 'pot calling kettle black' look. 'There's nothing you can do about children who are too stubborn to accept help.' He turned to Gavin, ganging up on me. 'Have you noticed a touch of immovability about our Cassie yet?'

'She certainly knows her own mind,' Gavin agreed.

I finished my last crunchy chip and stood to clear the plates. 'I'll take that as a compliment.'

Maman stood too and brought the fruit bowl over to the centre of the table. 'A fruit, a yoghurt? Sure, we have cheese too. In the bell, Cass.'

It was, of course, a proper haul of best French cheese, straight from the market, followed with a crunchy apple from my cousins' farm. 'Next time I come up,' Gavin said, 'I must bring you one of my mother's crowdie cakes.'

'You must visit,' Maman said. 'Not for investigating. Why do not you and Cassandre come over to France for one of my spring shows? The Poitevin is very pretty then, with the first leaves, and the woods full of *primevère* – primroses, no, not the ones you have here, primroses on a tall stalk, that smell of butter, and the violets everywhere, and the leaves of *peupliers*.' She sketched a tall, thin tree with her hands. 'They are almost purple, transparent. And sure it is warmer, already like summer here. This cold, brrrr, and the wind that never ceases. I think, Dermot, we are needing a holiday.'

'As soon as this review is over,' Dad said.

We drank our coffee through in the sitting room, with its dark-green Chinese carpet and Maman's grand piano, then I rose. 'Maman, Dad, thank you, but we'd better get going. Cat's on his own.'

'I have work too,' Gavin said.

We exited in a general shower of thanks and see you on Sunday. I collapsed in the front seat of the car, feeling like I'd been through a mangle. 'Well done.'

'A pity I'm driving,' Gavin said. 'I'd have liked that stiff whisky your dad offered.' He gave me a sideways smile. 'I take it that I go swimming if I call you Cassie aboard *Khalida*.'

'You do.'

'And I can wear my full Highland dress on Sunday?'

'Dagger and all. It'll be a proper French lunch, so don't bother about breakfast, and be prepared for it to last at least three hours.'

'Do you wear a pretty dress?'

'*The* pretty dress.' I only had one, and he'd already seen it. I wondered if I should be buying another. I might consult Maman on that one. Dresses weren't my thing.

The lights were on in Magnie's cottage, down by the shore. I remembered Magnie's offer of 'a special dram'. Someone's moonshine ... 'If you can keep your policeman hat off, I can get you a dram. Turn right here.'

Chapter Twenty-three

We bumped down the gravel track. Magnie's was a traditional cottage, the same shape as a Viking longhouse, and probably built on the foundations of one. The whitewash was so thick that I could use the gleam from it for navigation on a moonlit night; the door was painted blue each year as he was doing his wooden skiff, and the house was surrounded by sheds which gave a general impression of drunk men holding each other up. For now, the fruit bushes between the white stone paths were bare twigs, and the hens which usually clucked round the door must be shut up in their house at the back. I pushed the door open, stepped over the rubber boots, and gave the traditional greeting: 'Aye, aye, is anybody home?'

Magnie was in the kitchen, wearing his at-home gansey, circa 1970, blue pattern and white hoops with the white stained tobacco-colour with peat smoke, and a hole in each elbow. His scarlet slippers were bright against the coco-matting floor. The cream-coloured Rayburn glowed in one corner, with the kettle hissing gently on its black top. His Siamese cat was sitting on the table, very upright, her large ears flicking round at us, sapphire eyes haughty; stripey Tigger took up most of the two-person couch. 'We're just done a meal with Maman and Dad,' I said, 'and Gavin is needing a dram.'

'Ah,' Magnie said. He nodded at Gavin. 'You're off duty?'

'In so far as a policeman ever is,' Gavin agreed cautiously. 'Just a driver's dram. It wouldn't look good if the visiting DI failed the breathalyser.' He sat down beside

Tigger, and stretched out a hand to the Siamese, who ignored it. 'You kept her then.'

'It took a while for her to settle down. Pitched battles, there were, and while Tigger was too much of a gentleman to hurt a lady, she had no qualms about going for him. Now the pair of them can sit in the same room. We'll see them on the same couch yet, come the February blizzards.' He reached three glasses down from the dresser and went through into the back porch. 'I'm given up the drink, but I'll join you with this one.' He returned with the half-filled glasses. 'Lay your lip to that, and tell me what you think.'

It smelt good, with a hint of the peatiness of my favourite Laphroaig, and the taste was smooth. 'Nice.'

Gavin drank, nodded in appreciation, and took another sip. His eyes went up to Magnie's. 'That's very good.' He took a third sip. 'I don't recognise it. Ardmore, maybe, some kind of special edition?' He took another long inhale. 'Twelve years old at least.'

'Fifteen,' I said. Things were falling into place. I looked across at Magnie, and he nodded. Ivor, working in the distillery, and John Georgeson, with his storeroom. John Georgeson's annoyance at south firms exploiting the Shetland name. 'Peerie creditors are always the last to get paid, when a firm goes under. All those Shetland folk who'd bought a bottle of whisky would just have lost their money when the receivers moved in. Unless ... unless a couple of folk got together, one inside the brewery with lists of who'd ordered what, and access to the labels, and one outside it, with a warehouse to store the barrel the local folk had paid for until the fifteen years were up.'

I saw Gavin's face as he digested this, and made him a grimace of apology. I'd never expected to put him in so awkward a position. I'd thought Magnie had got hold of someone's special home brew, illegal but not related to this case. Now it seemed we had John Georgeson and Ivor Hughson in partnership, and John Georgeson had more to lose if Ivor had threatened to spill the beans. Perhaps his death had been a case of rogues falling out …

'It's no' legal,' Magnie agreed, 'but it's no' theft either.' He sat down in his armchair on the other side of the Rayburn, and looked straight at Gavin. 'Those folk had paid for their bottles, and they got them.'

I could see Gavin considering the legal argument of the firm's assets, and deciding not to bother. The simple justice appealed to the countryman in him. 'How did they get them?'

Magnie rose again and brought through a bottle. Lunna Bridge Whisky, the label said, in blue, with what looked like John Georgeson's house and bridge drawn below. 'It just arrived at the door, one day when I was out. No invoice, no note.'

Gavin settled back on the couch, patted his lap for Tigger, and took another sip. 'It's very good. I'll look out for it when the stuff the receivers got comes on the market.'

Magnie lifted his glass. 'Your good health, both of you.'

ᚴ

As we came out into the cold dark, the sky was thick with clouds, the moon hidden; the wind had freshened from the north. I saw Magnie's head go up. 'You might want to make good time back to Scalloway.'

'Snow coming,' I agreed. I hoped Gavin's hired car had decent tyres. We'd only got as far as the Co-op when there was a drumming on the car roof, and hail bounced in the headlights: the snow laying a ground for itself. I craned over my shoulder to see our parallel lines of black in the bobbled white. Not deep yet, but there was another half hour between us and *Khalida*, and then Gavin had to go over the hill to Lerwick. I sat silent, letting him concentrate on the road.

The houses of Voe slipped by. The dark shoulders of the Lang Kames on each side were ghostly with hail. Then the first flakes swirled across the windscreen, and soon we were enclosed in whirling white. Gavin slowed down to twenty, fifteen. There was another car half a mile ahead of us; by the time we reached where it had been, its black tracks had been swallowed by the snow, leaving only the powdery white.

Outside the window, the flakes thickened and slid down the glass, leaving it water-clear. Gavin snicked the windscreen wipers to double speed and slowed to a crawl between the white-blotched banks. His brows were creased; he leant forwards, eyes searching for the road ahead. Sandwater, Catfirth, the loch of Girlsta, Wadbister. The flakes thinned. We came at last into Tingwall, between fields iced Christmas cake white. Gavin flicked a look at the narrow valley road, and remained on the main highway. Six miles to go.

We came around the final bend at last and down the long hill into Scalloway. Snow patched the road and verges, the wind scouring the flakes to create sculpted drifts between bare patches. The heather was tussocked white. Below us, the sandstone-red castle stood out above its pier. Gavin came smoothly along the main street and slid to a halt outside the marina gate. 'I'll get back to Lerwick before I'm snowed in here. Good night, *beannachd leat.*'

The cold air stung as I got out of the warm car. I slithered along the pontoon, undid the padlock, and swung quickly aboard *Khalida*. My first thought was to start the engine, then I fed Cat, apologised for leaving him so long (though he seemed to have been happily curled up in my bunk), drew the curtains against the sliding flakes, put on an extra jumper, made a cup of drinking chocolate, and sat down on the couch to consider. By now the cabin was warm from the putting engine, and the glow of the oil lamp flickered on my varnished wood and the books on the shelf above my berth.

I felt as if I'd learned too much. Jeemie's trade in stolen goods, and his connection with Ivor; Magnie's whisky. If Ivor had known Jeemie was receiving stolen goods, he might have threatened to tell the police – but why? And if he was implicated in delivering the whisky to the folk who'd bought it, he couldn't finger John Georgeson without exposing himself.

It was after nine, and it had been a long day. I switched my detective head off and began boiling the kettle for my hot water bottle. I was just about to fill it when the marina gate clanged. The pontoon rocked to footsteps silenced by snow. Then there was a sharp crack, like a firework. It sounded so close that for a second I thought something had broken on *Khalida*'s foredeck. Ripples lapped against her bow, as if the pontoon had moved. Then I realised it was a gunshot. I peeked around the edge of the curtain.

The swirling snow had stopped. The half-moon shone on whiteness: the slatted pontoon, the boats under their smooth blankets, the shore washed by gleaming water, with a dark line where the salt stopped the snow from lying. The boating club roof was blanketed four inches thick.

There was nobody between *Khalida* and the marina gate. I crossed the cabin and looked out of the other side. Darkness had dimmed the bright colours of the New Street houses; above them, each castle turret wore a white cap. Nothing, though I could hear ripples still. I eased the forehatch up and looked out. Two metres away, in the centre of the walkway, a black shape sprawled at the end of a line of footprints.

He was still moving, arms clutched around his chest,

legs clenched in a protective spasm. There was nobody else in sight, just the line of boats between their pontoon fingers, and the only sound was my engine chugging away, and the splurt of water with each piston thrust. I reached back for my phone and jacket, swung out through the foredeck hatch, crossed the guardrails, and lowered myself down onto the walkway. *Breathing, blood, consciousness.* Movement meant breath. I knelt beside him. The silvery light was too dim to show blood on his dark jacket, but I could feel it wet under my fingers, and he breathed with a horrid bubbling noise that suggested the bullet had gone into a lung. A sucking wound. The air smelled of fireworks. *Reassure the casualty. Ask permission.* 'I'm Cass,' I said, 'I've done first aid training. You've been shot. Just lie still. Is it okay to help you?'

The man groaned and made a tiny nodding movement of the head.

There was a plastic bag among the stuff in my pocket. 'I think you've been shot in the lung. I'm going to slide this bag over the wound.' I turned the bag clean-side out and lifted his jacket, gansey, shirt, T-shirt, just enough to slide it in over the wound, then smoothed them down again, and twisted his jacket hem until it was bandage tight. 'Now you hold that there, while I call for help.'

Nobody dialled 999 in Shetland; it got you a call centre in Inverness, where you had to spell every name twice. I'd learned the Gilbert Bain Hospital number phoning to ask about Anders, last summer. I punched it and spoke clearly. 'I need an ambulance fast, to Scalloway, at the marina beside the boating club. A man has been shot in the chest. I think it's a sucking wound.'

Bless the woman, she didn't waste time asking for my name or address, but got on to the cavalry first. I sat with one hand clamping the man's clasped hands down, keeping the precious air in his lungs, and in less than a minute a paramedic called me back. I told him what I could, and turned back to the man. 'The ambulance is coming. Hang in there.'

'Cass.' His voice was so faint that I had to lean over to hear him. He turned his head to me, and the light caught his face, so that I saw him at last: Hubert Inkster. He spoke urgently, with the last of his strength: '*Bridge.* Saw her.' Then his head rolled away from me, and he jack-knifed into a ball around his shattered chest. I laid my hand on his neck pulse, counting the beats and praying for help to come soon. The ambulance would pass Gavin, picking his way between fans of snow. A gunshot wound; the ambulance might automatically notify the police. I felt horribly vulnerable, knowing there was someone with a gun close at hand. Not very close; only Hubert's footsteps trailed from the marina gate. I scanned the dark sea wall, the corner of the boating club, the whitened shore, for signs of movement. Nothing. But the person who'd shot him must have seen that he wasn't dead, heard me calling for help. My scarlet jacket, his black one, made us targets against the snow, but I daren't move him to safety.

His pulse was slowing. He needed oxygen in his lungs, warmth, blood, the neon-lit expertise of the hospital. I took off my jacket and laid it over him. 'Stay awake, Hubert. They'll be here soon. Hubert, stay awake.' But he didn't speak again.

At last, blue flashing lights reflected off the snow-covered hills that cradled the road to Lerwick; then the lights themselves came around the corner and inched towards me, several sets, an ambulance followed by police cars. They came down the hill past the quarry, and were gone for a long moment in the valley. Behind the fisheries college, an engine started up; a dark car slid along behind the shore wall, sidled between the Shetland Bus shed and Norway House and disappeared into the cluster of streets. At last the blue lights re-appeared, breasting the hill into the village and descending to the little roundabout. I followed the reflection of them as they passed between the houses. They came out at last, splitting the night with their clear brightness, coming steadily along the sea road towards us.

'The ambulance is here now,' I said to Hubert. His breathing was slower, slower, as if every centimetre of air burned as it went into his lungs. 'Hang in there.' Then, just as I was rising to let them in, the clouds went over the moon again. I heard him draw a horrible, rattling breath in the coldly glimmering dark. '*Bridge*,' he repeated, and died.

Wed 8th January

High Water at Scalloway UT	*01.54, 1.4m*
Low Water	*07.42, 0.9 m*
High Water	*14.05, 1.5m*
Low Water	*20.35, 0.7m*
Moonset	*00.46*
Sunrise	*09.03*
Moonrise	*11.05*
Sunset	*17.11*

Moon waxing crescent.

Der lippenings from da gaet, but nane from da grave.
There are expectations on the path, but none in the grave –
death is final.

232

Chapter Twenty-three

The first officer at the gate sat me in a police car while the paramedics worked on Hubert. I knew it was useless. He had died there, with my hand on his neck and my jacket spread over him. I was cold with sitting there, my jeans snow-soaked, shivering with shock, and I felt sick. I'd had enough of this police business. In the past year, I'd seen a lifetime's worth of bodies. I extended my palms for their cotton-wool swabs and tape, then huddled a white cotton blanket around me and listened to the feet tramping on the pontoon. When Gavin opened the car door, I didn't want to look at him.

'You're okay?'

I nodded.

'We're going to have to search *Khalida*, in the morning.' His voice was carefully neutral. 'The only other footprints on the pontoon are yours. We have to check you don't have the gun. Can you sleep somewhere else, tonight?'

I understood. Because of him, I had to be proved innocent. I made my voice as neutral as his. 'I'll stay aboard *Sule*, with Reidar. You'll need to let me call Cat, and get me some food for him.'

Slowly, I uncurled myself and came out of the police car. Gavin put out a hand towards me, then drew it back. Outside, the moonlight had been replaced with floodlighting, rigged up on a cable from a van with a chugging generator, and the silence was broken by the crackling of police radios. It was bitterly cold.

Then I heard Reidar's voice, questioning, and the

paramedic, authoritative: 'Just stay on board your own boat, please, sir. There's been an accident.'

'Cass?' another voice said sharply.

'Anders!' I wanted to hurl myself into his arms, back into my security of sails and engines and voyages far from land, far from the police world. 'I'm here, I'm fine.'

They both turned towards me. There was a police officer at the head of the gangplank, blocking the marina gate. Beyond him, Hubert's prints stretched along the pontoon to where two officers were busy erecting a white tent over his body.

'Don't worry, Cass,' Reidar called. 'We will be with you in five minutes.' A brief conversation, then they lowered *Sule*'s rubber dinghy on its davits. I watched them row for the slip, beach the dinghy, walk the ten yards towards me. I met them half-way and flung myself into Anders' arms. He closed them reassuringly around me. He smelt of engines and salt and Norwegian aquavit. I clung to him for a moment, then stepped back. 'Have you just arrived?'

'Two hours ago. I was sleeping when all the noise began.'

'And Rat?'

'Of course, aboard *Sule*. What about you, are you barred from *Khalida*?'

'I need to get Cat.' I turned to Gavin, watching with that shut-off look. 'Cat hates dinghies. I'll have to go myself and put him in his basket, to take him over to *Sule*.'

'I'll send Sergeant Peterson with you. She can take your statement aboard *Sule*.' He wouldn't be allowed to take it, of course. Be damned to their rules. I wanted to stamp and scream as if I was three again, but if they had to invade my home to clear me, to clear Gavin, then there was nothing I could do, except be reasonable about it. 'I'll get her to take photos before you go aboard. Can you get clothes too, please, and let us have these ones?'

234

There was nothing I could say, nothing I could do about it. Guilty until proved innocent. I knew he minded as much as I did.

He turned to call, 'Freya!' I made a face into the darkness. Sergeant Peterson was the original ice maiden. She had pale, straight hair held back in a pony-tail, and green eyes like a mermaid's, looking with the indifference of another species on human folly. We'd crossed paths on the longship case, and again in the witches murders, and not taken to each other. Gavin murmured instructions to her, and she nodded and followed us to the pier. I was gloomily pleased to see she balanced herself on the grey rubber side of Reidar's inflatable as if she expected to go swimming at any moment. The men rowed to *Khalida*'s stern, and Sergeant Peterson clambered aboard first. Camera flashes dazzled on the snow in the cockpit. There would only be my prints from coming aboard, half-covered. At last she beckoned me forward, allowing me onto my own boat at last. Knowing it wasn't Gavin's fault didn't help the rage building inside me as she watched every move I made: switching off the still-chugging engine, lighting a candle, Cat's basket, Cat himself, miaowing indignantly at this late interruption, two tins of food. I turned my back on her and changed into clean clothes, and she gathered what I was wearing into a white bag. Then, in silence, we clambered back into the dinghy, rowed to *Sule*, and came aboard.

After the snow-cold outdoors, it was blissfully warm. I set Cat's basket down on the U-shaped settee. 'Rat?'

Rat wriggled out of the sleeping bag in the forepeak. He was only just smaller than Cat, with glossy black and white fur, magnificent whiskers, and an intelligent expression. He whiffled in my face by way of greeting, hooked his way down my front, tail waggling, and leapt for the fiddle that held Reidar's cookery books on their shelf. I let Cat out of his basket. Cat patted up a paw, Rat dodged it, and within seconds they were playing their old game of chasing each other up into the forepeak, round the hanging locker, along the fiddles, across the engine box, over the chart table and cooker, and back to the forepeak. Anders sat down on the settee, and held his hand out. 'Come and sit down, Cass, and tell us what has happened.'

I was stretching my hand out to him when I saw the blood on it, crusted red-brown, and recoiled, holding my hand away from me as if it was contaminated.

'There is hot water in the heads,' Anders said, indicating into the forecabin.

The pump system chugged into action as I turned the tap. I filled the basin and plunged my hands in, then lathered them with gel, scrubbed with the brush and rinsed again. It was too dim to see if they were clean yet; I soaped and scrubbed again, then dried them, came out into the light and dropped beside Anders on the settee.

He was just younger than me, Anders, twenty-eight, and stunningly handsome, in a young Norse god way: silver-gilt hair, a straight nose, beautiful cheekbones, and a neat seafaring beard. He was also a star with any engine, even my ancient Volvo Penta, which was why his father was keen on keeping him in the family boatyard. His mother was keen on marrying him off to a nice Norwegian girl who lived in a house and had a job which she'd give up for children. There were a couple of obstacles to these ambitions: he'd become hooked enough on sailing to dream of long voyages, and he was a nerd. To make his eyes light up, all you had to do was mention an odd knocking noise in the injector lines. He was also, I'd discovered during the longship case, a secret devotee of those war games you played with exquisitely painted figures, which is not generally a woman-puller, and a lot of girls also objected to Rat; Sergeant Peterson, for example, was looking decidedly uneasy as he and Cat hurtled along the settee towards her. I didn't mind him; I wasn't afraid of mice, and Rat was clean, intelligent, and generally trustworthy aboard a boat, if you kept the biscuit jar shut, and the light airs sails stowed away where he couldn't nest in them.

Rat and Cat did a last circuit, then curled up together in Reidar's bunk, Rat's head pillowed on Cat's belly. Sergeant Peterson shut her pink-gloss lips on what she'd been about to say, and sat down. Reidar began making hot chocolate. Anders gave my hand a squeeze and sat back, motioning Sergeant Peterson forwards. 'You will want to ask questions.'

I ignored Sergeant Peterson taking out her black notebook. 'But what are you doing here?'

'I have come over for your Up Helly Aa. I worked over Christmas and New Year, so that I could have this week off.'

'Oh, excellent!' My voice felt as if I was saying the right things on auto-pilot. My hands were clean under Reidar's cabin LED lighting, but I felt as if the blood was still there. 'Have you got tickets for a hall?'

'For the boating club, the same as you. We will dance together yet.'

'Questions,' Reidar grumbled. 'Drink your chocolate first.' He distributed the little cups and produced a plate of stem ginger biscuits, warm from the oven. 'These are good for shock.'

I took two. 'Thank you, Reidar.'

Sergeant Peterson cleared her throat, then took me through the evening, moment by moment: the shot, looking out from each side and seeing nothing, then from the forepeak, to see Hubert lying there. 'Except I didn't know then who it was.' Yes, he'd been just conscious. I'd done what I could to stop the bleeding. She seemed deeply suspicious of me phoning the hospital, who naturally didn't record calls. I repeated that I'd seen nobody, heard nobody: there had been nothing but my engine, the ripples against the hull, and the wind thrumming in the rigging. Nobody had set foot on the pontoon other than Hubert. I was sure of that: 'I remember his tracks, coming straight forward.'

'Did you smell anything?'

I nodded. 'Fireworks. Gunpowder, I suppose.'

'You see,' Sergeant Peterson said, 'the initial impression is that he was shot at close range. His murderer was two metres or less away from him.'

'But that's impossible!' I thought it over. 'Unless someone was hiding in one of the boats on the other side of the pontoon. I couldn't see them till I opened the forrard hatch. They'd have time to come out, shoot, and nip back in. I didn't rush straight out. I looked from the windows first. Half a minute, maybe.'

Sergeant Peterson shook her head. 'The police have checked every boat on the pontoon. The only ones with disturbed snow are your yacht and –' she looked across at Reidar, 'yours, sir.'

Reidar held out his hand. 'Reidar Pedersen.'

'Mr Pedersen. We'll look again once it gets light, of course.'

In the meantime, her look said, I was the obvious suspect, and only Gavin vouching for me was keeping me out of clink. She turned to Reidar. 'What about you, Mr Pedersen, did you know the dead man?'

He shook his head. 'I am starting to make contacts of course, for my business, but in Lerwick and here in Scalloway only. I would not have come across him.'

'And you didn't see or hear anything suspicious? Not even the shot?'

Reidar shook his head. 'I was listening to music, through headphones. I saw only the blue lights, and then felt the feet on the pontoon.'

'Mr Johansen?'

'I only arrived from Norway two hours ago, on a

fishing boat. I was asleep.'

The ice maiden moved on. 'What did you think his words meant?' She read them from her notebook. 'Bridge – saw her. Bridge.'

I spread my hands, shook my head. The Georgesons lived at Bridge House. John Georgeson had ordered the bairns away from the bridge, when they tried to play njuggles there.

'A name?' she pursued. 'It didn't sound as if he was trying to say Bridget?'

Saw her. 'It might have been.' I tried to hear it again in my head. 'I don't think so. Bridget's an unusual name here in Shetland.'

Her eyes flared, as if she knew something I didn't. 'You don't know any Bridgets?'

'Not that I can think of.'

'Did you never hear your teacher's first name?'

'We just called her Georgeson in the playground, but it did begin with a B – was she a Bridget? No, that's not right ...' Memory stirred. 'Brede, that was it, like the sister in *Across the Barricades.*'

'That was what the family called her. Actually, she was Bridget. Her schoolmates called her Bridget, or Bridge.'

I was silent, digesting that. Hubert too would have called her Bridge. But where might he have seen her, that he needed to tell me? Not going into Ivor and Julie's house, on the night Ivor had returned, for Hubert had still been south then.

'And there's nothing else you noticed.'

I shook my head.

'Mr Johansen? Mr Pedersen?'

'Nothing.'

She rose, and dipped in her pocket for a card. 'You've had a very upsetting experience tonight, Ms Lynch.' She held the white square of card towards me. *Professional counselling,* it read. 'If you feel you need to talk to

239

someone about it, then here are some numbers you can ring.'

I'd brought a boat home over a thousand miles of the Atlantic alone, with a dead man haunting me. She laid the card on the table. 'I'll leave you to get some sleep.'

Sleep? After Sergeant Peterson had left, we sat huddled together around the table, Anders' shoulder warm against mine. The ginger had settled my stomach, but my face was numb. I kept seeing the way Hubert had lain there, curled tight on the white snow, like a discarded bundle of clothes; but then, I reminded myself, that was what his body was: clothing his spirit wouldn't need for now, until it was raised as a glorious body on the Last Day. For now, he wouldn't care about the indignity of lying there all night, behind the screens, until forensics could be flown in from south. *Bridge ... saw her.* That was what he'd come to tell me, but it didn't make any sense.

We didn't talk much. Reidar made toddies, fragrant with lime and Malibu; we drank them while the blue lights flashed outside, the feet came and went on the pontoon, the radios crackled. Once I tried to move, to let Anders go to bed, but he pulled a downie over me and put his arm round my shoulders to hold me there. 'I'm not sleepy. You will only have nightmares, anyway. Relax, and go to sleep if you wish.'

I didn't sleep, but I was contented just to lean back against him, eyes closed, to breathe in the familiar smell of oily wool, to know that I was with friends who didn't expect me to talk. From time to time he and Reidar chatted over me, Anders in Norwegian and Reidar in Danish, discussing the plans for the opening, the Up Helly Aa, the work Anders had just finished in his father's yard, the boats lined up for the rest of January. As the night wore through, they fell silent. Reidar went to his bunk, in the quarterberth, leaving Anders and I on the couch. I knew by his softer breathing, the heaviness of his arm, when he slept.

Every so often I heard Gavin's voice outside, but he came in only once, when the light crept at last over the east hill. We were eating breakfast, porridge with salt and cream. 'I can't stop. I'll be interviewing all day.' His grey eyes scanned my face. 'You're okay?'

I nodded; but I knew that he could see that I wasn't. His face was bleak. I saw again the look I'd seen in the longship case: this is my job. This is who I am. There was no compromise possible. I wanted to reach towards him, but I still felt sick inside. I didn't want to deal with death any more. As he turned away from me, I felt as if something was tearing inside me. I didn't know how to go about fixing this. *I knew I had to make an effort, or we'd be over,* Julie had said, and gone sailing. I rose as he went out of the door, and followed him into the cockpit. There were a dozen officers on the pontoon, and in this still air they'd hear every word I said, yet I didn't want to lie to him by pretending that everything was all right. I could feel Hubert's blood on my hands still.

Gavin turned, but said nothing. I could only look back, struggling for words that would say what I meant without laying my feelings bare to the people surrounding us. 'Phone me later, if you get time.'

His face lightened. He nodded. 'You have a good day.' His voice softened so that I could only just hear it; a tinge of red stole into his cheeks. 'Prayer helps.'

He turned away and became absorbed into his world, and I went back below. *Prayer helps ...* If I was to stay with him, I had to learn to cope, and cope on my own; he had enough to deal with, without having a tantrum from his girlfriend too.

I dragged my way into college. In that witch business in October my classmates had been shy of me; now, they knew me better, and I was greeted with a flurry of questions: 'Come on, Cass, what's happening?' 'Wha does your policeman reckon did it?' 'Is it right that Hubert Inkster's dead?'

Peter burst in over them. He was normally a quiet soul, but the excitement of the approaching Scalloway Fire Festival was giving him confidence, for he was in the Jarl Squad this year, the lead squad, which wore Viking costume. He'd been growing the beard since October, and had dodged all our attempts to trap admissions about the colour of the galley. 'Is it really right that he was shot from close to but with only his ain footprints ahint him?'

I gave a short account of what I'd seen, which naturally didn't satisfy them.

'He was shot from a boat then,' Kevin said. 'Someone hiding in one of the boats that was left.'

I shook my head. 'The police searched them all, and there was nobody aboard.'

'Could you walk along the very edge of the pontoon, holding on to the bows of the boats?'

We all visualised the white plastic rim of the wooden walkway.

'You'd be awful noticeable,' Jimmy objected, 'clinging like a crab to the boat pulpits. Besides, there arena enough boats there ee now to get all the way along like that.'

'And where would you go once you'd shot him?'

'Someone came in on a boat, then. Shot him and went away again.'

'I'd have heard the motor,' I said. 'We'd have seen the boat on the pontoon, with all the ones that are ashore for winter.'

They all agreed that yes, we would have, except for Peter, who had that dawning light expression.

'I ken!' he broke in. 'Listen, all of you, this is a good idea. It's one of this sub-aqua folk. They took the pistol in a waterproof bag, and swam ower to the pontoon, shot him, then just swam away.'

The lecturer came in then, and we had to get down to work. But between calculating boat weight and balance, the idea kept surfacing. The water was icy, you had less than five minutes if you went overboard, but a diver in a proper thermal wet suit could do it. Say he'd been waiting, black on the black shoreline, for Ivor's car to arrive, and slipped into the water as soon as it came. *Then why not shoot him there?* the voice of reason asked. Because ... because I might come straight out at the sound of the pistol, and see his car driving off? But a car had driven past, and without its lights I couldn't see anything more: size, colour, certainly not numberplate.

I imagined a dark-clad person slipping into the water, swimming the fifty metres to the marina, bobbing up beside the pontoon and waiting for Hubert to almost get to me, then shooting. Immediately, the figure would duck back under and speed back to shore ... no. I was pretty sure I'd have seen any movement on shore. But if they'd come to the far side of the pontoon, they could have gone out around the breakwater where I wouldn't see them. They could have swum past the fisheries college to the car park, and driven away.

First we'd needed a horseman; now we needed a deep-sea diver. I shook away the thought of a njuggle sneaking up, pistol in hoof, and concentrated on cargo distribution.

It was an odd day. The snow fell at intervals, pouring down like a white river, blotting out everything but the window frame, then clearing again to brilliant sunshine. The hills around us were like a stage set for a very expensive version of *The Snow Queen*, with the glittering snow smoothed over each tussock of grass. I couldn't see the marina from any of the classrooms, but I could see in

243

my mind's eye the white-suited figures going aboard my *Khalida*. They'd start at the forepeak, where my steps had led from, and lift the sails and bunk cushions, haul out the anchor chain and look underneath it. Then they'd move back: nothing to search in the heads or hanging locker, just the cabin floor to lift; then the main cabin. They'd look under the sole, and in each of the lockers. In imagination I heard the clatter as they took the pans from below the cooker, lined tins up on the table. They'd open each of my plastic boxes to check through my clothes, and undo my bunk to get underneath the mattress to the storage space below. They'd unhook the steps and check around the engine. Then they'd investigate the cockpit lockers: fenders, the gas bottle, ropes, flares, the liferaft, the spare anchor chain. I wondered if Gavin would be there, or if he'd turn it over to another officer, as he had with interviewing me.

As we broke for lunch, Kevin sidled up to me. 'Cass, I don't suppose I could borrow your black suit?'

I looked blankly at him. He gestured with his hands. 'The black suit you wear for sailing, the Musto onesie one.' He coloured. 'It's for Up Helly Aa.'

I made a face. Although I had the new one that Maman and Dad had given me for Christmas, I'd planned on keeping it good by wearing the old one most of the time. 'Can you keep it safe from sparks?' The procession was death on clothing.

Kevin's face fell, then brightened. 'Nobody wears the full costume for the procession anyway. I could wear black breeks for that, if you'd let me borrow it for the acts.'

'It'll be awful short in the legs on you.' I only came up to Kevin's chin.

'You'll never see that with rubber boots on. Thanks, Cass.'

Chapter Twenty-four

The moon had risen when I came back to *Khalida*, glimmering with a silvery radiance between heavy clouds. The pontoon was busy with people working around the neon-white tent. I looked at the empty berths for signs of a diver's hold on the pontoon rim or projecting fingers. The snow on each was smooth and unbroken. If a diver had shot Hubert, he'd bobbed in the water. I shook my head. It had been a better shot than that. And the idea of an extra motorboat was definitely out; it would have been higher than the finger pontoon arms, and I'd have seen it, especially if it had then backed out and roared off as the police arrived ... I shoved my curiosity away.

Cat wasn't aboard *Sule*, nor Rat; the men must have taken them over to the café. The officer at the marina gate checked on his radio, and said that I could go aboard my boat again. Hubert's footprints were lost under the new falls of snow, criss-crossed by official boots, although I could see in my mind's eye where they still were, frozen intact under the layers of white stars. *Prayer helps ... Eternal rest grant unto him, O Lord, and let perpetual light shine upon him ...*

Aboard *Khalida*, I swept the trampled snow from my decks and shovelled it from the cockpit before going below. I wanted to clean my home after the police intrusion, but I knew I'd be wanted at the café, and a walk would clear my head.

I paused at the marina gate, suddenly uneasy. Something was different. I looked back along the boats, but nothing rang a bell. It would come back to me. I headed across to Main Street, striding out along Port Arthur Road as if I could run away from my thoughts. *Eternal rest grant unto him, O Lord ...*

The café windows were lit up to show the armchairs in position, and the tables spread with my starched cloths. Cat and Rat were curled up in front of the stove, and a cinnamon pastry smell drifted out of the door. A pair of women and a toddler paused to look in; the toddler pressed his nose to the glass and shouted, 'Dass!'

I crossed the road. 'Inga! We're no' open yet, but I'm sure you can come in.'

'I come in,' Peerie Charlie said. His small rubber boots clattered on my polished wooden floor as he charged to the biggest armchair and clambered up on it, feet sticking straight out.

'We thought we needed to speak to you,' Inga said, pulling her woollen hat and gloves off. 'You mind Susan, don't you?'

'It's a braw twartree years since I was trying to keep the three of you out of trouble,' Susan said. I'd have known her, though; dark eyes just like Inga's, and dark hair, though hers was threaded with grey.

'Take a seat,' Reidar said. 'I will bring coffee, and a pastry.'

I collapsed gratefully into one of the armchairs. Breakfast felt a long time ago. Peerie Charlie clambered on top of me. 'I share chair, Dass.'

'We had the police round this morning,' Inga said. 'No' your policeman in the kilt, he's likely no' allowed to investigate you. The blonde Peterson lass and another one with her. Luckily for you, I'd no balled oot last year's calendar.'

I gave her the blank look that deserved.

'Alibis. The weekend Ivor came back was Lilian's wedding.'

Lilian was one of Inga's hockey team, and the entire

squad had spent the Wednesday and Thursday decorating the hall with ribbons in the team colours; then of course the wedding had been on the Friday and Saturday evenings, in the traditional Shetland fashion: the Friday after the actual wedding, and the Saturday just for the fun of it. I remembered it all vividly, because big Charlie had been away, and I'd babysat for all four nights. I'd had all three children for Wednesday and Thursday, then I'd picked Peerie Charlie up from the wedding nights mid-evening, and taken him home, jagged with tiredness after an exciting day. There was no possibility whatever of me having gone south then to kill Ivor and sail his boat back, or take his car down south; I'd been far too busy arguing about bedtimes.

'He even got Vaila and Dawn in and asked, casual-like, who'd babysat for them for Lilian's wedding, and after a bit of argument they agreed it had been you. You'd insisted on reading Dawn *Swallows and Amazons* as her bedtime story instead of *The Hunger Games*, and wouldn't let them watch a second film because of school tomorrow.'

I didn't need reminded. The four evenings were seared into my memory. I just hadn't realised it was that weekend. 'So I'm in the clear for Ivor.'

Reidar came over with a tray of mugs and a pot of coffee. There was a pause while everyone was served with coffee, and lemonade was found for Peerie Charlie, then Anders passed round a dish of pastries. I picked an apricot-centred one with plenty of sugar and bit in ravenously. Inga waited until the men had gone back into the kitchen, then leaned forward.

'He asked a load o' questions about your relations with Hubert. "None," I told him. "She'd ken him to speak to, at the marina, but as for having some secret affair with him, well, why on earth should she? They're both free and old enough to ken their own business." He looked kinda sheepish-wye at that, and Freya Peterson closed her notebook, and the pair of them trundled off.'

'Thanks.'

'And I brought Susan along because this needs sorted.' She nodded to her sister, who reddened.

'I'm no' sure what help I can be, but Inga just said to tell you about Ivor and Julie.' She turned the flower-patterned cup in her hands. I nodded encouragingly. 'I was all through the school with them. We were all in the same class. All the lasses fancied Ivor, no' just Julie. Bridge Georgeson was keen on him an' all. An' Hubert was aye keen on Julie, but she never looked at him. It was Ivor she wanted or nobody, but she had no chance.' She fished in her bag and brought out a school photo, three rows of bairns in their best Fair Isle ganseys. I took it from her. Susan was on the end, with two neat dark plaits. Hubert was behind her, smiling anxiously for the camera, a child who was keen to get it right. Ivor was in the middle, with fashionably long hair and a cheeky grin. I wouldn't have turned my back on him. Beside him, Julie was pudgy and plain, but smug-looking, the child whose hand would be up first. Miss Georgeson was in the front row, all sparkling dark eyes and rosy cheeks like a Dutch doll. Susan put a finger on her. 'Bridge was lively and fun, and Julie was just …' She struggled for the word. 'Devoted. She was aye the cleverest of us. Ivor got Julie to do his homework, but it was Bridge he asked if he wanted to do something wild, like the time they climbed up on the school roof.'

'So … when did Julie's devotion start paying off?'

'Well, he wasn't interested when we were teenagers, then he went off to uni, and we reckoned that was why Julie went to Aberdeen when she coulda gone to Edinburgh. They were in the same hall, but he was out partying while she was getting the best grades of our year. Then he got a flat, an' she'd go round and clean up, cook meals. There was a row with Bridge about that. I mind. By then, you see, he and Bridge were kinda steady, and

248

Bridge objected to Julie looking after her man, and Ivor said if she hated it that much then she could come and do it, and she told him to get lost. Next thing, he and Julie were an item, and she was choosing wedding dresses.'

'You didn't like her?'

Susan grimaced. 'I thought she was stupid. She shoulda got over it in primary school. She wouldna believe it, but you could see Ivor would have other girls behind her back. And he did. This Serco lass was the latest in a long line. It kinda soured Bridge an' all. After a few "I don't care" flings, she never went out with anyone else. She said she was too busy doing her teaching practice – that's a killer year, believe me – then her placement, with you twa in the class.'

She paused to drink her coffee. 'The sad thing is, I can see it now, that Ivor woulda been better off with Bridge, going adventuring together, and Julie woulda been just the wife for Hubert, sorting him out and gingering him up instead of letting him moulder away in a falling-down croft house.' Her face went white, and her eyes filled with tears. 'Poor Hubert. I hope they catch whaever did yon.'

The personalities were coming clearer. 'Can you try … give me one word for each of them. What they were like.'

Susan considered. 'Julie, efficient. She wanted Ivor and she got him.'

'Suppose she'd found evidence he'd got another girl? That could have turned all that devotion to hatred. Might she have snapped, and killed him?'

Susan shook her head. 'She's closed her eyes to them all these years. Bridge was the one for fireworks. Light blue touch paper and stand well clear.'

Inga grinned. 'Cass kens that. She was the one holding the match.'

'Julie never lost the rag. She was steady and determined, like one of those road roller machines. She

249

decided what she wanted, and worked and planned until she got it. I was eyeing up babygros already, for next spring.'

I jerked my head up, surprised. 'Is she …?'

'Na, na. But she was talking, in the summer, of them starting a family, before she got too old. So I was expecting the maternity leave to start at Christmas, whether Ivor liked it or not.'

'What was Ivor like? One word for him.'

'Laid back. Anything for a quiet life. Selfish – no, self-centred. He expected Julie's world to revolve around him.' She thought a bit more. 'Frustrated. Always expected the world to be more exciting than the daily grind. Full of new schemes for the rainbow tomorrow.'

'Hubert?'

'Devoted. He'd have done anything for Julie.' She glanced towards the kitchen and lowered her voice. 'Listen, Julie phoned me this morning. She wanted someone to talk to. Hubert visited her yesterday. He called in at the college, just after eleven, and she had a class about to come in, so she couldn't speak, but she said he seemed upset. He said he'd phone her later, but he didn't.'

'Upset about what?'

'She said he was asking her questions about the partnership between Ivor and Robert-John, what exactly was involved. She thought he was trying to find out if she was going to be okay financially.'

'Her workplace isn't great for a sympathetic chat.'

'Hubert wouldn't think of that. She couldn't remember his exact questions. She was knocked sideways by his death. "He was always there for me," she said.'

She sat back, spreading her hands in a 'that's all' gesture. There was a silence. 'Does that help?' Inga asked, at last.

I was beginning to have a wild idea of *why* and *who*, but I didn't believe the *how*. 'I'm no' sure. Thanks,

Susan.'

Inga stood and held out a hand to Peerie Charlie. 'Come on, peeriebreeks. We need to go and get the lasses. Thanks for the coffee, Reidar.' She pressed a tenner into my hand. 'Stick that in the till for me, once you're open.'

I walked out into the darkening street with them, and was just going back in when my phone rang. It was Gavin.

'*Feasgar mhath.*' I was glad he'd greeted me in Gaelic. 'How have you got on today?'

'Fine.' My voice was pitched too high.

'I hope the search didn't give you too much tidying.'

'No, it was okay.' He could hear in my voice that I meant it was as okay as it could be. I tried to make it warmer. 'Anyway, I'm too busy helping Reidar to tidy. How about you?'

'I'm tired to my very bones. I've spent all day talking, and now I have a pile of paperwork. Goodness knows when I'll get to bed.' His voice became self-conscious. 'I've been offered a ticket for the Fire Festival, at the boating club. Is that where you're going?'

'Yes.' *Make an effort* ... 'How about watching the procession together? I can explain the in-jokes, if I know them.'

'That'd be good. What time?'

'Seven o'clock, I think – I'll find out, and phone you. If it's seven, maybe meet at half six?'

'I should manage that.'

'Warm clothes,' I warned him. 'Two jumpers, a fire-proof jacket and at least three pairs of socks. The cold just seeps up from the ground when you're standing around.'

'You're telling a policeman about standing around in the cold?'

'Right enough,' I conceded, 'it doesn't last as long as a football match. Goodnight then.'

'*Beannachd leat.*'

I understood, but it hurt. I kicked a stone across the car

park, brooding, then jumped as Anders called me.

'Cass! You should not be hanging about in the dark here on your own.'

He was likely right. I came back into the cafe and put my pinnie on. 'What now?'

Reidar passed me a mixing bowl. 'Another set of cakes for the freezer. And there is a stew cooking for tea, if you are hungry.'

Stew sounded good.

'And then,' Anders added, 'you can tell us all about what you are mixed up in now.'

'I'm not mixed up.'

'Someone is doing their best to make sure you are.'

I hadn't thought of it like that. 'You think Hubert's death was setting me up?'

'No deaths,' Reidar rumbled. 'No discussions, until we have eaten.'

Chapter Twenty-five

We spent what was left of the afternoon baking. By six o' clock I was ravenous. Reidar swathed a heavy enamel casserole in a towel and I held it while we drove back to the marina.

As we got out of the car I realised what was missing. During the autumn there had been half a dozen little skiffs here, ten-foot rowing boats which had migrated back to their owners' sheds to hibernate for the winter; all except two, a solid wooden double-pointed one that it would take more than even a Shetland gale to shift, with a stout rope from the bow around a couple of breeze blocks, and a green fibreglass effort with a pram bow, upside-down, with a rope over her. The wooden one was still here, but there was only a faint outline in the snow where the fibreglass one been. The rope lay like a snake over the other boat's side.

I stopped dead, and Anders bumped into me. 'What is it?'

I pointed to the space. 'A skiff's missing.' She'd been a lightweight thing, with wheels on her transom, easily manhandled in silence by one person, especially if the water was close by. She was low enough to lie in the dark water between two pontoon fingers, long enough for a person to huddle down in. 'That's how Hubert was shot. Someone was waiting in a boat.'

The person had sculled silently out to the pontoon, and sneaked into a vacant berth at the end, not far past where that Cass had her *Khalida* moored. He or she had waited for him to arrive, and shot at point-blank range; then, in the moment it took for me to come out they'd slipped the skiff out of the marina and around the breakwater. I'd felt the ripples against *Khalida*'s hull.

I walked around the marina wall and along the boating club deck. Yes, there was the skiff, bobbing gently against the pier. I didn't suppose there would be any fingerprints, because even the most innocent citizen would naturally have worn gloves in this cold, but I didn't touch her, just in case.

I hauled my phone out of my pocket and phoned Gavin. 'I've found your murderer's getaway boat.' I said, and described it.

'Interesting,' Gavin said. 'Can you show it to one of the officers on duty?'

'Sure.'

It was a new officer on the marina gate, and I recognised him straight away. He was the young man who'd tried to keep me off my own ship in the longship case, and mistook me for a mischievous boy when I climbed the castle walls to get away from a murderer. He recognised me too, and greeted me with professional bonhomie. 'Hello, miss.'

'Evening. I've got a boat to show you,' I said. I gestured to the space where the skiff had been. 'It was the space here that I noticed. It was here until a couple of days ago, anyway. Then I looked over here.' I led him to the boating club pier, and showed him the skiff. 'She's tied with a proper bowline.' I smiled sweetly at him. 'Of course you'll need to move her before Friday, or you may find she's caught light from the galley.'

I left him to it, and headed for *Sule*.

Reidar's stew was wonderful. He'd made it with best Scalloway Meat Co. Ltd. beef, simmered with carrots and a dash of wine, and served it up with potatoes mashed to a creamy consistency, and flavoured with nutmeg. We ate around the table, with Cat purring in my lap and Rat perched on Anders' shoulder. Then there were biscuits and tea, and gradually the peace of the boat took over: the wood creaking, the gentle tap of the waves on the hull, the slush of snow sliding down the windows. Every so often a car came along the Port Arthur road and into the college, or turned in at the boating club. At last I leaned forward with a sigh. 'I should go and write my notes up from today.'

Anders shook his head. 'The story first.'

'It's too muddled in my head,' I grumbled. All the same, I did my best: the foursome of Ivor, Bridget, Julie, Hubert; the affair with Donna and Julie's attempt to save the marriage; the problems with Robert-John; Ivor's voyage down with Hubert, the arrival of Donna, the quarrel with Hubert, with Donna, with Julie; Ivor's return through the Caledonian Canal to Shetland, the note on the table, his departure on the ferry the next night. I explained his involvement in the missing cask of whisky, and his dodgy dealings with Jeemie. I tried to remember who had been where when, and who might be able to hoist a body on one of Gavin's ponies to transport it up the hill. My throat was dry when I'd finished. I poured myself another cup of tea and leaned back with an over-to-you gesture.

'It is very complicated,' Reidar said. 'It is like one of those Agatha Christie stories.'

'No,' Anders said. 'You are too cold, Cass, in your unheated cabin, you are not thinking straight. Your policeman would have thought of it the moment the wife, Julie, admitted she had quarrelled with her husband, and left him. Would he go on his own around this point of Ardnamurchan, which even you treat with respect?'

I sat up with a jerk which made Cat miaow indignantly, and dig his claws in. Of course he wouldn't. Tackle Ardnamurchan, single-handed, when he was used to at least one crew member aboard, and then go through the twenty-nine locks of the Caledonian Canal without another pair of hands to handle ropes and rig fenders? No way. He'd do what I had done, sail back up the west coast. There had been no sprig of heather on his boat's bow because she hadn't earned it.

And that meant he'd spent those days without Julie messing about in the area surrounding Gavin's loch: Mallaig, the bottom of Skye, Loch Nevis, Kyle Rhea. He'd never left it. He'd been killed where we'd found him, by someone who then sailed the boat home.

I should have thought of it, of course. It was just that the idea of someone else sailing Ivor's boat hadn't occurred to me, any more than I'd expect to take over someone else's house. I was silent for a moment, considering it.

The idea of Ivor having died where we found him was much neater. No borrowing horses or driving bodies about, just 'Let's climb up to that cave.' A blow on the head, a stab in the heart, poison in a drink. Then the survivor upped anchor and headed for Shetland. Inga's mother-in-law saw someone, after dark, in Ivor's red sailing overalls, driving Ivor's car and going into Ivor's house. That should have rung alarm bells. People left their oilskins aboard. That person scrambled some clothes into a bag, left a note on the table, took the car on the ferry that night and then dumped it in the morning, as if Ivor had gone south, leaving no forwarding address.

'Someone who knew Ivor well enough to imitate his

handwriting,' Reidar said.

Julie, of course. Donna. Robert-John, and Maya. Jeemie might have a sample, from the removals. John Georgeson might, from the whisky affair, and what he knew his sons and daughter might also know.

'I can see Jeemie as a forger, and he was from Walls. They're good sailors.' I thought about the rest of the list. 'I don't see Donna sailing a yacht home.'

'No,' Reidar agreed. 'But she had a strong motive for killing him. She loved him and he'd betrayed her.'

'All the same, she could only have done it if she killed him here.'

Anders shifted Rat to his other shoulder. 'Could his wife sail?'

I shook my head. 'She's used to boats, but she's never crewed at Brae. She had only one night aboard before the row, not long enough for her to learn to set the sails, and she's too sensible to think she could pick it up on an epic voyage like that.'

'The Georgesons?'

'John Georgeson's brother has a Sigma 33, and they've all crewed for him. John Georgeson might even have a boat of his own in Lerwick. I don't know all the fleet there. Robert-John's a good hand in a boat.'

The long way home would be a challenge for him, but I had no doubt he could do it, if there was enough at stake. Maya'd been on his uncle's boat at regattas too. *An intelligent woman* ... yes, intelligent enough to learn how to work the sails and instruments. If they'd worked together that meant it had been deliberate; they'd gone south intending to kill him. They'd left the business van there, brought the yacht home, and then Robert had returned to the mainland with the car, in Ivor's name, and come home in his own van.

'And Hubert Inkster, of course.' Hubert could sail, and he knew the boat. He and Ivor had planned the trip together, so he'd know all about the tides, the lights, places to stop for a breather. 'But if Hubert killed Ivor, then who killed Hubert?'

'That will be what is keeping your policeman busy,' Reidar said. 'Alibis. And given the weather last night, it will be everyone saying they stayed at home, watching the television, with the curtains shut on the snow.'

It sounded likely.

'What about the gun?' Anders asked. 'Your laws are strict, are they not? The police will know who has a licence.'

I'd thought about this too, in the watches of last night. 'I think, actually, that it might have been Ivor's. He had a pistol that he used for starting races, at the regatta, and I'd thought it was just a starting gun.' I hadn't cared to look closely at it. 'But perhaps it was a real one.'

'So everyone knew he had it.'

'Hubert, and Robert-John, and Julie, of course, but the person who killed him could have seen it on board, and taken it.'

I was getting too comfortable. I called Cat and headed back to *Khalida*. I'd just got the hatch open when the first flake fell, drifting down in a spiral around me, the second, then a dancing swirl of them; then, with a sudden rattle of halyards, the wind got up, and the snow poured down like smoke from the north, blotting out the school, the street of coloured houses, the pier with the castle, then sweeping across the water to envelop us. I dived into the cabin and saw through the windows the way the near shore disappeared into this same white whirl. We could have been alone at sea, Cat and I, our gold-lit cabin lost in spindrift.

I put a hot water bottle into my bed, and ran the engine while I did a coloured mind-map of today's lectures, then I renewed the hot water bottle, brushed my teeth, and got into my thermals. Never again would I spend a winter in the northern hemisphere, I vowed to myself. I'd head for the Caribbean come next September. I wriggled into my berth and lay for a moment, pondering. What had Hubert wanted to tell me? *Bridge – saw her.* Bridget Georgeson. Maya, Donna, Julie. John Georgeson lived at Bridge House, Voe. Hubert could have been telling me he'd seen Miss Georgeson, or he could have been saying he'd seen one of the others at Bridge House. Not Miss Georgeson; there would be nothing odd about her visiting her father. Nor could I see any link between Donna and John Georgeson, nor Julie and him. Maya, now, that was different. She wanted at all costs to save her husband and children, little Annemarie and the unborn baby. She might have gone to John Georgeson, secretly, while Robert-John was out, to beg the help he was too proud to ask for.

Bridge ... saw her.

Then, dazzlingly, it came to me. Bridge. The Skye Bridge. He'd been crossing on Thursday, and seen *her,* Ivor's yacht, on the water below, with her distinctive green dodgers, heading for home up the west coast, just as we'd surmised, when according to the plan they'd worked out, Ivor should have been making his way up Loch Ness.

He'd seen the person at the helm.

Thursday 9th January

High Water at Scalloway UT	*02.53, 1.3 m*
Low Water	*08.59, 1.0 m*
High Water	*15.12, 1.4 m*
Low Water	*21.54, 0.9 m*
Moonset	*02.05*
Sunrise	*09.03*
Moonrise	*11.24*
Sunset	*17.13*

Moon first quarter

You dunna tak ling amang da drewie-lines.
You don't take ling (a deep sea fish) among seaweed (close to shore). Fig, you need to make an effort to get a worthwhile result.

Chapter Twenty-six

It was bitterly cold when I awoke, and the condensation on the inside of the window had frozen into frost ferns. I hauled my warmest clothes over my thermals and set off for a hot shower straight away, envying Cat his thick fur. The tide was almost out; the shingle-sand glistened dark between the pewter-grey sea and the snow-covered upper shore. Little wading birds darted about the clear portion of beach.

Antoine pounced on me as I came back. His hair was standing on end as if he was harassed.

'I have the entire Jarl Squad here for breakfast tomorrow, and not a French breakfast of a croissant, a coffee, but the full Scottish, with bacon and eggs, and fried bread, and even blood pudding, for breakfast, what horror. And now one of my girls has phoned in sick, so if you can help out, I will be grateful. You cannot cook, of course, but you do not need certificates to serve plates.'

'I've got intermediate food handling.' It had been running at Train Shetland, a four-day course, and Reidar had suggested I sign up. Antoine snorted. Intermediate food handling didn't compare with a proper French waiter's apprenticeship. 'You have black clothes for waiting in?'

'No problem.' I'd got some from the charity shop, for this evening, where I'd be handing out Reidar's best baking at the ceremonial naming of the Up Helly Aa galley, the Viking longship which would be at the heart of tomorrow's celebrations.

'Then I will see you tomorrow, as early as possible.

There are to be speeches, so no doubt it will take half the morning.'

After my classes I headed up to the café. Cat came with me as far as the breakwater, pouncing on the snow, scooping it with his paws and making flurries as he chased his tail, then he decided it was too wet and cold, and raced back home, slipping in the gap in Reidar's forehatch to join Rat, who'd also been left behind. I scrunched briskly on. Prince Olav's slip glistened with ice, and the net over the shed roof made a faint pattern under the smooth snow. When I got nearer to the shop then the crunching snow had been turned to grey ice by passing rubber boots, walking shoes, buggy wheels.

The shop was in Up Helly Aa mode. The window was full of home-made shields and helmets with cardboard raven wings (the nursery Viking project) surrounding a miniature galley. There was a poster on the door promising a 7 a.m. opening tomorrow to sell programmes, and a home-made 'hours to go' countdown on the counter, alongside a stack of horned Viking helmets in authentic plastic. The girl behind the counter wore a long kirtle under a Viking-style apron pinned with oval brooches. I got two tins of catfood and was just hesitating over the choice of cat biscuits when a woman behind me spoke.

'So, now, did you hear Jeemie o' Grobsness is been hauled into the police station to talk about stolen jewellery?'

I turned round. It was an older woman in a parka, sparked with farm mud, and of course she wasn't talking to me, but to another woman of the same age, in a town coat, with a loaded wicker basket. I turned away and listened.

'Stolen jewellery! Never.'

'Yea,' insisted the country woman. 'I heard it from our Janette's oldest lass, that helps with the cleaning at the police station. The policeman with the kilt visited him twa days ago, and got suspicious, and after that they searched the "missing items" file in the station, and came up with several things in his shop. Then the police confronted him with the evidence, and he admitted it.'

'Never! Wha were they stolen from?'

'Folk all over Shetland. An you ken this, he did it through this Facebook that all the bairns are aye on.' *It's even got a Facebook page, the man's a great one for his computers*, Magnie had said. A quick glance showed me half the shop was listening, breath-held. 'It seems he was "friends" with the whole of Shetland. All he had to do was look out for holiday photos, to let him ken what houses were empty.'

I thought of the photos I'd seen of people smiling from a hotel balcony in the Canary Islands, from a ski slope on a Swiss alp, from a market in sunny Africa. *Having a wonderful time here ...*

'Then he just broke into the house and took things that widna be missed.' *What's security like?* Gavin had asked. I imagined Jeemie arriving at a darkened house in his dark car, and slipping silently through an unlocked back door or cludgie window. I thought he'd like the power buzz of roaming through the house without the owners knowing; maybe even, if it was an isolated house, drinking a cup of tea in their sitting room before he searched for things that wouldn't be missed immediately: a grandmother's engagement ring, pretty, old-fashioned, not hugely valuable as jewellery goes, but worth several hundred pounds, and never worn, just kept safely in a box for sentiment's sake. Prowling through people's houses, learning all their secrets ...

'Never!' the town woman repeated. 'Well, I dinna ken what folk are coming to nowadays.'

'Our Ruby said that the police had that much stolen stuff that they'd likely have to hold a display of it all in the Town Hall, and get folk to come and identify what was theirs.'

Our Ruby, I thought, was using her imagination now. The countrywoman trailed off in a round of appreciative murmurs. I chose the medium-priced cat biscuits and headed to the counter, thinking. Last Wednesday, Jeemie had said, for the girl selling Julie's gimmel ring, and presumably he dated the items just after he'd stolen them, so that he wouldn't be caught out by an owner saying, 'Oh, no, I polished that just before we went away on holiday.' That meant he'd taken it while Julie was in Tenerife over Christmas. Donna had been telling the truth when she insisted Ivor had never given her a ring; unless Jeemie'd stolen it from Donna.

Prowling through people's houses, learning all their secrets ... but that was three months after Ivor's death. I didn't see how it linked in. I paid the Viking girl, and came out into the cold.

Reidar and Anders had been busy. The armchairs were all in place, with little tables invitingly beside them, the peat stove glowed in its corner. A clock ticked between china huntsmen on the mantelpiece, and the windowsill was bright with pots of blue hyacinths. Reidar got me writing menus in my best French script, while he concocted chocolate cakes bulging with whipped cream and decorated with slices of strawberry. Anders was making croissants under his direction, rolling out, adding slivers of butter, folding over, rolling again. Once I'd done the menu cards I was initiated into the mysteries of creating *pains au chocolat.* It was peaceful, familiar, standing shoulder to shoulder with Anders again, and we reminisced of voyages we'd done and discussed how far two people could actually take my *Khalida*, while Reidar directed us like a benevolent giant. When the clock chimed five we drew a deep breath and looked around with pride at the cold store filled with trays of dough triangles and rectangles ready to bake, the cakes on their shelves, the plastic containers filled with biscuits. Reidar put an arm around my shoulders, and clapped Anders on the back. 'Tomorrow will be a success. Now we must eat, then it will be time to get to the boating club.'

The snow had stopped again, and the sky was clear, with the stars ruled over by the silver moon. We ate the remains of yesterday's stew aboard *Sule*, mopping our plates with thick slices of crusty bread, then I nipped back to *Khalida* for my blacks, and we headed to the boating club together.

We weren't invited to the naming ceremony, but from the buzz in the bar afterwards as the folk swarmed in, it had gone really well, with speeches from all concerned. The Guizer Jarl had invited the 'clerk o'works', the leader of the boys who'd built the galley, to fix the nameplate on, and she'd been named after the Jarl's wife, 'in appreciation of their lengthy marriage and consistent support.'

Evening refreshments weren't usual, but Reidar had offered to supply 'eight o'clocks' as advertisement for tomorrow's opening. I circulated with trayfuls of fancies, wished the Jarl squad luck for tomorrow, and headed for *Khalida* at half past nine, when the last of the food was gone, dog-tired, and with my feet aching far more than they'd ever done after a double watch on a tall ship.

'It went well though,' Reidar said. 'It was excellent advertisement. While the men are doing the official bit, we will see the wives tomorrow.'

Friday 10th January
Scalloway Fire Festival

High Water at Scalloway UT	*03.53, 1.3 m*
Low Water	*10.28, 1.0 m*
High Water	*16.29, 1.3 m*
Low Water	*23.06, 0.9 m*
Moonset	*03.21*
Sunrise	*09.01*
Moonrise	*11.47*
Sunset	*15.24*

Moon first quarter

Ros a fair day at night.
Congratulate yourself on a fine day only when it's finally over.

Chapter Twenty-seven

The snow lay overnight, but the wind had fallen, so it wasn't as cold as I'd feared. I re-filled my hot water bottle at 4 a.m., then Cat and I slept snugly until the first light began to creep into the cabin. I looked across at the clock: half past seven.

It was going to be a most beautiful day, crisp and clear. The sky was that pale winter colour, like a distilled essence of summer blue, and the water glimmered in answer. The snow stretched clean across the hills, as if they'd been newly sprinkled with caster sugar. A dunter bobbed up beside the shore, smart as a twenties young man-about-town with his white jacket and black and green yachting cap, tilted his head and commented, 'Cor, cor!'

I waved Reidar and Anders off, headed into the college canteen, and was soon busy laying tables while Antoine and his minions raced around in the kitchen. Then we heard a storm of cheering, a drift of music, and we all piled out to watch the procession, the Vikings leading their galley from the blue-doored galley shed above the Minister's steps, flanked on each side by three flickering torches.

She was a bonny sight, just bigger than my *Khalida*, with sides striped in dark red and white, and a silver head carved with scales and jagged teeth. A narrow blue glass eye like a snake's stared over my head. There were shields along her length, in the same dark red, embossed with a pattern of three silver fish twined with Celtic lines. The short mast was of polished wood, with the horizontal yard hoisted to the top, and the red sail furled in loops below the crow's nest basket. The raven pennant fluttered above her. At her stern, she had a silver forked tail, curved over to show the last dark-tipped dorsal spikes.

Her crew were equally magnificent. Everywhere I looked there were Vikings, with dark red cloaks, chainmail tunics over their kirtles, dark fur boots and rounded black helmets, ornamented in silver over the brow. It took me a moment to recognise my classmate Peter among them; I'd always thought of him as weedily built, but in his Viking rig-out he looked about ten feet tall, and broad in the chest as any raiding oarsman. The circular brooch that held his cloak had the same fish design as the shields. There were boys too, the sons of squad members brought along to enjoy the great day, ranging from teenage right down to a toddler in a miniature chain mail tunic, and their daughters were the gaggle of Viking princesses sitting in the galley, in dresses of dark red velvet.

The Guizer Jarl was a magnificent sight. The upright raven's wings held by silver clasps to his helmet made him a foot taller than his followers, and he brandished a double-headed axe. His chain mail had a leather grid pattern over it, and brooches fastened his cloak. He stood steady in the moving galley, head high, axe raised. When it came to a halt, two Vikings scurried forward with a set of steps, and he swung himself down onto the ground, where the rest of the squad had made ceremonial lines at the door of the college. There was a storm of cheering: the Vikings rattled their axe-shafts on the ground, or clashed their shields together, and as he came through the crowd the Guizer Jarl paused to greet, to smile, to wave, like a royal procession. This was his day, after seventeen years of helping to organize the procession, to be spent visiting schools, the nursery, the old folks' home with his squad. There'd be a senior citizens' tea-and-homebakes afternoon in the boating club, then a night he'd never forget: the procession, the galley burning, and going round the halls with his squad afterwards.

For now, he led his Vikings into the college for their first engagement. We slipped into the foyer to join the college in welcoming our Jarl. There was a hearty singing of the traditional march, *From grand old Viking centuries Up Helly Aa has come*, followed by the squad's own theme song, specially composed by members, with tongue-twister words and a refrain of 'da boaniest jarl dat ivir der wis'. After that the head of the college made a lengthy speech, with a number of sly references to salmon farming and football teams, the Jarl replied, and at last they all trooped into the canteen for breakfast, and I was too busy to worry about anything else.

I was just coaxing the Viking princesses to more scrambled eggs with smoked salmon when a voice I recognised said, 'Aye aye, Cass. Are you seen the galley yet?'

It was Shaela, one of my sailing pupils from Brae. She was looking scarily grown-up. Her long, dark hair was loose, held from her brow by two plaits; a white fur muff hung from a silver cord around her neck, and a tortoise-back brooch at her throat fastened a full-length cloak ornamented by two lines of Fair Isle-patterned braid in maroon and silver.

'Shaela! I didna ken you! You look gorgeous.'

'Me uncle Kenny is the Jarl. He's a Hearts fan, so everything's in maroon and white.' She giggled. 'The galley has a surprise – just you wait.'

It was after ten when breakfast was over. The Vikings formed their lines again, and the Jarl marched through them. Once he'd joined the princesses and miniature boy Vikings in the boat, he raised his axe. There was a huge cheer from the crowd. The dragon's blue eyes flashed. It gave a wheeze, then smoke belched from its mouth, accompanied by delighted squeals from the princesses. Shaela gave me a grin and a thumbs-up. The Vikings formed a phalanx around the galley, the accordionists and fiddler took up their stations at the front, and played the opening bars of the Up Helly Aa march. I found the words uncoiling in my throat, though I wouldn't have been able to say them, and joined in with a will as I followed the galley along Main Street to where my next spell of waitressing awaited.

The galley stopped at the Burn Beach for photographs: the Jarl in his galley, the princesses, the galley, the whole squad around the galley, personal photos of each squad member with his family. The flashes bounced off Reidar's cream-painted walls. At last the band struck up again, and the Jarl squad marched off with a swirl of cloaks towards the waiting bus, which trailed streamers of maroon and white. They would sing their songs, and march round the school halls, and cheering bairns in home-made feathered helmets would respond with a peerie play, or a song of their own, and a great time would be had by everyone. We'd see the pictures in next week's *Shetland Times*: a beaming Jarl presenting a miniature of his shield to the primary school's head-teacher, or a bearded Viking hugging his granny at the care centre.

In the café, the rush began, as Jarl Squad families who'd been hanging around since nine this morning decided they needed a cup of coffee and a fancy. Neither Reidar's official waitress, Amy, nor I, had time to look up until Reidar sent me out, just after twelve. 'Go and take a break, Cass. Study the Bill.'

It was set up in pride of place, the traditional Bill, a board headed with a painting of a white and maroon galley under full sail, swirling in foaming seas beside Scalloway Castle, and a portrait of the Jarl holding his shield. Below, the muster time was given: *The Guizer Jarl decrees that Guizers will muster at Lover's Loan at 6.30 p.m. Procession will move off at 7 p.m. prompt.* Beneath that was a paragraph of writing, with in-jokes highlighted in red. While I was out, I nipped into the shop and bought a programme, an A5 booklet with a colour photo of the Jarl on the front, and photos of all the squads inside. Kevin's seemed to be called 'Which Witch?' – that answered my suspicions about what it was about, and why he'd wanted my black suit.

The squad bus returned at one, while I was in the midst of serving up plates of creamy yellow pumpkin soup and plump bacon rolls; it seemed they'd been invited to lunch aboard the blue and white accommodation barge for the Totale workers. After that, one woman told me, they'd be off to Hamnavoe school, then back to the boating club for the senior citizens' party.

Reidar wasn't staying open in the evening tonight; everyone would be out partying. He sent me home early: 'For you have had a long day already, and you must be able to dance tonight.'

It was still daylight as I set off back to the pontoon. The quarter moon hung like a child's cut out against the darkening sky. Music echoed across the water from the boating club, and a lot of cheering. It was the traditional Fire Festival senior citizens' party, and by the sound of it a very good time was being had by all. I made a cup of tea and wriggled into my berth to rest for a bit. It would be a long night.

ᚼ

It was a bonny, bonny evening. The sky above the hills was midnight blue, with the stars ice-cold, and the planets bright as diamonds: Venus, Mars, Jupiter. High in the west the moon sailed, a golden halfpenny. A cold breath of air touched our faces as we stood on the shore road waiting for light-up. A crack, and the maroon fired red sparks into the air; the streetlights dwindled to blackness.

We smelt the torches before we saw them, a drift of paraffin, then the fixed brightness of the flare behind the shop and houses gave way to red flickering and the billowing smoke rising. The band began playing, but was drowned by cheers as the procession began to move, the trail of smoke and the red glow in the sky silhouetting the waterfront houses as if they were aflame.

I don't know what Gavin had expected, but his mouth dropped open as the first Vikings marched towards us, the galley swaying behind them on its metal trolley. 'They're like real Viking raiders. No wonder they struck terror into all the coast-dwellers. Imagine seeing that lot charging up the beach towards you.' Then the policeman came in. 'Those axes must be in breach of the offensive weapons act.'

'Bound to be,' I agreed.

'And what about the torches?' He watched as a scrap of sacking detached itself from one torch and swirled upwards, glowing red. 'On a windy night there must be sparks everywhere.'

'Health and safety is that you watch the back of the person in front of you, and put out any sparks that land on them.'

The galley's smoke-belching mechanism was still working; the blue eyes lit up balefully. The first Vikings were last year's Jarl Squad, mustering the procession; then came the galley, surrounded by its maroon-cloaked warriors. The brass band marched behind it, between the rows of torches. Every time it paused to change tune there was a roar of 'Uggi uggi uggi!' from the head of the procession, answered by 'Oy oy oy!' from the tail.

'Uggi?' Gavin murmured in my ear.

'Traditional Viking war cry,' I lied briskly. 'And have you noticed the half-bottles being quietly passed round? *Hit's a dry festival, du kens.*'

272

'I'd noticed.'

'At least they allow women in this one,' I said consolingly. 'All the country ones do. It's just Lerwick that's still men only. The next South Mainland one is even having a woman Jarl.'

Behind the Vikings came the rest of the guizers, a double snake of flickering orange torches. There were a hundred and fifty of them, made up of squads of around a dozen people, each dressed for their 'act'. The Jarl Squad was squad 1; they were followed by furry creatures mixed with council workers in blue boiler suits and yellow hard hats with SIC in black tape on the front; the next squad was obviously based on local happenings, for the glinting masks were photographs blown up to life-size, with ganseys, jeans and yellow boots below. There were doctors and nurses next, the nurses acted by men with curly blonde wigs and enormous false breasts. I risked a glance at Gavin, but his face was carefully blank, as if he was on duty. There were black and white suits next, then men with space hoppers. The next lot were in black, with the alphabet letters on their chests, and after them came a bunch in coloured hoodies with scarves tied round their foreheads, kung fu-style. Then my heart gave a jolt, and for a moment I couldn't breathe. There, in the procession, was the devil-figure that had surfaced in my dreams since the autumn, even though I knew he was no more than a costume. Several green-faced witches capered behind him. Gavin touched my arm and nodded across the road. 'There we are.'

It was indubitably us: Gavin in his kilt, with an orange 'See you Jimmy' wig, and me in a dark boiler suit and lifejacket with CASS written down one side. They'd done my scar with lipstick, and made me a good deal curvier.

'Just wait till I see Kevin,' I said. *Just a fun*, indeed.

'Your classmates? This must be Socks the moonwalking pony.'

273

The fur suits were chestnut, dapple grey, black and white, with flowing tails and horse heads worn like hats, so that the faces peered out from the pony's chest. Among them were men in butcher aprons and white net hats, with huge choppers tucked into their belts. 'I don't think I want to ask,' I said.

The next lot made the buxom nurses seem positively tame. It was some sort of beauty competition, with the men playing the women hamming it up for all they were worth. Low-cut blouses clung to breasts like nuclear missiles, there were golden curls, fishnet tights and enough make-up to paint a sixty-footer. Last of all – I knew there would be one – was the squad who'd gone for black face paint and nylon afro wigs. Some were visibly what even I recognised as the Village People, and the others were in a one-piece jumpsuit, pale blue with wide lapels. I watched from the corner of my eye as Gavin's mouth dropped. 'It's considered perfectly okay up here.'

He shook his head. 'So long as they know not to do it on the mainland.'

The galley had reached the top of the boating club slip now, and while it was being manoeuvred into position, and the barrel-float raft was detached from its wheels, the Jarl squad led the long procession back down inside itself, so that there were four lines of torches flickering past us. The heat stung my cheeks. As they marched, the snow began again, great white flakes that caught the rising torchlight and gleamed like rubies as they fell. Now as the Jarl Squad came back up to the head of the procession they continued, to form a line along the breakwater. The marching torches stilled, the flames rose upwards. The band had gone up to its platform on the boating club balcony, and loudspeakers blared the march across the water: *From grand old Viking centuries Up Helly Aa has come.* Then they changed to a slow, proud air: *Waves the raven banner o'er us, as our Viking ship we sail ...* When it ended there was silence

274

broken only by the waves against the pier. The Jarl stepped forward in his boat and raised his axe once more.

'Three cheers for the galley builders!'

The torches jerked skywards as the guizers cheered. The sound echoed off the houses at the other side of the bay.

'Three cheers for the torch makers!'

One of the Jarl squad stepped forward for the next one. 'Three cheers for the Guizer Jarl!'

The last cheers were led by the Jarl again: 'Three cheers for Up Helly Aa!' He clambered out of his warship and gave her a last, long look. The bugle sounded and there was another moment of stillness before the long line of fire along the waterfront began to flow forward to the galley. Each torchbearer came up to her, threw his great matchstick, and ducked back; we heard the thump and rumble of the torches being thrown into her, then her timbers crackling. She caught quickly; the heat was so intense that the last of the procession had to throw their torches in from ten metres back. A heave on the ropes that led seaward, and she rushed down the slip into the water, embracing her own element for her first and last voyage. The flames that blazed from inside her turned the still water to molten gold.

The band struck up: *The Norseman's home on days gone by, was on the rolling sea ...* The whole village sang her lament, watching as the fire crept stealthy fingers up the mast, caught the sail; it exploded in flames, leaving the crow's nest charred and the raven banner starting to blacken. The orange tongues licked up the spined neck and around the coiled tail until she was a mass of fire. Glowing sparks rose up into the sky. Then the burning torches made their way through her sides first, leaving the black oars like ribs, until they too dissolved in the white heat. The mast fell at last, the curved tail, the dragon head, with a final hiss at her death blow, and the proud galley was a

275

bonfire floating in the sea.

Gavin gave a long sigh, as if he'd been holding his breath. I slipped my arm into his, and we stood there for a moment, silent. Behind us, the chattering crowd began to disperse: the squads to their bus, and whichever pub they'd chosen to get their full costume on and fortify themselves further before their first hall, the folk to get out of their spark-proof jackets and warmest breeks and into their party clothes. Nobody in Scalloway would be staying home tonight. A confusion of buses blocked the street.

I felt a hand on my shoulder, and turned to see Reidar. 'I've made hot chocolate,' he rumbled, 'with a touch of brandy in it to keep out the cold. Come aboard.'

We trooped after him. *Sule*'s cabin was blissfully warm. I relaxed into the plastic cushions with a sigh.

'It was a good burning,' Anders said. 'I had seen photos, of course, but they do not give an idea of the scale of it all, of how spectacular it is.'

'And now we dance all night?' Gavin asked.

'In between squad acts.'

I drank my chocolate and left the men to it while I slipped aboard *Khalida* to change and make an attempt at make-up. Maman had given me the essentials, but I wasn't convinced. Foundation just seemed to make my tanned skin an unhealthy colour, although it did smooth the scar a little, and I hadn't quite got the hang of how much blusher, or where exactly to put it. I didn't achieve the porcelain doll look that would mask every young girl's face in the hall tonight, but Gavin would know I'd tried. I didn't own any jewellery, but my dress was pretty, black sprigged with flowers. Georgette, Maman had called it, a light material that swirled around my ankles and flowed like water as I moved. It was only two hundred yards to the boating club, but I wasn't slithering through the snow in sandals. I pulled my rubber boots back on and put my sandals in my pocket. I wasn't sure I'd be able to dance in them, but I could kick them off and go barefoot if need be.

Being a well brought up Scot, Gavin didn't whistle or compliment, but his smile told me he appreciated my effort to look bonny. 'Time to go?'

'We don't want to miss the first act.'

Chapter Twenty-eight

We gave our tickets in at the door, found space at a table that had a front-on view of the central space, where the acts would take place, but wasn't too close to the band, and settled down to read the programme. It gave a transcript of the Bill I'd admired that morning, a list of the squad names, suitably cryptic, and photographs. There were twelve squads in all. I pointed Kevin out. 'We share an engine. He was the one being me.'

A microphone wheezed into life; the band leader leaned forward. 'Well, folk, let's start the night off with a Boston. Let's see everyone on the floor noo, for a Boston Two-step, and dinna say you don't ken it, fir I winna believe that. Take your partners, please, for a Boston Two-step.'

I thought the Boston was ingrained in me from my youth, but I wasn't going to be first on the floor; and besides, I had three men here to share my dances among, and I wasn't going to ask one up first. *The policeman's girlfriend* ... Gavin turned as if he'd read the thought. 'I'll ask you to dance the minute there are enough couples to keep us from being conspicuous. Freya warned me that the Shetland version of every country dance is different from the Scottish one.'

'It's danced three times, so you'll get a chance to watch.'

He watched gravely through the first dance. 'It looks the same, except that you sway where our lady would birl under the man's arm. Shall we try it?'

I was annoyed to find myself trembling as we took the two steps to the floor. It was only a dance, Cass, get a grip.

As we joined hands and stood side by side, waiting for the second chunk of music to begin, I could hear his breathing, slightly quickened, as he could hear mine; then we were walking together, steps matching, less awkward than I'd feared. Three steps and a hop forward, three and a hop back, then sideways, and as we met again he swirled me into a waltz hold. I could feel the roughness of his tweed sleeve against my back through the thin material of my dress, and the warmth of his hand on my waist. He held me close enough so that I was secure, yet not so tightly that I felt constrained. His breath was warm on my hair, and I could feel his chest rise and fall as we swayed to one side, the other, again, then he spun me off into the polka steps, *one, two, three, one, two, three*. He was a good dancer. I thought about that and fell over my own feet. His arm tightened, steadying me, then relaxed.

'The annual Police Ball,' he said into my hair, 'and every wedding in the Highlands, to say nothing of being taught in school. My feet think in fours.'

'We were taught too, but I've no' used it much since.'

'I thought daily hornpipes were de rigeur on a tall ship.'

'Not since the days of Captain Bligh. We do Norwegian square dances sometimes, if there's a fiddler aboard.'

As we separated at last I was vexed to find myself blushing, and not quite able to look at him. Then the band leader pulled his microphone towards him again: 'Please take your seats, ladies and gentlemen, for squad number 7. Squad number 7, Fifty shades of the Doctor.'

The fiddle-box carrier (a youngster whose job was to collect and distribute props, and count all squad members onto the bus before it left each venue) scurried across the floor with the CD. There was a moment of clicks and hisses, then the *Dr Who* theme tune engulfed us. The doctors and nurses I'd noticed in the procession strode on, swinging their stethoscopes. They were followed by a selection of costumes, each topped by a photograph mask. I didn't know any of the people, but everyone else did, judging by the laughter at the other tables. Their complaints included an irresistible fascination for drink, not being able to pass a bonny woman in the street, and toenails that meant they had difficulty getting their rubber boots on. The doctors gave increasingly daft prescriptions, then there was a blare and crackle from the loudspeakers and in rolled a flashing-lights Dalek. 'Exterminate! Exterminate!' it gobbled, in traditional fashion, covered the doctors in silly string, and chased the entire cast from the hall. A pause for applause, then they all came back in, and the band leader announced the squad dance: 'The Polly Glide.'

'The *what?*' Gavin murmured in my ear.

I cast back in my memory. 'I think it's one you do in lines.' As the music began, my feet remembered. A march forwards, reverse, sideways, back sideways, then a complicated pattern of toe-pointing, a galumph forwards, and you began again. I was just about to say, 'Do you want to give it a go?' when Anders rose and caught my hand.

'Come, Cass, it is a night to be foolish.' He swung his arm around my waist and before I knew it we were between another two couples, stepping forward, back, sideways, and it felt entirely natural to be messing about with Anders like this again, a strange extension of scrambling about sailing boats. By the end of it we were both breathless and laughing as we dropped back into our seats.

'Squad 11, Miss Shetland,' the band leader announced, and the blue-movie women with the fishnets strolled in, simpering in front of the judges, who were girls dressed as crofters in boiler suits, yellow wellies, and toorie caps. One towed a life-size stuffed collie. The women swayed round the floor to a fiddle waltz, then, with a drum roll, the traditional striptease tune began, and 'Miss Scalloway' shimmied in, golden curls, high heels, gloves. He'd kept his beard on, just in case someone thought he was taking this seriously. I sank a little lower in my seat, but Gavin was laughing and cheering with the rest of the audience as 'Miss Scalloway' stripped down to a very ornate bikini. It wasn't a pretty sight; he had to be the hairiest man I'd ever seen. The judges were impressed and came forward with his prize, which had me laughing at last: an extra-large tube of Veet hair remover.

The squad dance was an eightsome reel. Anders and Gavin were grabbed by a couple of young women in very short dresses, and I steered Reidar round the intricacies of left hand and right, setting to your partner, the reel of three. I felt absurdly self-conscious when it came to my turn to be in the middle, and ended up clapping and turning counter-clockwise, against the way of the dancers circling me, eyes looking at the floor. Gavin set neatly, with none of the overdone raised-arm stuff, and when it was our turn to birl he spun me round with balanced control, placing me exactly in front of his opposite number for the next set and spin. His kilt pleats swayed as he stepped the reel of three; my dress floated about my legs as he spun me again. Then there was the final 'shaking hands' round, and a last birl with Reidar which was more of a galumph that took us sideways into Anders and his partner, so that we ended the dance in a flurry of apologies.

Gavin thanked his partner, and came back to our table. 'A long cold drink?'

'Oh, yes please. A bitter lemon with loads of ice.'

He went off to the bar, and I decided it was time for a breath of fresh air, and a quick look across at *Khalida*. Too many people would know she'd probably be unguarded tonight.

I slipped out of the front door and into the shadows of the wall facing the marina. The thump, thump of the band had begun again, blessedly muffled. Squad 7's bus was parked in the dinghy space, and another bus crunched along Port Arthur Road towards me, slowed at the club and turned in just past it: the next squad arriving. Along the pontoon, all was still. I took two breaths of the ice-cold air, and was just about to go back in when there was a shuffle at the corner of the club, and the broad shoulders of Laurence Georgeson loomed up in front of me. His dark brows met in a scowl, his mouth sneered. I turned my head away, hoping he wouldn't recognise me, and tried to move around him. He stood solidly, blocking my way.

'Well, now, I think I ken your face this time.' His eyes lingered on my scar; he gave a sour smile. 'You didn't wait for your weight.'

Damn.

He leaned forward, breathing beer in my face. 'And just why were you poking around our warehouse?'

Another dark suit, just as bulky, came up behind him: Peter Georgeson, as black-avised as his brother, and in just as friendly a mood. 'Our father would like a word with you.' He clamped an elephant-seal flipper on my shoulder. 'I think you should come with us.'

I thought not. They were between me and the club door, but I reckoned I could outrun them, even in these shoes. I shrugged sulkily and took two steps forward, as if I was obeying. I felt them relax. I spun around and ran for it: around this side of the clubhouse, onto the balcony at the back, and over the top of the railing.

Surprise had given me fifty metres grace. There was a shout behind me, then only one set of running footsteps; one of them must have gone back around the front, and if I wasn't quick I'd find myself trapped between them, here at the back of the club, with the dark water glimmering. I let myself down from the railing, and felt the jar from the heeled shoes stab up my ankles. If I was fast I'd make it behind the college without being seen.

My luck was out. The bus I'd seen had backed right to the railing, leaving no room for me to get behind. I heard my follower's shoes thud dully on the wooden balcony. He'd be on me soon; and the brother who'd come round the front would be in sight any second.

I ran for the open doorway of the bus. Most of the squad were still aboard, collecting up their gear or having a last long swig from their half bottles, but a couple were almost at the boating club door, and two, dressed as policemen, stood at the bus door. I dodged behind them, and Peter Georgeson strode past, looking beyond the bus. I started up the bus steps and ran straight into myself coming down: my dark sailing suit, the lifejacket with CASS down one side, my photograph fronting a wig with a long, dark plait. This Cass was a good head taller than me.

'Kevin?' I said. I leapt onto the step beside him. '*Shooosh*,' I breathed. 'There's someone after me.' Lawrence Georgeson had come around the corner, looking towards the club door, as if he thought I'd dodged past the guizers. His brother shook his head. Both heads turned to the bus.

'I need to get to Gavin.' Kevin's glittering eyes looked blank behind the mask. I claimed him without thinking. 'My policeman. It's those two, the Georgeson brothers.'

He shoved me behind him, into the bus. 'Shut the door,' he ordered the driver, and stood between the seats, raising his voice. 'Boys, we need to get Cass into the hall without anyone seeing her.'

'Nae borrer,' said a voice I recognised as Jimmy's. 'They'll be a black bag somewye. Come on, Andy, you have one. Brian, do you have your tulley?'

The bus driver fished under his seat and brought out a handful of black bags; a policeman produced a Swiss Army knife. Jimmy handed him a bag. 'Cut holes for her head an' arms. Wha has the green gear?'

'It's here,' a girl's voice said. I looked round into a green face and warty nose. 'I'm Gwen, Kevin's girlfriend.' The face paint wouldn't let her flush, but her voice was excited. 'Is someone after you? Have you found out this murderer?' Bless the lass, she was already fumbling in her handbag. 'Wipe this all over your face.' She was already moving as she spoke, thrusting a pat of face paint into my hand, and a dampened sponge. 'You can have me hat an' cloak, I'll keep the wig. We'll need to hurry, they'll be announcing us any minute.'

Brian handed me the black bag, and began working on a second one. I wiped the green facepaint all over my carefully done make-up, hauled the plastic bag over my frock, and tied Gwen's cloak around my neck. Gwen whisked a hairbrush from her bag and backcombed my hair, then put her hat on my head, and there we were, a pair of pantomime witches ready for our cue, not a moment too soon. There was a thump at the door of the bus.

'Yea, let him in,' Kevin said, and the bus driver shrugged. The doors wheezed open, and Laurence Georgeson lumbered forward. He filled the bus door completely. 'I'm looking for Cass Lynch,' he announced.

The boys in the bus burst into a chorus of whistles, the girls made 'oooh' noises. Kevin shimmied forward. 'That's me, darling. You want any villains detected, I'm your woman.'

Georgeson was momentarily at a loss. 'Cass Lynch?'

'It's on me lifejacket, see?' Kevin pointed. 'CASS.'

Then Georgeson got it. 'Dinna mess me about, I want the real one. We ken she's in here.'

Kevin blocked his way, and told the exact truth with a coolness I wouldn't have expected of my quiet fellow engine-destroyer. 'This bus is for the members of our squad, an' the real Cass is no' in that. Now you'll have to let us out, or we're going to keep the hall waiting, and that'll never do. Come on, boys.'

The busload of guizers surged forwards, and Georgeson was forced to step aside. I felt his scrutiny as I passed him in a surge of green-faced, black-hatted witches, with my heart thumping like an engine piston. Peter Georgeson had come out to the steps of the bus. He gave us a suspicious glance. Gwen shoved right up to him. 'Let us past, we're on. Come on, Angie.' She took my arm and swept me past him. He looked at the last of the squad straggling out of the bus, looked back at me, the smallest of the bunch by several inches, and reached out a massive fist to grab my arm.

Right on cue, the band leader announced us: 'Put your hands together for squad number 8, squad 8.'

'That's us! Come on!' She shoved Peter's arm aside and hauled me into the club. The loudspeakers burst into 'Black Magic Woman'. 'Follow the other witches.'

For crying out loud ... It was one of those nightmares where you're on stage with no idea what the script is, or what your lines are, and I definitely didn't do theatricals, but the Georgeson brothers were right behind me, and following the other witches out into the clear space in the middle of the hall was the only way to get myself back to Gavin and safety. I took a deep breath, and came into the spotlights. Three witches were wheeling a cauldron made out of one of those blue plastic barrels, almost chest height, and from the effort they were making, surprisingly heavy in spite of the wheels; the rest were crouching, cackling and rubbing their hands in best witchy tradition, so I did likewise. This wasn't a time to be shy. My first cackle startled me with its volume.

Gavin was still at the bar as we came in. He turned to watch us. I passed close to him and cackled again. His head came up instantly; a long look, then I knew he'd recognised me. His eyes went quickly round the room, found the two Georgesons, like a pair of mobmen in their black suits, and came back to me. I nodded. Message understood.

We were circling round the cauldron now. Suddenly there was a bang and a flash from it, and the devil character rose out of it, waving his hands. We witches went round him, cringing, while he waved a whip about. Then there was another flash, and Kevin-Cass leapt out of the cauldron too, and proceeded to run round us, trailing a line of jib sheets tied together, until we witches were trussed to the cauldron, with the devil in the middle of us. Kevin blew a whistle, and the Gavin character and a squad of policemen entered at the gallop and did a dance routine before unmasking the devil, who turned out to be the Leader of Shetland Islands Council (another photograph). We witches went into a pleading routine, blaming him for making us do it. The police seemed inclined to let us go, but the Gavin character strode forwards, lifted the hat of one witch, and flipped down a mask inside it – Helen Budge, Head of Education. The other witches lifted their hats and flipped down masks which looked like more council people, including Vaila Wishart, who was the chair of the Education committee. There were cheers from the audience; Scalloway school had been the first casualty in a round of closures. The policemen unfurled blue and white 'Communities United for Rural Education' banners, plastic handcuffs were produced, and we were marched off. My heart began to thump again; for all they were plastic, the cuffs were strong enough to hamper me if a Georgeson grabbed me – but surely they wouldn't dare, right under Gavin's nose?

The policeman who'd collared me was taking an age to find the key for my cuffs, making a comedy performance of it, patting each of his dozen police jacket pockets. In the shadows, the Georgesons moved forwards. I stood mast-still, fighting down my impatience. He found the key at last, and fumbled my handcuffs off. I sensed rather than

287

saw the movement of a dark arm behind me. A heavy hand came down on my shoulder. I ducked away from it and pushed forwards onto the floor, just as the squad dance was being announced. Perfect. I slid across the floor to Gavin, at the bar.

'The Georgeson brothers say their father wants a word with me.'

'Presumably they've now matched up the stupid boy in a boiler suit with Cass Lynch, girl detective. The sort of people who act first, then let their brains catch up. The father didn't get where he is by doing that.' He took his change and carried the two drinks back to our table. 'Are you asking me up for your squad dance, before you change?' He held his hand out. 'Or are you going to stay green all night?'

'It isn't easy being green. I'm not sure I remember how to do a Pride of Erin.'

'You said that about the Polly Glide, and your feet remembered fine.' He swept me into a waltz hold. 'I haven't managed to tell you yet.'

'Tell me what?' I stepped, crossed, pointed my toe, reversed the movement. We spread our linked hands, pulled back from each other, then pulled in again, so that our faces were very close, looking along our shoulders into each other's eyes.

'You mentioned the horse harness,' he said. Retreat, advance again. 'And the Lerwick Gala items.' A last sway, and we were back into waltz hold, gliding round. 'This is most dreadfully unromantic,' Gavin complained. His arm was warm around my waist, his hand firm on my back. 'Our first waltz, and I'm talking shop.'

'I don't have a fan to flutter. Go on, the Lerwick Gala stuff.'

'*The Purloined Letter.*'

I gave him a blank look.

'Three barrels,' he said simply, stepping nearly

forwards without even looking at his feet, 'among cartoon cut outs, with the front one labelled "Lucky Dip".'

Light dawned. We did the spread arms, stepping back, stepping forwards bit again. 'And one of the empties smelt of whisky?' I asked, along out lined-up shoulders.

He nodded, and turned me under his arm. 'It's funny how people don't seem to count receivers or creditors or insurance or tax officials as actual owners. He was very offended that I called it theft.'

'It's not exactly theft. He gave it to the people who'd bought it.'

'Yes. Unless forensics can match the whisky profile to the recovered Lunna Bridge, there's no actual evidence of anything.'

'You didn't mention Magnie?' I asked, alarmed.

He shook his head. 'I saw no bottle, I tasted no whisky. I think it'll just be quietly dropped.'

My feet had remembered the complicated step-cross pattern now. I could leave them to get on with it. 'Shetlanders have had years of ignoring the ranselmen to take what the sea brings.'

'Ranselmen?'

'The Customs Officers.' I remembered a radio broadcast we'd listened to in secondary. 'There was this ship wrecked, *Gudrun*, and all that was left to salvage was some spars and a keg of brandy the seawater had got into.'

'Flotsam, jetsam, laggan.'

'A wreck. The customs officials weren't happy. There was a court case, but the only men who'd been seen at the ship just happened to have left on a whaling ship.'

'One benefit of living on an island,' Gavin agreed. We spun round in the waltz again, steps matching neatly. He was making me into a better dancer than I remembered myself being. I was sorry that the black plastic bag prevented my skirt from swirling out as we swung.

'The entire community must have helped clear the

ship,' I said, once we were back to criss-cross stepping. 'She had a full cargo of wine, flour, tea-sets, all sort of stuff.'

'It's odd talking to someone with a green face,' Gavin complained. 'What about the crew?'

I remembered the broadcast, and put on a story-telling voice. 'All dead aboard, and the captain sitting at the table with a gold ring apo' his finger.'

My policeman raised his brows. 'Sitting?'

'Or there's a rumour they were murdered, but our teacher didn't believe that one. She made us listen to the story in groups and sort out first-hand evidence from rumour.'

'What first hand evidence did you have?'

'Oh, the records from Hay and Co – they were the shipping agents. The gold ring was right, because they sent it back to the widow. Anyway, there's a saying up in Nesting, where she went ashore, "Dey're gotten a Gudrun there", meaning a windfall.'

'I don't suppose I'd have time to go to the archives tomorrow. Maybe some other time.' He sighed. 'The world is too full of interesting stories. Why would they have been murdered anyway?'

'You canna rob the sea of her prize. Shu'll tak a life in revenge.' I remembered what I'd meant to tell him. 'I heard about Jeemie, in the shop.'

'Yes. That took up most of yesterday.'

'So if Jeemie is out of it, and Georgeson senior, then who …?'

'Still under consideration. Tomorrow.' The tune ended; Gavin held me still in waltz hold, ready for the second bout. 'You see, I'm learning. At home, we do each dance only once.' He smiled at me. 'We dance rather well together, don't you think?'

'On easy dances,' I agreed cautiously. 'I wouldn't offer to do an exhibition tango.'

'It's good having someone who's the right height for me. At the police ball, all the female officers are as tall as me anyway, so once they're in high heels I feel like I'm steering a giraffe round the floor.'

We stepped and twirled round the floor in silence for the next stage, while I contemplated that. I'd never thought of myself being the right height before. I'd got good at stretching or clambering up to holds designed for six-foot men. I could wedge myself into small spaces, and I'd never complained about a sea-berth being too short. Yet here we were with his shoulder the height above mine that meant my arm fitted comfortably under it, and our strides matching. His grey eyes caught mine, with that teasing glint, but he didn't speak, just smiled and kept dancing, his arm firm round my waist, his hand warm around mine, and I was contented.

ᛁ

He'd just drawn me back to join Reidar and Anders when there was a drum roll from the band: 'Put your hands together, please, for squad number 6, squad 6.'

A crash of heavy metal music, and the fiddle box boy came in with a construction labelled 'The Tunnel of Doom'. Behind him, an even smaller boy struggled with 'The Hoop of Horror'. A pause, then three men in motor-biking leathers boinged into the room on orange spacehoppers. We laughed and clapped as they hopped round, contemplating the obstacles, then lined up ready to try them. There was a shrilling of whistles, and a set of neon waistcoats charged in, brandishing clipboards labelled 'Health and Safety Audit.' Heads were shaken, mouths pursed, then the H&S people issued the bikers with purple helmets and swimming goggles. They stood

291

back; the bikers revved up their spacehoppers, and two men with lawnmowers disappeared into the other side of the tunnels. The bikers went in; the tape ended in loud whirring noises, clanks, and screams; the mowing men came out of the front of the tunnels, bedaubed with fake blood and with rather horribly realistic severed limbs dangling from the mower blades.

We laughed and clapped, then I went to the toilets to remove the green face paint. Without it, without the make-up, my face was scrubbed and red, the scar horribly visible. *We dance rather well together* ... All the same, I'd wanted to do him credit. I made a face at myself, and returned just in time for the squad dance, a St Bernard's Waltz. Anders took me up for it. 'And how did you come to be green in the first place?'

I explained. My feet knew this dance without me even having to think about it. He held me tighter than Gavin had in the waltz, but I didn't mind. We belonged, Anders and I, and I was tired, so tired, it was good to have his shoulder to lean on ...

'Hey!' he said, in my ear. 'I know that you can sleep on a clothes rail, but it is not polite to doze while you are dancing.'

I shook myself awake. 'Sorry. It's been a long day waitressing.'

He spun me in an extra circle as the first set of music ended. 'Pretend you are on watch on a tall ship.'

I put my hand over a huge yawn. 'I can't.'

'Then talk to me. Tell me all your plans for this year. Somewhere warm.'

That woke me up a little, but not quite enough; I kept yawning through the next squad, the one we'd spotted as Socks, the moonwalking pony. The ponies were auditioning for a cute pony advert, and any that didn't make the grade were handed over to the butchers, and taken behind a screen. There were thumping noises and whinnies, then the butchers came out carrying Spam tins. Rainbow and Vaila wouldn't have liked it, and my eyelids were heavy, so heavy ... then I jerked awake as I found myself falling forwards. 'I'm sorry, I think it's probably my bedtime.'

Gavin glanced at his watch. 'I'll have a busy day tomorrow. I'll walk you to your gate.'

Anders and Reidar flicked a glance at each other. I could tell exactly what they were thinking: if this was to be a romantic moment, they didn't want to spoil it, but if Gavin was going to abandon me at the gate, they wanted to make sure I came to no harm. 'How about you two?' I asked.

'I am tired too,' Reidar said. I wasn't surprised; he'd been on his feet all day.

'Waiting at tables and being a baker is much harder than taking an engine apart,' Anders agreed.

'We're a set of wimps,' I said. 'Everyone else will be up until dawn. You haven't even seen the Jarl Squad.'

'What do they do?' Gavin asked, cautiously. 'Rape and pillage?'

'They sing the Up Helly Aa songs, and the squad song.'

Gavin waved one hand. 'They were very impressive at the burning. I really do have to work tomorrow.' He smiled at me. 'I shouldn't feel relieved you don't want to dance all night.'

'I couldn't.' As I walked across the floor, I was swaying as if I was drunk; or maybe it was the world swaying around me. Gavin gave me his arm; my hand curled around the rough tweed, stone-steady. Outside, the cold was biting after the warmth of the club, but even that didn't wake me up. The moon shone above us, ringed with a frost halo. Anders and Reidar went on first, Gavin and I behind them, side by side, steps matching. At the gate, Gavin leaned forward to kiss me on the cheek, quickly, lightly, just as I'd kissed him. We said goodnight, *beannachd leat,* speak tomorrow. He walked briskly to his car, and I locked the gate and stumbled forward to *Sule.* Cat didn't want to leave the warmth of Anders' sleeping bag, where he and Rat were curled up, but by the time I'd renewed the hot water bottle I'd tucked into my berth to pre-warm my thermals and two downies, brushed my teeth, and wriggled into my bunk, he'd slipped in through the forrard hatch, finished his supper, and was ready to curl in beside me. We were out cold in less than a minute.

Saturday 11th January

High Water at Scalloway UT	*05.11, 1.3 m*
Low Water	*11.39, 1.0 m*
High Water	*17.40, 1.3 m*
Low Water	*00.03, 0.9 m*
Moonset	*04.31*
Sunrise	*08.59*
Moonrise	*12.16*
Sunset	*15.26*

Moon first quarter

Der surely some whaup ipo da raep
There's some hidden motive or undisclosed reason.

Chapter Twenty-nine

Someone was following me. I could hear the footsteps, soft on the pavement, as if the person wore unseasonal canvas shoes so that they could move unheard. Like an echo, when I paused, they paused, but not quite quickly enough; when I went on, a little faster, they hurried after me, yet when I looked over my shoulder there was nobody there in the dusk.

I cursed my hurry. Anders had gone off to a Warhammer game, and I should have waited for Reidar to finish preparations for tomorrow, but I'd been worried about Cat, left alone all day while I waitressed, and it was just past five, with people in the shops and street, discussing last's night's triumph. I'd come past the brightly lit shops, the open car park with the Shetland Bus Memorial in the centre, and come around the corner at the first of the sheds. It was there I'd heard the echo. I'd gone on, past the Walter and Joan Grey Eventide Home, past the Bus men's repair shed; the red of Norway House was on my right, its windows dark. On my left, the water lapped at the rusted slip. I came out into the centre of the road. 'Who's there?'

There was no reply. The echo stilled. I remembered Hubert, lying in the snow on the marina pontoon with the blood bubbling over his chest, and felt a cold slither climbing up my spine. The long street between me and *Khalida* stretched before me. I could run back to the old folks' home, where there'd be a warden on duty, but the footsteps had been behind me.

Then a hooded shadow moved in the blacker shadow of

the nearest doorway, not twenty yards from me. A woman's voice breathed my name: 'Cass, wait! I want to talk to you.'

I paused, turned, and realised I'd made a mistake, for she was holding a gun in her hand, pointed straight at me. She wasn't going to do the 'murderer confesses all' chat, like an Agatha Christie. She was going to shoot me at point-blank range, as she'd shot Hubert. It took a good shot to hit a moving target. I leapt sideways, then turned and ran, the lights of the Walter and Joan Grey bright before my eyes.

There was a queer crack, and I was flung backwards, a searing pain in my belly. My head hit the ground with a bang that half stunned me. My side was wet – I was bleeding and hurting, and a shadow was gliding over the road beside me with a shadow gun in its hand, like something from a film, except the gritty pavement under my cheek, the hardness under my hip, made it real. I tried to get up, but my arms had no strength. I could only move in slow motion, as if I was in a nightmare. The shadow on the ground by my head looked over its shoulder, as if it heard something that the drumming in my ears shut out, then I was grabbed under the shoulders and half dragged, half tumbled down Prince Olav's slipway.

'You shouldn't move me,' a voice in my head was protesting. 'The first rule of first aid, don't move the casualty. Airways, bleeding, consciousness. I'm losing enough blood, and you're hurting me ...' Over it, I was thinking. If she thought she'd got me with her first bullet, she wouldn't shoot again. It took all the resolution I could muster to go limp, let myself be hauled like this, down the sharp rocks of the shore and towards the cold water of the sea. I could feel the wave motion trembling through the beach, and the pebbles were wet as my hands brushed them. *Born to be drowned* ... the shoosh of the waves was getting closer, then I felt the shock of icy water on my face. The fog that filled my brain cleared for a moment. My oilskins held out the water for a few seconds, then the chill fingers crept around my collar and down to my breastbone. My heart tensed with shock for a moment, then resumed the beat that thumped through my chest, echoed in my ears.

All the time I was praying, praying incoherently for help. Now I was lying half-in the water. I felt her hand on my head, and took a long, silent breath, mouth open to gulp in as much air as I could, lungs filling to the very bottom, as if I was Maman preparing for one of her lovely runs of sound, like a lark's trill on a summer day. The hand clamped on my head; my face went down into the water. Count, Cass, count. Pearl divers could stay down for unbelievably long times. I felt a larger wave come over me, lift me, and glory be, she automatically stepped back from it, and I was able to sneak another long breath, salt-smelling, my own sea that was both foe and friend, that would clean the wound and stop the bleeding if she would only leave me lying here. The hand came back to my head, grasping my hair. My nose went down into the swirling sand.

Then there was light. I saw it even through my closed eyelids, dazzling through the dark: a car stopping, using the car park to turn in. The clutching fingers let my hair go. I felt the stones move as she turned and ran, and let my hands grasp the wet pebbles to haul myself out of there, inch by painful inch, gasping for breath, with the snatching wave receding from my shoulders, my waist. The wind was colder than the water had been. I didn't have long to get help.

The car had turned and gone, the driver looking over his shoulder while his searchlights had blazed over the sea. Heaven send she didn't come back to make sure I was finished off. Heaven send my oilskin jacket pocket had kept my phone dry. I rolled onto my back, ignoring the waves washing over my legs, and fumbled the velcro open. *Please, Lord…* It lit up as I touched the button. I manoeuvred my other hand to my face and pulled my glove off with my teeth.

The black waves a metre from me came and went, and there was a singing in the air. The screen was blurring in front of my eyes. Airways, bleeding, consciousness. I swapped the phone into my bare hand, then fumbled a fold of my jacket tight around my body and pushed against it, keeping my hand there while I worked the phone. One click of the centre button, up one, another click, and I should have 'contacts'. I'd re-saved Gavin as A Gavin, just to save scrolling through. Another click, to open his name, and then the green button. My hand was shaking, my mouth was filling with blood. I turned my head to spit it away. One ring – two – three – oh, Gavin, I need you, pick up – and then at last his voice was saying 'Cass?' and with my last rags of consciousness I found myself going into the formula I'd learned by heart, although I'd never yet needed to use it: 'Mayday, mayday.' I was struggling for breath now, and a red mist swum in front of my eyes. He needed to know where I was. That was the most urgent thing. I used the last rags of my strength to speak clearly. 'I'm on the beach. Prince Olav slipway.' Bless him, he didn't ask questions or try to interrupt. 'I'm bleeding badly.' I should tell him who. 'Julie shot me. Julie. *M'aidez.*'

Then the darkness washed over me.

ᚺ

The time passed as if I was dreaming. I thought I heard Cat's almost silent miaow, then felt a rough tongue licking the salt from my face. The waves came up me, chilling my

300

hands, soaking my clothes. I couldn't feel my legs any more, but there was warm fur against my cheek. A njuggle hovered just at the edge of my vision. The trickster, the mill-dweller, the killer. There was something I had to remember, but it was lost in the darkness. Julie's voice. Then there were sirens, in the distance first, faint through the singing in my ears, then closer, splitting the quiet night with their clamour. Cat leapt away. Blue flashing light spilling over the wall above me, then the white glare of a searchlight raking the beach. Shouting. I felt the pebbles under me vibrate to running feet. Now I was surrounded by people with the antiseptic smell of medics. Someone was kneeling beside me; competent hands were unclasping my grip on my jacket. I heard an indrawn breath.

'Don't cut my gansey,' I managed to murmur.

Someone was at my head. 'Cass, can you hear me?' It was Gavin's voice. I tried to move my hand, and his fingers grasped mine. 'Hang on, Cass. Keep talking to me.'

'Julie,' I said. 'She shot me.' A hand clamped a bandage pad to my side. I closed my eyes for a moment, breathing deeply against the pain. When I opened them again, Gavin's face was hovering over me, calm as if he was in church; but his eyes were filled with anxiety. 'Be fine,' I promised him. '*Cat.* Here. Ask Reidar – look for him.'

'I'll get an officer to go.' I heard him giving instructions: she's worried about her cat. It would have been following her. Not following, my head contradicted, waiting for me.

'Won't come to a stranger.' My voice didn't sound like my own. 'Knows his way home. I just want to be sure he gets there.'

Gavin's voice turned away from me again. 'The café where the museum was. Tell Reidar what's happened, and ask if he'll come and check on Cat.'

'Julie.'

Gavin's face hung over my eyes, his shoulders lost in white mist, as if he was hovering in the air. 'Are you sure?'

I tried to nod, and felt the pain spasm down my side. 'Certain.' The hands holding the pad lifted for a moment, then pressed again. Dear God, it hurt so that I could barely think of anything else. The sweat was cold on my forehead. 'I recognised her voice.' I forced the words out of my memory. 'She said, "Cass, wait. I want to talk to you." Julie. Dragged me here – was going to hold my face under water – car came.'

Gavin turned away again. 'Go and pick up Mrs Julie Hughson, and take her to Lerwick. No arrest, we'd just like her to answer a few questions. Recommend she has a lawyer. I'll see Cass safe to hospital then come along.'

I heard the feet tramp up the beach. 'Grievous bodily harm. Attempted murder.'

'We don't know you're grievous yet,' Gavin said. I felt him move back, though his hand still held mine. Another face loomed over me.

'Cass, can you move your legs?'

'Cold,' I said, and did my best.

'Arms?'

'Yes.' I demonstrated.

'Take a few deep breaths for me.'

I had breathed deep for Julie. I could do it again, though the effort hurt. The paramedic spoke softly into my face. 'We're going to lift you onto the stretcher now. Don't try to help us, just lie limp. We'll do everything. Just relax, you're going to be fine.'

They laid a plastic stretcher beside me on the beach, and lifted me onto it. An explosion of pain. There was a cold sweat on my forehead, and the stretcher was hard beneath me. Straps were secured over my body. Then I felt them lifting me between them, slanting me as we went up the beach. The stretcher levelled out. There was a clicking of catches, and the movement changed to rolling. Up into the ambulance. I opened my eyes again, and the white ceiling swam above me. A plastic mask was pressed over my nose. 'Just focus on breathing now. In, out, in out.' I was so sleepy, so very sleepy. Gavin would make sure Cat was okay. The hospital would make sure I was okay. I gave up the fight to stay conscious, and let the mist descend once more.

ᚺ

When I awoke, I wasn't sure where I was. A white ceiling, a green curtain drawn around me, a ticking machine on my left, with an array of red lights and figures, and a clear tube drawn down to a butterfly of plasters on my elbow. I seemed to be wearing a shapeless green cotton nightdress whose sleeves came halfway down my arm. Then I remembered. Julie had shot me.

Gavin had sent officers to arrest her. Good. I thought about being attempted murdered and decided against it. I'd lost a fair bit of blood, and I'd have some bonny bruises from the way Julie had lumped me down the beach, but I could breathe, and there was no more blood in my mouth. I hadn't inhaled any water, and although I'd been shudderingly cold I shouldn't have developed hypothermia in so short a time. I wriggled my toes experimentally, and found they moved when asked. Fingers, ditto. No frostbite, then. I only had the gunshot wound to deal with, and even that didn't hurt as much as it had. The stabbing pain had subsided to a dull ache. That was probably painkillers. I'd gambled on her not being able to hit a moving target accurately, and I'd been lucky.

I let my eyes travel slowly round the room. It was a

small room, and mine was the only bed in it. There was a green plastic armchair on my left, and a locker on my right. The table had a green-capped jug of water, placed tantalisingly out of reach. The blinds were drawn, white horizontal blinds made out of broad semi-transparent stripes. Across from me there were various white cabinets on the white walls, and a sink with several admonitory posters stuck around it. The door was propped open, and that hospital-at-night hush breathed in: machines ticking, someone muttering, a bed creaking as someone else turned over, the distant hum of voices comparing notes, the occasional pad of trainer-shod feet down the corridor. If I closed my eyes and added the creak of masts and the shoosh of waves, I could pretend I was on a tall ship at night.

There was probably a clock somewhere, but I couldn't see it, and they'd taken my watch off. I considered the orange light slipping between the blinds, and supposed it was still night, but other than that I couldn't tell, and that was surprisingly disorientating. Then a nurse came in, a tall woman of about my own age, dressed in a mid-blue uniform. 'Hello, Cass. How are you feeling now?'

'Okay.' I considered that for a moment. 'Thirsty.'

She checked the chart that hung at the end of the bed. 'You're allowed 50ml of water every half hour.' She poured me a mouthful of water into a plastic nip glass, lifted a remote control from the end of the bed, and raised my head up. I drank, gratefully, rolling each sip around the dry inside of my mouth.

'How am I?'

'Stable,' she said, 'and lucky, considering you were shot at close range. You spent the night in theatre – but the consultant will tell you all about that in the morning, when he does his round. You can go back to sleep now.'

She glided out, leaving me to contemplate the ceiling. Julie ... I'd got her all wrong. I'd been distracted by the trickster njuggle; I should have remembered the other side of it, the ruthless creature that lured you on its back and plunged down into the waters with you. She'd fallen in love with Ivor at school, and not looked at anyone else. She'd gone to university with him, kept being there until finally he'd noticed her. I'd taken it as love. Now I looked at it the other way round: suppose it had been a man who'd fallen in love with a girl who wasn't interested, followed her to university, kept being there ... wouldn't you call that obsessive, instead of touching devotion, and tell him to get a life? Well, then. She'd wanted Ivor and she'd been determined to have him. She'd got him in the end; but it wasn't happily ever after. He'd remained the charmer she'd fallen for, charming other women, and the sea had taken him away from her too, sailing at weekends, holidays abroad. There hadn't been children to give her love to.

What had Inga's mother-in-law said about children? That was why they'd quarrelled. Julie was worried about the clock ticking, and wanted to try IVF, and Ivor wouldn't hear of it. That was Julie's version. But why should she want to have children in a marriage where the two people had drifted so far apart? That was just my supposition, of course; one partner constantly having affairs didn't sound like a happy marriage to me. Perhaps she did still love him, and thought a child would bring them together again.

My head was starting to hurt. I didn't do people. I did wind, and waves, tides and currents. I did setting of sails and steering a course. Then I remembered Anders, back in the summer: *Think the way you would naturally think. Think where you would place them on a watch.*

Very well. Ivor. A good sailor, a good navigator, a feel for the sea, but a risk-taker. I'd put him high up on the watch, but not as the leader, because he'd put the prize above the ship's safety. I remembered what I'd thought before: an idealist. *Full of new schemes for the rainbow tomorrow*, Susan had said. What had his scheme been this time, to get away from the collapse of his partnership with Robert-John?

Julie. The word that kept coming back was efficiency. Nothing in her appearance, her speech, suggested *flair*, the ability to feel how things were. She'd got where she was by meticulous attention to detail, by organisation, by dogged persistence. She'd be valuable wherever you put her: she'd plot a course, create a watch rota that let every one of a hundred and fifty trainees try every aspect of the ship, organise the ship's stores. What she wouldn't be able to do was feel the ship moving through the water, know by instinct how to trim the sails or the course. If it wasn't in a book, she wouldn't be able to do it.

I kept thinking. She'd married Ivor, and it hadn't worked. She didn't have children to make the new centre of her life, so she'd got a career instead. You didn't need to be touchy-feely in college lecturing; what was needed was well-prepared lessons, timely marking, good delivery of a good syllabus. She was tipped to become the Shetland College's first female principal. You didn't get that high without throwing your full determination into it. Now, why couldn't she pursue that and keep Ivor too? The answer surfaced slowly in my drug-fuzzed brain: he'd gone from an asset to a liability. She was an IT teacher; computing, book-keeping, accountancy. It would be child's play to her to inspect Ivor's books. She might have been trying to check on his love life, or just doing a normal household finances balance, but either way it wouldn't take her two minutes to see that things were going badly wrong. Soon there would be a smash. Would the College appoint the wife of a bankrupt embezzler as their principal? Having eroded away her love, Ivor was all set to destroy her ambition, the prize and culmination of her career.

306

And then Donna had come on the scene. Ivor had pursued her, and told her he was leaving his wife for her, only it turned out he'd never got round to telling the wife about it. Donna'd said Ivor had said he had told her, but then she discovered the wife was still coming on holiday in Scotland with him, as if nothing had happened. Now suppose ... suppose Ivor was telling the truth. Just suppose that the marriage really had drifted apart. He'd never been truly in love with Julie anyway. Now he'd met shy, childish, trusting Donna, and fallen for her, really fallen for her, and he wanted to begin all over again, in his rainbow tomorrow. I considered Donna in my mind's eye. Certainly not watch leader material. Honest, willing, trusting. Give her a task within her capabilities, and it would be done. Loyal, dutiful. She'd be there on deck for the first stroke of eight bells, and wouldn't leave until the next eight bells had finished chiming. The backbone of any ship's crew.

I considered that picture, vaguely depressed. Was that really what men wanted, the perfect helpmeet, the Victorian wife? He for God only, she for God in him? Sweet, trusting, clever only in her own sphere. I sighed, and continued reasoning. Ivor had really fallen in love with Donna, and when she precipitated a decision by coming to Shetland, he meant what he'd said. He told Julie he was leaving her. He was going to set up home, in Shetland, under Julie's nose, with a girl only just too old to be his daughter.

I added one more characteristic to Julie. She was proud. She had a sense of what she owed herself: in her appearance, in her teaching, in her organization. She wouldn't let herself down. Now she was going to be let down, publicly, by the husband she'd secured in spite of everyone telling her to give up and find someone else. To her fears for her triumphant career achievement would be added personal rage.

Ivor had to go, and go in a way that would leave her all she wanted. All that formidable competence would be trained on achieving that object. She'd have read up on murders; the police would find that in her computer, unless she'd also read up – and of course she would have – on destroying your tracks. She'd have found out all the things forensics can see when they have a body to work on, or the suspicion of a death in a house: a hair, a fragment of skin, taking up floorboards and analysing pipe bends for minute particles of blood. Very well then, she'd leave the body elsewhere, where it would be quickly destroyed and where, if it was found, nobody would link it up with Ivor. She'd pretend he'd done the note-on-the-table act, and if she was tight-lipped and obviously not wanting to talk about it, nobody would pry. She wouldn't report him missing; why should she? He'd left her because she wanted a child (a neat touch, giving that version to a crony of Inga's mother-in-law, to make sure it spread all over Shetland, and a nice, sympathetic, womanly reason too), and she didn't want to talk about it, she'd just throw herself into her work. If the embezzlement came out – and it might not, given Robert-John's relationship with his father, which she'd know all about, through Ivor – then that was an extra reason for him to run. Poor Julie, left holding the can. If he'd gone like that, leaving her in it, there'd be no whispering about how 'she must have known an' all'. The College interviewing body might even have a touch of sympathy vote towards her application.

But how could she have done it? Killing him, yes; easily. All she had to do was suggest a picnic up on the hill slopes: 'Is that a cave up there? Why don't we walk up?' A blow on the head, poison in his coffee. She was the person who could most easily have impersonated him in the house, then taken the ferry down with his car; she flew back from Inverness the next day. All she had to do was get a bus from Aberdeen to Inverness and get on her flight.

But – the stumbling block to her guilt all along – she couldn't have brought the boat back. Even with murder as a spur, she couldn't have sailed back. I just didn't believe it. Not only did she have to hoist the sails and set them, but she'd have had to trim them not only efficiently but well; Ivor's return had made almost as good time as I had.

My brain had reached an impasse. Hubert, then; maybe they had done it together. She'd shot him so that he wouldn't give her away. No, I didn't believe that either. Julie was a loner, who walked by herself. I could see her at a staff do, with the party yet not of them, watching their drunken laughter with cool eyes. Besides, murder wasn't a game to let others in on. I let my head loll on the rubberised pillow and closed my eyes. I was almost asleep again when I heard my own voice, back in Gavin's sitting room: *It's frighteningly easy ... You could get yourself into such trouble ...*

Instantly I was awake. I heard the fire crackle, saw the chart and books spread before me on the floor. '*Cass, bairn, you're behind the times,*' Kenny had said, and then Gavin had got out his iPad, with my route already marked, compass course, distance, times. Computers were Julie's business. The fancy chart plotter that had been removed from Ivor's boat would have been child's play to her. She'd have set it to work out all the calculations: distance, course to steer against tide-set. I'd been thinking of Ivor's yacht as a sailing boat, and Julie couldn't sail, but any driver could steer a motor boat, and Ivor's yacht had a good engine. She could have punched the route into the plotter, linked it up to the wheel, set the speed at six knots, and never touched the steering again until Brae marina. It was a crazy idea, but for someone who didn't know enough about the sea to know it was mad, it would seem perfectly feasible. I heard my voice again: *People do it ...* People who weren't used to the sea took boats they'd just bought second-hand out into the North Sea with only a land map to guide them. Julie would have heard plenty of talk about this yacht sailing off to Norway, that yacht going to Faroe. She'd think it was easy.

I wondered how afraid she'd been, once she was alone in the wastes of the North Sea, with only the grey tumbling waves around her, and no land in sight. Maybe her faith in her mastery of the boat gadgetry had been so complete that she'd gone below and slept, leaving the boat to get on with it. Powering forward at a steady six knots, no wonder she had made good time.

Then, arriving in Brae after dark, she'd berthed the boat and gone home in Ivor's oilskins. She'd banged the car door to make sure her neighbour would register him being home, put the lights on. She'd gone before anyone was up to recognise her, or come to the door. She'd skulked around Shetland all day, then got on the boat, gone straight to her sleeping pod, put one of those daylight-excluding masks over her face to make sure she wasn't recognised by anyone she knew, and slept until the call for drivers to go to their vehicles. If she had been recognised, it wouldn't matter much, for there wasn't going to be a police enquiry. She was just a woman whose husband had left her. No police, no courts, no fuss.

Word would spread, of course. Her final revenge on Donna would be knowing that Ivor's other woman would find out that Ivor had left her too, without even a goodbye message.

Bridge ... saw her. Ivor's boat, with her highly recognisable green dodgers, coming up the west coast under engine. Hubert had seen her, and not thought about it, until I'd mentioned that she'd come home via the Caledonian Canal, and asked about heather. He hadn't known what to say, so he'd gone to ask Julie about it, at college. It seemed out of character that she should suddenly confide in Susan; maybe she knew Herbert would have been seen visiting her, so that she had to get

310

her version of what he'd wanted to know in first. Hubert had to go; and who was more likely to have taken Ivor's pistol than his wife, who'd cleared out his boat?

I wondered how cool she'd remain under hostile police questioning.

Sunday 12th January

High Water at Scalloway UT	*05.59, 1.3m*
Low Water	*12.29, 1.0m*
High Water	*18.31, 1.3m*
Low Water	*00.54, 0.9m*
Moonset	*05.34*
Sunrise	*08.58*
Moonrise	*12.53*
Sunset	*15.28*

Moon first quarter.

Dem at wants ta kiss i da dark'll aye finn da mooth.
Where there's a will, there's a way.

Chapter Thirty

Visitors began at half past ten, as soon as the consultant and his entourage had inspected the ward. Maman and Dad were first.

'They would not let us in any sooner,' Maman said. Her eyes were red-rimmed under the careful make-up. 'They just kept saying that you were stable, then, this morning, that you would be fine, but you would need clothes.'

'I do,' I said. The clothes I'd come in were crumpled in a bag in a locker, wet with blood and seawater.

'So I went aboard your boat, and found what I thought you would need.' She brandished a carrier bag. 'I hope you do not mind.'

I smiled at her. 'If my own Maman can't rummage around in my clothes boxes, who can?' I looked inside. 'Oh, bless you, my toothbrush as well.'

'Then we came in and waited.' Her dark eyes looked me over. 'You seem as if you will be fine.'

I nodded. 'They said they'll let me out tomorrow.'

'You wouldn't think, now,' Dad suggested, 'of coming home to the warm to convalesce? Cat would like it, sure he would.'

I knew they'd ask. 'I'll be fine. I'm acclimatised. Besides, I've got to finish my course.' I could see Maman wasn't happy. 'If it gets very cold, Reidar would let me stay aboard his boat. He has heating.'

They weren't reassured, but this wasn't a dire enough emergency to warrant living ashore.

'And your nice policeman phoned, with his apologies,'

Maman said, 'and he hopes he will lunch with us another time. He is busy arresting the person who shot you.'

'Good.'

The afternoon brought Reidar and Anders. By that time I'd explained myself to the elderly lady in the next bed, managed a shower, shakily, lain down for a bit, and got myself dressed, one item of clothing at a time. I'd need to speed that up when I got home. Reidar was inclined to blame himself.

'I knew I should not have let you go out alone.'

'As if you could have stopped her,' Anders said. He laid a large block of fruit and nut chocolate on the bed. 'Cat is fine, Cass, but missing you. When will they let you out?'

'Tomorrow.'

'Rat and I will come and fetch you.'

'Rat will have to wait in the car. The hospital would have a fit.'

'And I will leave *Khalida*'s engine running before I come, so that your home will be warm for you to return to, and Reidar will bring dinner, so that you can just rest.'

Men from my own world. 'Thank you, Anders.'

They had just gone when Gavin arrived at last, with a khaki canvas grip slung over one shoulder, and a Thornton's bag which he laid in my lap: several bars of their Sicilian lemon mousse. His grey eyes scanned me, noting the bulge where the bandage was. 'They seem to think you're doing fine.'

'Home tomorrow. The surgeon said I'm a tough cookie, and lucky with it. Vital bits were only grazed. They sewed up the holes, bunged me full of antibiotics, and left me to sleep it off.' I shifted, gently. 'It swees.'

He sat down and took my hand, our fingers meshing naturally, as if we'd been together for years. 'I asked for a couple of days' leave, just to make sure you're properly on your feet again, but it seems a trial I'm involved in has been brought forward, and I have to be there.' He grimaced. 'Police work is like that.'

I nodded. 'I know.' His fingers were warm around mine. 'Life at sea is like that too. You go when the wind says you can.'

He nodded. 'It can be easier, sometimes, to get leave at short notice. If you got a text, say, to tell you that a particular ship is about to have two days in La Rochelle or Dublin.'

'That could work,' I agreed. 'Assuming I get a tall ship.'

'You'll get one.'

The lady in the next-door bed was absorbed in giving what looked like her daughter a full run-down of her latest symptoms. I spoke softly. 'Just an academic question, of course, but have you locked Julie up, and thrown away the key?'

Gavin rose. 'Are you well enough to see me off the ward?' He helped me ease myself upwards and gave me his arm again, as he had after the dance. Walking hurt, but a nurse smiled and nodded in approval as I hirpled past. We came past the reception desk and into the quiet of the stairs.

'She's saying nothing,' Gavin said. 'She just asked for a lawyer, then sat tight. So we're focusing on evidence. We'll chase up the Inverness end, see if we can prove she really wasn't there. Her work computer has her logged on in the college in Lerwick on the evening of Hubert's death, with timings that mean she could have switched it on, driven over, shot him, and driven back to switch it off. Her own computer will have the details of the eBay sale of the chart plotter, and we should be able to recover the boat's track from that, though it's only circumstantially helpful. If we're really lucky, it was switched on as they came into our loch. That would be harder for her to talk away. She might have had to buy more fuel, if Ivor hadn't refuelled

315

in Mallaig; we'll check out Plockton and Kinlochbervie.'

'Did you know it was her?'

'Not know. She was my front-runner, if only on statistics. It usually is the spouse.'

'I thought she couldn't have done it. I just never thought of using a yacht as a motorboat.'

He smiled. 'I didn't have your sailing bias. The idea of her killing Ivor where we found him and motoring home occurred to me as soon as she changed her story. We questioned her again yesterday morning, but we didn't have anything to hold her on. Now we do: your accusation.'

'My word against hers.'

Gavin's voice was confident. 'Now we're looking we'll find the evidence. Just one credit card transaction in the wrong place will do it. She wasn't thinking of a police investigation.' He changed tack. 'Is Cat okay?'

'Missing me.'

'I'll miss you too.' We'd been leaning against the stair-well bannister; now he turned me to face him. 'My part in all this is wound up now. I go back on the 18.25 flight.'

I felt a rush of dismay. 'Today?'

He made a face. 'Spring in France sounded good. If you're not half-way round the world on a tall ship.' He bent forward to kiss me, a brief touching of lips that left us both trembling. There was a long pause while we looked at each other, then we kissed properly, passionately, as if we'd always been lovers, and only jumped apart when footsteps clattered on the stairs above us.

'Take care of yourself,' I said. '*Beannachd leat.*'

'I'll see you soon.'

I watched as he went down the stairs, footsteps light and unhurried. At the bottom he stopped and tilted his head to look up at me. 'Keep away from murderers until you've healed.'

'I'll do my best,' I promised.

316

I knew what the letter was straight away, by the stamped address on it: **Stiftelsen Fullriggeren _Sørlandet_ | The Ship _Sørlandet_** Skippergaten 55 | N-4611 Kristiansand | Norway. My hands shook and my heart thumped as I opened it. Below the stamped heading and my address were half a dozen lines:

Dear Cass,

Congratulations on your college course. I remember you very well from your previous voyages, and will be delighted to welcome you back aboard _Sørlandet_. We are now in the process of assembling the crew for this year's voyages, which will start in April. We are considering you for the post of third mate/navigation officer, which would involve looking after equipment, passage planning with me, and standing the 8-12 watch. I will contact you soon with an interview date, initially by phone, then here in Kristiansand.

With best wishes,
Gunnar Halvorsen, Captain.

I picked up Cat and hugged him. 'You'll like it, Cat. Life aboard a tall ship.' Then I dived for my computer. www.sørlandet.org. _Unforgettable sailing trips,_ it said. April and May were taken up with weekend trips out from her home port of Kristiansand, then June and July was the Tall Ships Race: Kristiansand, Stavanger, Belfast, then back to Alesund and a fortnight of sailing through the fjords before the regatta across the North Sea.

My heart sang at the names. I picked up my mobile and

sent off a text to Gavin: Sørlandet *wants me! How about meeting in Norway or Belfast? Have u seen the fjords?*

I paused, then added *x*

APPENDIX: CASS'S PASSAGE PLAN

Scalloway to Gavin's loch
Distance: 270 nautical miles
Time @ 5 knots = 2 days 6 hours.
ETA: to arrive at point of Rona for 06.30, 23 December.
Arrive at loch head **14.10**.

Hazards:

1) Tides round Sumburgh: avoid by going straight out from Scalloway, heading 235° to keep clear of Cape Wrath. Fair water from 4 hours before HW Dover to 3 hours after HW Dover – pushing me to east, but then will push westwards. Avoid 2 hours each side of LW.

2) Submarine zone in Minch – keep to sides of channel

3) Tides at Kyleakin (Skye Bridge) and Kyle Rhea: on **23 December** HW Kyle of Lochalsh = 09.39, 22.21. First of East-going tide HW -3, but weak for five hours so be at Skye Bridge between 6:10 and 12:10 – **no later.** Best between 09.10 and 10.10.

4) Wind turbines in Kyle Rhea

5) Two rocks in Gavin's loch: Sgeir Ulibhe day marked, Ellice shoal not.

6) Narrows into head of loch – ask for escort boat?

Saturday 21ˢᵗ December

Scalloway, UT:

LW	04.52, 0.7
HW	11.12, 1.7m,
LW	17.27, 0.6,
HW	23.43, 1.5
Sunrise	09.15
Moonset	10.28
Sunset	14.51
Moonrise	20.05

Gibbous moon, last of spring tides.
Winter solstice.

ETD: Leave Scalloway 05.30 Saturday 21ˢᵗ December.

Sunrise 09.07, but will have quarter moon, sets 10:28.

Course: 234°T, 144 nms.

Lerwick LW 06.52, 0.7 HW 13.12, 1.7m, so should get fair tides for next 7 hours southwards from Sumburgh head. Tide at 09.00 slack at Roost.

Might just see loom of Fair Isle lights.

Sunset 14.51, moonrise 20.05.

Passing 12.5nms of Noup Head lighthouse, **fl w 30 secs**, elevation 79 m, range 22M. White tower 24m high. ETA 21.00

Might also see Brough Head light, **fl 3w 25 secs**, elevation 52m, 18M

Bolt hole: Stromness, east-going stream 18.12 to 00.10.
Clyde Cruising Club p28

WPT2 KDUR: Kyle of Durness light.
(WPT co-ordinates) **58°41'91 N 05°03'04W**
Fl **r w alt every 2 minutes**. Visible 43 kilometres / 26
miles. Should see from 04:30.
Approaching coast, keep in 21+ fathoms of water.
ETA 09.30 Sunday 22nd December.
Bolt hole: Durness Bay/Loch Eriboll.

Sunday 22nd December

Ullapool, UT:
LW	03.35, 1.6
HW	09.24, 4.8
LW	16.09, 1.6
HW	22.02, 4.5
Sunrise	09.11
Moonset	10.55
Sunset	15.27
Moonrise	21.38

Waning gibbous moon.

Course: 208°T, 56.7 nms.

Butt of Lewis light to starboard, fl w every 5 secs.
Elevation 52 m, range 25 nms, red brick tower 37m high.

Bolt holes: Kinlochbervie – sheltered all winds. Imray
p131; Loch Nedd, Imray p118, 121, 122.

Pass between
Stoerhead light, fl W every 15 secs, elevation 59m, range
24 miles. White tower 14 m high.
and Tiumpan Head light fl 2 W every 15 secs, elevation

55m, range 25 nms, white tower 21m high

WPT3 STRH Stoer Lighthouse. **58°16'38 N 05° 27'21 W**
ETA: 15.00 at Raffin Bay, 3nms on from Stoer
Lighthouse. Shingle beach.

Bolt hole: Lochinver, Imray p116.
Sunset 15.27, moonrise 21.38.
STOP FOR A REST.

Leave at 21.00 to be back on course for
WPT 4 RURD: Rubha Reidh light, **fl (4) W 15 secs**,
elevation 37m, height 25m, white circular tower. **57°
52'34N 05 °50'96W**
ETA: 02.00 Monday 23 December

Course: 177°, 31.9nms.
*Continue past Gairloch, Loch Torridon, hugging mainland
shore, well away from the scatter of rocks north of Rona.*
Bolt hole: Gairloch, Loch Torridon, Imray p 91.

***Rona light, fl W every 12 secs**, elevation 69m, range
19nms, white tower 13m high. Passing it 06.30.* **57° 36'94
N 05°54'24 W**
Now into inner Sound of Sleat.

WPT5 CRWL: Crowlin islands lighthouse, **fl w 6 secs,**
32m, 6M, **57°20'67 N 05°53'04 W.** Imray p 84
ETA: 08.00 Monday 23 December

Sunrise 09.07, moonset 11.15.
Course: 133°T, 6nm.
Bolt hole: Plockton, Imray, p 80

WPT6 SKYB: Skye Bridge. Flashing p and s buoys, lit, +
lights on bridge. 4 knot current. **57°17'09 N 05° 44'81 W**

Imray p74-6
ETA: 09.10 Monday 23 December

Continue into Loch na Beiste and Loch Alsh.
WPT7 ALSH: Turning for Kyle Rhea light. fl **WRG 3s**
7m 11-8M **57°16'29 N 05°37'94 W** Imray p71-2
Course: 96°T, 3.8nm
This heading until Kyle Rhea light visible, then turn to
starboard.
ETA: 10.00

Course: 204°T, 2.3nms
WPT8: KREA: Kyle Rhea light. fl **WRG 3s** 7m 11-8M
57°14'18 N 05°39'74 W
ETA: 10.30

Course: 168°T, 1.3nms
WPT9: end of Kyle Rhea **57°12'84 N 05°39'20 W**
ETA: 10.50

Course: 215°T, 3.8nms
WPT10: SDGL: Sandaig islands light – **fl 6 s** 12m 8M
leave well to port. **57°09'78 N 05°43'28 W**
ETA: 11.35 Monday 23 December. Now off entrance to
Gavin's loch. Imray p69-70

Eyeball pilotage.
Course: 130°T for 2.0nms, hugging north shore to avoid
Sgeir Ulibhe
WPT11 SGUL: Sgeir Ulibhe, marked, unlit buoy on
skerry. **57°08.44 N 05°40'36 W**
ETA 12.00

Continue down loch, keeping central – 3.3nms at 109°T,
WPT12: LHRN, 2.1 nms at 141°T, **57°07'37 N 05°34'58**

W
ETA 12.40

Steer for south side of loch, towards Barrisdale, to avoid Ellice Shoal, unmarked.
WPT13 ISLD: islands marking entrance to inner loch.
57°05'65 N 05°32'31 W
ETA 13.10

Steer roughly 74°, avoiding Barrisdale point, Caolas Mor point and island.
WPT14 SKRY: **57°06'72 N 05°25'50 W**
ETA 14.00 Now 10 mins to head of loch.

At Skiary, head 103°T towards Narrows. Chart datum 0.2 – need tide to get through. Going in on falling tide -get escort boat, be very careful, or anchor until tide rising.
LW Mallaig 15.59, **2.2m. = 0.7 m of water under keel. Will only be about 1.1 -1.5 at 14.00.**

Anchorage in tidal pool at head of loch. Sheltered north and south, may be exposed in E and W winds.
ETA: Arrive head of loch 14.10.

*Very important author's note: This is Cass's passage plan, worked out on paper, and based entirely on these dates and tides. **It is not under any circumstances to be used for real-life navigation, and the author is not in any way responsible for the safety of anyone who so uses it.***

A Note on Shetland

Shetland has its own very distinctive language, *Shetlan* or *Shetlandic*, which derives from Old Norse and Old Scots. In *Death on a Longship,* Magnie's first words to Cass are,

'Cass, well, for the love of mercy. Norroway, at this season? Yea, yea, we'll find you a berth. Where are you?'

Written in west-side Shetlan (each district is slightly different), it would have looked like this:

'Cass, weel, fir da love o' mercy. Norroway, at dis saeson? Yea, yea, we'll fin dee a bert. Quaur is du?''

Th becomes a *d* sound in *dis* (this), *da* (the), *dee* and *du* (originally thee and thou, now you), *wh* becomes *qu* (*quaur*, where), the vowel sounds are altered (well to *weel*, season to *saeson,* find *to fin)*, the verbs are slightly different (quaur <u>is</u> du?) and the whole looks unintelligible to most folk from outwith Shetland, and *twartree* (a few) within it too.

So, rather than writing in the way my characters would speak, I've tried to catch the rhythm and some of the distinctive usages of Shetlan while keeping it intelligible to *soothmoothers*, or people who've come in by boat through the South Mouth of Bressay Sound into Lerwick, and by extension, anyone living south of Fair Isle.

There are also many Shetlan words that my characters would naturally use, and here, to help you, are *some o' dem*. No Shetland person would ever use the Scots *wee*; to them, something small would be *peerie*, or, if it was very small, *peerie mootie*. They'd *caa* sheep in a *park*, that is, herd them up in a field – *moorit* sheep, coloured black, brown, fawn. They'd take a *skiff* (a small rowing boat) out along the *banks* (cliffs) or on the *voe* (sea inlet), with the *tirricks* (Arctic terns) crying above them, and the *selkies* (seals) watching. Hungry folk are *black fanted* (because they've forgotten their *faerdie maet*, the snack that would have kept them going) and upset folk *greet* (cry). An older housewife like Jessie would have her *makkin*, (knitting) *belt* buckled around her waist, and her *reestit* (smoke-dried) *mutton* hanging above the Rayburn. And finally... my favourite Shetland verb, which I didn't manage to work in this novel, but which is too good not to share: *to kettle*. As in: *Wir cat's just kettled. Four ketlings, twa strippet and twa black and quite.* I'll leave you to work that one out on your own ... or, of course, you could consult Joanie Graham's *Shetland Dictionary*, if your local bookshop hasn't *just selt* their last copy *dastreen*.

The diminutives Magnie (Magnus) and Gibbie (Gilbert) may also seem strange to non-Shetland ears. In a traditional country family (I can't speak for *toonie* Lerwick habits) the oldest son would often be called after his father or grandfather, and be distinguished from that father and grandfather and perhaps a cousin or two as well, by his own version of their shared name. Or, of course, by a *Peerie* in front of it, which would stick for life, like the *eart kyent* (well-known) guitarist Peerie Willie Johnson, who recently celebrated his 80th birthday. There was also a patronymic system, which meant that a Peter's four sons, Peter, Andrew, John, and Matthew, would all have the surname Peterson, and so would his son Peter's children. Andrew's children, however, would have the surname Anderson, John's would be Johnson, and Matthew's would be Matthewson. The Scots ministers stamped this out in the nineteenth century, but in one district you can have a lot of *folk* with the same surname, and so they're distinguished by their house name: *Magnie o' Strom, Peter o' da Knowe.*

Glossary

For those who like to look up unfamiliar words as they go, here's a glossary of Scots and Shetlan words.

aa: all
an aa: as well
aabody: everybody
aawye: everywhere
ahint: behind
ain: own
amang: among
anyroad: anyway
ashet: large serving dish
auld: old
aye: always
bairn: child
ball (verb): throw out
banks: sea cliffs, or peatbanks, the slice of moor where peats are cast
bannock: flat triangular scone
birl, birling: paired spinning round in a dance
blinkie: torch
blootered: very drunk
boanie: pretty, good looking
breeks: trousers
brigstanes: flagged stones at the door of a crofthouse
bruck: rubbish
caa: round up
canna: can't
clarted: thickly covered
cludgie: toilet
cowp: capsize
cratur: creature
crofthouse: the long, low traditional house set in its own land

daander: to travel uncertainly or in a leisurely fashion

darrow: a hand fishing line

dastreen: yesterday evening

de-crofted: land that has been taken out of agricultural use, e.g. for a house site

dee: you du is also you, depending on the grammar of the sentence – they're equivalent to thee and thou. Like French, you would only use dee or du to one friend; several people, or an adult if you're a younger person, would be you.

denner: midday meal

didna: didn't

dinna: don't

dis: this

doesna: doesn't

doon: down

drewie lines: a type of seaweed made of long strands

duke: duck

dukey-hole: pond for ducks

du kens: you know

dyck, dyke: a wall, generally drystane, i.e. built without cement

ee now: right now

eela: fishing, generally these days a competition

everywye: everywhere

fae, frae: from

faersome: frightening

faither, usually faider: father

fanted: hungry, often **black fanted**: absolutely starving

folk: people

gansey: a knitted jumper

geen: gone

gluff: fright

greff: the area in front of a peat bank

gret: cried

guid: good

guid kens: God knows
hae: have
hadna: hadn't
harled: exterior plaster using small stones
heid: head
hoosie: little house, usually for bairns
howk: to search among: I *howked* ida box o' auld claes.
isna: isn't
just: just
ken, kent: know, knew
kirk: church
kirkyard: graveyard
knowe: hillock
Lerook: Lerwick
lem: china
likit: liked
lintie: skylark
lipper: a cheeky or harum-scarum child, generally affectionate
mad: annoyed
mair: more
makkin belt: a knitting belt with a padded oval, perforated for holding the 'wires' or knitting needles.
mam: mum
mareel: sea phosphorescence, caused by plankton, which makes every wave break in a curl of gold sparks
meids: shore features to line up against each other to pinpoint a spot on the water
midder: mother
mind: remember
moorit: coloured brown or black, usually used of sheep
mooritoog: earwig
muckle: big – as in Muckle Roe, the big red island. Vikings were very literal in their names, and almost all Shetland names come from the Norse.
muckle biscuit: large water biscuit, for putting cheese on

na: no, or more emphatically, **naa**
needna: needn't
Norroway: the old Shetland pronunciation of Norway
o': of
oot: out
ower: over
park: fenced field
peat: brick-like lump of dried peat earth, used as fuel
peerie: small
peerie biscuit: small sweet biscuit
Peeriebreeks: affectionate name for a small thing, person or animal
piltick: a sea fish common in Shetland waters
pinnie: apron
postie: postman
quen: when
redding up: tidying
reestit mutton: wind-dried shanks of mutton
riggit: dressed, sometimes with the sense dressed up
roadymen: men working on the roads
roog: a pile of peats
rummle: untidy scattering
Santy: Santa Claus
scaddy man's heids: sea urchins
scattald: common grazing land
scuppered: put paid to, done for
selkie: seal, or seal person who came ashore at night, cast his/her skin and became human
Setturday: Saturday
shalder: oystercatcher
sho: she
shoulda: should have, usually said shoulda
shouldna: shouldn't have
SIBC: Shetland Islands Broadcasting Company, the independent radio station
skafe: squint

skerry: a rock in the sea
smoorikins: kisses
snicked: move a switch that makes a clicking noise
snyirked: made a squeaking or rattling noise
solan: gannet
somewye: somewhere
sooking up: sucking up
soothified: behaving like someone from outwith Shetland
spew: be sick
spewings: piles of sick
splatched: walked in a splashy way with wet feet, or in water
steekit mist: thick mist
swack: smart, fine
swee: to sting (of injury)
tak: take
tatties: potatoes
tay: tea, or meal eaten in the evening
tink: think
tirricks: Arctic terns
trows: trolls
tushker: L-shaped spade for cutting peat
twa: two
twartree: a small number, several
tulley: pocket knife
unken: unknown
vexed: sorry or sympathetic "I was that vexed to hear that."
vee-lined: lined with wood planking
voe: sea inlet
voehead: the landwards end of a sea inlet
waander: wander
waar: seaweed
whatna: what
wasna: wasn't
wha's: who is

whit: what
whitteret: weasel
wi': with
wir: we've – in Shetlan grammar, we are is sometimes we have
wir: our
wife: woman, not necessarily married
wouldna: would not
yaird: enclosed area around or near the croft house
yoal: a traditional clinker-built six-oared rowing boat.

Also by Marsali Taylor

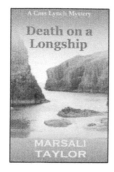
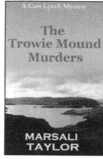
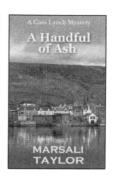

For more information about **Marsali Taylor**
and other **Accent Press** titles
please visit

www.accentpress.co.uk

https://www.facebook.com/marsali.taylor?fref=ts

Lightning Source UK Ltd.
Milton Keynes UK
UKOW06n2323180915

258883UK00001B/2/P